THE CODEX LACRIMAE

A.J. CARLISLE

THE CODEX LACRIMAE

A.J. CARLISLE

—— PART 2: ——

THE JOURNEY
TO MIMIR'S WELL

BEING THE FIRST PART OF
THE ARTIFACTS OF DESTINY

IngramSpark
La Vergne, Tennessee

Credits:
Front & Back Cover, and Spine Design
Cakamura
https://99designs.com/profiles/cakamura/services
Original concepts by Adriana, Seth, Sophia, & A.J. Carlisle;
2019 Interior Redesign, text, & formatting by
Marraii Design / Natasa Marovic
Interior ePub & POD Design by A.J. Carlisle & Marraii Design/Natasa Marovic
Author Picture: Monty Nuss Photography
Interior Artwork (Map & 12 Plates): Copyright 2017 by A.J. Carlisle

Book Layout @ 2019 BookDesignTemplates.com and Marraii Design

The Codex Lacrimae, Part II: The Journey to Mimir's Well / A.J. Carlisle
With Illustrations by the author.

Print ISBN: 978-0-578-45401-6
eISBN: 978-0-578-45402-3

Reviews for A.J. Carlisle's
The Codex Lacrimae

The Codex Lacrimae, Part 1:
The Mariner's Daughter & Doomed Knight
(2012, & Revised Edition, 2016)

"This is the beginning of a truly extraordinary and epic series that melds Norse mythology with human history and the legends of the Grail Knights. The characters, the scope and complexity of the story, the skillfully rendered beauty and horrors of the worlds, and the stunning story itself completely overshadows every other work of fantasy I have ever read—including Tolkien. This is truly a 'must-read' for everyone who likes fantasy in any of its forms.

—TAHLIA NEWLAND, editor, & founder of
Awesome Indies Book Reviews

"... dynamic adventure with a wide cast of characters interweaving Christians, Muslims, Jews, and Norse mythology in the medieval Middle East with the central character being a beautiful young Venetian woman!"

—CELESTE GARDNER, Amazon.com

"... an intriguing blend of alternate reality and fantasy, featuring a young woman set to inherit magical powers, and a young man who may or may not be evil incarnate."

—*KIRKUS REVIEWS*

The Codex Lacrimae, Part 2: *The Book of Tears* (2013, 1st Edition)

"... Carlisle is a master of spinning a yarn while creating a rich fantasy physic and metaphysic. The fire of genius is everywhere—the freshness of the characters, the evocation of medieval backgrounds, the endearing romance of Clarinda and Aurelius, and the originality of its Arthurian-Norse mythology."

—CHARLES SMITH, Professor of English Emeritus,
Colorado State University, Fort Collins
Amazon.com

FOR SOPHIA, ADRIANA, AND SETH
There aren't enough words to express the gratefulness
and good fortune I feel for having you in my life—
I dedicate this work to you with love, & I hope you enjoy
the continuing adventures of Clarinda and Ríg
as they travel through the Nine Worlds!

Also, with deep appreciation to Bob Thixton, Dick Duane, and
Peter Jones at Pinder Lane & Garon Brooke
for all the years of support

Contents

Illustrations

MAP: Clarinda and Rig's Worlds:
Mediterranean Lands & Europe of 12th Century

BOOK THREE

THE DESERT
ON MIDGARD

CHAPTER 1

A Lore Master's Third Rune Gate

i. The Boy from Byzantium

It's too quiet.

Jacob frowned and slowed to a jog. His hand grasped the pommel of the sword at his hip. He'd borrowed the blade to replace the one Marcus had taken, and he'd made good time reaching the hospital wing of the Krak des Chevaliers. He need only find the physician Brother Belvedere, convey Ibn-Khaldun's request for help, and there still might be a chance to join Ríg's fight against the intruders.

Despite the urgency, he slowed to a stealthy pace. Some instinct screamed of danger in the infirmary.

Where are the physicians and monks who were working here?

Something felt terribly wrong, and as he drew near, it began to smell even worse. An acrid odor filled the air, part musky perfume and part coppery smoke. His eyes began to water and his stomach tightened.

It smells like when they burned a plague ship in the Golden Horn. It's human beings burning.

The memory ignited his determination, a resolve fueled by fear for his mother.

Move, Jacob. Ima was in this section.

He clenched his teeth and fought the impulse to flee. If this foreboding proved true, his first real sword-fight might come even sooner than expected.

Moments ago, a flash of eerie, aquamarine light had bathed this entire section of the Hospitaller castle. He'd thought that the warrior-monks were practicing some kind of secret warding-off ritual before the siege of two armies began in earnest, but now he realized that the disquieting sight had been nothing of the kind.

Anxiety shifted into battle readiness as he crept down the hallway, stepping over incandescent chunks of limestone, concrete blocks, and some smaller feathered forms he couldn't initially identify, then realized were dead birds.

That glaucous, blue-tinged glow must have been a massive explosion!

Rubble lay on the ground beneath a destroyed window and scorch marks blackened the corridor's walls for some distance beyond it.

This is bizarre. How do dead birds come to be in the middle of a castle? Were the knights keeping them as message carriers?

He stepped over a cluster of pigeons that lay amidst the wreckage, their grayish, plump bodies blown inward from some point outside.

More destruction and gigantic holes in the walls awaited around the corner. Even worse, to his right rose a ceiling-to-floor mound of limestone debris that blocked the hallway leading to his mother Rebecca's room.

Oh, Ima, *what happened here?*

This wasn't just one explosion, but a series of them, and the detonations seemed to get worse the closer he got to the main ward. He'd planned to check on his mother while getting Master Belvedere, but now he wasn't sure what to do.

Think, think. Go back and find another way?

No. He still felt too uncertain about the labyrinth of passages. Searching for an alternate path might mean a fatal delay. He needed to try to find Belvedere and make sure the area where he'd last seen his mother was truly impassable.

He took the one direction that did seem clear, into the hospital wing. The boy's nape prickled as he entered the burned antechamber of the ward. Small fires burned and guttered amongst the broken tables and cots. Jacob blinked rapidly against the smoky haze, wondering at the strange shapes visible in the weak late afternoon sunlight. He'd seen the light, but heard nothing. How, he wondered, could there be all this destruction and no sound?

His habitual frown deepened into a scowl. Given the evidence, only one deduction could explain an explosion with no sound; however, if true, that reason would remove all logic from a long-held view of the world.

There's got to be a rational explanation. Remember what Mordecai said, 'look past the smoke.'

He didn't want to admit that he sensed the supernatural. To him, the so-called occult arts were simply a form of entertainment, a means for a host of charlatans in Constantinople to make a quick *bezant* from gullible passersby. In his thirteen years of life in the Genoese Quarter, the boy had seen enough of conjurers, soothsayers, astrologers, and would-be necromancers to learn one thing about thaumaturgy: there were no miracles or supernatural forces.

He wasn't cynical, just realistic. The Roman population's opinions of sorcery alternated between contempt and veneration—a crazy paradox. At one moment, Byzantines would pride themselves on their Greek Orthodoxy, dutifully pray in the basilica, and piously declaim that there was only one mystical part of their lives: the sacramental conversion of bread and wine into the Body and Blood of Christ. Then, in the next hour after Mass, the same parishioners might be found paying ridiculous sums of money for any kind of roadside diversion that had the faintest whiff of sorcery about it. They'd wait in lines or gather in crowded alleys to see hooded mages make provocatively dressed assistants disappear and reappear. They'd *ooh* and *aah* at illusionists' shell games, fire eating, or rope tricks. They'd patronize apothecaries who sold every drug imaginable: vials of health elixirs, luck potions, sexual stimulants, and especially poison (and, sometimes, a combination of the last two, if the money was right and the abused spouse were desperate enough).

Meanwhile, Greek Orthodox preachers stood on stone benches or monument steps, engaging anyone who'd listen in arguments about the True Nature of the Christians' Triune God: the Father, Son, and Holy Spirit. In the imperial city, such sermonizing was no joke—contemplating the question of 'was Christ more human, or more God?' could occupy a Byzantine all day!

Jacob stared at the phosphorescently glowing rubble around him, trying to pretend that there was some logical explanation for this destruction. Childhood exposure to supposed magics that had always ended with disappointment when he'd uncovered the deception.

Two years ago, a dark-cloaked man, showering sparks from his hands and proclaiming that he was Dardo the Magnificent, had emerged from a cloud in Leukothea's Alley and proceeded to give an amazing performance. For the first time in his life, Jacob had believed in magic, but when in great excitement, he'd told his master so, Rabbi Mordecai had said, shaking his head in disappointment, not even bothering to look up from a scroll. "*Bah!* You should know better, Jacob. Tomorrow, when this Dardo appears, look past the smoke."

The next morning Jacob had done as instructed and noticed the baker's niece, Melanie, closing a vent in the side of her building that belched smoke into the street. Then Dardo cursed as the Chinese fire-sticks burned his wrists and he cast them onto the cobbles close to Jacob. A second's scrutiny later, he saw that Dardo was, in actuality, Melanie's ne'er-do-well uncle, Deimos.

Jacob scalded his shin on a smoking chunk of rubble and winced.

'Look past the smoke.' There's an explanation here, Jacob: find it!

With every magic trick since Dardo, Jacob had been successful in figuring out the fraud and chicanery behind a host of so-called supernatural phenomena. There was always something.

Exotically, there had been the day when Jacob had passed the bead-curtained entrance opening onto Hypatia the Enchantress's shop, a narrow and dark place, filled with curios and antiques, and where a teenaged acquaintance's mother spent every day at a velvet-covered table predicting customer's futures, her gigantically bosomed form crouched over a faux-crystal ball as she conducted what séances she could before going to sell her body at night in the brothel next door. Jacob had been delivering a bolt of cloth to Hypatia when a customer entered. She'd cast the boy hurriedly out of sight, eager to make a sale and convince the man that his long-dead wife was returning for a conversation. Trying to be a good neighbor, the boy hadn't felt comfortable interrupting the séance; however, during the quarter-hour beneath the table, he'd realized that she was anything but a medium for otherworldly forces. Instead, she'd muttered nonsense words and used her hands to employ a variety of noise-making devices to imitate the rapping responses of the dead. Jacob had endured the spectacle until Hypatia placed a suggestive hand onto the man's thigh—neighbor or not, the boy had howled in his best imitation of a ghost and dashed from the shop without looking back at the two figures who'd become entangled in his overthrown tablecloth.

There's always something. Look for it, and know it when you see it, even if it's not what you expect. You simply can't have a massive explosion like this without any sound!

That certitude made him pause. There had been one

inexplicable preternatural moment that he still couldn't explain, even a year later. No, he reconsidered; there were two instances, and both involving a woman who'd become a friend.

Sølvmora's pirate ships and her horoscope.

The astrologer, Sølvmora the Witch, a truly stunning woman, oval-faced, long-lashed, and raven-haired, who wore revealing purple gowns that somehow barely managed to cover her cleavage, consistently went out of her way to speak with Jacob. She lived down by the waterfront and was perhaps the only member of the Genoese Quarter's would-be magical community who Jacob thought might possess something of the supernatural. She'd made her name by appearing at the docks the night before the emperor's fleet was to sail into the Black Sea after three pirate ships, telling them, "Wait only two weeks and a pirate ship will return to you—of three will come one."

She'd convinced the *hoplitarch* to delay their departure and had been proven correct when only one of the pirate ships returned to the harbor, its occupants stricken by bubonic plague.

Jacob had watched the ship burn, put to the torch long-distance by a well-aimed cast from a Byzantine-fire laden trebuchet. The boy had turned on the dock in time to see Sølvmora observing the same scene from the porch of her shop. However, rather than showing any kind of elation at the verification of her soothsaying, she'd turned away in sadness from the flames, not even opening the door when the general had come to thank her with a small bag of silver.

Another time, Jacob and his friend, Owena, had once dared to enter her rotunda-shaped shop, and sat for a horoscope reading that had left both youths momentarily shaken. After seating the children on an amazingly smooth section of granite flooring—whose stone had been inscribed with symbols of the Twelve Houses of the Zodiac—Sølvmora had asked the children's birthdays, and then she'd made nonsensical predictions for each of them. The moment still amused Jacob to this day.

For Owena—his best friend, and the daughter of a Welsh blacksmith who operated a forge a few storefronts around the corner from Jacob's home—the witch had predicted, "Your true love will be lost on road to Huntsmen's Night, but reunion comes if Sampo-Friend finds heritage and true might."

For Jacob, Sølvmora made a similar attempt at prophecy, with a slant toward the theatrical: "When a sword sings and Kullervo's skin flames molten, in healers' hall shall Jacob Davidson take the work of Ilmarinen."

The two youths had asked her what she meant by such soothsaying, but Sølvmora had grown strangely silent. She'd dumped the scrying bones and feathers into a wooden bowl and shooed Jacob and Owena from the shop.

... the same parishioners might be found paying ridiculous sums of money for any kind of roadside diversion that had the faintest whiff of sorcery...

ii. A Lore-Master's Third Rune Gate

The opinion that supernatural phenomena were nothing more than charlatans' tricks had seemed reasonable until a few seconds ago. This blasted section of the Krak felt like a burned and scored passageway to ... *Gehenna*.

There, he'd thought it. This part of the castle could easily be a multi-roomed tomb in Hell.

He preferred not to consider places as good or evil—such notions applied only to people and actions—yet, here, in the gloom of the ruined medical wing of one of the *nazaros'* Crusader castles, and hundreds of leagues from his former home in the center of the Byzantine Empire, Jacob couldn't deny what his senses were telling him. Even though he couldn't yet see it, he unmistakably felt an otherworldly presence coming toward him through the smoky rooms, a darkness so filled with hatred and malevolence that, like a miasma of poisonous air, it constricted his chest.

He flinched at a creak, and then leapt backward at the groan of thousands of pounds of stone pushing against some unseen framing timber. The sound grew louder and finally thundered into a resounding crash as a large section of nearby wall collapsed.

What happened here? Where is everybody? Surely they didn't all rush to fight by Ríg at the front gate! A dismaying thought, but also a likelihood because of the priority the knights gave to war.

He shook his head in mystified disgust. These military orders might proclaim that they gave equal time to praying and fighting, but for monks who called themselves Hospitallers, somebody should have stayed to care for the bedridden patients! He reminded himself not to be too judgmental; after all, he's wanted to follow Ríg when he'd jumped out that window, too.

Ravens cawed somewhere outside. Their mournful cries tightened Jacob's stomach with an intimation of grief. Were they upset, or ... sad?

He turned a corner, and then stopped. *Mystery solved.* He'd reached the gigantic hall of the main ward. *I should think for a moment before judging*, he told himself. Santini might have killed his father at Mecina, but this time the *nazaros* themselves had suffered.

He took a breath to steady himself. Besides being completely wrong in his assessment of the situation, there was too much devastation to take in. The physicians weren't off fighting. They had stayed with their patients to the end. It was quiet because they were all dead.

He drew his blade.

There might be something supernatural in the air, but in the physical realm he beheld only the blood and deaths of men.

Corpses and fragments of bodies were strewn upon the blackened limestone floor and many blasted shapes lay, sat, and even sprawled upside-down amidst the wrecked furnishings, as if they'd died instantly, caught in some kind of massive explosion.

And I heard nothing!

Jacob couldn't reconcile the destruction around him with the fact that there'd been no sound of a blast, but only that eerie, flaring blue-green luminescence that he'd seen upon exiting the stairwell from the upper gallery.

An hour ago, he'd been there helping Ríg and Master Ibn-Khaldun. Now, all the people they'd saved, the monks, the doctors ... they're all dead.

The ravens screamed outside, a haunting counterpoint to the near quiet in the hospital.

Nearby, small embers spat sparks into the silence from splintered bedframes. Occasionally, they burst into flames. Jacob squinted into the smoke and groaned when he saw a fallen doorway blocking the passage to the pilgrims' cells on the other side of the ward.

How am I supposed to get to Ima now?

He inhaled a shallow breath to quell rising nausea, but coughed at the acrid odor of burned flesh.

I can't ... stop! Focus!

He reviewed a narrow list of options that wavered between fight or flight.

Yes, run! Even if you don't know the way, run back the way you came and find Ima! Fool—stop panicking. What if she's already here among all these dead men and women? What if she's unconscious and needs help?

No, do the right thing. You can't ignore this disaster just to get to Ima's side. Somebody might still be alive and injured here!

Tears welled in his eyes. The internal debate was pointless. Jacob might not know what happened in this hospital, but he knew himself. He'd made his decision the moment he'd seen the carnage in the ward.

Keep it together, and move, *Jacob!* The imaginary voice of the rabbi he'd once hoped to become held urgency in it, and the hoped-for sagacity from years of study strained to assert control in the face of the boy's first wartime experience.

Resolved, he obeyed his future self, moving from one body to another, seeking for any sign of life among the corpses. He found none.

Your sword practice and daydreams are over. Stay alert. Whoever did this might still be somewhere in this vast hall. You're either ready to fight, or, as Ima jokes, all you've been doing these past few years is playing with your sword.

After the thirtieth body, though, he began to lose hope and shifted to tallying the number of dead. The act imposed some order on a suddenly chaotic and violent world. There was no one to help here, not anymore. The place of healing had turned into a tomb.

I can count them, though, and then report the number of dead to Khajen ibn-Khaldun. That I can do.

Determined not to succumb to fear, he still prayed that there'd be a survivor, and that Yahweh wouldn't let his mother be the next body he rolled over.

Someone moaned nearby. Hope flashed. He snapped his head around, then grunted in alarm—the moan had been his own. He returned his attention to the body before him and recoiled from the sight.

Is this the thirty-fourth dead man, or thirty-fifth? Fool! How'd you not notice the robe's a different color? You can't fit it like that ... he's ... **it** *...it belongs to someone else! Oh, please, don't let this be happening ... don't. I can't do this, Ima, please, please, don't be one of these—*

Fully in shock, he dropped the severed and burnt arm he'd

been trying to push into the chest cavity of a dead Hospitaller. Then he crumpled to his hands and knees and emptied his stomach into a broken porcelain basin.

He hurled the oversized bowl in disgust. But in his haste to scramble away from the armless victim, he tumbled over the leg of another body and cracked his elbow on the bloody floor.

The sharp pain cleared his mind, and as he popped to his feet, anger overwhelmed the nausea and shock.

His sword lay nearby, dropped at some point while he'd rushed around the room. He focused on the gleaming steel, the blade something clean and familiar in this world of blood and smoke and fiery ruin. He grabbed the hilt and wiped his mouth with the sleeve of his free arm.

Enough, Jacob. Be a man. Fight. Where are the ones who did this?

He stumbled over another inert form, and though this time remained upright, he slowed to navigate more carefully between the chunks of superheated limestone.

Another curiosity drew his attention: as with the dead pigeons in the entry corridor, here lay many birds, wings spread as if they'd dropped from the air while in mid-flight. Strangely, whatever force destroyed the ward had left their plumage unburnt.

Jacob reached the apparent source of the main explosion, a hole that yawned where the south wall and window used to be. He gulped at the cool late-afternoon air, letting the mild breeze refresh him while he tried to sort his thoughts. Half the wall had gone, and what was left of it seemed to have blown into the room.

Impossible. Surely someone heard an explosion?

Though the courtyard lacked evidence for the cause of the explosion—no incendiary devices, no wreckage, and (strangest of all) no Hospitallers running in alarm to the area—the lifeless shapes of pigeons, kingfishers, and grey shrikes littered the cobblestones.

And, where'd all these dead birds come from? As dead and broken as the men and women here, all dead ...

A slight fluttering at the top of a turreted tower across the yards caught his eye. Two gigantic ravens peered at him from their perch, no longer screaming, but identical in their surprising heights to the ones he'd seen in Ibn-Khaldun's chambers when he'd first met Ríg. Were they the same birds?

But unlike that frightening moment when those ravens had burst into the scriptorium to confront the young Hospitaller, rather than swooping upon Jacob, both birds spread their massive wings and took to the sky, passing overhead and out of sight.

Why did they survive and all these other birds die? Stop! Can't worry about dead birds or even dead people, anymore—go find your mother!

Preoccupied and numb, he retraced his steps through the ward, determined to find a way through the maze of the Krak's hallways to his mother's room.

A burly figure's helmeted head slammed into the boy's abdomen.

Despite the sword still clutched in his hand, Jacob grunted, stunned. The short stranger grasped the boy's tunic, lifted him bodily from the floor, and hurled Jacob into the opposite wall!

CHAPTER 2

The Reunion of Arch-Mage Dietrich & Brother Braunen

"*Ein anderer Mensch? Bah!*" roared the deep-voiced boy who'd thrown him. "*Sie! Wo sind Perceval und Palomides?* Where's Taliesin? I can *smell* all of them!"

"*Halt, Dietrich!*" Urged a different, raspy male voice from nearby. "Let him go—I think he's Rebecca's son!"

"*Was? Oh, dann sagen Sie ihm, um mir aus dem Weg, Braunen!*" the figure shouted, still rushing at Jacob.

He caught the boy by the collar and threatened in a low

voice, "Do you hear? Tell me where Perceval and Palomides are, or your mother will suffer for your silence!"

Jacob hurtled upward at the yank, stunned at the shorter youth's strength.

When only halfway to his feet, the attacker thrust Jacob against the wall so hard that he lost his breath. Through his daze, he finally realized that it wasn't a mere boy who gripped his shoulders.

Instead, Jacob stared into the fierce, narrowed eyes of a stout, heavily bearded man. A film of masonry dust and smears of still-wet blood covered the short stranger's black-leather jerkin. A chain-mail tartan that reached almost to the shin of his knee-high, hobnailed boots hid his legs. A sheathed broadsword with ornate hilt was strapped to his back.

"You've the stink of codex magic, too," Dietrich growled, looking upward at the stunned boy. "If Arthur's knights are here, then the Lore Master's close. Where are they?"

Jacob flinched at the dwarf's breath, which smelled like rotten seaweed.

"Tell me, boy! Are you a Codex Wielder? I've killed your kind before, and won't hesitate again. Where are Taliesin the Bard and Merlin of Carmarthen? They sided against me, in the end, and their fate is sealed."

"I ... don't know who they are!" Jacob gasped.

"Enough, Dietrich!" wheezed the other man, whom Jacob noticed with some relief to be an elderly, kind-faced Hospitaller.

The old man's spindly fingers clutched at the dwarf's jerkin. "I repeat, let him go!"

"*Nein*, Braunen! I spent at least six years in *Annen Verden!*" Dietrich retorted. "I don't know what trick Taliesin and Merlin played, but I've escaped that prison. Midgard yet stands, so there must still be time—I need only a new staff and the Sampo remade!"

"Indeed?" the Hospitaller murmured. "I tell you, you'll find neither Taliesin, Merlin, nor a Sampo by doing violence to this boy. Leave him be. Or, would you have me as an enemy, too, Master Dwarf?"

Dietrich frowned, then angrily pushed the boy from him.

"No ... no, Braunen. I'd not have you as an enemy."

Jacob choked as air returned to his lungs.

"*Gut, das ist gut,*" the ancient knight replied calmly. Leaning heavily on an ornately carved cane of polished ash wood, he placed himself between the boy and dwarf. Jacob caught only parts of their subsequent conversation, spoken quickly in German and some other language he couldn't identify.

"I'll repay your good decision with information," Braunen continued. "As I began to say before you stormed from Lady Rebecca's room—"

"Rebecca?" Jacob interrupted, at least clearly understanding that name. "My mother's safe?"

Braunen waved him away with a flip of the cane, saying, "*Bah!* She's on her way, Boy. Quiet, now, I'm speaking!"

Braunen shifted Jacob slightly from the dimensional plane. Jacob didn't realize it, but for him time slowed and stretched. He remained against the wall—hearing all but unable to move—and the distortion of time and space imparted a glittering aspect to the forms of the men that made Jacob's eyes ache, like when one stares too long at shimmering waves under a noonday sun.

Dietrich the Arch-Mage felt the phase, and raised an eyebrow. "You fear the boy, Braunen?"

The old man shrugged. "I have plans for him, as well as for all within this castle."

"We'd best talk quickly, then. If not undone, that spell will make him discorporate ere long." The dwarf peered closely at Jacob. "There's something about this one ... in his mind."

"Enough, Dietrich," Braunen interrupted. "You're correct. We must be quick about this. I've many places to be, and many fires to tend. Arch-Mage, you've seriously misreckoned how long you've been gone. Time, time passes ... strangely in the Otherworld. *Verstehen Sie?* Where only a few years may have passed for you in Annen Verden, centuries have passed on this plane."

Dietrich snorted. The comments finally distracted from his preoccupation with Jacob, and a true smile flashed through the storm of his emotions. "*Bitte*, Braunen. No jokes. I've just returned."

"I'm not in jest. We're no longer anywhere near Cad Camlan. The Knights, the Huntsmen, the Witches, and Druids—they're all gone. That moment is lost, Dietrich. Yours and Veröld Martröd's plans were undone at the Fields of Burning Night. You must accept that Taliesin, Merlin, and their king succeeded in denying you the prize—"

"*Their* king?" Dietrich snapped. "Perhaps he was Merlin's king, but not Taliesin's. Taliesin and Arthur were enemies until the last moment! Something ... some*one* changed Taliesin's mind, and I think it must have been Verdandi—"

"They succeeded —" Braunen repeated, then crooked a robed arm and coughed heavily into it. "I say, they succeeded in denying you the prize back *then*. Pay heed to the present. Look around you, Dwarf. Don't you see this masonry? How different in design and shape human buildings have become since you last walked Mediterranean lands?"

Dietrich's hand flashed in Jacob's direction, and part of the boy's frozen mind flinched, but the dwarf only splayed his fingers upon the limestone wall.

"*Hmmph*," Dietrich muttered. "If I'm displaced by centuries, you lie about it being the future, not if this wall's any indication." He withdrew his hand and glanced at his fingertips.

"Yet, civilization rarely moves in reverse, so why's this building so crude?" the dwarf continued thoughtfully. "If I'm indeed in the future, and if this stonework's a guide to the lack of advancement, there may yet be a way to accomplish the task, even without Taliesin. *Ja, ja*. There's respectable rock here, but the Romans built better in their temples, their civic centers. *Hmmph*. By Niflheim, come to think of it, even the Greeks built better."

His voice momentarily without anger, Dietrich continued softly. "Do you remember those days, Braunen? I saw Emperor Justinian's basilica a few months before Cad Camlan." He grunted. "I'll allow that *that* building was a decent bit of Midgardian stonework."

"Hagia Sophia still rises above Justinian's city," the old man said, "half a millennium after Amari's and your flight through the cistern. I believe that even the *runeporte* you and Taliesin made within the basilica walls remains intact ..." Braunen's lips pursed mischievously. "It still functions. I know that Urd used it recently."

"A Norn used one of my portals? The world has changed."

"To the victors go the spoils," Braunen said. "Everything that was yours, belongs now to the Fated Three."

"*Hmmph*. Don't try to bait me, Braunen. Unlike Taliesin, I know your ways."

"You were angry a moment ago, confused," the old man said, putting both hands on his cane and leaning forward. "Perhaps you thought Taliesin had seen the error of *his* ways, eh? That he regretted his decision, and opened a *runeporte* to pull his best friend back from Annen Verden? Poor Dietrich. How disappointed you must have been to see only me when the smoke from this blast cleared."

"I mean it—watch your tone, Druid," Dietrich murmured. "Besides, the idea's not so far-fetched. He might have realized he'd made a mistake."

"*Mistake?*" Braunen chuckled. "Is that what you've been thinking all these years in your prison? That Taliesin made a mistake by tearing the Sampo from you and using the Codex Regius to cast you into Annen Verden?"

"Taliesin and I *were* friends, Braunen. We'd been in many battles before. Things happen. Things get ... confused. At the end of the fight, there were many things happening at once."

"That's some confusion," the old man snorted. "I must take greater care when I'm creating a *runeporte* to the Otherworld ... oh, silly me, I forgot. You *can't* make a mistake creating a *runeporte* to the Otherworld! You need to summon Youdic the Damned, and let him finish the rune-casting! Or, did you forget that little fact as the Codex Wielder and the Norns handed you over to Youdic to drag you into the Pit?"

"Stop saying that name!" Dietrich frowned, his usually ruddy features paling at the mention of Youdic. "Thirty years of friendship overturned in one moment of betrayal. Damn the Norns, and thrice-damn the Codices!"

"One moment of betrayal?" The old man chuckled and shook his head. "I repeat, you've not been gone six autumns, but six *hundred*."

Dietrich's eyes widened. "Six hundred? *Nein, nein*. That's not possible. I would've felt it."

"There's that arrogance," Braunen beamed. "I've missed that, I think. Well, whether you believe it or not, I'd say that's quite a lengthy 'moment,' eh?"

"Even for me, that stretch of time ... my kindred, the dwarf kingdoms ... *und* ... Traeg."

"The Nibelung still thrive," the old man assured him, "and Traeg's still alive, although I think that she's found a dwarf more to her liking and temperament."

"Andvari." Dietrich's face clouded again.

"Come now, Dietrich, you can't blame her," Braunen said. "Given all the reports of your liaisons with witches, succubi, and any of the students at the academy who'd 'take a walk' with you near your apartment by the underground sea, you really weren't in Traeg's bed often enough for the relationship to last—"

"She lives, though."

"She lives."

Braunen fell silent, then added softly, "Ever was I a better friend to you than Taliesin or Traeg, Master Dietrich."

"When things went your way," the dwarf said dismissively.

"I do like that best." Braunen sighed.

"Six hundred years ..." Dietrich held his hands before him, then examined what he could see of his body. "*Hmmph.* So be it. I live. I feel my magic within me. I've aged only six years, and I still have a job to do."

"*Gut,* let me tell you some of the events that matter, the ones concerning the Codex—"

Dietrich held up a hand. "Let's be honest, Braunen—Veröld, Taliesin, and I disagreed about many things, but the one thing we all were in accord about was not trusting you. Taliesin was the one who listened to your honeyed words. *Bei den Göttern!* You were the one who first introduced us to the witches! They were the ones who were our undoing."

"*Und,* you had your fun with many of those witches, didn't you?" Braunen shook his head. "Don't act an innocent here, Dietrich. I simply introduced you to Morgana, Sølvmora, and Amari; I didn't tell you to bed them all, then try to use them against their own Coven! That was your faulty judgment. I told you to use them against the druids, to use the plans of both witch and warlock for your own purpose—"

"Honeyed words *und* too damn many witches," Dietrich interrupted, still reflecting. "Too many temptations for my dwarves, Mogthasir's Huntsmen, and Taliesin's knights. *Huh.* If we include Verdandi and Skuld, probably too many witches for even Taliesin himself." He glared at Braunen.

"What?" The old man grumbled, irritated at the dwarf's sudden silence. "Don't give me a look like the Balor-Dirk. Do you have something to say to me, Arch-Mage?"

"*Sie waren richtig*, Braunen."

Braunen smiled, revealing yellowed and decayed teeth, and then put a finger in his ear. "Eh? Would you repeat that? It had the tone of an apology. My hearing's been ... "

"Damn your ears, I said you were correct!" Dietrich snapped. "We should've remained united with your kind. Your druids might have been able to counter Taliesin when he went after Mogthrasir and me. They certainly helped us when we fought Njörd and his *fossegrim* and *strömkarlen* for the sarsen stones at Emain Ablach."

The dwarf's glare returned. "Stop gloating, you goat. Perhaps we *would* have listened to you more carefully, if we could have trusted you. If we didn't have to double-think all your words, nor spend so much time trying to avoid your snares."

"Call my words what you will, I never lied to you!" Braunen retorted. "*Und* look where you both ended up by *not* heeding my counsel. Tell me, did you see the almighty Veröld Martröd or Taliesin while you wandered Otherworld?"

"They were exiled there, too?" Dietrich asked, stunned.

"Mighty are the Norns, and great was their hatred for the Codices and the Sampos," Braunen said. "I'd bet Taliesin's thirty pieces of silver that you didn't see any of the Norns in Otherworld, either."

"*Bah!* Taliesin didn't betray me for coins," Dietrich groused. "More likely it was the promise of burying himself in Verdandi's cleavage or Skuld's grotto, if you know what I mean."

"Hah! Oh, Dietrich, would that you listened to me," Braunen mused, then he spoke slowly, as if savoring a memory. "As many do, you thought the Norns were crones simply huddled around Mimir's Well, watching ... *heh!* Watching over the Nine Worlds while cobwebs and dust gathered in their brains, bodies, and lower regions. Fool. I warned you. The Norns are almost ageless, and they can be just as tempting in flesh and mind as any witch from the Coven of Mists."

"Taliesin," the dwarf muttered, ignoring the comment and focusing on his own pain as he spoke to empty space. "What in Grimnir's Name were you thinking? Was it truly a woman's wiles that turned you against us?" He regarded Braunen pointedly. "I didn't agree with it, but Taliesin and I had a plan. The battle was almost over, and then the Codex Wielder changed everything when Mogthrasir revealed himself as Surtur's agent. Even then, even then, he and I could have held off both Mogthrasir and destroyed the Codices. No, someone got to him. Only the Norns had the power to change Taliesin's mind, and the only Norns I ever saw him with were Verdandi and Skuld."

"I tell you, Arch-Mage, it was neither of them," Braunen clicked the cane on the ground in finality. "In fact, I know that—far from opposing any of your efforts—those two Norns were so besotted with the idea of making Taliesin their own that they'd even persuaded Mimir to look the other way. Mimir! *Verstehen Sie?* At the end, those two Norns *and* Mimir were willing to let you, Veröld, and a disguised Mogthrasir do what you could to destroy the Codices."

"That makes no sense," Dietrich said. "I recall now that Taliesin and Merlin were chanting together, that Youdic appeared to complete the *runeporte* and cast me into Annen Verden, but I saw only Verdandi and Skuld there at the end of the battle. They did nothing but watch him make the *runeporte* that exiled me!"

"*Ja, ja,*" Braunen agreed, "but isn't that the curious thing? Two of the three Sisters of Fate are present with their supposed mortal enemies, you, Veröld Martröd, Taliesin, and Mogthrasir, and they do *nothing?*"

"It's not beyond belief," Dietrich said. "Taliesin was appealing to many women—"

"Did your mind rot in the forests, fool?" Braunen snapped. "There's none so appealing that any Norn would forget her hatred of the Codices for the sake of a man, any man. *Nein,* Dietrich. For the answer, look not to the Norns who lusted after Taliesin, but the one whom *he* desired. Look to Urd when you seek vengeance! All those witches are drawn to the Codex Light like moths to a flame—but, only one of the Fated Three held his heart. Only one could have the power and restraint to use his attraction to achieve her own ends and then destroy him and his codices when all his allies were gone. Only one of the Norn's possessed a beauty that outshone even Verdandi and Skuld."

"Urd."

"Urd. Taliesin probably had no chance when she asked him to betray you. She must have clouded his mind with the Norn's Voice, then rewarded him with the pleasures of her body after he and Youdic the Damned cast you and your friends into the Otherworld."

Dietrich didn't reply, again assessing the chambers and hallway.

"Well, since I'm obviously boring you, enough of this. As I said, I have things—" Braunen stopped speaking and gave a rheumy-eyed glance at Jacob.

The old man paused and stared. Was the boy listening? More, had he somehow managed to move an eyelid? Impossible. Jacob stood outside of time and space.

You will not surprise me, boy. I have plans that call for you and your mother in one place, at one time, and that time and place isn't now! He grunted, disturbed. Just in case he had missed something in his assessment of Jacob, it seemed best to end this conversation soon.

Braunen returned his attention to Dietrich. "I'll tell you this much, Arch-Mage: you, indeed, sense truly about Taliesin and the Knights. Of that group, Perceval and Palomides *are* nearby, though their faces are different from the enemies you remember."

"Returned recently, as I was?" Dietrich shook his head. "I'm confused, Braunen. I don't understand. You said I've been gone six hundred years, and that Urd killed Taliesin and destroyed the Codices. But, only a Lore Master's magic could've wrenched me from *Annen Verden*. A Lore Master at the height of his powers with all the Artifacts of Destiny at his command. Before he ... did what he did, Taliesin and I slew all of them. Together, we made sure that none were left alive. If the Norns ... if *Urd* allied with Taliesin after he cast Mogthrasir into the pit and me into Annen Verden, who brought me back?"

"*Nein.* You misunderstand, both in what happened to Taliesin *and* the fate of Arthur's Knights. Veröld Martröd and Mogthrasir were defeated, yes, but Taliesin ... Taliesin vanished. My question about whether you saw him in the Otherworld sprang from irritation. I lost Sight of him after the battle, and last saw him clutching Urd as they transported from the field.

"But," the old man shook his cane in warning at Dietrich, "I tell you this: Perceval and Palomides *never* departed this realm, and your return to this place, along with this destruction..." Braunen's voice tapered off. He shook his head, then raised a blue-veined hand to indicate the smoldering corpses and blasted medical hall. The old Hospitaller chuckled. "Believe me or not, when you look at all of this destruction, these horrible deaths, know this: there's *no* intention behind any of this magic!"

Dietrich's bushy eyebrows narrowed.

"*Nein.* What you see comes from the goading of a squirrel, and the momentary irritation of a *new* Lore Master —"

"*Was ist das?*" The dwarf erupted. "A squirrel? Ratatosk?"

"None other. You're fortunate that this new Codex Wielder's young and prone to mistakes, else you'd still be in the bogs of *Annen Verden* looking for a Rune Gate home."

"A new Lore Master?" Dietrich repeated, digesting the information. "*Und*, he's not Taliesin?"

"Call him an heir."

"*Jaaa* ... that explains why I'm here on Midgard and not Nidaveller." Dietrich's expression grew alarmed. "Then the Codices weren't destroyed."

Braunen shrugged. "The Book of Tears is almost fully returned. I know not of what happened to the others. I believe that the Norns either destroyed them or hid them."

"*Hmmph.* So, who is this would-be Codex Wielder, and why hasn't Ratatosk ordered a witch to kill him?"

"The squirrel tried to, I think, and this crude attempt at a rune-gate was misdirected sorcery from the new Lore Master's annoyance with an apprentice Norn—"

"Apprentice Norn?" Dietrich laughed. "Honeyed words, again, Braunen? Always your words seem to drip with lies. There's no such thing as an apprentice Norn! Urd, Skuld, and Verdandi are eternal. They'd slay anyone who sought to replace them."

"I tire of repeating myself. You are returned by the unlearned sorcery of a new Lore Master. Believe me or not, but I'd remind you of how you've just spent six centuries thinking about how you should've listened to me."

"What's his name? Give me his name, and tell me what in Odin's Name Ratatosk is doing with either a Codex Wielder or a Norn. He hates both of their kinds!"

"I'll reserve the boy's identity for another time. *Und*, as ever, one can't be sure of Ratatosk's true allegiance until it's too late. He enjoys playing with mortals almost as much as I do."

Something caught the old man's eye and he glanced at Jacob.

Creator be damned and sit at my left hand, did the boy blink again?

He smacked his lips, casting a calculating look at Jacob. "I feel dry and need a drink. Go, Dwarf. Get out of here."

"*Aber*, I still need—"

"*Bah!* I've said enough, Dietrich. I've already told you more than's my custom."

"You *und* your damned games, Braunen."

The Hospitaller smiled thinly. "It appears that one consequence of those games was to bring you back, wasn't it? No, no, I tell you, *enough*, Dwarf. You begin to remind me why we had a falling out all those years ago. I can't explain anything more here. I've duties to attend, and our paths weren't yet meant to cross. Go!"

"I need a staff," Dietrich protested. "Even that cane of yours could be used to fashion a decent *runeporte* to—"

"*Go!* Go, I say, before I take this cane and rap it over your thick head! Maybe send you to the deepest part of *Sheol*, eh? Would you like that, Master Dwarf? Think you that Annen Verden was a nightmare? Come to my home, Dietrich. Come to where my master lives!

"No, no, no." Braunen shook his head in the way that elders do when obstinacy becomes habit. "I think you'll find there's enough work to be done *here* without trying to take revenge on the Norns or Arthur's knights."

"I need to get back to my people," Dietrich said. "They need to be warned that the Codices weren't destroyed."

"Don't worry about getting back to Nidaveller. Not yet! All will be well. I tell you, already caskets built in the antique style approach this castle—caskets whose contents will make a rune gate that rivals the one over the Niflheim Sea! *Und*, I can't reveal my plans, but I will give you this much: whatever you might think you sense, avoid the scriptorium. I've plans there that will brook no interference. Besides, the young man who can help you most was recently in a fight near the Inner Ward. They'll bring him to the pilgrim cells."

"I'm going to neither an outer ward nor pilgrim cells, Braunen," Dietrich muttered insistently, "*und* certainly not when I know that something's wrong *here*. I smell Taliesin's stink— high codex magic—everywhere in this area, *these* rooms."

"Why wouldn't you? His heir's been walking these floors for years. However, the boy's not in this hospital at the moment. You're wasting both of our time, Master Dietrich. Trust me in this: take a look at the Inner Ward, ask for where they've taken 'Ríg,' and your path will become clear."

"Trust you?" Dietrich barked a laugh and shook his head. "*Nein, nein.* I saw what happened to Mogthrasir when he trusted you. Taliesin and the Norns tore him apart, then remade him into something ... else."

"Mogthrasir trusted too much in Surtur's and the witches' promises," Braunen corrected, "and you need to listen carefully to my words. I didn't say trust me completely, Dietrich. I said trust me in *this*, and take a Look."

While he spoke, the Hospitaller gave the dwarf a long, considering gaze, and the dwarf took a half step backward in deference. Though still irritated, he put hands on hips and glared at Braunen. "Oh, very well, I'll take a moment to See!"

In an obvious attempt to calm himself, he inhaled deeply, crossed burly arms over his barrel chest, and shut his eyes. "Ah. *Ja, sehr gut* ... very good. We are on Midgard, and the other worlds seem unharmed. *Und* ... Hela's here? *Und* Fafnir? That old worm still flies? *Hmmph.* I thought him slain by Sigurd and holding pride of place among Hela's Dead." The dwarf's eyes widened. "*Was? Was ist das? Nein—das ist unmöglich.* Not possible. Very distant, I can See ... Veröld Martröd?"

"He's not fully returned," Braunen said, "but I've Seen him, too. He gathers strength in northern Italic lands, where a city's risen from lagoons since last you walked there."

"Perhaps all isn't lost, then." Dietrich mused, then lowered his chin, concentrating.

"*Und,* there are witches remaining on this world? *Ja* ... they flicker in the Sight just as weakly as Veröld Martröd, but they're alive. *Hei*, now, Cerys just appeared! *Und*, I sense another. *Aber*, *welche hexe?* Which witch? Nimue? *Nein*. She's still lost. Amari of the Mountain? *Nein*. Not on this plane, at least. Ah ... *ja*." He inhaled deeply and opened his eyes. "She's disguised, barely flickering in my eye, but it can be no other: it's the witch, Sølvmora. But, in Constantinople? *Hmmm*. That's nowhere near any of the Nordic ranges she usually haunts. How far are we from southern Gaul, Braunen?"

The Hospitaller smiled again. "Hundreds of leagues distant, and far, far eastward."

"*Hmmph*. No matter, hopefully I'll not be dealing with witches again anytime soon, but Sølvmora was an enchantress not soon forgotten, on the field of battle, nor in the bedchamber."

Dietrich inhaled yet again, and seemed to savor whatever scent he'd found. "Ha! There they are! I *am* close. I can smell both Codex and Sampo. Nearby, but just out of reach, as they sometimes were of old." He sniffed again, and then opened his eyes abruptly. "*Und ... was ist das?* Two Huntsmen, also?" He looked questioningly at the Hospitaller. "They've come back? What game's being played here, Braunen?"

"Too many games to explain for one so recently returned," the old Hospitaller cautioned.

"Ah, *ja*. I understand. I mean, I *don't* understand, but no matter. I've a Sampo to hunt. I intend to finish my task, so I repeat the warning I gave you before the Fields of Burning Night: stay out of my way."

"As ever, I respect your wishes, Arch-Mage," Braunen replied. "I spoke up here only because I have need of this child. I didn't want you harming him. He will do some ... work for me."

Dietrich whispered a rune that allowed him to match the temporal distortion, and then made a show of straightening the boy's tunic before shoving Jacob at the Hospitaller. "Well, then. Here you go. See, Braunen? No harm done. He'll be fine, and you can carry on with whatever you're doing, as I go to complete the work Taliesin and I began."

"*Ich würde zu keinem anderen Zweck, alter Freund zu fragen,*" murmured the Hospitaller.

"We're not friends, Braunen!" Dietrich said, raising a warning finger.

"It's so good to see you again, too, Arch-Mage," Braunen replied dryly with a slight bow. "May you have better luck this time in your quest."

Dietrich started to say something else, but the Hospitaller snapped his fingers, and restored Jacob both to the normal flow of time and into his proper dimension.

CHAPTER 3

The Dawdling Hospitaller

The return of Jacob's motion and words coincided with his mother, Rebecca, walking unsteadily around the corner. Her eyes lit first upon the old man.

"Finally, Brother Nicholas, there you are!"

Jacob's relief at seeing her combined with a realization that she'd seen neither Dietrich's violent interactions, nor his threats.

She appeared dazed but rejoiced at seeing her son stumbling toward her as the dwarf helped the boy to his feet.

"Ah, you did find him, Brother Nicholas," she said, repeating the old knight's name. "And, you're still here, Master Dietrich?

Well, here's my one remaining pride—my son, Jacob. Jacob, this is Master Dietrich."

"We just met. A fine, strapping lad he is, too, Milady," Dietrich said gruffly. He brought a heavily gauntleted glove onto Jacob's shoulder. "Reminds me of some ... knights I used to know. He's all right, just a little dusty from taking a fall, aren't you, son?"

Jacob winced at the dwarf's slap, but checked his anger. From the way Dietrich's fingers dug into his flesh, the dwarf seemed willing to make good on his earlier threat. Jacob wouldn't put his mother in harm's way for the satisfaction of an angry retort.

Instead, the boy simply shrugged off the dwarf's hold, knelt, and retrieved his sword. He embraced Rebecca, and held her for a long moment. Whatever the two men were discussing didn't seem to concern him, and his mother looked deathly ill. Her well-being took priority over all else.

"*Ima!*" he said, holding her shoulders as he stepped back to look down at her. "Are you well? What happened here?" His questions tumbled after one another in his relief. "I thought you were in a room behind that collapsed section over there?"

"Oh, Jacob, I don't know. I don't know. The room is beyond that pile, but we came another way. Brother Nicholas gave me an elixir that he brewed—"

"No, not I!" interrupted the old Hospitaller sharply, rapping his cane on the stone floor. "Belvedere made it! I merely delivered it to you according to his instructions."

Rebecca paused, regarding the old man curiously, then continued. "Yes, well, wherever it came from, I began responding to the medicine better than anything I've taken before."

"Do you think it's the cure that Ibn-Khaldun's trying to find for you, *Ima?*" Jacob asked, unable to hide the excitement in his voice.

"I don't know, but we can hope. Anyway, Belvedere thought I was responding so well, that he moved me from the general ward to a pilgrim's cell." She sighed and waved an exasperated hand, "Then, Brother Nicholas came to check on me, we saw a flash of blue-green, and Dietrich appeared—"

"*Und*, 'Brother Nicolas,' *Frau* David-son, I must be off," Dietrich snapped. He inclined his head toward the group and strode away in the direction from which Jacob had come.

"Oh, Lord," Rebecca murmured, moving past the knight. Her eyes widened at the sight of the destroyed ward beyond her son's shoulder.

She approached the nearest corpse, but Jacob caught her under the elbow before she stumbled over a post that protruded from a ruined bed frame.

"No, *Ima*, no. I don't care how you think you were doing, you look exhausted now. You should be back in bed, and ... I already checked here. There's no one left alive."

"No one?" She turned toward him, horrified. "But, there were at least forty men in here."

"Thirty-six were killed by the blast," he said. "I've seen no one else."

"Oh, Jacob, no!" Rebecca looked in confusion at Braunen. "But, we heard nothing Brother Nicholas! How could this happen without us hearing any kind of explosion?"

The monk gazed at the dead bodies and ruined ward, his eyes unreadable. "This seems to be the Devil's work." He turned to Jacob with a glint in his eye. "Don't you think so, boy?"

"It's war," Jacob replied, keeping his own ideas about the mystery to himself. "But, I'm not sure how this happened with no one hearing it."

The old man grunted. "It's a mystery that will be solved, Lady Rebecca, I promise."

"*Ima*, I want to stay with you," Jacob said, "but I can't. I'm supposed to get a doctor to Master Khajen to help Brother Mercedier."

"I'll be fine, Jacob. Go with Brother Nicholas. He's a doctor."

The old man raised his cane and swung it like a pendulum before him. "Well, *heh*, it may take a while with these crippled legs, but, *ja*, of course, I'll go with you, Jacob. Good to meet you, boy, even amid such horror."

He extended a wrinkled hand, liver-spotted and shaking with palsy. Jacob, confused that Dietrich had called him Braunen while his mother knew him as Brother Nicholas, shook it reluctantly and took stock of the stranger.

Whatever his name, the Hospitaller seemed of an extreme age in a time when most people seemed to die by their mid-thirties. Jacob guessed that Braunen was well into his seventies, with a bald head, thinly arched white eyebrows, and brooding dark eyes of indeterminate color.

"Your mother's been telling me many extraordinary things about you."

"Hello," Jacob said, feeling cautious. "Thank you for helping me with ... Master Dietrich. You're really a physician here? I didn't see you earlier."

"I just arrived at the castle, but I know human beings inside and out," the old knight assured him.

"Oh, good." Jacob gave a nervous glance backward, but Dietrich was truly gone.

He gathered his thoughts, remembering his mission. Other Hospitallers must be coming soon, and if they weren't, he could tell Grand Master Arcadian himself to resolve the situation and tend to the bodies here. He focused on the fact that his mother was safe.

"Khajen ibn-Khaldun asked me to find a physician to help Brother Mercedier," Jacob said.

"The Grand Master's brother?"

"Yes, he's upstairs in Father Arcadian's solarium. He was injured during a sortie and not recovering from surgery. Brother Mercedier's condition is worsening, and Master Ibn-Khaldun wanted Brother Belvedere to come help him. I think that they've got to do another operation."

Concern marked the doctor's careworn face. "Well, I fear that I'm the only one here who can help. See that poor knight there? That was Brother Belvedere."

Jacob, shocked, looked at the corpse, then again at the Hospitaller. "But, the elixir? Didn't he give my mother the potion?"

"Quite so. He prepared the potion, and gave them to me for safekeeping. I have the remaining vials here—why don't you take them?

Jacob took the proffered four green-glassed phials and put them in one of the pouches at his waist while the old man continued talking.

"Belvedere started to give me a tour of the area before he checked on a patient. That's when I noticed your mother in one of the pilgrim cells and began speaking with her ... *hmmm*, a cell now beyond that pile of rubble back there. I'm glad we found another way around."

"Would you come, then?" Jacob asked, regretting that there'd be no chance now to follow Ríg, but determined not to fail Ibn-Khaldun's request. If necessary, he'd *carry* this elderly doctor back to the solarium where Brother Mercedier lay.

"Yes, of course. I'll go immediately. W e can't have the second-in-command disabled while two armies wait outside, can we?"

"No, sir, we can't."

"I'll tend to things here," Rebecca said, moving in the direction of the ruined ward.

"Where are you going, *Ima*? You need to get to bed."

"Not with all these poor men dead," Rebecca exclaimed, but her raised voice brought on another coughing fit. "We ... we need to get help. Someone to collect the bodies."

"*Ima*, we're heading upstairs to the Grand Master's chambers. I'll tell Father Arcadian what happened, and there will be many knights here shortly. Please, go to bed so I know that you're safe."

"I ... of course, Son. You are correct. I'll go back to my room, but please, be careful."

"We should be going," the old Hospitaller said. "Please, Jacob, lead the way."

Jacob saw how unsteady the man seemed to be.

"Perhaps you follow when you can. I'll run ahead and—"

"Please, boy. From the state of things here, most of the castle's preparing for war. Even if you got to Arcadian first, there might not be anyone to spare to run back for me. Come. I haven't been assigned here long, so I'm still getting to know my way around the place. Lead the way. I really think we should go together." Braunen reached a hand to Jacob's shoulder for support and nodded at the boy's mother. "Farewell, Rebecca."

"Goodbye, and thank you again for the visit."

Stymied, but unable to argue with his elder's logic, Jacob moved slowly with the decrepit knight toward the stairs. "I appreciate you checking on my mother," he said as he tried to curb his patience. *At this rate, we're not going to get back to the solarium until two dawns from now!*

"It was my pleasure," the knight replied, smacking his lips. "So thirsty, but it can wait until we reach the Grand Master. It can wait. Your mother. *Ja*, we had a good conversation, mostly about places and people we both knew in Constantinople."

"People you both knew? That's amazing, Father ... I mean, Brother—" Jacob was at a loss what to call the man. Moreover, it surprised him that his mother and this strange knight should have mutual acquaintances. There were too many riddles in this hospital ward to digest at once.

"Forgive me, sir, but what *is* your name?" the boy asked. "Dietrich called you 'Braunen,' but my mother called you 'Brother Nicholas.'"

"Ah, *ja*. Dietrich knew me as Brother Braunen when we first met back in the northern lands. That was a long time ago, before I joined the Hospitallers and took my Christian name."

"So long ago that it feels like 'centuries?'" Jacob asked, echoing part of the conversation that had confused him.

"You heard that, eh? *Sie verstehen Deutsch?*"

Jacob shrugged. "*Das wenige, was ich gelernt arbeitet das Geschäft in Konstantinopel.*"

"Ah. Your mother told me about your cloth shop in the city." Braunen hesitated. "As for meeting Dietrich, *ja*, it was so many years ago that it feels like centuries. What else did you hear?"

"I'm sorry for listening, but I didn't know what to make of Dietrich after he attacked me. Don't worry. I couldn't understand most of what you were talking about, but I thought I heard something about King Arthur."

"Arthur? I don't recall mentioning him."

"Yes, you did—when you were joking about Arthur, Merlin, and Taliesin."

The Hospitaller's eyes narrowed. "Joking?"

"You each mentioned Cad Camlan, but I must have gotten the tenses wrong because you both made it sound as if you were there."

To his chagrin, Braunen said nothing in reply. The old man was breathing heavily, and seemed to struggle with the simple exertion of walking.

"Cad Camlan?" Jacob repeated after a moment. "The battlefield in Britain where Arthur fell to Mordred? Hundreds of years ago? That's what I thought I heard you two talking about."

"Ah, that," Braunen halted and smiled. He peered closely at Jacob, flicked the hand holding the cane, and frowned when nothing happened.

"No, don't stop walking!" Jacob urged, trying not to scream. *We're never going to get there!*

"Eh? What's that?"

"I mean, let's just keep going. We're almost at the stairs."

"Cad Camlan?"

"Yes, yes," Jacob said, holding the old man's elbow as they moved forward again.

"I'm afraid you're correct about the joking, Jacob, but not in the way you think. That exchange was just a bit of scriptorium humor. I thought you had the air of learning about you. I'm impressed that you know Deutsch, let alone heard of the Arthurian legend here in the East."

"It's a captivating tale, and where else but the East?" Jacob appreciated the compliment about his education and tried to remain patient. He had to remember that any of the other physicians who could help Mercedier were dead, and that this old man had saved Jacob from whatever violence Dietrich had intended.

"Arthur and Merlin might be sleeping," the boy said, "but, wasn't the Holy Grail brought back to the East, to these lands?" He shrugged. "My teacher and I heard some say that the Grail even made its way back to Jerusalem under Sir Perceval's care."

"*Mmmm*, possibly, but others also say that Perceval failed at the last. Do you believe that the Grail's in the Holy Land?"

Jacob frowned. "I'm Jewish, and perhaps not the most qualified person to discuss the Cup of Christ. I'm not sure it exists."

"Come, come, we are educated men, are we not? You speak well and there seems to be some intelligence behind those eyes. Surely, you can guess, *hmmm*?" Braunen said, letting Jacob pass him to start ascending the stairwell. "Wait, *bitte*. Perhaps you could walk behind me? In case I fall? *Vielen Dank*."

Chagrined, Jacob waited for the stooped man to start climbing the stairs, a process that seemed to take a half hour.

"Now, to continue," Braunen said at the end of another coughing bout on the top landing. "Where were we? Ah, *ja*.

When questioning the Grail's existence, surely you can at least appreciate it as an artifact? A treasure to be valued and curious about?"

"I really wouldn't know enough to make a guess," Jacob pointed to the left, acutely feeling the press of time.

There are over two thousand people in this castle ... is there no one in these hallways that I can send to Ibn-Khaldun?

"I believe the solarium's this way. We really need to get there," he said, agonizing inside.

"No need to speak rudely," Braunen said curtly. "I'm going as fast as I can. *Heh.* You reach my age and try running around castles at suppertime!"

"Sorry, I just want to help Brother Mercedier."

"Good, good. So do I. We can go now. I've caught my breath. The Grail?"

For Yahweh's sake, forget about the damn Grail! What about your dead brethren? Why. Are. You. Walking. So. Slowly?

"The Grail," Jacob repeated, striving for patience while keeping pace with the physician. "What little I learned about it was last year in a Byzantine library. I was a scribe there. The tale about Arthur came by way of Gildas the Wise's account, and even learning about that source was accidental. My teacher was hosting an old friend of his from Cordoba, who'd just returned from Britannia. He told us the story, then Rabbi Mordecai, my friend Arella, and I spent a couple weeks researching it in the synagogue's archives. What about you? You're Christian, Brother, what do you think about the Grail's location?"

"A Christian? Oh, yes, yes, I'm ... I'm ..." he coughed again, then hacked violently and spit a wad of black phlegm on the floor. "A Christian. *Ja. Gut.*" He smiled through crooked teeth. "Sometimes, boy, I'm *so* consumed with Christianity that I give thought to little else." Braunen wiped the back of his hand across his mouth.

Still feeling ill from the sights in the ward, Jacob regretted his question. He should've known better than to bring up the topic of religion in a castle full of zealots. It was like being in Byzantium with the stone-bench preachers; one couldn't even mention Christianity without risking raptured fervor in some believers!

"In fact," Braunen said, "I have thought so much about Jesus of Nazareth that I feel as if I were present when the legionaries nailed Him to the Holy Rood at Golgotha."

Braunen chuckled, and then jerked a thumb toward the shadowed stairwell behind them. "But, no, Jacob, while I'm a believer in my own vocation, it might surprise you, but my mind about the Grail is close to yours, my ... religious beliefs notwithstanding. However, Dietrich back there—he's the one whom we should have asked."

"Dietrich?" Jacob exclaimed, completely nonplussed. "But, he's a—"

"*Ja, was ist es?*" Braunen prodded, his dark eyes glittering with amusement as they continued down the hallway. "I mean, I'm interested. What do you think he is?"

"A brute!" Jacob finished. "I'm sorry, but even if he's your friend, he seems to be a warrior, and certainly not interested in learning or books."

"*Ja*, I suppose he did appear that way to you, but he's under considerable ... stress. Let me simply say that Dietrich is, indeed, a scholar—he's always tried to be more warrior-like than his circumstances allowed, and now he finds himself displaced from the times and peoples he's familiar with." Braunen considered his words. "When I think about it, he ought to do very well here in this castle where monks are also knights! I assure you, he's spent more time with the lore of Arthur and his knights than anyone I've ever met."

Jacob fell quiet, remembering the dwarf's manner, which hadn't seemed scholarly in the least.

The old man raised the cane again, this time overtly waving it in front of Jacob's face.

"Why do you keep doing that?" the boy asked, surprised.

"*Eh*? Keep doing what?"

Jacob mimicked the sweeping hand motion, then added, "You keep putting the cane near me and waving it strangely, like some magicians I used to see back in Byzantium."

"Like this?" Braunen repeated the action. The old man frowned, obviously unable now to freeze space-time around the boy as he'd done while speaking with Dietrich.

"Yes, what are you doing?"

"*Bah!* It's the palsy—you'd think that your mother would've taught you better manners than making fun of old folk! *Hmmph*! Implying that a respectable Hospitaller knight like me is a sorcerer of all things ..." Braunen snorted, then moved off again, continuing to mutter.

For all of Braunen's patriarchal overbearing (mixed with a dose of repeated flattery at Jacob's intelligence), the boy wasn't fooled. Something was wrong here, wrong with this man, but he just didn't know what it was, and he simply didn't know enough about these westerners' ways to make an educated guess.

For all his suspicions, though, the supernatural presence he'd felt earlier seemed to have disappeared, and this Hospitaller's crotchety demeanor was making the boy feel foolish for even asking questions.

He shouldn't have been eavesdropping, anyway, but it had mattered little that he did. From the boy's perspective, the conversation between the Hospitaller and dwarf had occurred quickly, and even the boy's gift for languages hadn't helped him follow everything the reunited friends had said.

Besides Cad Camlan, the only other words that the two men had repeatedly used were the terms 'Sampo' and 'Taliesin,' neither of which meant anything to him. He also thought there'd been mention of Sølvmora a few times, but that seemed impossible, so he dismissed the thought as mistranslating on his part. Then there was the constant reference to codexes, witches, and druids, but given what Braunen had just explained about the men's common literary interests, it made a certain sense that they might discuss books. Perhaps the old knight had sent the dwarf to the Krak's vast library? As for the witches and druids, rumors of their existence fascinated even Jacob sometimes.

The boy shrugged away the problem for the same reason he'd temporarily shelved the mysteries of the explosion and dead birds. His mission was clear: he simply needed to get this doctor back to Master Ibn-Khaldun so that both physicians could help Brother Mercedier!

"So," Jacob said, focusing on the one thing he could clarify. "Your name's no longer Braunen, but Brother Nicholas?"

The doddering knight stopped at the stairwell that led to Grand Master Arcadian's chambers and assessed the boy. His eyes gleamed in the half-light, all irritation gone.

"I think we're going to get along just fine, Jacob, so let's not be so formal with Father This or Brother That. Are you able to do that?"

"Of course."

The Hospitaller winked, then clasped a shaky hand on the boy's shoulder before leading Jacob up the final flight of steps. "Good, good. Why don't you simply call me what my friends do? I prefer the name Old Nick."

CHAPTER 4

The Orphans
of Mecina

After Ríg and the other knights departed in haste to pursue the intruders at the gate, Father Arcadian, his brother, Mercedier, and Khajen ibn-Khaldun found themselves alone in the Grand Master's quarters.

"Ahh — that's it!" Mercedier groaned, when Ibn-Khaldun examined the old soldier's side.

Ibn-Khaldun nodded, replacing the coverlet over the man. He looked at Arcadian. "Let's have a drink, shall we?"

"*Mon Dieu* — a farewell toast? Am I dying, Khajen?" Mercedier asked.

"No, we just need a moment of rest," Ibn-Khaldun said. Arcadian motioned that he'd get the drinks and Ibn-Khaldun returned to his seat. "I'll have to go back inside, but I don't think that this is the poisoning I feared. I felt a slight protrusion just under the surface." He pointed at Mercedier's abdomen. "At your age, you're lucky to be alive after that battle and a fall like that."

"I know it," Mercedier watched Arcadian poured two goblets of wine and a cup of cold, saffron-laced tea. "Why go back inside, though? What about a magic potion? That made me sleep before."

"Let's try these drinks first, eh?" Ibn-Khaldun raised his cup. "To surviving another siege."

The brothers seconded him, and all took long, thoughtful sips.

Arcadian put his drink on the night table. "Well, I'll say it if no one else will," the Grand Master said. "There are too many similarities here to Mecina for my liking."

"Except," Mercedier qualified, "we have five times the castle and twenty times the people compared to back then."

"I'd add a small point," Ibn-Khaldun added, "but it is a point, nevertheless. In this instance, *we're* the ones besieged and not serving as a relief force, and there are *two* armies outside the walls, not one."

"Then, you add your own bit of mystery to the danger by arriving with a 'magic book' meant for young Santini," Arcadian said, thoughtfully appraising the scholar. "No, old friend, no. There's too much similarity here for coincidence, and too many coincidences with the prophecies we heard at Mecina."

"What?" Mercedier asked. "That troubadour's song?" He shook his head and grimaced at the pain. "Nonsense, Arcadian. Soothsayer or *non*, Eric the Mariner was a gibbering idiot. I said it back then, and I repeat it now: *absurde.*"

Ibn-Khaldun recalled the dawn of that morning five years ago at Mecina, when he, Arcadian, and Mercedier had approached the scored limestone of the demolished curtain wall.

Against a backdrop of fires blazing high from the castle, a colorfully dressed jester sat playing a fiddle on a pile of rubble. The music drifted, hauntingly beautiful over a ruined landscape still filled with the sounds of injured and dying people, the shouts of rescue personnel, burning buildings, and even the hastening clip-clop of horses being led to safer pastures.

The musician turned to the approaching Hospitallers, and the small contingent saw that he seemed blind, the shadows cast by a foppish hat didn't conceal a linen rag across his left eye. Moreover, the performer radiated pain. He appeared to be a person completely shattered by war, whose pockmarked and thinly black-bearded face, ragged clothing, and haggard aspect made for an altogether strange counterpoint to the exquisite melodies flowing from the strings of his Hardanger fiddle.

The trio dismounted the stallions and hiked up the pile of rubble.

"*Bonjour, messieurs!*" The jester said with a flourishing bow. He grandiosely doffed the fancy hat, but overthrew and lost it into a nearby fire. He frowned as the article briefly blazed, then shrugged and spread his hands.

"*Je suis Eric le Marin*—Eric the Seafarer— *et c'est Frett, un ami de longue date et tout un harpiste accomplie, jongleur, et zitherer!*"

Mercedier grunted. "You're alone, *mon ami*. Were you—"

"*Seul?*" The man croaked. "*Certainement pas!* Frett and I entertain together, always." He leaned forward to speak in a stage whisper, his voice gaining in strength. "*Et, entre nous cinq, nous espérons que vous venez de meilleure humeur que les Sarrasins qui vient de quitter ici.*" ("And just between the five of us, we hope you're in a better mood than the Saracens who just departed here !")

"I think the man over here is ... *was* Frett." Ibn-Khaldun said, nodding at a corpse slumped to the side of the boulder.

"*Qu'est-ce que c'est?*" Eric asked in alarm, following the Muslim's eyes until his own came to rest on the body of his friend. "Ah, Frett, *non, non, non!* No sleeping now! A song, a song!"

"Did you ... drag him here?" The grandmaster asked. "From the castle?"

"No, no, that would be mad, would it not?" Eric replied conversationally, even while he strained to lift Frett's body into an upright position.

"If he were dead," the jongleur continued, "why, I'd have left him in the courtyard on Santini's pyre, just like all the others did. There are enough corpses back there for both the *Sidhe* and Nightmare Lord to feast upon. Our friends piled them on the flames before they took their walk to the Genoese ships. To the sea. Hah! Don't worry about us. He's just tired and feeling a bit ... displaced. We're glad to see you. It means that we can start fixing everything, rebuild our home.

Eric's tugging on his friend's unmoving torso dislodged Frett's head, and the troubadour bolted to catch it before the decapitated thing rolled down the slope.

"*Non, non, non ...*" he said fiercely. "You need to be back here on the shoulders, Frett, stop falling off—"

"Enough!" Mercedier shouted, intercepting the man's wrist as Eric tried to complete his work. The soldier's tone quieted as he took the head from Eric, and returned it to the ground in proximity to the corpse. He covered both with a discarded cloak. "Enough, *ami*. Enough. He's gone."

"*Non,*" Eric wrenched away and hoisted his fiddle under his chin. He drew the bow across the strings on the mother-of-pearl fingerboard. "I can still hear the song he taught us during the siege. A soothsaying song, or I'm a fool. Listen. I'll prove it:

Sur la Barbe de Mimir, dans la Jeunesse des Mondes,
De Crânes de Jotuns, à la Dent de Ran Coralliens,
Cherché les Aesir—les frères, Vili, Vé, et Odin—
La Sagesse Antique, Neuf Reliques en Ruine.

Dessous de Givré Pins, sur un loin Côte Ardeur,
Près de Glade Elfique, par la Porte Surtur,
Frappe le Marteau du Volund—voir Destins Enlacés!—
Par le Forgeron Sampo, Codices Neuf récuperés ...

The effort seemed to exhaust the fiddler. He stopped abruptly, and returned in a heap to his boulder. "There's more, but it's dark and sad, and this is a bad enough day already. Oh, just leave the wretched youth be," the survivor pleaded, then pressed a palm against his temple. *"Oh, très bien, je vais leur dire, si vous voulez être tranquille!"*

Arcadian and Mercedier exchanged glances.

"Who are you telling to be quiet?" Mercedier asked.

"The *Sidhe*."

"The *Shee*?" The cynical Frenchman repeated. "What's that?"

"Not what, *who*, and they're in my head, all the time now." Eric's bow dangled limply in his slack hand. He exhaled slowly. "I think the Nightmare Lord is partial to musicians—oh, how these *Sidhe* wail! His sendings barely let Frett or I sleep for more than a couple hours at a time once the siege began." He paused. "*Et*, I confess: Frett didn't make up the song. I did. I just tried to write what the *Sidhe* were screaming in my mind all ... the ... time. I soothsay to you: Santini's fall becomes *your* ruin if you bring him with you! Hela walks this land, Surtur begins his bid for freedom, and the boy must face them alone."

Eric shook his head, his voice so calm and rationale in its tone that Ibn-Khaldun forced himself to remember the seeming madness of a few moments earlier.

" 'A deluded child,' " the troubadour continued. "That's what Veröld Martröd called him in the end. I think only I heard the words. The Nightmare Lord's so far away, but he's returning, he's returning. They'll all return, now. Urd didn't have the heart to end it at the Fields of Burning Night, and now all the enemies will return. Ancient enemies."

He cast a long gaze at the smoldering curtain wall. "Monsieur Martröd's *Sidhe* have been repeating much the same thing, mocking the boy, taunting us all." Eric raised his voice. "I soothsay thus: Santini was orphaned while still at home, but knew it not—let reality catch him and take its due. Such is the nature of sacred quests, eh? Interfere, though, and worlds will be worse for it later—doomed. He was not meant to be here, nor to survive this siege. All is changed. The worlds will burn with a fire like the heart of Creation itself ...”

"Ignore him, he's crazy," Mercedier said, nodding to where a fountain still splashed peacefully on corpses floating in its waters. "Look at this place—everything seems doomed, and Santini's lying through there, dead."

"...this is the world that awaits us all," Eric continued in disgust, "both *franj* and Saracen alike. My dear, dear Frett—why did you have to stay up so late and play with those nasty *Sidhe*? They came for him, they came for Santini and you distracted them. You ... lost your head!"

The jester barked a laugh, then saw Arcadian and Mercedier tightening the reins on their stallions and convulsed into sobs. "You go? You leave poor Frett and his Eric? Ah, *c'est une bonne chose, ce qui est bon. Je comprends. Nous ne sommes plus comme un couple heureux. Nous sommes actuellement trois.*" ("Ah, that's a good thing, for the best. I understand. We no longer live as a happy couple. We are now three.")

He leaned against the boulder and again took up the instrument. "You'll find Santini in there. My last warning to you, a gift of the *Sidhe* screaming their frustration in my head: beware his finding a book that weeps, or a sword that sings— each alone is chaos. Together? Murder and madness that can be healed only by a cup of blood!"

The fiddler returned to his music, his words receding into a titter. "A cup of blood, the chrism of kings. *Et*, that's only three of six, before the line that bars all nine ... *Ha!* Break time's over, Frett! Grab your harp, and get to work, you Lazybones."

He began to play again, but while the Hospitaller brothers moved on to ascend the hill that led to the destroyed front gate, Ibn-Khaldun remained to listen. This time, he noticed, along with repeating the first verses, Eric the Seafarer finished the song.

"That man's broken by war," Mercedier muttered when Ibn-Khaldun rejoined him. The Muslim scholar said nothing, still thoughtfully regarding Eric.

"He seems to soothsay well," Ibn-Khaldun observed. "Those images seemed specific."

"*Vraiment,* Khajen? Really?" Mercedier blanched, then in a slightly mocking tone recited the first verse:

Upon Ymir's Beard, in World's Youth,
From Jotun's Skulls, to Ran's Coral Tooth,
Sought the Aesir—Odin, Vili, and Ve—
Nine Runed Relics, Wisdom's Way.

"That's prophesying to you? It sounds like gibberish!"

The old man's eyebrows raised in amusement. "For gibberish, you repeated it quite well."

"Bah. I'm still a monk, and I do listen, Khajen." He jerked a thumb at the mourning jester. "I tell you, he's in shock from losing his friend, and his words are *absurde.*"

"We'll see."

"Wait. What are you doing? Where are you going now?"

"Back to Eric for a moment. To write it down."

"*Mon Dieu*, Khajen. This place is a war zone. Can we at least get inside the castle and see for ourselves?"

"Look around, *mon ami*, the battle's over, and no one's going anywhere. I'll be back shortly. Something tells me that this song is important. Something in the man's … presence."

Mercedier and Arcadian waited for him to return, but it was a quarter hour before he joined them. Even with shorthand, it took many tries until Eric could repeat the song in its entirety, rather than fragmented phrases.

"*Finis?*" Mercedier asked.

"For now—I may speak to him again on the way out. *Merci.*"

The trio passed through the gigantic smoking gap in the wall next to the ruined front gate and emerged into a nightmarish scene.

Hospitallers seemed to be everywhere; the white crosses on their black robes and surcoats the only symbol of order in the chaos.

Pinkish-white smoke billowed into the lightening, rose-colored skies of dawn as the kitchens and stables continued to burn. Some castle servants ran in panic past the blazing timbers and hay bales that fueled the fires, while more composed knights carried bodies to mass graves in the nearby Syrian hills.

"You, friends!" Arcadian shouted, signaling two of the knights. "What are your names?"

"Manegold of Brescia, Grand Master!" The nearest man replied, his tone clipped and martial.

"Bruno de Lucca, Grand Master!" replied the other.

"Where's Brother Santini?"

Against a backdrop of fires blazing high from the castle,
a colorfully dressed jester sat playing a fiddle on a pile of rubble...

"Dead, Grand Master!" Bruno nodded at another knight. The man took his place at the stretcher and trotting over to talk. "Dead—and this castle would have fallen to the Saracens a fortnight past, if not for him. You'll find his remains on that pile." He pointed at the gigantic pyre visible through the half-collapsed timbers of an interior gate.

"What garrison did he hail from?" Mercedier asked. "The Krak's lists hold no record of the man."

Bruno shrugged. "We don't know, *monsieur*, and we didn't much care."

"Didn't care?" Mercedier began, but Manegold stepped in front of his friend.

"What he means," Manegold explained, "is that we didn't know him, either. We never even saw his face—stayed hooded the entire siege, he did."

"It didn't matter what he looked like, or where he was from, did it?" Bruno countered, moving around his friend to get in front of Manegold. "No, Grand Master, what mattered is what Santini *did*. We would've followed that man into Hell. In fact, I'd say we did follow him into Hell!"

"Some precision, *s'il vous plaît*," Ibn-Khaldun said dryly.

"Who is he?" Bruno asked, apparently noticing the elderly Muslim for the first time. "What is he doing here?"

"You mentioned Hell," Arcadian prompted, ignoring the man's question.

"*Oui, oui, je m'excuse, Grand Maître*," Manegold answered, glowering at the other knight. "What he means is that, last night, Islamic miners tried to enter by digging under the curtain wall. When it collapsed, Santini led the defense until we pushed the

Saracens back. Santini didn't stop there, though. He took a hundred of us into the camp, and we captured Lord Turan-Shah—"

"Saladin's brother?" Ibn-Khaldun asked. "He started this siege?"

"*Oui*, and for no reason, Monsieur!" Bruno's disbelief made his voice tremble with rage. "The Krak's a half-day distant and filled with knights—Mecina is, was, a monastery that happens to have a drawbridge." He shook his head. "No, there was no reason to attack us ..."

"*Assez de ce genre de discours*," Mercedier interrupted sharply. "We need to know what happened."

"*Oui, oui*. Bruno, please, let me tell them. You're too emotional about this, the Grand Master and his party simply want to—"

"*Hommes d'armes, maintenant!*" Mercedier ordered sharply.

Both soldiers straightened at the martial call to order, and Manegold spoke quickly. "Sorry, Sir. Once we had Turan-Shah in custody, the siege was almost settled peacefully. Santini's raiding party returned and *le grand homme* brought Turan-Shah to the battlements so Saladin would have no choice but to negotiate. Unfortunately, the knight holding Turan-Shah slit his throat while they talked, and threw the body off the wall. Killed him right in the middle of the negotiation. Santini slew the murderer and screamed at Saladin that he'd not meant for his brother to die. Saladin didn't listen. He rode away, enraged beyond reason—"

"Rightly so," Arcadian murmured. "Such behavior is not acceptable by any standard of warfare, and certainly not for Hospitallers."

"You can guess the rest," Manegold motioned to the fires and dead bodies around them. "A full assault followed, combining forces of Turan-Shah's siege army and Saladin's newly arrived men, who brought trebuchets and other siege engines. He personally led an assault through the breached wall and met Santini past the pile of rubble and fought him in hand-to-hand combat."

"From reports about Santini," Mercedier said, "I'd have thought he'd have posed more of a challenge to Saladin. Reports are that the fight ended almost when it began."

"He *did* fight differently, now that I think about it" the knight agreed, "but perhaps the two weeks of constant battle had exhausted him." He shrugged, looked for permission to withdraw from Mercedier, and upon getting assent, motioned to Bruno. With curt bows, they returned to the task of collecting bodies.

The trio from the Krak entered the central courtyard where a pyre burned, the corpses piled upon it mixed with the remains of broken stable fencing to create a blaze that soared into the sky thrice a man's height.

Ibn-Khaldun noticed two females near a Hospitaller knight who stood in front of the bonfire. The pale-skinned and jet-black-haired woman said something earnestly to him, while the bronze-skinned and blond-haired, cloaked girl leaned forward and kissed the man on the cheek. Both women cast a dark look at the newcomers, then swept robes about their figures and withdrew into the shadows of an access tunnel. They were gone before Ibn-Khaldun and his companions reached the area.

Except for the crackling flames, there was an unnerving

quiet in the courtyard that contrasted with the flurry of activity that marked all the other parts of the castle. Mercedier and the Muslim scholar took in the scene, realizing that the knight himself must have dragged the twenty or so bodies to the bonfire.

On one of the ramparts, two gigantic ravens peered at the Hospitallers then, making gurgling caws that sent a shiver down Ibn-Khaldun's spine, the birds soared into the air.

"*Mon Dieu, ce sont des corbeaux énormes,*" Mercedier muttered. "It must be my eyes, but they seemed as large as us!"

The old scholar watched the ravens disappear around a gutted turret, then grunted, "This entire place seems abandoned by Allah. I don't like the portents here."

"It's the aftermath of war, Khajen," Arcadian said, "no omens anymore, just carrion crows."

Mercedier shook his head, in agreement with Ibn-Khaldun. "Those were damned big crows, Arcadian."

The trio approached the dark-cloaked and cowled Hospitaller, but he didn't look at them. The enormous knight stood over the charred remains of one of the corpses lying upside down on the blaze, a gaping socket where the dead man's head used to be.

The Hospitaller poked idly at the chest of the burning, blackened body, murmuring words that sounded to Ibn-Khaldun like, "*Che sono io, che sono io,*" and "*famiglia.*"

The Muslim scholar knew Italian from many years of interacting with Venetian and Genoese traders, so when he came to stand before the man while Arcadian and Mercedier went to see where the dark-cloaked women went, he asked gently of him, "*Perché dici, 'che sono io?'* ("Why do you say, 'that's me?'")

The man didn't answer, but merely continued to chop into the smoldering, blackened body with the end of his sword.

Ibn-Khaldun realized he was quietly sobbing, and something about his voice didn't sound right, didn't fit the sight before him. He frowned, unable to reconcile the dissonance between what he saw and what he heard. Standing there amidst the castle ruins, it was as if the wind carried the keening sounds of a grieving child through this fractured frame of a gigantic man.

Ibn-Khaldun started to step forward and realized that somebody else remained alive in this courtyard. A small form wriggled frantically in the mass of corpses that lay strewn between the portcullis and the cistern fountain. He peered through the smoke at a youth of no more than eight summers.

The boy scrambled backward on the ground near the base of the north wall's colonnade, seeking protection beneath the limp arms and hands of a prone man and woman. "*Réveillez, réparer!*" The child repeatedly muttered the words in a fierce desperate voice. "*Réveillez, réparer! Réveillez, réparer!*"

The couple held each other in death, the man with a spear jutting from his chest and the woman curled on her side in a pool of blood. Her hand still clutched at the man's tunic as if trying to save him from the killing wound.

The boy spoke the language of the Franks, but the urgency in his piercing voice and the agitated way he tried to burrow between his parents chilled Ibn-Khaldun, a veteran of over a hundred battles.

"*Réveillez, réparer! Réveillez, réparer!*"

The child wasn't crying but held an expression of determination in his face as he urged his parents to "wake up," and for someone to "fix them." Over and over the boy repeated the words, as if by that mantra, he'd bring his blasted mother and father back to life. He saw Ibn-Khaldun, his eyes widened, and he began howling in panic, the *"réveillez!"* and *"réparer!"* spoken so quickly and with even greater insistence that the Muslim scholar stumbled as he backed away. Horrified, he realized that the boy must think him to be one of the brown-skinned men who had slain his parents, now returned to do more harm.

The boy turned away and began to cry with heaving shrieks, pulling harder on his father's arm while pushing himself as hard as he could into the slashed corpse of his mother, ignoring the blood smearing over his clothing as he huddled close.

The fiddler could be heard nearby, the music created by his fast-moving bow turning into a screeching punishment of strings.

The black-cloaked Hospitaller suddenly appeared, no longer by the pyre but kneeling beside Ibn-Khaldun. *"S'il vous plait, Monsieur,* I can help," the knight said, the authority and maturity in his voice completely different from the incoherent ramblings of just a few seconds past.

Surprised and alarmed, Ibn-Khaldun looked closely at him, able now to see golden-brown eyes that seemed to survey everything at once beneath a mantle of sandy brown hair.

Ibn-Khaldun guessed that the lad couldn't be more than thirteen or fourteen, although his size reminded Ibn-Khaldun of the stories he'd heard tell of the ancestors of the *franj* who'd invaded this land—centuries before the Crusades. Those peoples had been known as the Northmen, or Vikings. Until this moment, the elderly scholar had always viewed such tales with reservation. Now, seeing in this youth a descendant of some gigantic and mightily muscled warrior, he knew that the legends had more than a grain of truth.

"And your name, my friend?"

"Call me ... Ríg."

Ibn-Khaldun appraised him quietly, sensing falsehood. "If you're trying to conceal your identity, Brother Santini, you'll have to learn to lie better than that."

"*Qu'est que-c'est?*" Ríg asked, astonished, his face flushing with anger. "What did you call me?"

"A liar." Ibn-Khaldun replied. "But, a liar for a good reason, I believe." He nodded at the uppermost corpse on the pyre. "Why the pretense? Why do you allow that headless man to take your name?"

"I don't know what you're talking about—my name's Ríg."

Ibn-Khaldun pursed his lips. "Very well, 'Ríg,' call yourself what you will." He paused. "Do you see those two men over there? Those two Hospitallers talking with that sentry?"

"*Oui.* The elder one wears a grand master's robes."

"He is a grand master. His name's Arcadian, from the Krak des Chevaliers—the man with him is his brother, Mercedier. They're intelligent fellows, and they're going to run into something of a problem when they meet you. You see, they have just heard three different men identify you as Servius Aurelius Santini—"

"Impossible!" Ríg said, but fear seemed to shake his confidence.

"—all of whom said that they'd seen you at different times during the siege without your hood." Ibn-Khaldun lied as easily as the youth had done, sure that he'd guessed correctly. "Those two are my friends, Ríg, and they're honorable men. They'll protect your secret if you give good reason—I can help with this, but not if you lie. Not to me, nor to them." He hesitated. "Nor, I think, to yourself. We must all hear the truth."

Ríg said nothing for a long moment, his silence and presence almost unnerving the old man. Ibn-Khaldun steeled himself against the involuntary reaction. It seemed impossible to him that a youth of thirteen summers should command such a response from a scholar five times that age! But, if the boy persisted in his lie, there really was nothing that Ibn-Khaldun could do to help him.

Even though the old man sensed that Ríg did need some kind of help, without Ibn-Khaldun's endorsement, Arcadian and Mercedier simply would not believe that someone Ríg's age could be the warrior who'd held off one of Saladin's armies for two weeks.

No, they'd let 'Ríg' return to the ranks of Mecina's surviving novices. Those members would be relocated to the Hospitaller mother-house in Jerusalem for eventual reassignment. Ibn-Khaldun and the two brothers would return to their regular duties at the Krak, and the events of this siege would become another legend in an ancient land already laden with myths and fantastic tales.

For some reason that he couldn't explain even to himself, Ibn-Khaldun couldn't let that happen—besides the chill he'd felt when he'd heard Eric the Seafarer sing his prophecies, the old man simply felt a need to discover the truth behind this particular mystery.

"How do I know that I can trust you?" Ríg asked.

"You don't," Ibn-Khaldun replied, and then pointed to his desert *bedouin* robes. "But, I have lived among westerners in one of their strongest castles for almost forty years, and I'm trusted in the Hospitallers' highest councils. Surely those facts might give you some assurance that I know how to keep confidences?"

"My family will be killed if ... if the truth of this day were to get back to Europe."

Ibn-Khaldun's eyes narrowed. "Saladin has a long reach throughout the Levant, son, but I hardly think—"

Ríg turned again to the bonfire, still deciding something. Then, he said, "No, not Saladin. These matters are imperial ..." He expelled a harsh laugh. "Imperial, Venetian, Genoese ... God, even slavers! What was my father thinking?"

"Oh, Orí, Orí, Orí!" the boy wailed nearby. "Oh, Orí—*réparer! Ma mère! Mon père!*"

Ibn-Khaldun gave a questioning look. "Well, Ríg, he seems to want to call you 'Orí.' Which name is it?"

"Aur ... Aur —" the boy screamed, mistaking the Muslim scholar's words as a goad for correct pronunciation. He gulped, then strained to enunciate between sobs, "Aur... aur... lius—"

"Marcus, Marcus, stop, please!" Ríg moved towards the boy, concern etching furrows into his features. "*Il est vrai. C'est moi,*" the knight said in a hushing tone as he reached forward to embrace the boy, "*Oui, oui ...* it's me, Orí. It's Aurelius. *Oui.*"

"Orí, Orí, Orí!" the boy confirmed fiercely, hugging the knight to him in gratitude.

"Indeed?" Ibn-Khaldun regarded the youths, taking in the elder boy with a skeptical eye. "My understanding was that Servius Aurelius Santini is that corpse over there, the one burned and without a head."

"It should have been me—he had no right to take my name!" the youth snarled, then paused, as if sensing that any more violent expressions on his part would send the grieving child back into hysteria. He collected himself with almost superhuman control.

"I mean," Ríg inhaled, "that's what my uncle wanted everyone to think. Uncle Servius knew Saladin wouldn't rest or make peace until I was dead, and then we had to think about the family back in Sicily ... or wherever my family is now. There are networks between your people and mine. Networks that reach to Sicily and beyond, *monsieur*."

The young knight nodded at the topmost figure on the pyre. "He gave his life for me. For our family. And, my name ... well, Santini has to be dead now. Forever." He held a hand out to the frightened boy, who'd quieted immediately upon seeing the newcomer stand beside Ibn-Khaldun.

"He's lost his parents," Ibn-Khaldun said. "He's in shock and we need to get him out of there."

"I know—I saw it happen. His name is Marcus," the young Hospitaller said. "I've gotten to know him over the last few days." Ríg indicated the dead couple that Marcus kept clutching.

"They were fine ..." His voice caught with emotion, but then with a grimace he continued, "his parents were fine until a trebuchet's fireball hit after the miners collapsed the wall. Their names were Jonathan and Desdemona. They secured Marcus under those wagons over there, but then the final assault broke through the wall and we were all in for it. I was fighting near my uncle and couldn't get to this side of the yard in time."

He reached forward again, speaking softly. "Marcus, it's me, you're going to be fine; we'll get you out of here."

"Orí, Orí, Orí, Orí!" the boy cried. "*Réparer! Réparer!*"

"We *will* fix things, *mon ami*," Aurelius said softly, grasping both shoulders of the boy and making Marcus look him in the eyes. "Just not them, and not here. We'll fix our lives, but not here. We have to go. You have to let them go."

"Orí?" Ibn-Khaldun asked.

"There's something wrong with his head—he speaks in loops many times, and can't say 'Aurelius.' We finally settled on Orí."

"Where will you go?"

The youth pulled his robe over his head and tossed it onto the fire where his uncle's body still burned. Underneath he wore a heavily soiled and bloodstained tunic over a chain-mail vest. "We're going to lose ourselves in the crowds leaving by the west gate, and then go south to Jerusalem." Aurelius secured his sword in its scabbard, then clasped Marcus's bloody hand.

The boy finally let go of his parent's arms, and let Aurelius help him to his feet.

"Is that where your family is?"

"No, they're back in Sicily."

"I'm sorry ... I'm confused." Ibn-Khaldun nodded at the burning clothing. "Those were the robes of a Hospitaller sergeant-at-arms. You seem ... young for that rank."

Aurelius shrugged. "He was one of the first to die up on the battlements...after I killed the intruders, I took his clothing."

"And kept your hood on the rest of the siege? *Le Capuchon Hospitaller?*"

"Let's go, Marcus." Aurelius gently ran a hand over the back of the boy's head. Still crying, Marcus kept whispering, "wake up" and "fix it." The repetition of *"réveillez!"* and *"réparer"* took on something of an eerie quality, set as they were against the distorted strains coming from Eric's fiddle on the other side of the rubble heap.

The horror of these children's situation struck at Ibn-Khaldun's heart. "Wait, I have an idea. I live in another castle, to the east. It's about five times the size of this one and much better occupied and defended."

"I'll put no faith in the defense of any castle after the past two weeks," Aurelius said coldly, but there seemed to be a hesitation in his voice and he didn't hasten to leave. Ibn-Khaldun guessed that he would listen because he really had no plan and didn't know where to go.

"Nor would I," the Muslim scholar agreed, "but I've lived there for over forty years, and still walk about to tell the tale."

"You mentioned that earlier." Aurelius said, reassessing the Muslim scholar before him. "The Hospitallers really let you live in a Christian castle?"

"*Oui*, and more than just live—I run the library and educate the novices. The castle is called the Krak des Chevaliers, and it's the largest frontier outpost between Antioch and Jerusalem. We have a large scriptorium and over two thousand men-at-arms ..."

More sounds of clinking swords brought Ibn-Khaldun's thoughts back to the present. He looked steadily at Mercedier.

"I thought I heard swordplay earlier, but that might have been men in the yards. That's pitched battle. It's begun."

"That was quite a sprint," Mercedier grunted. "If they were heading toward the front gate, that's some distance, even for a teenager. I didn't think he could reach them in time."

He paused. "Do either of you want to take bets on if Ríg and Marcus take them all out before Perdieu shows up?"

"The boy said there were at least nine Assassins," Arcadian cautioned. "We should perhaps hope that they both return with skin intact."

"I disagree with you about that fiddler being *absurde*," Ibn-Khaldun said to Mercedier, needing to distract himself from concern at the youths' peril while they awaited the other physicians. "Except for this 'Codex Lacrimae' and my experience of the last six months, I have no proof for what I'm thinking. I believe, though—and I've thought long and hard about little else for that entire time—that Eric the Seafarer's prediction might not be as peculiar as we once thought."

"Eric the ... oh, the madman at Mecina. He *was* strange, though, wasn't he?" Mercedier murmured. "Even if he hadn't lost his friend, I generally don't trust jesters."

"That's a bit ironic, isn't it?"

"Watch it," Mercedier tried to grin, but couldn't because of the pain in his abdomen.

"Do you remember the song, Khajen?" Arcadian asked, knowing the answer.

"I know it, but I'll not sing it." Ibn-Khaldun didn't mention how much he'd heard of the Lay of the Codex Lacrimae during his flight of the last six months! He cleared his throat, then recited:

Upon Ymir's Beard, in World's Youth,
From Jotun's Skulls, to Ran's Coral Tooth,
Sought the Aesir—Odin, Vili, and Ve—
Nine Runed Relics, Wisdom's Way.
'Neath Frosted Pines, distant Shoals Aflame,
In Elven Glade, from Muspelheim
Smote Volund's Anvil—Dooms Entwine!—
In Sampo Hearth, tonged Codices Nine.

Quires Gathered, split Monk-Squire,
Trebled Witches, hewed Flesh-Cut's ire,
'Pon Glass-Walled mage, Dark Cauldron seethes,
In Kenned Ink, Moult-Feather sheathes,
As Gamble-Bones roll, clatter Merchants' Greed,
'Til Ruler's Halo, looms on Wave-Steed.
On Otherworld's Wake, falls Face-Shield night,
Lest Gemmed-Pin's truth, match Codex Might,
By Starred Path's chart, burn Creation's Light.

Nine songs magical sing I,
Goblet-sipped from Bestla's mead,
As Sibyls' Coven and Druids Nigh,
Doom Fate's Daughter and Last Son's need!

"I thought there was some mention of a codex," Arcadian said.

Ibn-Khaldun grunted, then sipped at his tea. "In two places, with 'Codices Nine,' and 'Codex Might.'"

"That was five years ago," Mercedier protested. "Couldn't this all be just coincidence?"

"We can allow for that, of course," Ibn-Khaldun said.

"The entire battle and siege of Mecina was strange," Arcadian mused. "I have been the first to protect him from Baron Perdieu's questions, but I myself have never understood Aurelius's story about his uncle sacrificing himself to Saladin—"

" —and none of us have ever pressed the point with the lad," Mercedier said. "I think we were all relieved that he took to the regimen of study and training that we set for him. Once he became Ríg it was simply a matter of making a new life for him, and then you and Sara adopted Marcus."

"You two worked the closest with Aurelius," Arcadian said. "I know that he never brought his family up with me, although there were many times that I made opportunity to talk about them."

"Nor has he spoken with me," Ibn-Khaldun said, "and I have been a bit more insistent at times because I really wanted to understand."

He glanced at the night table near Arcadian where the Codex Lacrimae rested.

"We all might come to regret not asking certain questions," he added quietly, recalling the full phrase that Aurelius spoke in front of the pyre as he chopped the tip of his sword into his burning uncle.

Per la nostra famiglia, che sono io! "For our family, that's me!"

Loud shouts and the blowing of horns came from the front gate of the inner ward.

Ibn-Khaldun and Arcadian rose to their feet, and walked to the three great bay windows that overlooked the upper ward and courtyards of the castle interior.

Ríg's fighting style was easily identifiable and he was making quick work of some cloaked figures that were moving in and out of the long halls arched portals. Two attackers dropped from the roof but, again, Ríg evaded one and did something to another that made the man drop to the ground.

Ibn-Khaldun gasped. A half-naked Marcus stood suddenly next to Ríg. They fought side-by-side before getting separated. An archer appeared at one end of the walkway and fired at Ibn-Khaldun's son.

The distance was too great for the observers to make out exactly what happened next, but Ríg threw something in the air between the archer and victim and, although Marcus lurched backward and fell to the ground, he quickly stood and tackled one of the intruders down the sloping green that led to the stables.

Arcadian looked at Ibn-Khaldun. "Go," he said simply. "I'll have the physicians tend to Mercedier when they get here."

The Muslim scholar moved quickly across the floor toward the door, glancing at Mercedier as he spoke. "When Jacob brings Belvedere, tell him to forget the poison—we'll need to reopen—sorry, Mercedier—and flush the wound again. Have him look for a piece of metal or glass that's worked its way to the surface since the surgery."

"I will," the grandmaster assured him. "Go tend to your boys."

Ibn-Khaldun passed into the stairwell with the speed of a man half his age.

CHAPTER 5

Saladin and Fafnir: A Survivor Revealed

As the day aged outside the walls of the Krak des Chevaliers and the al-Ansariyah Mountains purpled into dusk, Saladin knew fear.

It didn't matter to the emir that his fifty-man, mounted honor guard waited nearby, nor that the rest of his army made the final siege preparations on flatlands where the Homs Gap opened onto the Orontes River Valley; Saladin was a seasoned enough veteran to know trouble when he saw it, and this eastern commander known only as 'Fafnir' was definitely trouble.

The shadows of the easterner's cloak flowed wildly in the breeze, making it unclear where the material ended and the horse began, but it evoked an unmistakable menace. Every few moments, those same desultory air currents carried a foul odor across the space between Fafnir and Saladin, its repulsive smell making the sultan almost gag and his eyes water.

When Fafnir spoke, his deep and resonant voice rumbled across the space like distant thunder that promises a storm impossible to outrace, the sound audible both in Saladin's ears and, he imagined, his *mind*.

It seemed to Saladin as if it were not a man astride a horse before him, but a strange, four-legged, creature. A winged shape crouched languidly on the bluff, whose pinion length couldn't be measured in distance, but rather by the radius of the putrescent odor it cast.

Worst of all, besides arriving at the rendezvous upon a carrion wind, the enigmatic commander had not even lowered his cowl upon first meeting Saladin—an insulting display of arrogance!

Saladin considered himself a modest man, but knew that his was the modesty of the powerful. It had been almost twenty years since anyone approached him with Fafnir's kind of casual demeanor. Didn't the eastern ruler realize the prominence Saladin held in the Levant and Middle East? That Saladin himself controlled Egypt? That he had personally abolished the Fatimid Caliphate in Cairo, an empire that had endured in these regions for over two hundred and fifty years? Didn't Fafnir know that for the past five years Saladin had been hounding the Crusaders up and down the Levant, rallying thousands of Arabs by the promise of driving the Frankish occupiers into the Great Sea and back to their own lands?

No. This eastern ruler seemed to know none of these things, or perhaps they simply didn't impress him. As it was, Fafnir had amplified the insult of not lowering his cowl by offering a strange token of friendship: a leather bag filled with Frankish scalps. Disgusted, Saladin hadn't touched the bag, letting an adjunct take it as he glared at his military counterpart.

"Lord Fafnir, I appreciate the … goodwill gesture, but I am not Shirkūh," he'd said, referring to his uncle, who'd once received a similar sack of battle trophies. "And you're certainly not Nur ad-Din."

"Perhaps not," Fafnir agreed, his hand stretched vaguely behind him, "but, as with Nur ad-Din, I, too, come with military aid in your time of need."

"You know something of my family's past, Lord Fafnir, but this isn't the Battle of Bilbays." Saladin tightened the gloves on his hands and adjusted the rein on his stallion, as if making ready to leave. "Further, in this instance, I'd remind you that *I'm* the one besieging the *franj*, and unlike my uncle, not waiting months in northern Egypt for a relief force."

He didn't mention the fact that the bag of *nazaro* skull-skins seemed a small amount in comparison to the number who'd fall in his *jihad* against the Crusaders.

Instead, he merely said, "In any event, I don't approve of such tokens."

"Salah ad-Dīn Yusuf ibn Ayyub …" Fafnir began patiently. "May I call you Yusuf?"

"No, I think not."

"Ah." A moment's pause, then Fafnir resumed. "To business, then. You say that Morpeth and Farbauti are no longer with you? That they poisoned your brother?

"Hamzah al-Adil lives, but your envoys have fled. Their tent burst into flames shortly after sunset, and they're nowhere to be found," Saladin replied. "They will be killed upon sight if they enter my camp again—"

He interrupted himself, and frowned thoughtfully toward his aide who stood to one side, still holding the leather bag. "I didn't ask: were their scalps among those others in the bag?"

"Unfortunately, no." Fafnir said, his rueful smile barely visible in the gloom.

"Pity. If you'd included them, I might have been more willing to continue this alliance."

"I wasn't aware that Morpeth and Farbauti's behavior had anything to do with our alliance, Salah ad-Dīn Yusuf. Rather, I thought your use of my army of ten thousand might outweigh any crimes of two mere negotiators."

Ten thousand men? Saladin started, but carefully didn't reveal his surprise. *How in Allah's Name could my scouts miss that big of an army? Would Fafnir lie to my face? But, why? There's no gain here for a lie. Careful, Yusuf. If he's indeed brought that many men, I need to play this correctly, lest the situation reverse itself. Instead of just besieging the Krak, I may have a war on two fronts.*

The Egyptian ruler was disconcerted, but he checked his unease as tightly as the reins on the stallion beneath him, steadily regarding his supposed ally. "I have kept our meeting, even with their absence," he said aloud, "but perhaps you overstate your numbers? I'm told that you command little more than two thousand soldiers."

Fafnir shrugged. "You've seen how far one might trust the words of Farbauti and Morpeth. I revealed neither my entire plans to them, nor the forces I might bring to bear."

"*Might* bring? Then the rest of your army hasn't yet arrived?"

"I didn't say that," Fafnir said.

He's not lying. But, ten thousand men? Where are they? My scouts reported encampments and deployments of two thousand men. My scouts, who have fought with me since I took Cairo fifteen years ago. "Such a thing is needful to know, Lord Fafnir."

"Well, now you know."

"I disagree. My scouts have reported the men in your encampments to the east number not ten thousand, but barely two."

"They aren't looking in the correct places, then."

Saladin stared. "You seem to think I'm jesting. My plans call for the siege to begin the dawn after tomorrow's, but I need to know all aspects of my ... of our offensive. I will need to know that the entirety of the gap and river plain around the Krak are covered. I need to know that your eastern contingents of at least two thousand will be there to complete the encirclement of the Krak, matching the three thousand I have with me. Your ranks were to cut off any relief force that might come to the Hospitallers—"

"What's all this, Sultan? Are you worried?" Fafnir chuckled. "I thought better of you."

Saladin took a moment to curb his irritation. Then, he said, "Not worried. I've led battles and even sieges that defeated these *franj* with fewer men, *but* the Krak des Chevaliers is a respectable fortress. I began this siege based on reports from Damascus that numbered your army at two thousand men —"

"Ah, and now you wonder how not even your *tali'a* scouts nor *darraja* guards have seen anything to support my claims of ten thousand bodies?" Fafnir paused. "You might even wonder if you'll defeat these Crusaders, only to see their presence replaced by my people?" Fafnir shook his head. "I tell you, whether you see them now, my forces will be at your side when you need them, and we will return to eastern lands after securing the price of our support."

Fafnir brought his stallion in a sideways trot to a closer position to the Muslim ruler. "Tell me, Ruler of Egypt, did Farbauti or Morpeth mention to you an item that they sought?"

"They were after something," Saladin began cautiously, "an item in the Krak, I believe."

"Long has this object been pursued," Fafnir said.

"A treasure of some kind?"

"Of some kind, yes." Fafnir was only a few *arsh* from him, but Saladin still couldn't see the man's features beneath the cowl. "I foresee things, Saladin. You'll be regarded as mighty both of your people and by those in the kingdoms across the Great Sea," Fafnir said. "These things are ripples in Mimir's Well. You can increase those realms—and perhaps live longer—if you aid me in this small matter."

"Help you find this thing that Farbauti and Morpeth were searching for?"

"Your people call it the 'Dark Book.' Have you heard of it?"

"A myth," Saladin snorted, disappointed at his ally's gullibility. "A tale to tell children who haven't obeyed their parents."

"Perhaps it is a myth," Fafnir mused, "but, perhaps not. I tell you that, like all myths, this one has some basis in truth."

"I have no interest in this," Saladin found it difficult to remain civil. He needed Fafnir's army if here were to complete the siege to begin his final push against all Crusaders in this land. "We're waging a war here, not imagining fanciful quests like those Scheherazade told to King Shahryar." He straightened in his saddle. "I'll not be spending a thousand and one nights at this siege."

Fafnir chuckled. "Think what you will, Salah ad-Dīn Yusuf, but I'd suggest that you don't have to believe in the thing to tell your troops to look for it. The book is not a magic lamp, nor guarded by a *djinni*. It's of use primarily only to those for whom I seek it, and I can assure you that they live far, far from these fields."

"When we breach this cursed citadel, my soldiers will be more interested in making it a regional seat for *me*, than in any search for a book. Such matters are meaningless to them."

"We have come to an impasse, then, O Great Saladin. Besides the book, the material things you mention are of little interest to *me*, and it seems as if you might bargain for naught else." Fafnir paused. "Tell me, what if I mentioned Servius Aurelius Santini?"

"He's dead," Saladin said flatly. "I slew him myself at Mecina almost five years ago." He shook his head wearily. "This discussion bores me. I wonder for the thousandth time why I agreed to enter into this alliance when such men as Farbauti and Morpeth were brokering the transaction."

"Santini is alive, and he dwells in the Krak des Chevaliers."

Turan, my brother. I've failed you. The thought came unbidden, rushing from a long-closed part of Saladin. He stared for a long moment at Fafnir. "That can't be true," Saladin protested, even though a mystery he'd long dwelt on was now solved. As with the claim of ten thousand men, in his heart, he knew that Fafnir told him the truth.

Still, he asked, "Do you have any proof?"

"In seeking to avenge your brother's death, you slew another at Mecina, the wrong man." Fafnir obviously took some pleasure in this revelation. "I often make the same mistake with these Westerners. They all look the same, don't they?" The cowled man hesitated, then continued. "But, this was an intentional deception. A man posing as Santini's uncle, in turn, pretended to be the real Santini so that the boy could live to fight another day."

"Boy?" Saladin shook his head, still not understanding. "Santini was no boy, but a man."

"He was barely thirteen years old—"

"Impossible!"

"—his blood line is almost pure Viking, and one of his distant ancestors was one of the Northmen who conquered the Frankish lands."

"No, Santini was a giant of a man."

"He still is," Fafnir said.

Old doubts about whom he'd slain at Mecina coursed through Saladin like a dry torch immersed in oil and ignited by his ally's words. "If this were found to be true, what are the conditions for a continued alliance?"

"I change nothing, nor should you. In this, the words of Farbauti and Morpeth still govern: I want the Dark Book, or as it is more properly known, the Codex Lacrimae." Fafnir paused and Saladin could almost hear the smile in the man's voice, "And you may have the castle, as many Hospitaller survivors as you need for bargaining with the Leper King in Jerusalem, and, of course, Servius Aurelius Santini."

"Alive," Saladin said. "I want him alive so that I myself might slay him."

All the memories returned. He recalled the moment when he'd personally led his men across the rubble pile of Mecina's collapsed curtain wall. In the courtyard of the upper ward he'd beheld the curious sight of Santini punching another westerner, even though both were clad in the robes of the Hospitaller Order. The man who'd fallen had sandy-blond hair, and of a size that the sultan originally thought him to the be the dreaded *Le Capuchon Hospitaller* himself. But, then the knight who *was* cowled, who'd defeated the other and remained standing, had launched himself madly at Saladin, knocking him somehow from his steed and screaming something in the language of the *franj*. He would never forget those words, because they were the last ones that Santini had uttered before Saladin slew him.

"Tell me, Lord Fafnir," Saladin asked, "what does this mean: '*Pour notre famille, je dois devenir quelqu'un d'autre?*' "

"*For our family, I must become someone else?*" the dark-robed man translated, confusion in his voice.

"That's what I've been told." Saladin said thoughtfully, recalling how he'd decapitated Santini and then had to flee the castle lest he himself be captured.

He wondered. What if that fallen man, the gigantic youth who'd been punched and who'd lain prone on the ground, instead, were the famed Hospitaller enemy?

Had Saladin indeed killed the wrong man at Mecina?

"I must get back to my camp," Fafnir said abruptly. "When will you begin the assault, Salah ad-Dīn Yusuf?"

"Tomorrow we'll be finished with construction of the siege engines," Saladin replied as he lightly kicked the flanks of his horse. "We'll strike the day after next, ere the dawn."

"I'll have my men ready," Fafnir agreed, grabbing the reins of his own mount. "Tell your generals and commanders of the Codex Lacrimae. It will most likely be in the library of the castle, and guarded by one of your people, a 'Khajen Ibn Khaldun.' Get the book, and bring it to me at the end of the battle. I promise that you'll have Santini within your reach by day's end."

"Ibn-Khaldun?" Saladin repeated in disbelief, but the dark commander was gone, retreating down the hillside with the sound of pounding hooves. The emir turned his own steed and looked heavenward, watching the sun disappear behind tendrils of approaching rain clouds.

He made a nickering sound to the horse, then galloped away with his men falling in behind. Soon only the rumble of thunder could be heard upon the wind-swept plain.

CHAPTER 6

Morpeth Strikes

The opponent with whom Marcus rolled down the grassy slope was dead by their second tumble—the boy had yanked as hard as he could on his attacker's head and broken the man's neck.

"Hurt, hurt—Orí! Orí! Orí!" Marcus muttered as he staggered to his feet, ignoring the horses that stamped nearby. He heard the alarmed cries of some members of the crowd of pilgrims below, people who were starting to realize there was a fight on the hill by the loggia and had moved toward the action. The incline of that hill prevented Marcus from seeing what had happened to Aurelius, but the boy saw the archer who'd wounded him running away.

Focusing on the archer, Marcus relaxed as he always did in battle, and waited for the moment when he'd see eight or ten duplicates of the enemy Hospitaller appear. The archer's image remained single, however, moving quickly toward the southwest castle courtyards.

Marcus frowned, uncomfortable about this new aspect of the *Jeu de Bataille*, or Battle Game. Except for Aurelius and himself, he'd never met anyone who could reduce their presence in his sight to just one version, and he wondered if this enemy's ability was why the archer's arrow had succeeded in nicking Aurelius back at the loggia. Marcus had thrown a dagger to intercept the projectile, yet it had still found its mark.

"Marcus—go find Brother Perdieu!" Squire Pellion shouted at him, trying to catch a group of Hospitallers that chased the archer. "I left him at the top of the hill, helping Ríg,"

"*Bonjour*, Pellion!" Marcus shouted, even as he shook his head. "*Non, non, non. Nous devons obtenir l'homme mauvais.* We have to get the bad man!"

Pellion slowed, and tried to shoo Marcus back up the hill. "No, Marcus! *Laissez ici!* Others are coming—" The boy stopped when he saw that Marcus continued to trot after the group of knights with sword at the ready.

"*Nous devons obtenir l'homme mauvais. We have to get the bad man ...*" Marcus kept repeating under his breath as he moved forward.

Pellion knew that look. Or, rather, he knew what it meant when Marcus wouldn't look at him. His friend wasn't going to relent. "Oh, for God's sake, get dressed, then!" Pellion groaned, sheathing his own sword quickly and whipping off his short cloak. He tossed it at the trotting boy.

Marcus grinned, and slipped his head through the hooded garment. Though now he appeared somewhat clothed, except that he still lacked shoes. *"Nous devons obtenir—"*

"Oui!" Pellion exclaimed. *"Je sais, et nous le ferons!* But, it's full on, Marcus. No mercy, and this isn't a game. They're a dangerous group, and the archer's the worst. Rig's alive, but *que homme mauvais* took him down."

"Non, Orí not hurt! Orí not hurt!"

Even in crisis, Pellion winced. Marcus looked stricken at the news, and his face had paled.

Both boys sprinted after the Hospitallers who chased the traitor. They need not have hurried. As Pellion and Marcus rounded the corner and came into the entry hallway to the kitchen areas, the archer rose with a dagger in hand, having just slain the fifth and last of the pursuing knights.

He chuckled when he saw the two youths enter the corridor.

"Oh, *das ist gut! Das ist sehr gut!"* Morpeth said excitedly, beckoning with bloodstained hands. "Not one, but *two* of Santini's friends! Come along, now—let's end this. Fulfill the damn prophecy and bring a Codex back into the Nine Worlds. We just need one of you dead, boys!"

"Bad man! Bad man!" Marcus shouted, raising his sword.

Something shifted in the air between the archer and him, and, thankfully, the boy now saw *six* Morpeths flash into sight, with a seventh and eighth shimmering in his peripheral vision.

Here was familiar territory, and a return to the Battle Game he knew!

"Marcus, hold on!" Pellion cautioned, too aware that this enemy archer had just slain five experienced knights. "Let me give you an opening to—"

"Orí, Orí, Orí!" Marcus yelled, dashing past Pellion as he committed to a sequence of engagement that began with Morpeth-Five and Morpeth-Six before returning to Morpeths One through Four.

He felt an excited pitch in his stomach at the risk he was taking in leaving the still-shimmering Morpeths-Seven and Eight until later, but he'd already anticipated that they could resolve into another Morpeth One and Two after the first second of battle. He still needed to make the first moves to see where the game took him.

His blade clanged onto Morpeth Five's upraised dagger, and the man made a motion with this other hand. Marcus laughed—Morpeth-Seven *had* become One!—and the boy reacted instantly, jerking his blade sideways with a still supinated wrist that deflected the second cruelly shaped knife in the new Morpeth One's left hand.

In the same smooth motion, Marcus dropped at a backward angle, his speed outmatching his surprised opponent while he kicked his bare foot solidly into a different Morpeth-Four's jaw and acrobatically flipped off a splayed left hand to alight gracefully on his feet, waiting momentarily for newly created Morpeths Two, Three, and Five to resolve into their own actions, or split again into different potentialities.

He squared himself, and prepared to lunge, shouting, "*Maintenant, Pellion, maintenant!*" Marcus hoped that his friend would go after the same Morpeth-Three that Marcus had decided was the main threat. He'd been correct, and his blade flicked close to Morpeth Three. The man grunted, stumbled backward a step, and glowered at the swiftly moving Marcus.

"That's not possi— " Morpeth began, then frowned, reconsidering the boy.

Marcus stepped back. The game had changed again, and the enemy archer's duplicates suddenly resolved into a single combatant, without any other potential Morpeths dotting the courtyard. The boy inhaled, remaining calm as he calculated his next move in the game. He'd feared the possibility when he'd seen the man running across the lawns, but now he was certain. This opponent *could* calm himself enough to control his own timelines!

Marcus steeled himself as he did when Aurelius and he had trained in true earnest. If Marcus could fight and defeat his best friend when Aurelius became a singularity in the Battle Game, then he felt confident that he could defeat this assassin.

It bothered him, though, that Morpeth could apparently center himself in much the same way that Aurelius did, because until the Battle of Mecina and his first meeting with Servius Aurelius Santini, no one had been able to resolve himself or herself into a single person in Marcus's vision.

For the first eight years of his life, Marcus had become used to seeing duplicate, triplicate, and multiple versions of people he met, versions whose numbers varied depending on the situation.

If he were in a calm, sedentary environment, the number of images around any given person was usually three or four, the potentiality of each move that that person's future self could make governed by the person's limited movement. But, in battle situations, when a person's movement was fluid and changing, the duplicates could reach a bewildering ten or twelve possibilities!

Bewildering to others, that is, but not to Marcus, who'd been born with this strange ability and long ago become accustomed to it. He'd grown up in the south of France on a Burgundian estate, the youngest of two children, and his sister had been the first one to realize what was happening to him.

"*Il voit trop vite, Mère*," Denissa had observed one morning when Marcus, his mother Desdemona, and Denissa were riding in a carriage. They were returning from a shopping day in Carcassonne.

Both women were seated across from the boy, watching him giggle uncontrollably as he watched people walking by in the crowded town.

"He *sees* too quickly?" Mère asked incredulously. "What does that mean, Denissa?"

Marcus's head had swiveled, and even though to him her seconds'-old comment seemed to have taken place five or ten minutes in the past, his eyes took in his sister adoringly as he nodded at her. Denissa, indeed, knew what he was feeling. Then he returned to people-watching outside.

"Just what I said," Denissa said. "I think that Marcus sees things move faster than we can, so fast that he can predict what's going to happen before it actually does happen. Look at him laughing. I think he sees hundreds of people out there, where there are only perhaps twenty or thirty at the market."

"Don't be ridiculous," Mère said. "He's just being silly. He'll grow out of it."

"He's not being silly, Mère," Denissa said, shaking her head. "He's enjoying himself, but he's also learning how to be around more people than we can see."

"He does like to be around people," Desdemona smiled at how much joy Marcus seemed to be taking in watching the townspeople going to and fro on market day.

"It's more than that. I catch him looking to each side of me when we're alone, like he's seeing where I'm going to go, or what I'm going to say, and I can't beat him anymore when we're fencing. He's also stopped me from dropping things and tripping, and it's happening often enough that I think he's seeing things happen before they happen."

"Denissa! I'll not have you calling him a warlock, or accusing him of seeing things we can't see. If you're not careful, you'll have us accused of following Cathari ways and persecuted by the Church!"

"I didn't say anything like that," Denissa replied, calmly dismissing her mother's fears as she thought about her brother. "I do think that that's why he speaks the way he does."

"Because he sees more quickly? How would that affect his speech?"

"Because, don't you see? Everything's more quick for him, and I don't think he knows how to slow down enough for others to understand him." Denissa caught Marcus's eye again and smiled, winking at him. "I don't think he wants to slow down. It's all a game to him, Mère. We should be grateful for that, I think."

It's all a game to him, Mère.

Marcus smiled at the memory of her, but then stopped thinking of his sister as Morpeth started to replicate into seven images, the villain's attention obviously distracted by Pellion joining the fray.

Pellion's entrance was aggressive and fast, complementing Marcus's thrust with a flurry of overhead *remise* slashes at Morpeth's midsection intended to distract the man and give Marcus an opening.

Marcus smiled, correctly chose Morpeth Three when Pellion was struggling with Morpeth Five, and prepared to lunge when Morpeth Seven left an opening.

In real time, both boys moved with surpassing speed, their swords appearing to some of the pilgrims who'd begun to gather as a series of well-placed strikes that still nevertheless failed to leave a wound.

The archer easily matched every thrust with long daggers and, after a half-dozen defensive parries, he struck back.

Marcus dodged again, attempting a *passata sotto* on Morpeth, but it was then the archer's turn to surprise him.

Resolving into a singular figure, Morpeth Five hammered his elbow into Marcus's forehead as the boy tried to straighten upward from his attempted evasion of Morpeth Two's kick.

Marcus stumbled slightly, stunned, and, remaining a singularity and incredibly fast, the traitorous Hospitaller delivered a swift kick to the chest.

The impact hurled Marcus into the wall of the corridor.

Still spinning, Morpeth landed in a half-stoop beneath Pellion's incoming swing. Although the boy anticipated what happened next, the squire had neither Marcus's agility nor speed, and simply couldn't reverse his sword in time to block both of the daggers that Morpeth thrust upwards from his crouched position. To his credit, Pellion managed to deflect one of the knives, but the other one plunged deeply into his side.

Morpeth grunted as he heaved into Pellion. As Marcus scrambled forward to help, an explosion burst from his friend's abdomen, its concussion throwing Marcus on his rear and spattering blood over the entire area.

Pellion dropped to the floor, his body smoking from whatever the archer had done with the blade. Morpeth spun from the fallen boy and faced Marcus, the steel of his dagger glowing redder than molten lava.

The killer extended a hand and the hilt of Pellion's sword flew into it! The same reddish glare that flickered off the man's dagger flared up this new length of steel, warlock-fire limning the sword's sharp edges in crimson flames.

"*Pellion! Pellion! O, vous homme mauvais! Vous homme mauvais!*" Marcus exclaimed, tears blurring his eyes while he fell into an *en garde* position, instinctively noting that Morpeth's exultation had made a prism of his images, splintering the enemy into ten duplicates and possible lines of attack. Marcus scanned Pellion's body. His friend still breathed, but he couldn't tell the severity of the injury to his side.

"*C'est la magie maléfique!* That's black magic! Black magic!" Marcus cried, nodding at the blazing sword in Morpeth's hand. "*Marcus rêvé de la magie de couleur arc-en-ciel! La magie de couleur arc-en-ciel!*"

"Stuttering idiot," Morpeth snarled in disgust as he attacked. "I'll give you rainbow-colored magic to dream of!" Morpeth's sword thrust moved with the same contempt as his voice, a *balestra* hop that blurred into a direct lunge at the boy's heart.

"Il voit trop vite, Mère," Denissa said as the family returned from Carcassonne.
"He sees things faster than we can..."

Impossibly, Marcus counterattacked with an *in quartata* move that tapped Morpeth Eight's blade a hair's breadth to the side. Rather than following through with his own strike, Marcus correctly foresaw Morpeth's anger resolving his ten selves into one, and the boy whirled balletically, allowing his blade to swing in a precise arc behind him. The tip sliced across Morpeth's left cheek, finally drawing blood.

Enraged, the *faux*-Hospitaller made his own reverse move, turning the momentum of his lunge into a counterclockwise spin whose kick lashed at Marcus's head. His boot caught empty air as Marcus ducked, then shot upward. The boy's shoulder caught the underside of Morpeth's outstretched leg and flipped the man toward the wall.

Morpeth landed on his feet, but Marcus was already on the other side of the corridor, retrieving a sword from one of the fallen knights. There was only one Morpeth now, with no hint of any others forthcoming. Marcus didn't care. He'd spent a lifetime adapting to a slowed down existence for the sake and pleasure of living among family and friends. If an enemy wanted to fight him at true Battle Speed, the boy would accommodate him. In his heart, that's the only game he truly wanted to play, and even Aurelius had never beaten him when they were fully engaged.

Non. Let the real game start. All he wanted to do was get Pellion to the hospital, and check on Aurelius. Both desires meant that he needed to defeat this bad man. Marcus relaxed, and rather than viewing others in duplicate versions, he turned the Sight inward upon himself.

"You're fast, Boy," Morpeth observed as Marcus again

squared himself, "almost elven-quick, but I've slain elves and Sampo-users who are faster! Come now, and join your friend!"

For one of the few times in recent memory, Marcus said nothing. With both blades well-positioned in his hands, he took the offensive, rushing at Morpeth in a fury whose hotness matched the coruscating weapons of the Huntsman of Muspelheim.

Clarinda's Gambit, Fatima's Ruse

Shortly before Ríg leapt from Arcadian's chamber to pursue the Assassins, in another part of the Krak des Chevaliers, the face of Brother Adelbert, the Krak's Master of the Stores, turned cherry-red with agitation.

"*O, le Diable nous prendre pour des idiots, Frère Jeremiah!*" he exclaimed, his hands on hips as he stood in the middle of the entry ramp of the lower ward, just within the front gate.

Jeremiah leaned on his cane, and rolled his eyes in exasperation. "That's overstating things, I think, Adelbert," the elderly scholar said. "The devil's not going to take us for idiots. You know Fatima. This is Ibn-Khaldun's daughter—"

"I don't know these other Saracens and, besides, we're under siege. I will not allow their entry!"

A small group of *bedouin* stood before the two Hospitallers—as well as six soldiers from Saladin's camp under a flag of truce—with Fatima, Khalil, and a gigantic kaftan-clad nomad most prominent.

Behind the group, and braying loudly in the interior courtyard of the front gate, seven donkeys shifted in the harnesses of six large carts that bore pine coffins, the last of which carried two ebony wooded sarcophagi.

"We're at <u>war</u>," Adelbert repeated, his voice almost a sneer as he waved a disparaging hand. "Shouldn't we be putting heathen *into* coffins, rather than helping them bring their dead into the castle?"

"Brother Adelbert, please," Jeremiah kept to his own crotchety nature but unknowingly adopted the same irritated tone that everyone eventually took with the store master. "I need to return to the Warden Tower for a meeting with Father Arcadian. I just told you: this woman isn't some anonymous *bedouin*, she's Master Ibn-Khaldun's daughter. We'll make an accommodation. I'm leaving."

"*Non!* There are procedures to follow. I will need to check the coffins before they pass."

Jeremiah stared at the man, then turned to Fatima and Khalil. "Well, children, you'll need to let him check the coffins—I'm sorry, but Adelbert's correct about one thing: we are under siege."

"*Certainement*," Fatima said.

"Very well," Jeremiah said, moving slowly to one side. "Well, what are you waiting for? Get on with your procedure, Adelbert."

But Adelbert's attention was on Fatima. He asked suspiciously, "*Parlez-vous française?*"

"*Oui, je suis la fille de mon père, monsieur,*" Fatima replied, amusedly looking directly into Adelbert's eyes.

Surprisingly, her flirtation disarmed the rigid monk. Khalil raised a hand to his mouth, hiding a smile as his wife batted her eyelashes at the disconcerted bureaucrat. The man started to blush in response to Fatima's beauty and bold manner.

"Adelbert! If you please," Jeremiah said impatiently, "get on with it."

"*Bien sûr,*" Fatima added calmly, "and, just so I'm sure—you'll *both* be the ones telling my father about the desecration of the bodies?"

"Of course," Jeremiah said, mirroring her casual tone. Then, startled, he glanced at her. "*Attends. Qu'est-ce que c'est?* What was that?"

"I just wanted to be clear when I report this conversation to my father and Grand Master Arcadian. You two will be the ones personally responsible for desecrating the remains of Ibn-Khaldun's son and those of his retainers? He'll be heartbroken, but I know that the grief of one Muslim family matters little when measured against the needs of a *nazaro* fortress in wartime ..."

"Wait! What's this?" Jeremiah repeated, apparently mortified, and looking sidelong at Adelbert before returning attention to Fatima.

Then the old man surprised her. He smiled and gave an

exaggerated wink that his Hospitaller brethren couldn't see! "Did you say 'desecration?'" Jeremiah exclaimed, dramatically playing along with Fatima's ruse, but his horror seemed almost too pronounced.

Oh, Allah, Fatima thought. *Poor Jeremiah's trying to help me. He's a dear, but overdoing it.* Such an attempt could undo all of Clarinda's plans. There was nothing for it, though, but to continue and hope that the gambit would work. If Jeremiah did indeed suspect something, Fatima hoped that the old man didn't give up her and her companions in an attempt to help them.

"Yes, the bodies have already been wrapped in the ceremonial *kaftans*—" she began, but got interrupted again by Jeremiah's emotional reaction. He shouted at Khalil and the gigantic warrior because the men were prying the lids off two of the foremost coffins.

"You there!" The elderly scholar shouted, his voice shaking. "*Vous, là-bas—attendez!*"

Discombobulated, Jeremiah slapped Adelbert's arm with his cane.

"*Oww!* Jeremiah what are you—"

"Adelbert, stop that man, for God's sake! If Arcadian hears of this, I wouldn't want to be you!"

Confused, but reacting to Jeremiah's urgency, Adelbert dashed to Khalil and put an arresting hand on the man's arm. The giant, too, halted in the middle of peeling back the white linen cloth that exposed two faces.

In the coffin Khalil had opened lay the dark-brown, mortally slashed face of a young man in his mid-twenties; and in the coffin before the giant, the suntanned features of a beautiful teenaged girl were now forever still.

"I said, *attendez!*" Jeremiah yelled, again slapping his cane on Adelbert's shoulder as Khalil moved to the third of the six coffins with the short crowbar in hand. "Wait!"

"*Oww!*" Adelbert flinched, pushing away the cane. "Enough, Jeremiah! I'm not one of your novices. Keep that cane away from me!"

Jeremiah grumbled and stood before Fatima. "Now, young lady, what's this about a desecration?"

Adelbert exclaimed in complete disbelief, "Oh, *allons*, Jeremiah, just because *cette belle femme*—"

"*Tais-toi, Adelbert!*" Jeremiah cut him off, again raising the cane. "Shut. Up!"

"There are death-rites that must be observed," Fatima explained. "We brought Thaqib, my brother there—we brought him quickly because we were so close to the Krak and our father. He really should have been buried where he fell, but we're still within the twenty-four hours since his death ..." Tears came to her eyes. "We thought we might bury him in the cemetery here?"

"You're not thinking to inter them on Christian grounds?" Adelbert said in horror, the trauma on his face almost making Khalil burst out loud in laughter. The *shaykh* was glad for the *keffiyeh* on his head that he'd wrapped over his mouth.

Fatima kept her attention on Jeremiah, and when he looked back at her, she dropped her head in what she hoped look like shame.

"Adelbert ... enough," Jeremiah said, his voice commanding. "Master Khaldun has great esteem here, and this is a matter best left to the decision of Grand Master Arcadian, or perhaps Brother Damian." He motioned to Khalil and the gigantic man to put the lids back on the coffins, and continued. "I couldn't help but notice—that woman ... that girl, she's not a *bedouin*. She looked Italian."

Fatima wiped her eyes, and then nodded. "Yes, her name was Clarinda Trevisan—a merchant's daughter from Venice whom we met in Caesarea. She fell in the raid, along with the others."

Khalil secured his coffin, and stood aside as Jeremiah continued to stand near it.

"And ... that was your brother, or is he in one of the more ... decorative coffins?"

"No, that was a trusted bodyguard. My brother and his wife are in the black ones at the back," Fatima said, motioning to Khalil and the giant.

Crowbars in hand, both men moved hurriedly to comply, and Jeremiah almost turned apoplectic, sputtering at them again to stop. Fatima repeated in Arabic the order that she'd earlier given, and all the *bedouin* looked questioningly at the old Hospitaller.

"Please," Jeremiah said, "just take them inside." He glanced at Saladin's warriors. "Tell the soldiers we continue to honor the flag of truce, and that they may return the way they came. Our *saqalibas* will take the donkeys and carts into the castle."

Fatima did as requested, and the soldiers departed.

"But, Brother Jeremiah, I really must insist," Adelbert protested, "haven't you heard the story of the Trojan Horse? You can't just let—"

"Adelbert, take them personally if you want, leave two

guards with them always. I don't care what you do, but you'll get them to a safe place where they can wait for Master Khaldun to see them. Have the *saqalibas* bring them to the stables via the main gate."

"Oh, now *that* is completely unacceptable! There's a perfectly good service tunnel off the—"

"Adelbert!" Jeremiah roared, turning fully on the store master. "They *pass*. Bring them to the stables via the main gate. I have to go—I'll tell Master Khaldun that his family awaits him, and will take full responsibility for them."

The elderly scholar bowed curtly to the *bedouin* couple and stomped his way up the entry ramp, muttering under his breath as he went.

Adelbert frowned, looked at Fatima and Khalil, and then bade two of the Hospitaller guards to serve as escort for them and the five carts.

"*Excuse moi*, Frère Adelbert," Fatima said, "but you act as if we don't know each other. You <u>do</u> recall that Khalil and I've been here before? That we've *all* met many times?"

The master of stores stared icily at her, replying simply, "*Oui*." He sniffed. "Mind the bumps—until the battle begins, the last thing we want is to block the ramp with … dead heathen."

He turned on his heel, not waiting to see if the group followed and obviously trusting that the Hospitaller guards would tend to any problems that might arise on the long ramp to the inner gate.

The *saqaliba* servants began leading the donkeys up the cobbled ramp, and Fatima glanced at Khalil who nodded, then took the camel leads in hand while the giant warrior took the reins of the donkeys harnessed to the cart that held the two ebony sarcophogi. All moved steadily up the long passage.

The Hospitaller guards led them through the crowded area to the stables. Displaced villagers, working shepherds, fearful pilgrims, and steadfast knights were everywhere as they made their way through the crowds milling about the public campus.

Fatima was gratified by the sight, because her guess (and knowledge of the Krak) had been correct—if her party could just get past the guards at the gates, the personnel within the castle would be too occupied with the provisioning of these thousands of people to give some *bedouin* and coffins any prolonged thought.

Then she flushed in embarrassment, disgusted with herself. She'd used the fact of her brother's death—and the corpses of two of Saladin's soldiers who'd died on a recent scouting mission—in a deceptive ploy devised by Clarinda to get themselves, Genevieve, and the two caskets into the Krak.

Fatima wasn't sure how the Venetian girl had come up with the ruse, but it had worked exactly as Clarinda promised, the girl revealing a talent for predicting behavior and using guile and deceit that would have made Fatima suspicious if she'd not admired the girl so much for it!

She didn't know what potion Clarinda and Genevieve had taken to feign their deaths, but while the Hospitaller guards stood at the front of the stables, Fatima checked on both girls under the pretense of reciting the *salat-i-janazah*. Or, rather, she was prepared to explain that she was reciting the formal prayers for the dead if asked why she was prying open the coffin lids. But, again, no one noticed and no one asked.

Khalil saw the guards' preoccupation with people-watching and came close to her before speaking in Arabic: "Is Adelbert that blind?" he asked his wife. "We brought furniture and tapestries to your father the last time we were here. We even had donkeys and carts like we do now, and that was—what?—a year ago?"

"I've noticed that the eyes of some *franj* glaze when they see our skin color or clothes," Fatima agreed, "but having Brother Jeremiah there was very helpful." She looked appraisingly at Khalil. "Did you see him wink at me? I think he knew we were up to something, but trusted that it wouldn't harm his people or the castle."

"You practically grew up here," Khalil said. "Of course he trusts you. He's worked by your father's side for over five years."

"I'm still touched that he would let us pass without any kind of challenge." She gazed thoughtfully at Khalil. "As for Adelbert, I think I embarrassed him with my flirtation. I'm surprised that you weren't jealous, husband. Am I so losing my attractiveness to you that you'd let a westerner imagine such things about me?"

Khalil laughed. "You are my desert flower, Fatima. I don't get jealous when your smile and eyelashes get us all safely inside without them checking all the coffins!"

"That would've been a problem with the two black ones," Fatima agreed. "No one can get those things open."

Palomides ...

"What did you say, Fatima?" Khalil asked.

"That no one can get those caskets—"

"No, I heard that. After."

She looked at him in amusement. "I didn't say anything else, Khalil."

Palomides, you must take up the sword and stand beside both of Taliesin's heirs.

"There!" the *shaykh* exclaimed, whirling around. "Who said that?"

Fatima frowned, casting about, but saw only the stable area. "Khalil, what are you hearing? You did this yesterday in the Homs Gap."

He looked back at her, alarmed, then realized she was seriously concerned. "I ... nothing. I guess it's nothing." Self-consciously, he fingered Thaqib's amulet on his chest, acting as if the voice were anything but nothing.

Thaqib was supposed to take me up, but the Huntsmen slew him, the voice continued, *removed him from the game as they would strip any Lore Master of his allies.*

"Khalil?" Fatima said. "My love?"

You must be strong, and be prepared. Thaqib accepted me, but he's passed. It is up to you, Khalil. Santini will need all the allies he can, if he is to survive this siege. I am trapped between worlds, but I See thanks to the curse of the Druids of Rhydderch. Many forces work against Santini, and he will need you both in surviving the traps, and afterwards, if he's to find a defense against the Questing Beast.

"It's like ... it's as if I can feel Thaqib here," Khalil finally said, not trusting his mind and unsure how to tell Fatima what he was hearing. "There are too many family memories in this castle."

I fear that the Questing Beast was another name for the Nightmare Lord. A disguise. We must convince Santini to find him, Khalil. The Coven of the Mists and the Druids of Rhydderch are returning ...

The voice suddenly fell silent, and Khalil could again focus on his wife.

"I know what you mean," Fatima agreed, and then a motion caught her eye. She glanced at the giant, 'Abdullah.' The man had just started to brush down a donkey after he'd helped the servants disengage all the carts and tethered the camels. The coffin carts were lined up at the base of the vast, high-arched and barrel-vaulted wall on the western side of the stable. The animals and carts appeared small in the area filled with hundreds of horses.

"Abdullah!" she called, beckoning him to join her and Khalil.

The man acknowledged her, but gave the donkey a couple more casual strokes with the brush before making his way to the couple. When he drew near, the giant made sure that his back was to the guards, and then spoke urgently to Khalil.

"I don't like this, not one bit. Clarinda looked dead when I pulled the cloth away!" Alexander Stratioticus hissed. "Are you certain that she and Genevieve still live?"

"They're fine, Alex," Fatima assured him. "I don't know when they'll wake up, but they're both still breathing."

Alex inhaled deeply, visibly relaxing as he indicated the stables around them. "It worked. Clarinda was right, and we owe Saladin for the assistance. We're 'hiding in plain sight' and the two caskets are where she said they needed to be."

"Let's hope that Jeremiah delivers the news and father gets here quickly," Fatima said, her tone an implicit reminder of the cost that their ruse would have on Khajen ibn-Khaldun.

Khalil was sympathetic. "This isn't the way he should find out about Thaqib," he said, "I'm sorry, Fatima."

Fatima scanned the commons, expecting her father any second in flowing scholar's robes.

"No, but his daughter and son-in-law got into a castle besieged by two armies—we're as safe here as he'd have us be. He'll be saddened by Thaqib, but he'll also have to join the rest of us in getting used to it: that sadness will last a lifetime, my husband."

"After all this is over, we'll take him to where we buried him." Khalil paused. "He'll appreciate whatever ruse it took you to get into this castle, and I think even Thaqib would approve. We need to tend now to the living."

"I'd still like to see him sooner than later," Fatima said, returning to a survey of a castle whose environs she'd been familiar with since childhood. "The Warden Tower's right over there, and Jeremiah must've gotten there ten minutes ago. Where *is* Abby?"

"Abby?" Alex asked.

"My father," Fatima said. "I need to see him in person to talk about Thaqib. I *hate* this part of the plan!"

"Easy, my love," Khalil said, attempting some kind of reassurance. "We're in. Once we explain things to your father, he'll be able to explain things to the Powers-That-Be and we'll be able to help Clarinda do whatever it is she thinks she has to do here."

"Uh-oh, look," Alex said, rebinding the linen of his *keffiyeh* across his face. He nodded toward the kitchen area and saw that Brother Adelbert was rushing toward them with at least a half-dozen Hospitallers behind him.

"Guards!" the enraged Hospitaller Master of Stores screamed. "Brother Nicholas spoke truly! Seize those three liars immediately, and open all those coffins!"

BOOK FOUR

THE JOURNEY
TO MIMIR'S WELL

CHAPTER 1

The Caverns of Nidaveller

i. The Troubles of Arch-Mage Andvari

Of all things, it was a combination of Clarinda's knitting, Delling's apple-orange tarts, and Fabricia Trevisan's glassmaking skills that rekindled conversation between Aurelius and Clarinda.

Until those occasions, the two Italian youths had exchanged few words since departing the dwarf city of Nidafjöll earlier in the day. Aurelius remained angry about Clarinda's omission of her secret meeting with Mimir, the Norns, and Grimnir, informed as he'd been by Ratatosk that a covert conversation had revolved around him and the Codex Lacrimae. So, he'd completely avoided her, spending most of the first stage of the journey to the Crystal Caves walking beside Fenris, or talking with the leaders of the expedition, the Arch-Mage Andvari and his friend, Brigadier Halfdan.

Molto bene, she'd thought, *perché non voglio parlare con lui, neanche. Agendo come un pazzo infantile, e l'uccisione degli uccelli innocui perché aveva un capriccio!* ("Fine! I don't want to talk to him, either. Acting like an infantile idiot and killing innocent birds because of a temper tantrum!")

She'd had many variations of thoughts along that line, of course, but since Fenris, Andvari, Halfdan, and Aurelius seemed well on their way to becoming friends, Clarinda gladly left Santini alone. In spite of her determination to leave him be, however, moments of irritation persisted. At a rest stop by a series of broad pools in which everyone took turns refreshing themselves, she fumed by a wagon, her thumb worrying a peg in one of the side slats.

By Selvo's Loss, she thought, *I'll not be the first to break this silence. I've waited to trap pirates for longer than this before, and I don't lose ships because of impatience. Non! I'll wait for him to come to me.*

"How's the blanket coming along?" Ratatosk asked, sitting on his haunches and looking down at her from on top of the baggage cart.

Clarinda glared at him, and then crossed her arms under her breasts and turned away, muttering, "I'm not talking to you, either."

The squirrel didn't push the matter, and she returned to brooding.

Besides, I didn't do anything wrong! What makes Santini think he has a right to know everything I do, the instant I learn about it? That's not how it works. I'm training to be a Norn, for Odin's Sake! E, I've thought about this: Skuld was correct when she warned me at the council— things revealed too early can alter a future action for good or bad. I'll not take that risk merely because Mad-Monk Boy over there can't wait to get to Mimir's Well and ask all of them himself ... and I'll not be held hostage to his moods because his magic can kill flocks of birds when he stomps his foot and cries 'foul'!

Clarinda heard a splash, and inadvertently caught a glimpse of Aurelius without his tunic, sloshing water on his body. She turned away before he saw her, and stalked off, furious.

I'll not—I don't care how good-looking he is.

The annoyance surprised her because during the last ten hours she'd been able to distance herself from Santini. Aurelius might be getting to know others in the expedition, but Clarinda, was also making acquaintances. She'd remained near the center of the company, talking with Skade or knitting with Traeg.

The sea captain in her had even prompted making self-introductions to Brigadier Halfdan and many of the dwarf warriors under his command. Whether on a ship with sailors, or underground with a detachment of soldiers, Clarinda wasn't the kind of girl to sit on her hands and wait for someone's mood to improve before acting responsibly—she had to get familiar with these people in case they needed to rely on each other in battle.

But the effort of traveling combined with conversing all day had exhausted her. When the expedition began moving again after the half-hour break by the pools, Clarinda sat next to Traeg on the bench of the arch-mage's covered cart and rested her eyes.

She reflected on the start of the journey and how the expedition had grown to four times its original size in the time it took to meet the arch-mage.

After the argument with Aurelius that yielded dead birds dropping from a burst of Codex magic, Clarinda and Ratatosk had joined Aurelius, Fenris, Skade, and the wolves in meeting Andvari, and his wife, Traeg, at the top of the hill behind the seaside cottage.

To Clarinda's surprise, a platoon of thirty dwarves escorted the arch-mage and sorceress at the crossroads fronting the exit cave to Alfheim Way, a broad tunnel that led to the lower passages beneath the Scandinavian Mountains.

Clarinda had to reconsider her preconceived notions of arch-mages. The spouses conformed to neither the depictions of sorcerers she'd seen in illuminated manuscripts back in the Norn Grottoes, nor even to those scholars and priests she'd seen along the busy Venetian canals between St. Mark's Basilica and the Church of San Zaccaria.

Instead of a cloak and staff, Andvari seemed a typical miner, clad in a cream-colored tunic, brown breeches tucked into boots, and armed with only a long-handled iron pickaxe sheathed in a holster at his waist. The only departure he allowed from the work-dwarf image was a red-brown shoulder cape of velvet-like material, whose deep scallops reached to the middle of his thickly muscled chest and were fastened by a sizable silver medallion brooch that bore a pronounced triquerta symbol. Merry eyes glittered beneath bushy brown eyebrows and a beard of the same shade stretched to his silver belt buckle.

Andvari's spouse, Traeg, however, did fit Clarinda's stereotype of a sorcerer. Besides a roundish face that emphasized her warm and welcoming smile, and a linen kirtle of luminescent green that smoothed the lines of her plump figure, Traeg did carry a rather intimidating carved, short staff that would have proudly served as a focusing talisman for any respectable arch-mage. The matron's finely meshed headdress also pleasantly reminded the Venetian girl of the one her mother wore when going to work every morning in the glass shop.

No one could accuse Andvari of being unprepared. Thirteen long, oxen-harnessed carts had awaited the party, five of which were fully laden with provisions and fresh water, three with supplies and weapons, three with hay for the oxen and pack-mules, and the last two piled high with coverlets.

"... hardly seems like the 'small expedition' we requested, Andvari," Fenris growled as Clarinda arrived.

"It can't be helped, Master Fenris," replied Brigadier Halfdan. A clean-shaven dwarf, he glanced at the arch-mage, who nodded. "Besides the usual threat of rock-giants and *Wrothken*," the brigadier continued, "there have been increased raids by Falmorrian rebels throughout the lower tunnels, especially close to the *Kristallhöllen*."

"*Wrothken?*" Aurelius said. "Brigands?"

"*Ja*," Halfdan said, "but, not ordinary thieves. The *Wrothken* are kinfolk to the mountain trolls of the Jotunheim line. They're nasty business, and travel in gangs of five to eight."

"I see," Fenris said, understanding the need for a full patrol. "I've heard of them, but haven't yet met any. You feel that you've sufficient men here to defend against them?"

Halfdan gave a curt nod. "If it were only the *Wrothken*, I'd need only ten soldiers and half of these damn carts."

"These Falmorrian rebels worry you, then?" Skade said.

"The rebels, and a couple of other potential threats. Perhaps, Lord Andvari, you'd care to explain?"

"*Danke*, Halfdan," the wizard said, then opened his stance to the group. "We need to get underway, but it's important for you all to understand some things that have happened in Nidavaller recently. Things that may or may not affect this expedition into the mines." He rested his hand on the broadside blade of the pickaxe. "Now, I'll get to the rebels Brigadier Halfdan's worried about in a moment, but to my mind a greater threat lies in how the people back in Nidafjöll are reacting to false reports of *Wilde Jagd* incursions."

Aurelius studiously avoided looking in Clarinda's direction at the mention of Hela's army, but the Venetian girl felt him tense and saw the cautionary glance he cast at Fenris and Skade.

"Hordes?" Fenris asked.

"*Nein*. Single individuals, but even those testimonies are hearsay. That's the problem," Halfdan said before Andvari could respond. "Our military hasn't seen any evidence of an invasion force—"

"Just enough *ghasts* and *vampyrs* in the lower tiers to make mothers and fathers lock their doors tightly at night, and cause panic to simmer in the streets," Traeg said. "It's a shame. After the Battle of Niflheim two centuries ago, we'd thought we'd taken care of the runeporte that could allow Hela access to our tunnel system."

"It was taken care of," Andvari said, "and a primary goal of this trip will be to certify for myself the untruth of such rabble-rousing 'sightings.' I'll still not believe that Hela's crossed into our realm until I see a horde attacking for myself. *Nein, nein.* Hela's many things, but she's not a fool, and she'd not break a covenant she signed with her own blood."

"Which, then, leaves us only to tell you about the *Myrkridor,*" Halfdan sighed before turning his attention to a soldier who came to him with a clipboard.

The brigadier scanned the parchment, asked something of his captain, then scribbled a signature on the bottom with a proffered quill. The dwarf returned and began ordering the company to fall in lines and prepare for a march. "The expedition's ready, Andvari," Halfdan said. "We can go."

"*Myrkur Vistfólk?*" Skade cried, her exclamation running over Halfdan's words. "You've got Dark Dwellers appearing down here?"

"That sighting was confirmed, by me." Andvari said. "The creature surprised me, we battled briefly, but then it slipped away before I could finish it off."

"Odin's Beard," Skade muttered. "This is bad news. Give me a full invasion of the *Wilde Jagd* over that possibility anytime, Ancient One."

"What are *Myrkridor?*" Aurelius asked.

"Creatures whose fires make them seem spawned from some

pit in Muspelheim, but they're born of frost giants from Jotunheim," Fenris said. "They're savage, and almost unbeatable."

"Almost?"

"I've fought many creatures, Codex Wielder, but fighting *Myrkridor* isn't an experience I'd be willing to repeat anytime soon."

"Nor I," Skade said.

"*Bene*, so that's three problems," Clarinda stepped next to Aurelius so that the young knight couldn't readily ignore her any longer, nor could he easily get away from her in the press of wagons, oxen, and soldiers all around. "I've just arrived, so I apologize if I haven't caught everything."

"*Ehi, cosa fai?*" Santini asked, startled by her sudden proximity.

He'd been leaning against one of the wagons, but when he tried to move away, he inadvertently nudged his elbow into her left breast. He tried to move around her, but when she pretended to get out of the way his hand brushed against her rear. Blushing, he gave up and remained still, listening to Andvari.

She felt him glance at her, but not with anger. She almost felt sorry for him, but was also half amused; she needed him speaking to her again, and intended to use every means at her disposal to do it.

The group had been preoccupied with Andvari, Fenris, Traeg, and Halfdan, but because of Clarinda's interruption all eyes were now on the two Italian youths.

Acting unaware of Santini's discomfort, Clarinda continued her questioning of Andvari. "So, in short," she said, "you're telling us that we're embarking on what was supposed to be a quiet trip to one of Glittertind's entrances with a full military escort because of," she raised her forefinger, "*il primo problema,* the *Wrothken* brigands. Then, *secondo,* sightings of things that may or may not be members of the *Wilde Jagd. Terzo,* these *Myrkridor,* who are wandering the tunnels and terrorizing folks?" She raised a fourth finger. "*Bene.* Now, what about *il quarto problema,* the rebels? Who are they?"

"As far as we can tell," the arch-mage replied, casting a curious look between her and Aurelius, "the rebels are mostly former miners from the Galdhøpiggen section in the southern Scanes."

"Scanes?"

"The Scandinavian Mountains." He uncurled her thumb so all five digits splayed open. "*Quello che io considerano problema numero cinque* might be bundled with the rebellion."

"Your fifth problem?" Clarinda said, incredulous.

Her comment coincided with Aurelius's surprised, "*Tu parli italiano?*"

"We're dwarves, Norn," Andvari said gruffly to Clarinda. "We do nothing in half-measures, not even the amassing of problems." He regarded Aurelius with a dismissive eye. "*E, naturalmente, parliamo italiano!* We dwarves speak every language in the Nine Worlds, Boy! How else would we get any trading done?"

Those comments got even the dour Halfdan to smile, and after a grunt of disgust at the youths' apparent ignorance of basic realities, the arch-mage continued his story.

"The fifth problem. That's a mystery—a mystery whose solution will explain (and possibly dissolve) the growing rebellion: we have disappearing dwarves. One or two at a time, sometimes four or five, but never more than ten. Eventually, when the losses topped a thousand of their kinsmen and coworkers, the miners in the *Galdhøpiggen* section of the caves put down their picks and raised their axes against King Högni."

"What do you mean, disappearing, Arch-Mage?" Skade asked, misunderstanding. "Do you mean they're abandoning their work stations in the shafts and joining the rebellion?"

Nein, nein." Andvari gave a sharp wave of his hand. "I mean the disappearances have led to the rebellion ..."

"You're confusing everyone, Dear," Traeg interrupted. "What you should say, rather, is that the delay (or, some would say, lack) of government action about the missing miners has led to dwarves taking arms against the king."

"I'm with Skade in being a bit confused," Clarinda said. "What's the nature of these disappearances? I mean, are you talking about collapsed caves, abyssal drops, marauding Myrkridor, what?

"*Ja*, you grumpy dwarf," Skade added. "We've known each other far too long for this kind of roundabout. Most importantly, for us at least, is there a problem anywhere near the mines that lead to the *Kristallhöllen*?"

"Would that it were just a matter of cave-ins or falls down cliffs," the arch-mage said, including Fenris in his regard of Skade and Clarinda. "To answer your question: *nein*, but some of the activity I'm worried about is close to the Crystal Caves. Your request for guidance to the Glittertind *runeporte* had the merit of coincidence with my own plans. I like efficiency, and your need of a guide was well-timed with an investigation I'd already planned into the lower caverns."

"Ordered by the king?" Fenris guessed.

"*Ja*. King Högni isn't going to be coerced into any action by rebels, but he knows that the miners' fundamental complaints are valid. He and I were concerned about the repeated disappearances of the workers long before the rebellion began."

"Andvari was going to investigate by himself, but Högni wouldn't hear of it," Traeg smiled with pride and gazed fondly at the young soldiers bustling about in final preparations for the journey.

She winked and smiled at Skade and Clarinda. "So, now we have this escort of fine, handsome, and spectacularly muscled soldiers to keep us safe from all kinds of dangers!"

"Traeg, *bitte*." Andvari groaned. "A little decorum, if you would?"

"What do you think happened to the miners?" Clarinda asked.

"That's the mystery," Andvari said. "If the disappearances were clustered near the *Kristallhöllen* themselves, then I'd say that something was coming through the Rune Gate and abducting workers. Likewise, if the *Myrkridor* were responsible, there'd be ... residues of their passing that I could sense. Unfortunately, both of those hypotheses were dismantled almost when I made them. Too many of the losses occurred in caverns very distant from the Crystal Caves, and I didn't sense any of the dark energy one associates with the *Myrkur Vistfólk* at the abduction sites."

"But, are there any shared features?" Aurelius asked, still standing off to the side of Clarinda where she couldn't see him without turning fully from Andvari and Fenris. "I mean, were the workers mining in the same kinds of sections, like where ores are extracted for making *dvergar* steel, or near lodes of precious metals? Gems?"

Andvari shook his head. "A good question, but, the answer doesn't lie in those areas. Until recently, the only commonplace was that all the abductions were at remote sites. Most were near the end of tunnel systems that are in some places hundreds of leagues from each other."

"*Und* far from either of the capital cities—Nidafjöll here in the south, or Atlakvida in the north."

"Almost as if whomever's doing the abducting thought some dwarves wouldn't be noticed if the disappearances were far enough from each other?" Clarinda said.

"Abductions separated by space and time," Halfdan said. "Great distances within Nidaveller, and over a span of time. It was Master Andvari who first realized that there was a connection."

Andvari sighed. "Too much time. These disappearances occurred over seven years. That's why the rebellion is so strong. The resentment against the lack of response by the king had too much time to build. Complaints were made with the authorities, but for some reason the central miners' bureau never pieced together all the pieces of the puzzle."

"How many dwarves are now missing?" Fenris asked.

"Two thousand, five-hundred, and before you ask, the division's almost evenly broken between males and females."

"What?" Clarinda's eyes widened. "Twenty-five hundred dwarves? How didn't anybody notice that many gone? That's, what, almost three hundred and fifty dwarves taken a year?"

"That's why I said relatively," Andvari's tone was commiserative. "At any given time there are over forty-thousand dwarves working in the mines. No one except the workers and their immediate families realized that the disappearances might be caused by anything besides workplace accidents. It was only in recent months, when the absences couldn't be explained by falls into abysses or shaft collapses, that a pattern emerged."

"The frequency of disappearances started increasing?" Clarinda said.

"The rate, and the locations," Andvari confirmed. "One of the king's agents finally noticed that dwarf absences were occurring in more highly populated and well-lit tunnel sections. Those couldn't be explained away as easily as losses in the more remote, unexplored areas. The clerk brought it to my attention a couple days ago, I went to the king, and here we are."

Clarinda moved away from Aurelius, ending her little game, and then risked a glance at the young knight, trying to gauge the temperature between them. He watched both Andvari and Halfdan. His mind seemed completely preoccupied with the problem, and he didn't notice her.

"You've told us about raids by the *Wrothken*, and *Myrkridor* in the tunnels," Aurelius said, "but, I feel as if there's something else you're afraid of, something in the caves that's neither of the threats you believe might be abducting those miners."

Clarinda tracked his thoughts. "You think that all of your problems are connected to whatever's taking those miners."

"Or whomever," Andvari said. "I try not to link separate events, and on any given work-shift our miners face plenty of threats in the deep places of our world. But, the coincidence of the rebellion added to all these other factors has created unrest among all of the Nibelung, and both kings now face the possibility of open warfare amongst our people. That reality is astonishing, especially when you consider that in the lives of dwarves, a mere seven years is like the blink of an eye for such problems to arise."

The arch-mage looked intently at each of the companions. "Hence, this military escort, and my warning: don't wander from the group!"

ii. Into the Caves, and A Talk at the Way Station

The remainder of the meeting passed quickly. The sorcerer explained that the underground road to Mount Glittertind was long, with many stages that would require food and rest. Upon arrival at the *Kristallhöllen*, he told the travelers that they'd need special equipment to keep from going blind amid the brilliant crystal formations. Fenris's wolf pack made necessary the empty, twelfth and thirteenth carts so that the animals could ride under cover. The wizard laughingly told the group that while the oxen and packhorses would be provided with blinders, he'd not yet designed *starglassen* for wolves or any other creatures.

Once underway, the group moved at a relatively fast pace, considering the great number of soldiers, animals and baggage carts. Halfdan evenly divided his troops so that the dwarves guarded the front, middle, and rear of the train.

Andvari, Fenris, and Aurelius kept close to the brigadier. Clarinda remained apart from that quartet, so the males could have spent the first leg of the journey discussing everything from defensive tactics to the most preferred of pub ales. The two eldest dwarf brothers—Austri and Nordri—stayed close to the supply wagons, catching up on family matters with Sudri, Vestri, and the cook, Delling. (Austri took pains to make clear to anyone who'd listen for thirty seconds that the cook was a distant cousin, twice-removed.)

The members of Fenris's wolf pack loped where they would. Occasionally, Clarinda heard snatches of commands that Geri and Freki, the two lupine guardians of Yggdrassil, growled to the wolves, keeping them in line while Fenris conversed with Santini.

The pace set by all the dwarves surprised Clarinda. Despite their short legs, she almost had to trot at times to keep the leaders in sight, and she was grateful when Traeg and Skade seemed concerned enough for her well-being that they pulled her up on their wagon. Both women had sensed Clarinda's stormy mood, but after a couple of hours of watching her half-trot to keep up with the company, they'd decided enough was enough.

Ratatosk sulked.

When Clarinda made it clear back at Andvari's cottage that she wasn't going to begin the subterranean journey by killing Aurelius, the squirrel petulantly muttered something about that not being a surprise. He then hopped onto one of the carts and spent the rest of the time taunting various dwarves and wolves.

The first few hours were uneventful, marked by a long winding road through heavily populated caverns that housed everything from villages to mining operations. Eventually, the path became quiet and the air grew distinctly warmer. They approached a vast intersection paved in cobbled granite, whose squares were perfectly geometric and as smooth as hard glass. An odor of rotten eggs and the clanging of hundreds of hammers sulfur filled the air emanating from the right tunnel.

Near the din-filled tunnel, a few soot-covered dwarves pushed wheeled carts on a track that passed out of sight into another tunnel. The flickering flames of a blast furnace that must have filled an entire gallery painted this section's walls red-orange, and the shouts of working dwarves sounded amidst the hissing of smelting operations.

"That's one of the central foundries in all of Nidaveller!" Andvari shouted, urging the company to pass quickly when he and a few soldiers halted ore-laden mine cars.

The road became paved with richly red-veined marble, almost arabesque in its swirls and serpentine designs. Andvari seemed reassured by the sight, and exclaimed, "We're very close to our campsite, and should reach the *Kristallhöllen* by evening three days from now."

Andvari chose a gallery filled with pools illuminated by blue-green lights for the evening rest period. Clarinda guessed that the area was an often-used way station, because besides sleeping niches and holding pens carved from the rock formations, a great clay oven and cooking space dominated the far part of the cavern.

While the soldiers pitched tents and setting a watch, Delling and the four dwarf brothers unpacked. They spread linens on a flat stone slab and unrolled two leather-sheathed knife sets that seemed as wide as they were tall.

The cook and Vestri diced vegetables and meat while the helpers, Sudri and Nordri, all hustled and bustled, moving this way and that in such speedy responses to Delling's curt commands of "bring me more water," or "knead that dough." Ratatosk scampered under one of the wagons to avoid getting kicked aside in all the seemingly chaotic activity.

Delling and Vestri skinned ten braces of hares, diced onions and carrots, and the chefs' work soon filled the cavern with the promising aromas of stew and fresh-baked bread.

The other, non-military members of the company also busied themselves. When he'd finished helping Delling and Vestri set up the mobile kitchen, Austri tended to the oxen. Fenris loped off with his wolves to coordinate the making of a defensive ring with Halfdan's captains, and Andvari, Traeg, and the brigadier leaned over a gigantic parchment chart to pore over the next day's route.

After the briefing, Clarinda and Aurelius found themselves alone in the midst of all the activity. The young Hospitaller blushed when their eyes made contact and he quickly turned his attention to the modest stream where Delling's helpers retrieved the water.

"I'll get some more firewood for the night," Aurelius said to no one in particular, deliberately ignoring Clarinda. "There's a huge pile in that chute past that waterfall."

Ratatosk emerged from beneath a wheel and turned his head from side to side, then glanced up at the youth. "Who are you talking to, Santini?" the squirrel asked sarcastically.

Aurelius frowned, irritated at the animal but trying to ignore him, too. He moved quickly down the hill to the woodpile.

"You know what they say if you're hearing voices in your head —" Ratatosk warned as the youth passed from sight.

"I think you've said enough today," Clarinda said. "Do you remember the birds at Andvari's house? Let's try not to get him angry again for a while, eh? If anything, I've been doing things to try to make him smile."

Ratatosk reared upright on two hind legs and put a tiny paw on his own chest.

"If his scowl's any indication, you're failing miserably, Clare. And, I'm not joking about the voices. I'm in earnest. If he's hearing things, it might mean the Codex is taking control—"

"Basta!" Clarinda hissed, and then she, too, disappeared around the bend of the same path Aurelius had taken.

"—of his mind," Ratatosk finished. He looked at the empty path for a long moment, and then snorted, "Midgardians!" before returning to finish his nap under the cart.

Clarinda reached the cord of wood just as Aurelius turned with his first armful of logs. She noted his surprised expression with some satisfaction.

Besides her attempt at cornering him back at the crossroads, it was the first time they had come near each other since awakening in each other's arms in the Fenrir-Baude some fifteen hours ago that morning. The girl sensed that—although the knight was still quiet—he'd become more approachable.

While still not speaking, he nevertheless helped stack some of the logs in her arms. She also noticed appreciatively that he kept giving her what amounted to kindling while taking the much heavier loads for himself.

"I've been known to carry some heavy rope and sails," she

said after a few trips back and forth. "I'm a big girl—I can handle some of the larger logs."

"No argument here," Aurelius said, but continued to stack more thin sticks and branches into her arms.

"Not arguing will be a relief," she said, amused by his attempts to look everywhere but in her eyes. "It's no fun fighting."

"I'm not fighting."

"Good, because I'd hate to think you'd get mad about the Norns being mysterious and not telling us everything."

"They're—you're the Witches of Fate." He grunted as he stacked another log absurdly high against his chest so that she couldn't see his face. "I suppose you all think you have the right to keep secrets."

"There's that," she said, "but sometimes time plays a role."

"Time?"

"Servius, the Norns are more than just three women sitting around a pool. Time—our conception of it, our participation in it, our use of it ... how do I explain? Time is everything for them. For us. I can't say anything else at the moment, but you need to know that if I don't tell you something, I might be choosing to be secretive—"

He snarled at that and dumped his logs onto the pile near Delling's fire.

"—which, if you knew anything about women, any girl worth her weight in salt has the right to be, let alone if she's training to be a Norn!" She kept pace as he returned to the woodpile. "More often than not, though, revealing some secrets might simply be a matter of time."

He spun on her. "So, I'll wait for you to decide the moment to tell me about the Codex?"

"I think that you'll understand better when we get to Mimir's Well." She looked at the chute with the wood piled so high that they couldn't see the top of it. "Unless you're planning a bonfire that will cook everyone in the cave, don't you think we're done here?"

He glanced at the substantial pile they'd made near the oven, then dropped the stack in his arms.

"Where do you think all this wood comes from," she asked, genuinely curious, "and who stacks it?"

"We'll have to ask Andvari." He shrugged, falling back into sullen silence.

They parted, but she felt satisfied that they were at least speaking again. Whatever his irritation with her, she knew that a bond remained intact between them. They had a long trek ahead and she could afford to be patient. She'd grown up with sailors who sometimes went for days communicating in nothing more than grunts.

Sì, she smiled as she followed him to the group, a civil exchange of words was definitely a starting point!

iii. The Story of Fabricia and Angelo Trevisan

The next day passed uneventfully, and Clarinda was most relieved at the broadness and height of the tunnel they traveled, even though the road was descending more deeply into the depths of the Scandinavian Mountains. She'd gotten used to the ascents and descents within Glittertind, but for some reason when memorizing those paths she hadn't felt as claustrophobic as she felt here.

After the final leg of that day's journey, the setting up of a camp gave the comfort of familiarity. The flickering light of the blaze off the limestone walls reminded Clarinda of the Norn grottoes, and as she sat down near the cooks she made a plan to slip away and coordinate some events on Midgard, as well as check in on those awaiting her at Mimir's Well.

She had begun to devise a plan to facilitate Fatima's transport of Morpeth and Farbauti's caskets into the Krak des Chevaliers, and, unwilling to thought-speak in case the Codex Lacrimae had truly awakened and could eavesdrop (a distinct possibility, Urd had cautioned), she had to slip away to see the Norns and Mimir, who wanted direct reports of her interactions with Santini.

Before she did anything, though, she needed Santini fully speaking to her again.

She approached him after a supper of Seafarer's Pies that Delling and Vestri miraculously prepared in another way-station's gigantic ovens—a blend of smoked salmon, diced onions, and mushroom chunks mixed in a white wine sauce, then enclosed in freshly baked crusts. Biting into the flaky and buttery pies had been a pleasant surprise for Clarinda at the end of an otherwise boring day, and to a dwarf, the soldiers agreed that these kinds of meals were much better than the typical army rations.

After finishing her portion and washing it down with

honeymead, she politely listened to Andvari, Halfdan, Skade, and Fenris argue about some point of history regarding the Dark Elves. Many of the soldiers huddled in groups around their own campfires, and half of the dwarves were already asleep, needing rest before the second and third watches began.

When Aurelius left the group to prepare his bedding for the night, she went to speak with him.

"*Buona sera,*" she said, sitting on a boulder near the blankets. She withdrew a pair of knitting needles and yarn, and began working on the blanket she'd begun earlier in the day. After learning that Clarinda was interested in the fabrics that Traeg had stowed in one of the carts, the dwarvish woman had given her an extra set of needles and a skein of deep turquoise whose density and resiliency almost demanded that Clarinda fashion a blanket from it. She'd begun to do so while riding on the cart for part of the journey, thinking to herself that, with Aurelius sulking, she certainly wasn't going to spend all this time underground not doing something productive!

"*Buona sera,*" he replied cooly, not looking up as he made a pillow from some spare clothes rolled into a tunic. "We'll have to take Andvari's word for time, though. I'm starting to see how one loses track of days and nights in these caverns."

"The fire helps," she said. "I'd have never imagined that caves could be so beautiful."

He didn't say anything to that, but he also didn't leave. "The colors on the water and the rock—they remind me of the glassware my mother used to make."

"Your mother was a glassmaker?" He glanced at her, and his eyes widened as he saw what she was doing. "You knit?"

"Of course, I knit," she replied, staying focused on her work. She didn't want to reveal the trill of pleasure that his normal tone of voice sent through her. She'd missed the quieter moments of friendship between them that had started in Niflheim. "My mother taught me."

"My mother knits, too," he murmured. "What are you making?"

"A blanket for Traeg." She raised the needles. "She loaned me these, and it gave me something to do while you were off with the men."

He nodded at the foot of fabric she'd already completed. "You did that all since we've started?"

"When we've had breaks," she said, then held up the material. "This will be the width. Do you think it'll be big enough?"

Aurelius smiled. "She's a dwarf, Clarinda. I think if you keep going at that rate, she'll have a tent instead of a blanket for a gift."

"*Bene*," she replied, satisfied.

He paused, then prompted awkwardly, "You were … um, talking about your mother? That she was a glassmaker?"

"*Sì*." She remained focused on the knitting, and pleased again that he was making some effort to repair the rift his anger had created between them. "She inherited her father's shop and kept with it after marrying *Padre*. They—"

Traeg suddenly joined them, a platter in her hands piled high with a variety of desserts.

"Oh, my dears," she said in an excited voice, "Delling's outdone himself again. You've not really completed a meal until you've had one of his desserts. The apple-orange tarts are my favorite, but you won't be disappointed by the gingerbread or chocolate cakes."

Aurelius took a tart and gave her a measured look. "*Grazie*—I don't think that I've ever been on a journey so well-provisioned. He's quite a cook, isn't he?"

"You're welcome, and *ja*, he is—Delling's been with us almost one hundred and ten years. I can't remember a time when he's ever failed to please." She patted the paunch under her robes. "You might not have noticed, but Andvari and I take food very seriously."

Clarinda laughed. "Well, I hope I look as good as you do if I live to be seven hundred years old!" She took an almond-cream tart. "This looks delicious—*grazie*, Traeg."

Aurelius looked at both women. "I'm sorry—did you say seven hundred years' old?"

"She did, indeed, my dear," Traeg said with a grin, "and I must say that, even though I snared Andvari when I was a little past my first century, I do worry sometimes that he'll leave me for another, younger dwarf. He's almost nine hundred, you know!"

Aurelius smiled. "No ... no, I didn't know. I never would have guessed!" he said with disbelief and wonder in his voice.

"Long are the lives of dwarves, sweetie," Traeg said, and then, tapping her temple added, "and our memories are almost longer. I've got much to teach you, too, if you'd ever come speak with me, and quit hiding out with our wolfish friend over there."

Fenris, on his fifth Seafarer Pie looked up from his seat by the bonfire with a questioning expression. "What? Did you say something about me?" he asked when his mouth was empty enough to speak.

Traeg sighed. "No, just about men in general. You can run, but you can't hide. Eventually, you have to deal with us women-folk at the end of the day."

"Not always a bad thing," Andvari said, prodding the fire with a large stick.

"Oh, hush, old man." Traeg shook her head and looked at the youngsters. "Now, you two need to get on talking to each other," she said with a kind firmness. "The silence has been unbearable for the rest of us, and we've known each other for only half a day. Vent the smoke from the air, hmm?"

She moved on to the rest of the company who were lounging about the bonfire, telling stories and relaxing after the hard day's travel.

When Clarinda finished eating, she sat down on her blankets and returned her attention to Aurelius.

"I'm ... sorry for not telling you what I'd learned about the Codex sooner—"

"You still haven't told me anything." He took a breath. "I'm sorry, too ..." He paused, uncomfortable. "*Prego*. Finish your story about your mother. I've heard you tell me only about your father."

Surprised at an apology where she expected stubbornness, she said, "But, you've been angry at me all day. Don't you want to know what was said at the council?"

He frowned. "It's a council now? That makes me want to hear even less."

"Less?"

"Clarinda, I was angry because you didn't tell me something about the Codex, but I've come to suspect that, even if you were to tell me the worst possible thing, it wouldn't matter. I've decided none of this matters back in the real world—"

"Servius, it does matter! Believe me, we need to talk about what Mimir and Grimnir argued about, and the Norns, and what Ratatosk told me this morning—it matters so much that we'll probably be up half the night discussing things."

Contrary again to expectation, he smiled. "All the better then, to tell me now about your mother. You said she was a glassmaker? I thought you were all in the sea trade."

"On *Padre's* side, *sì*," she said, with mock exasperation. For all the casualness by which he'd postponed discussing the Codex, she believed that he was experiencing the same pleasure that she was in just talking with each other again.

"But before that part of their lives, before I came along, they had their first social outing at a party on All Soul's Day. Madre came from north of the city—the Isle of Murano."

"They met at a party?" he asked, intrigued. "Which feast?"

"*Alla festa dell'Epifania*, but that's not where they first met."

"Ah, Twelfth Night..." Aurelius said with a chuckle, remembering from his own childhood the Feast of the Epiphany that fell on the twelfth day after Christmas. "Did *La Befana*, the Old Witch, ever bring you lumps of coal?"

"*Naturalamente*," Clarinda began, then her eyes widened. "I mean, *non*—of course, not! Not lumps of coal ... presents! I was a good girl, Santini! There was always a fresh baked meat pie on the table for the evening dinner, and during the day *La Befana* put glasswork in my stocking—sometimes it might be pendants or beads, but whatever she left was always very delicate and precious." She grinned, relishing the moment. "When I was very young, I built quite a marble collection from *La Befana's* visits. I think the leather sack with them is still in my room somewhere at home."

"My mother would always make some kind of meat pie for that dinner, too," Aurelius said, "but I liked the antipasto the best, especially the prosciutto wrapped around cantaloupe slices—"

"Or, just prosciutto on its own—" Clarinda protested.

"With hot bread and butter!" Aurelius finished, and they both laughed as the memories of childhood holidays came too quickly to recount.

"*Hei!*" Fenris called. "Are you two going to hop in the sack together, or come over here by the fire?"

Both youths flushed and rose from the blankets, self-consciously aware of the eyes upon them.

O, Dio, how long has everybody been listening? Clarinda wondered.

"Clarinda was just telling me about Venetian glassmaking," Aurelius said.

"Indeed?" Andvari said. "Come, sit with us. We dwarves usually import glass from Midgard or Alfheim. I'd much appreciate an insider's view on the process."

"I'm afraid I might not be of much help, then," Clarinda said. She and Aurelius found places on the benches at the fire. "My mother made glass, not me." She nodded at the entrance cave. "Those blast furnaces back there reminded me of the times

Madre used to take me to *Nonno's* house on the island of Murano. *Nonno* was my grandfather. He made everything from eyeglass lenses and panes of stained glass to accents on enameled bowls ..."

"Ah, a true artisan," Austri commented, glancing at his brother, Vestri. "Do you hear that, Vestri? Craftsmanship by hand that lasts—not the kind that gets eaten after you make it."

"Easy, Austri," Delling rumbled, wiping his hands on his apron as he sat down. "You've just eaten three pies made by your brothers' and my hands. You start insulting the cooks, and we'll not be responsible for what you find in your next dish."

Austri muttered something, but stopped talking. Andvari nodded at Clarinda.

"Madre's specialty was making decorative vases. They were known throughout Europa. We sold them at fairs in Italia, in many towns north across the Alps in Francia, and even into Germania." She looked at Aurelius. "I may have taken over my father's ships, but those long trips were where I first learned about trade and the merchant's life. Ah, those vases. Besides having unique curves on the glassware, Madre also included a signature seam of transparent glass that ran clearly through the other colors." The girl traced imaginary curves in the air. "Like this. They were amazing. I'm not just saying this because I'm her daughter, but Madre worked the tubes and *bocche* vents like nobody before or since. Part of the talent lay in knowing how to use the heat of the three different furnaces to do everything from getting rid of the impurities, to pressing or casting shapes. Mostly, though, a real master like her just has a keen sense of timing and knows how to apply the heat when blowing the glass. Then, of course, we had such volume that she also knew how to run a very busy operation, with a lot of workers and monthly shipments to all part of Europe."

"It sounds highly profitable, and you sound very proud of her." Traeg said.

"Highly profitable, and I was ... am. We still have the glass factory, but it's being overseen by my uncle while we're at sea." Clarinda stared at the fire. "Like *Nonno*, *Madre* managed all the business aspects well, but she took the most pride in the craftsmanship. No one on the isle, no one in Italia, could replicate the clarity of that glass. *Nonno* and *Madre* kept its recipe secret, and they hid that secret in the safest place possible ..." She tapped the side of her forehead.

The dwarves who were still awake murmured appreciatively.

"The freemason guilds of Atlakvida keep similar secrets," Sudri said.

"Nay, Sudri." Nordri said. "I know you worked with them for a while, but they're an unruly lot, and given to blabbing." He rose to his feet and walked a bit unsteadily to the end of the wagon where the casks of wine and ale were kept. He continued to speak while he filled a vast pitcher with honeymead. "Nay, a freemason back home might say that they have a secret for mixing a certain kind of underwater cement, but you'd wrest that recipe from him—and the hidden sources for one or two rare ores you weren't even interested in—for the price of two ales and some jokes. A better comparison would be to the sword-smiths of Nidafjöll and the forging of *dvergar* steel. Now, that's a guild that knows how to keep things close to—"

"Sword smiths?" Sudri said. "You're saying that a bunch of

metal-stroking, would-be elf lovers can keep secrets better than our stone masons?" He shook his head. "You should be ashamed of yourself, brother. Here, though, since you're up, fill this ale again, and I'll tell you some things about—"

"*Hei*, my story, boys!" Clarinda said. She intercepted Nordri, took the pitcher of ale from his hand, and filled Sudri's leather stein before topping off those of a couple other dwarves, ending with Aurelius's and her own. She smiled. "I feel as if I'm back on my ship. Now, settle down and let me finish. I don't know the particulars of your guilds, but secrets are secrets, and I think that you're both correct, as you'll see in a moment." She glanced at Aurelius. "This is where my father comes into the story."

He clacked his stein against hers and raised it to include the group. "To your *Nonno* and parents." He took a sip, and said, "I was wondering how a sea-merchant and glass-maker met."

"Typically, for Venetians—and you'll appreciate this, fellows—the tale has to do with trade secrets and complex formulas. You see, my father, Angelo Trevisan ..." Clarinda stopped speaking. Her throat constricted and eyes filled with tears.

"It's fine, Clarinda," Aurelius said softly. "We can hear it another time—"

"*Non!*" She wiped her eyes. "I'm proud of this story." She inhaled deeply, then started again, taking in the dwarves. "My father, Angelo Trevisan. He passed away recently."

There were murmurs of condolences, but she pressed on with her story. "He ... Angelo grew up in one of the larger merchant families of Venice, where they build ships," she glanced at Aurelius, cleared her throat a final time, and qualified: "In the Castello district near the *Arsenale*. I grew up in the same *palazzo* he did, and our house has been in the family for generations."

"A palace?" One of the guardsmen asked, his eyes widening.

She paused, seeing confusion and not a little wonder on some of the dwarves' faces. "*Non*, a *palazzo*. It's a large house on the Grand Canal. It's still there, a bright place, with a large parlor where we do paperwork on the ground floor, a great room with a kitchen on the second, and a loggia on the third. The point is, *Padre's* family was very well off, and there was no reason for him to paddle a scull across the lagoon to Murano one night and try to steal the secrets to *Nonno's* glass works."

"How's that?" Andvari asked. He grunted. "He tried to steal from your grandfather?"

Clarinda laughed. "You've your *dvergar* steel down here, but, trust me, clear glass takes some doing on Midgard. It's very hard to come by, pricey when you do, and *Madre's* family had the clearest that there was. No haze, no fog, no distortion of any kind—just clear glass. But, as I said, the secret recipe for blowing that glass was only in *Nonno's* and *Madre's* heads, so there was no parchment for my father to find. All that Angelo got out of his night's journey was a sound thrashing by *Madre's* broomstick when she found him in the family parlor above the factory looking for the secret formula."

"Why would she marry the man, then?" Skade asked.

"That came later," Clarinda said. "*Primo*, after *Padre* stopped trying to crawl away, she and grandfather confronted Angelo to find out why he'd tried to steal from them. For all the blood that he wiped from his nose, Madre told me that she still noticed he was a very handsome fellow, and thought that this type of misadventure—"

"Crime," Skade corrected.

"—he was fifteen," Clarinda said, "so I call it a misadventure, a *scherzo*. After Angelo told them that he'd done it at the urging of some friends just to see if he could, Fabricia thought that he'd been given a good enough scare that he wouldn't be doing something like that again. *Nonno* wasn't so forgiving. He threatened to turn him over to the guild master who controlled the shipyards. That really put the fear in my father. He knew that kind of revelation would be a huge scandal for his family. So, like he always did, Angelo weighed his options, and decided it'd be better to tell everything. *Madre* and *Nonno* discovered that the idea had been a dare—a *sfido*—from one of his friends who lived on Murano."

"Ah—competitors," Austri said. "So, when they discovered that 'friend's' full name, your mother and grandfather realized that the 'dare' was in reality a ruse. Another glassmaking family had used the friendship of the boys to try to find your family's secret of the clear glass."

"*Precisamente*," Clarinda said. "My father was attracted to my mother, too, so he rightly decided that the friend who'd dared him wasn't much of a friend—"

"—and that your mother was a much better looking new friend," Aurelius said.

"*Grazie, sì. Era molto bella!* Very beautiful ... As you can guess, Angelo switched sides and agreed to help my family, and, hopefully, get the girl. Together, *Nonno*, *Madre*, and *Padre* got rid of the competitors on the island who'd tried to steal secrets from a neighbor and, because of the information, my grandfather not only got rid of them, but also used the moment to buy their property and become guild-master of the glass blowers."

She looked at Aurelius. "That autumn's All Soul's Festival on the Piazza San Marco was the first time they danced together, and they married a year later."

"*E, tua madre* remained with her family's glassmaking business?" Aurelius asked.

"*Sì,* but she also began to do all of the bookkeeping and finances for my father's family at the dockyards. When *Nonno* died, she took over the factory on Murano, and made *Padre* split time between our home there and the one in the Castello. By then, though, his brother—*mio zio* Verrocchio—had rejoined the family and become very involved in our maritime trade, so it all worked out." She paused. "That was our routine until a few years ago, when *Madre* passed away."

There were nods and compliments all around as she concluded, and some commiserative words at her loss.

The core group of Andvari and Traeg, Delling, and the four brothers were interested in making parallels between their own commercial practices and the Midgardian ones. In contrast, the handful of dwarvish soldiers who'd been listening appeared to be excited simply by nearness to the Venetian girl herself.

After hearing some of his men whispering, Halfdan explained that the soldiers were aware that the majority of people might spend their entire lives without meeting an aspect of Fate, let alone having a chance to become personally acquainted with a girl who'd been predicted to become the newest incarnation of Urd.

The conversation turned to the dwarves themselves, and

Andvari's face lit up when Aurelius asked about the history of the Nibelungs. The arch-mage gave many details about dwarvish history and the current state of affairs under the twin brother co-regents, Kings Högni and Gunnar.

From the brief sketch he outlined before bedtime, Clarinda learned that the Nibelung dwarves were an ancient race whose livelihood and culture depended almost entirely on the operations of the mines that opened into every one of the Nine Worlds. Most of their civilization existed even deeper in the earth than the capital cities of Atlakvida and Nidafjöll, Andvari explained that those lower levels were where most of the daily work of digging and extracting took place.

Also, beside the many foundries that smelted iron into the famed *dvergar* steel a host of other industries existed to serve the thousands of dwarves who inhabited the kingdom. At the heart of all those trades and businesses, dwarvish intermediaries and brokers worked with buyers and traders for selling dwarvish metals and gems in the other eight worlds.

Exhaustion eventually overtook the interest Clarinda had in Andvari's words. She watched Aurelius as the wizard spoke. He stared into the bonfire, and glanced at her only occasionally, but when he did, his eyes showed a pain that she'd not seen before.

Qual è il problema, now? she thought, reviewing in her mind what had been said in the past quarter hour. *All we've been discussing is business ... ah, business and family. We never finished that discussion we started in Hela's hall, did we? Hmmph. He's keeping secrets, too. A bit hypocritical to come after me for keeping my own counsel, and then not share what he's been through.*

Well, tonight wouldn't be the time to find out. It had been a good enough day, ending with a moment that seemed to make things right between them again.

Andvari used the talk of the lower mines to discuss the next day's route, then Aurelius rose to his feet and said that he'd better get some rest in preparation for the next day's journey.

That broke up the company for the evening, and as everybody settled down and checked on gear, Clarinda used the moment to slip into the shadows by the cavern entrance. She yawned and realized how much she appreciated the magic in Grimnir's staff that kept the Norns' voices out of her head. Without it she'd have little true rest.

While fingering the *Brisinga* necklace, she realized that, tired or not, she needed to implement her plan for getting the caskets into the Krak des Chevaliers. The ruse would require some play-acting on the parts of Fatima, Khalil, and Alex, as well as demand that she and Genevieve swallow doses of a potion she'd discovered through her studies in the grottoes.

I'll visit the Norns and Mimir sometime tomorrow, she thought. *Not much could have happened since I saw them last.*

When she was completely out of sight of the company—and especially as far as she could get from Santini—she focused on Midgard and the camp of Saladin, touched the jewels on the Brisinga and disappeared.

Except for the sentries, only wolves noticed Clarinda's return a few hours later. Everyone else was fast asleep. Geri and Freki raised their heads as she slipped under the blankets of her niche, but after she winked at them and indicated with a wave that all was well, they returned to their own slumber.

When she dreamed, though, Clarinda's sleep was restless, filled with a vision that didn't wake her, but which imparted dread like a fist around the heart.

In the dream, birds plummeted from a desert sky as a wall exploded in a fortress, its force slaying over forty men and women. Two figures appeared in the wreckage, one of whom felt as if he should be Old Nick, but whose features were too elderly and different from those of Evremar of Choques. A boy and a large dwarf whose aura crackled angrily with powerful energies accompanied the dark man. Clarinda could hear the old man and dwarf speaking, but try as she might, their words remained unintelligible.

She awakened, then, and looked across the gallery floor to Santini's slumbering form, visible as a shadowed lump against the flickering light of the small watchfire. The nearest of Halfdan's dwarf sentries glanced at her, rising to a half-crouch in alarm at her face, but she motioned him to return to his seat on the stone bench.

Reassured that all was well, she rolled over, secured her grip on the staff Grimnir had given her, and fell asleep. Her last thought was a question directed in thought-speech to Urd — who is Dietrich the Mad? — but in the haze of drowsiness, she'd forgotten that the magic in the staff blocked the Norns from communicating with her, and she with them. Then exhaustion overtook her, and she fell gratefully into a dreamless sleep for the rest of the night.

CHAPTER 2

Death in the Crystal Caves

From Clarinda's vantage, the next day's march was so uneventful that she repeatedly distracted herself by daydreams. She yearned to break from the company and transport herself to the Norn grottoes, and imagined herself reclining on the flow-rock in Mimir's Sanctum, sipping hot honeymead, and making some progress toward finding answers to her questions. If those answers weren't forthcoming from the reticent Seer or the Witches of Fate, at least she could be productive and research in the musty tomes and parchments of the scriptorium.

Why didn't she just go? Whatever she did while back in the Norn Grottoes would surely be more productive than this journey, and she knew that she could return to Andvari's group well before it reached its destination.

Anything would be better than this long, boring march!

The first eight hours were filled with nothing but a descent down a narrow, dimly lit, and steadily declining grey tunnel which induced a feeling of claustrophobia. There wasn't any room for walking on either side of the wagons, let alone pulling over for a proper rest stop where she could try to speak again with Aurelius.

She was irritated with him, too. Contrary to her expectations after the warmth he'd shown last night, this morning upon breaking camp, he'd stayed with the men. Once the caravan set off upon the subterranean road, there hadn't been a chance for anyone to move forward or backward from his or her respective places in line.

So stuck near the rear and walking slightly behind Traeg, Clarinda fingered the jewels of the *Brisinga* necklace beneath her tunic and fantasized about disappearing.

She sighed each time she felt this urge to leave, knowing she'd do nothing of the sort. She couldn't. *Primo*, she hadn't yet explained to Aurelius all the aspects of the *Brisinga* necklace (and how the Codex Lacrimae adversely affected it). If she just disappeared, he'd rightly believe that she was keeping more secrets from him. *Secondo*, she didn't want him or anyone else suspecting that her purpose was anything other than escorting Santini to Mimir's Well.

She just needed to be patient, endure this tunnel until the

end, and then find a way to get Santini to Mimir's Well after they passed through the *Kristallhöllen*. From that moment, she'd be able to rely on the Norns and Mimir to give what advice they could. Yet, even that thought brought up the *terzo* problem: Ratatosk's warning that the Witches of Fate and the Seer conspired against Santini.

She wanted to give the three sisters the update they'd requested, but her confidence in them had been shaken by the squirrel's words outside Andvari's cottage. Who should she believe anymore? She shrugged, knowing that constantly double-thinking everything would result in madness, and ultimately believing that she already knew the answer—she had to trust her heart and instincts; both were telling her to stay the course she'd charted with the Norns.

Andvari stopped the group when they came to an area where a bright light shone around the corner just ahead. The intersection seemed to be a major crossroads, the road they'd entered on splitting into four different directions. Three of the paths passed out of sight into side tunnels. However, the light that emanated from the fourth path—the road directly ahead— was so intense that just its reflection off the granite walls it hurt Clarinda's eyes.

Two rivers rushed along the walls on each side of the road that led into the glowing chamber, the waters black and cold-looking as they apparently rushed into the base of the rock walls themselves.

"We're here, my friends," the arch-mage said. He moved to the long wagons and directed Suđri and Vestri to start unbinding the wrappings on the *starglassen*. "Those waters are the beginning of the *Underjordisk Elv*—the Underground Rapids—and they feed into the great Døkk River that we'll be coming upon tomorrow, after we pass through the *Kristallhöllen* today."

He put his hands on his hips and surveyed the cavern in satisfaction. *"Ja, ja—das ist sehr gut.* We're very close to the realm of Alfheim and the *runeporte* to Glittertind here. Can you hear that thrumming?"

Clarinda and Aurelius both nodded, and Andvari continued. "That's the roar of the Franang Falls, as they appear in Alfheim. The falls are a seventh of a league beyond that wall where the river on the right is running. We're almost to the *runeporte,* but *Kinder* ... Children, I can't stress enough that you must keep the *starglassen* helms on your head. When you see the crystal formations, they may play tricks on your eyes, even with the filters on the lenses—some folk have even heard songs coming from them, like sirens on a river bank, but ignore ..."

Those were the last words that Clarinda and Aurelius heard Andvari speak peacefully on this journey through the Caverns of Nidaveller. A great rumbling shook the floor of the cavern, interrupting him. He instinctively swung around, looking toward the glowing northeast bend in the road that marked the beginning of the Crystal Caves.

Halfdan moved forward, a curt command and hand signal launching dwarves to the front of the cavern on each side of the exit tunnels. Fenris and the wolves growled.

The sound of many feet pounded down two of the darkened access tunnels, punctuated with familiar tip-tapping sounds, like bones clicking against pavement. Aurelius looked in alarm at Clarinda.

"That sounds like Modgud and—" Aurelius groaned, his hand moving to his sword-hilt.

" —the *Wilde Jagd!*" Skade finished, reaching to her quiver.

Clarinda raised her staff and looked to the northern tunnel.

Ratatosk's head snapped up from nibbling a hole in one of Delling's food storage sacks, and he leapt from the cart to his usual place around Clarinda's shoulders.

Halfdan himself joined the deployment of soldiers at the rear of the baggage train, commanding two dwarves to sprint up the ramp to ascertain if retreat was possible.

All the dwarves had drawn swords and axes, but Skade simply broke into a full sprint toward the central-right adit with the glowing walls, overtaking seven dwarf soldiers who were positioning themselves behind boulders, bows notched with arrows at the ready.

The Huntress correctly anticipated the first threat—five giants strode around the northernmost corner. Three times as high (and twice as wide) as Aurelius, the muscular titans were armored from head to foot in massive shingles of grey granite. Their weight seemed so ponderous that Clarinda wondered how the colossal men moved—but they advanced with such fierce speed that they were already halfway across the cavern floor, raising their great, spiked wooden clubs by the time Skade loosed five arrows at their faces.

Unless she'd seen it with her own eyes, Clarinda wouldn't have believed that anyone could move so quickly, let alone loose arrows with such accuracy.

Quartzite-faced round shields deflected a couple of the arrows, but three projectiles found their marks and plunged deeply into each warrior's right eye. The giants staggered backward and eight members of the wolf pack tore at their bare feet and legs. Thick slashes of red-black blood welled in the cuts made by claws and fangs, and the howling of angered giants and frenzied wolves filled the air.

Two more rock giants entered the chaos-filled chamber from the eastern tunnel. Though armored in stone and clad in the same pelted loin cloths as their compatriots, they wielded different variations on the clubs—one held a spiked mace, while the other had a quarterstaff with bladed ends. Runes embossed that weapon's hawthorn shaft; their crimson power emanated through a collection of skull etchings.

Clarinda's quarterstaff lurched in her hand.

"What's happening to your staff?" Santini asked, his sword and trident main gauche drawn. He'd taken a protective stance slightly ahead of the Norn.

"It's called Gungnir," she corrected, then realized that he didn't know anything about it yet. Curse these new perceptions! In times of panic, she found it increasingly difficult to keep a correct reckoning of the past, present, and future.

"That's another thing I didn't tell you about the meeting," Clarinda explained. "The old man ... Grimnir —" she hesitated, unsure how much she should reveal of what she'd witnessed at Mimir's Well. That moment was still in Aurelius's future, but he needed the knowledge now.

"Grimnir, he ..." she continued, "well, he 'melded' his weapon with mine, merged them. My staff's called Gungnir now, and it's part-magical spear, part rune-staff. Anyway, it's supposed to be a great help in a fight like this."

As if responding to her words, bright runes blazed along her two-handed quarterstaff. Well-formed Norse hieroglyphs covered every part of Gungnir's wooden surface. The characters flared with a brilliant yellow light that countered the blood-red malice radiating from the skull designs along the giant's staff.

Then the the shambling and shrieking forces of the *Wilde Jagd* assaulted the cavern on the north and east sides.

Clarinda looked at the horde and her heart felt heavy. In the seconds at the beginning of battle, she almost succumbed to a fear that this subterranean area would become a tomb. Members of the company had done battle with this enemy in Niflheim, but she didn't know how they'd even lifted a blade or bared a fang—the horror descending on their company in the forms of corpses, skeletons, *vampyrs*, and werewolves surpassed anything she could've imagined. Her mind seemed frozen in shock, but even through the immobilizing fear, she tried to make calculations.

If this force were part of the same army that previously attacked Aurelius, Fenris, and Skade, and if the horde continued to access the cavern through the two north and eastern cave mouths, then the layout of the gallery gave a slight advantage to her much smaller group. Thanks to Halfdan's quick deployment of his troops, instead of the hundreds that had swarmed through the trees and by the river in Niflheim, only five to eight enemies could enter this gallery at a time.

Besides, Clarinda thought, trying to find some cause for hope, *didn't Aurelius say that Skade and Fenris had done the wolf's share of the fighting back in Niflheim? We've got them as allies, plus Halfdan's troops, and Andvari, Traeg, and Austri's family.*

Clarinda took heart when the four dwarves raced together to the easternmost tunnel, and joined soldiers in hacking at every corpse and skeleton that tried to enter.

Combined with the swift moving members of Halfdan's patrol, the dwarves' efficiency at killing was remarkable, and the bodies of the enemy started piling high at the left-hand portal. Surprisingly, given their earlier arguing, Austri remained close to Vestri, but his two-sided axe was almost a blur. At the other side of the entrance, Norðri and Suðri used broadswords as long as the dwarves were tall to great effect.

Cold drafts whirled in great gusts through the cavern. Clarinda looked instinctively skyward, but saw only the frozen-icicle limestone formations of the ever-present stalactites.

Where were those strong breezes coming from?

The four brothers did a masterful job of defending their position with a few of the dwarf troops near one entrance, but then more of the ghastly forms flooded like a shrieking torrent into the cavern from the last two unguarded adits.

Now, I'm worried. They're coming through every entrance! Clarinda inhaled deeply, and steeled herself. The first line of the new entrants would be upon her soon. She'd not die without a fight.

The cavern's rock formations, boulders, and close quarters continued to work in the company's favor and, in many instances, the giants themselves proved a hindrance to their own forces. They took up so much physical space that Hela's *Død Bueskytteres*, the Death Archers, kept missing their targets. Some of the ghoulish bowmen's arrows bounced off the backs of the giants themselves, or burst into stalagmites where their intense heat set the limestone pillars aflame.

Yet, for all the limited access allowed by the tunnels and the two black-watered rivers that bounded the cavern, there still seemed to be too many for the company to successfully defend against.

"No," Clarinda heard Fenris say in disbelief. He stumbled forward and grabbed the back rails of one of the baggage carts.

"Lord Fenris, what's ...?" Halfdan began, then ducked in the opposite direction as a volley of arrows came between him and the ailing man.

The oxen started to whine, but that volley killed five of the animals yoked before the baggage carts, and they burst into flame.

A horrendous stench erupted from their blazing carcasses, and an oily smoke started to fill the area. Then four others were slain in the same manner, and the flames spread to many of the wagons, consuming wood, metal, and supplies in an inferno that lit up the area.

"Use the smoke and move!" Aurelius shouted, scanning behind them and seeing no one on the road where they'd entered the cave. "Andvari, Traeg! Let Halfdan and the rearguard take the tunnel, we need to follow Skade and take the attack to them!"

"Agreed, Midgardian," Halfdan shouted, not bothering to argue about chain-of-command when the Hospitaller had given the same orders he'd been starting to say. "Hela should be following the giants, so be careful after you break through that line—"

"No, not there—Halfdan, watch and ware: she's coming from behind!" the arch-mage screamed, leaping on a pile of boulders. "Clarinda and Aurelius, head along the river on the right side.

Our only hope lies directly ahead in the *Kristallhöllen*—the dead won't last long in that light."

"I bet those giants will, though," Clarinda muttered, remembering that the Crystal Caves' entrance was where the first five giants came from. She doubted that any part of the underground world could be denied those creatures.

"Brace yourself, Clarinda!" Aurelius said. "The three giants that Skade hurt, they're getting past—"

Traeg etched glowing sigils across the stone floor using the ironclad heel of her staff, while Andvari stood above his wife on a boulder in front of the foremost two carts, raised both hands high and chanted, *"Ved å de pakter dvergene, begon fra ditte halle!"*

Orange light leapt from Traeg's symbols, passed through her husband's body, and found release in eruptions of hot coruscating power that lanced from Andvari's fingertips. The fiery magic blasted into the faces of the three wounded giants who'd been rushing toward the company with Skade's arrows still jutting from their ruined eye sockets, and continued in a sweeping arc of mage-fire that enveloped the corpses shambling across the stalagmite-ridden floor toward him.

Upon contact with the light, the heads of the giants simply disappeared into smoldering ash, and their bodies toppled onto the skeletons trying to get past them to the dwarves; when the sorcerer's flame hit the cadavers, their pale flesh burst completely into flames, slowing those who pressed behind.

Now Traeg leapt to her husband's side, holding her staff defensively and swinging each end of it into the face or body of any enemy that came near—with each blow, more orange light exploded from her opponents, and Clarinda's eyes widened as she realized that Andvari's wife wielded enough raw power to be an arch-mage herself.

"Four giants left," Aurelius corrected himself, and nodded at Clarinda. "We do this together, back to back, but always making toward the Crystal Caves—*sei d'accordo?*"

"*Sì, d'accordo*, but if those giants get close, let me take the one with the glowing staff." She held up Gungnir, her confidence strong. She'd had years of experience fighting. Indeed, only a short while before, she'd battled Old Nick and his forces at the Battle of Caesarea!

"Tag the *vampyrs* in the forehead when possible," he added, giving a nod of agreement, "and the werewolves right in the heart. The corpses and skeletons are scary looking, but they don't move as fast as Hela would—"

"Oh, no, no, no!" Fenris moaned. His repeated negations (coming as they were from so strong a man) were almost as frightening as the approaching army of the dead. He fell hard against the back of the cart, his body sweating. "This can't be!"

"Now would be a good time to change into a wolf and help us, not her, Fenris," Aurelius urged, fearing what was happening. "Remember who you are!"

"Get ... away ... from ... me," Fenris roared.

The ferocity and self-hatred in his voice startled both the Hospitaller and Norn, and they stepped back. He raised a warding hand to Aurelius, who maintained his protective stance next to Clarinda.

"I know Andvari said to go right, but the brothers have held that entrance on the left—there's less of the enemy if we go that way. Let's try to join the brothers," the knight said in a low voice, "to the left of where Andvari's made that wall of fire."

Fenris stepped forward, then spun and grabbed Aurelius by both shoulders. The action was so quick that Aurelius found himself pinned by the man's great strength, unable to lift his sword.

"Aurelius, we are betrayed! That is not the way to Glittertind's *runeporte* at the end of the tunnel! The road has been changed!"

"Impossible," Andvari shouted, glaring at Fenris as he continued to mutter incantations.

"What? How can that be?" Aurelius felt the panic surging through the man's frame. "You can't know what the road is like—we haven't even gotten through the Crystal Caves." He didn't struggle, but said evenly, "Fenris, *bitte erlöse mich*."

Halfdan grabbed the large man's arm. "*Ja, alter Freund, können Sie steuern diese*. You can control it. Now, *Lassen Sie ihn*—please, release him."

Fenris dropped his arms in consternation and let the knight go, then glanced in the direction of the glowing corner before turning to both Hospitaller and brigadier.

"I thought I could control it, Halfdan, but she's gotten stronger. Something's coming from behind us, and ahead ..."

"What?"

The giant with the radiant-red quarterstaff swept Andvari aside. The impact sent the arch-mage crashing into the back of one of the burning carts. He somehow retained enough sense to keep rolling so that when he fell off the vehicle his clothes were only smoldering. Blood ran from a gash in his forehead.

"*Alte Wölf, waren Sie korrekt,*" he gasped. "Those aren't the *Kristallhöllen* ahead. This is a trap!"

"I knew it," Fenris growled, the skin on his face starting to twitch and shift.

"When we were in the long tunnel—something warped it," the wizard said, breathing heavily. He drew his axe. "I can't leave Traeg alone long. If all is lost, Codex Wielder, dive into the right-hand river—it leads directly to Franang Falls. Hold your breath, because it's an underground chute for almost a minute, with no air and just the rapids."

Then the dwarf ran to join his wife back at the boulders and flaming wall.

"No, Aurelius, Clarinda—you mustn't stray," Fenris growled through clenched teeth, clearly in agony but desperate to finish his thought. "Stay ... and fight here!" He staggered from them, his body jerked in paroxysms of pain. "Halfdan, tell them!"

"Like a puppet—Hela's taking control," the brigadier shouted as he leapt to help one of his dwarves defend against a *ghast* that had burst through one of the cavern walls to try an attack from behind.

"No, he knows that ..." Fenris groaned, frustration vying with pain in his voice as he swung on Aurelius.

"I'm not talking about me; it's you and Clarinda. Even ... even ... if you survived the Falls, I don't think you'll end up in Alfheim. I know Hela. If she's reoriented a *runeporte*, you can be sure that you'll be at Franang Falls as they appear in Svartalfheim, the Land of the Dark Elves. You can't go to Svartalfheim by yourself—those forests are as bad in their way as ... as ... Niflheim. It's where the Codices were created, the first place the Book of Tears will try to take you, to rid itself of you—"

The winds Clarinda noticed earlier became a tempest.

"That's why I know that reek," Fenris's head wrenched toward the tunnel they'd entered. "Run from me ... now, while you can. I feel her taking control ... and ... she wants you, Aurelius." He doubled over. "Ah, she's here, Hela's here!"

Fenris began to transform into his wolf form, hair sprouting from every pore on his skin. He loped in the direction of the rear tunnel, swaying and twitching as he fought to maintain control. "This way, my friends ... move! There might still be time to escape. She tricked even Andvari. Those aren't the true *Kristallhöllen* ahead. She's done something to the rune-gates. I'm not sure how, but the—"

"You've always misperceived my realm, Fenris, that's how."

Fenris jerked to a stop as if he'd run into a wall. Hela, clad in funereal black, emerged from the long stone corridor behind the party.

"Unbelievable," Hela said, taking in the group. "You're all here, just as they promised."

She waved a hand at Fenris and he rose slightly into the air, hovering in twitching resistance while she turned her attention to Aurelius and Clarinda.

Behind them, the rock giants were killing some of Fenris's wolf pack and the numbers of the shambling undead were starting to overwhelm the patrol dwarves at the cavern entrance opposite the four brothers. Four wolves were hurled overhead; they slammed into the ceiling high above and dropped lifelessly to the ground. Clarinda watched as one dwarf failed to stop a relentless cadaver from punching a hole through the center of his armor. The sounds of magical blasts from Andvari and Traeg continued, but none of the *Wilde Jagd* had entered the area yet where the Hospitaller and Norn stood.

"I'm confined neither to a tower, nor even to Niflheim," Hela continued. "Where pale shades roam from mortal graves, so, too, can I."

"You've violated an ancient covenant—" Andvari began, but the Dark Queen waved a dismissive hand.

"Blame your own kind for breaking covenants, Dwarf! Dietrich broke the covenants between earth and water when he and the druids tried to raise the Sarsen Stones, and I've a more recent permission for my presence here. One that supersedes all other agreements in how much it's favored by the Fates."

"What?" Traeg exclaimed. "The Norns wouldn't allow you to come here and switch a *runeporte!*"

"Perhaps, perhaps not," Hela turned from the arch-mages to the Hospitaller. "Death has come for you Servius Aurelius Santini. But, as I told you earlier, you need not die now. Return to my halls so that we might finish our conversation. My father has waited too long for it, but I think I'd have the Codex Lacrimae for my own."

Fenris remained immobile, suspended some feet above the ground, his face contorted in struggle against his invisible bonds. Hela walked past him and touched him lightly on the shoulder.

"Change, Brother—you're revolting as a man, but somewhat tolerable as a hound."

"Au … re … li … us—run!" Fenris howled, then any semblance of the man was lost to the wolf.

The knight needed no prompting; he'd watched in sick fascination as hair covered the exposed areas of Fenris's body. He grabbed Clarinda's arm to pull her away, and they both stumbled toward the battle and the backs of the dwarves who were fighting furiously to maintain their line against the swarming horde.

The skin on Fenris's face, forearms, and hands bulged, stretching from some internal pressure that was transforming him into his other, lupine self against his will. His warning had barely emerged when a series of growls erupted from lengthening fangs and a slavering maw. Still suspended in the air by Hela's magic, the wolf burst from his tunic and breeches as Aurelius and Clarinda backed toward one of the fast-flowing water channels.

They were trapped, pinned between the Wild Hunt, Hela, and the rushing water that led into a series of perilous underground chutes.

CHAPTER 3

The Battle of the Underjordisk Elv: Clarinda

"**N**ot that river, you fools!" Andvari shouted, noticing their predicament and thinking that they were heading toward the left watercourse.

The arch-mage hewed his way through the ranks of dead men between them, his large battle-axe glowing with orange fire. "I told you—get to the other waterway if you can, the *Underjordisk Elv*. After a minute of panicked swimming, it leads to Franang Falls, but you'll have to take a deep breath."

Skade ran past the burning carts and dead oxen, and hurled herself directly at Hela with a scream of rage. The force of her tackle drove the Queen of the Dead against a stalagmite.

"Leave him alone," the Huntress shouted, trying to stop her sister-in-law from completing the transformation of her husband.

Skade delivered a powerful backhanded slap at Hela, and then the two women were lost to Clarinda's sight as a rock giant swiped at her. The creature had moved so quickly that she'd scarcely realized she was its target, let alone devised any kind of defense.

Aurelius swung his sword at the descending hand, but the blade merely clanged against the creature's left forearm brace. The giant's hand brushed Clarinda's side and hurled her to the ground.

Though failing to completely defend her, Santini had diverted the giant's attention. It grasped Aurelius by both legs in one gigantic hand, and snatched him from Clarinda's side and lifted him into the air. The knight's sword dropped and clattered against a wall.

"Servius, hold on," she shouted.

"Not ... going ... anywhere, Clare!" he retorted, straining against the beast. He slashed at an exposed section of leathern flesh with his knife, and then fumbled for something at his waist.

"Bene, *tu Cacasenno*," she grunted as instinct and rage overtook fear. *Buon Dio.* Adrenalin surged. *Even while possibly dying he's so ... così ... così ... infuriare!*

"Prendi questo, *tu Faccia di merda*," she screamed at the rock giant, stabbing at its knee with her quarterstaff, driving it in with all her might.

A sapphire-colored explosion erupted at the touch of the

stave's iron-shod heel. It shattered the rock armor and pierced the exposed knee beneath. The monster's joint buckled and he roared in agony, his free hand pushing Clarinda into the cart behind her while he tried to assess the damaged leg. She fell against the side of the vehicle, the impact knocking the breath from her, and vainly tried to inhale as the rock giant came at her, slowed only a little by his lame leg.

"Don't-touch-her," Aurelius yelled, heaving against the giant's hand.

The giant's enormous fingers were still wrapped around his thighs, but somehow Santini freed the little hatchet from its waist holster. He brought the small hand-axe down hard onto the creature's wrist.

Clarinda watched, amazed, as the giant stopped mid-stride and bellowed in anguish, staring at its half-severed wrist. The Venetian girl tried to make sense of what had just happened. The weapon Aurelius had used was, indeed, only a small woodsman's hatchet.

The Hospitaller dropped to the ground, somersaulted, and sprang to his feet. He afforded her a glance as he sprinted toward the wounded titan. *Stai bene?* he asked her.

"*Mi?*" she replied, incredulous. "*Sto bene!* I'm fine!"

"You curse like a sailor," he said.

"*E ... e ...*" she gasped, unable to catch her breath, "I thought you were faster."

He frowned, and slowed a bit, taken aback. "Faster?"

"Well, he did catch you. *E*, why didn't you free yourself earlier, if you had that kind of wea—"

"Faster? Huh," he muttered, then leapt onto the rock giant's bloody forearm, passing from earshot. He scaled its bicep in two steps, hurled himself into the air, and brought the hatchet down with two hands in a smiting blow on the titan's skull.

The rock giant crashed lifelessly to the ground, carrying Aurelius with him, but the Hospitaller tumbled again, and came to his feet close to Clarinda.

"Was that fast enough?" he grinned.

"*Sei un furbetto e un fanfarone!*" she groaned, knowing that he wasn't really a smart-aleck nor a braggart, but strangely enjoying being near him even in a descending nightmare.

It was good to be alive after that fight, and she was beginning to think that they might even survive this attack.

"Clarinda, look out!" Aurelius shoved her aside.

Skade flew through the air where the Venetian girl had stood, catapulted into a cart bed by Hela's magic. Then the Queen of the Dead ordered Fenris to attack and the wolf charged them at full speed.

The Huntress regained her feet, leapt from the cart before Aurelius could raise his hatchet, and tackled her husband. Their combined momentum bore them careening into a group of skeletons making their way to Hela's side.

The last remaining rock giant waylaid Andvari and Traeg with a blast from his quarterstaff. They fell backward, the explosion detonating the boulders where they'd tried to muster a defense.

Geri and Freki leapt onto the giant simultaneously, but his armor proved enough of a defense against the two wolves that he had time to hurl them aside. Unencumbered, he advanced quickly toward the Norn and Hospitaller.

Before Clarinda could say anything to Aurelius, he'd retrieved his sword in his left hand and was running at the rock giant.

The dwarvish cook, Delling, had seen his master and mistress fall, and stood alone against the titan with only an axe in hand. The giant lifted his arm ready to swing the point of its red, skull-decorated stave at Delling when Aurelius hurled the hatchet as hard as he could at the monster's face. The tool smashed into the giant's forehead with a tremendous crack, and the creature staggered backwards a few steps.

Then, having struck, the hatchet flew back into Santini's hand! The knight stared at it, wondering briefly if the hatchet had also gotten bigger in the short time he'd owned it, but then a werewolf from the Wilde Jagd leapt on him and he had to defend himself.

The giant took advantage of the attack and rushed at Aurelius, but the hatchet dispatched the werewolf with a backhanded strike, and the Hospitaller turned to his gargantuan foe.

"*Sie sind nicht, was du warst, Taliesin, aber ich kenne dich,*" the giant roared, and swung his quarterstaff at the Hospitaller. Fell, reddish energies trailed behind the weapon with a supernatural might that made Clarinda sick to look at it.

"*Wir werden endlich gerächt werden!*" the giant screamed.

"What?" Clarinda shouted, disbelieving. Did the rock giant just call Aurelius 'Taliesin,' and that while he wasn't what he used to be, the rock giant still recognized him and would be 'avenged?'

Aurelius ducked the swinging stave, and then brought his hatchet upward to parry the return swipe. The hatchet stopped the blow with enough force to send a shudder through the

Hospitaller's arm. A yellowish flame erupted from the hatchet, its color similar to the runes glowing along Clarinda's weapon. Aurelius held fast, pushing forward and swinging his weapon in a sideways arc. This time, though, the giant blocked the strike.

Clarinda squinted through the flashing flames of power, tracking both combatants as they moved swiftly across the body-strewn cavern floor. Had she imagined ... no! There, and there! Hatchet and stave collided again, confirming her guess: whenever the monster's red-glowing quarterstaff collided with the hatchet, the crimson runes on its surface dimmed to a pale red.

"Servius, keep at it," she shouted. "The hatchet's affecting his staff!"

A group of skeletons ran between her and the knight, and while she defended herself against their jabbing spears, she lost track of Santini. But from the flashes of red and yellow light that marked their battle, she knew that he held his own against the titan.

Clarinda made short work of the skeletons—they seemed to explode whenever her staff hit them—but the winds continued to build, and two more skeletons tried to surprise her by ducking around one of the carts. She blasted them apart with her staff. She still couldn't see Aurelius, but noticed that the four dwarf brothers had stopped fighting and were holding hands in a circle in front of their entry portal to the cavern.

The brothers began to float and spin, increasing speed with every rotation. The air gusted through the cave and reached a high-pitched wail.

"Andvari, you cannot bring the Four Winds into Hel!" the Queen of the Dead screamed. "You will unmake the ancient covenants for the Ginnungagap!"

"You brought them when you changed the tunnels, Hel-Witch!" Andvari shouted, standing defiantly near the brothers, his back to Traeg who continued to battle any foe that came too close.

"This cavern wasn't Hel until you entered!" Traeg added.

"Hela, you're the only one threatened if Ginnungagap collapses!" Andvari continued, shaking his head in disgust. "Did you think that I'd travel with a Norn and a Codex Wielder and not bring the means to defend them? Fool's Daughter! My friends are the points of Creation!"

His voice was so hoarse with rage and so hotly did orange-flaming energies course around his frame that Clarinda almost didn't recognize the arch-mage.

"I am the Guardian of Nidaveller—how dare you transform any of my tunnels into a *runeporte!*" He looked to the four brothers, who were spinning so quickly now that their brightly colored tunics made for a rainbow-like, multihued blur. "*Nordri, Austri, Sudri og Vestri,*" he cried, "*blåse dem tilbake til Hel!*"

Comprehension dawned on Clarinda. "Nordri, Austri, Sudri and Vestri, blow them all back to Hel." The dwarves were literally their namesakes: North, East, South, and West ... the Four Winds!

Clarinda watched, awestruck, as the ceiling and parts of the stone road begin to crack. Even the bedrock of the mountains couldn't withstand the force of the tempest created by the four dwarves. Stalactites dropped everywhere, crashing into the cavern floor and posing as much a threat to allies as they did to the enemies. Fissures appeared above the cave entrance that the four brothers defended (and through which more members of the *Wilde Jagd* tried to stream).

Then the portal completely collapsed, ruptured by the hurricane forces in the caves. The shambling undead who were too slow-moving in that tunnel fell, permanently entombed under tons of granite.

The dwarves drew upon the two rivers to create cyclones devastating in the confined space. Water whipped through the air, lashing the entire cavern. The winds flung those of the Wild Hunt who still remained in the disintegrating gallery into the upper heights where dying bats' screeches echoed through the caverns.

A giant rushed past Santini's guard, slammed him across the chest with the stave, and tossed the knight like a child's doll through the air. A fist closed around Clarinda's heart at the sight of the nightmarish scene. Unbelievably, though, Aurelius managed to roll, turning what should have been a bone-breaking collision into new momentum, but when he scrambled to his feet a confused pain transformed his features.

Jeg er Codex Lacrimae, Servius Aurelius Santini, hva er din vilje?

Clarinda recoiled at the female voice. It resounded loudly in her mind, imposing its presence in a way that felt like a violation. Who was it? She snapped her head in Hela's direction, but the woman was preoccupied by Skade's battle with Fenris. The Venetian girl swung back to Aurelius. Perhaps she'd imagined the voice? Or, could there be a seductive siren among the *Wilde Jagd*, trying to distract the combatants?

They were trapped, pinned between the Wild Hunt, Hela,
and the rushing water that led into a series of perilous underground chutes.

No. It had reminded her too much of the thought-speech of the Norns and Mimir.

"Pellion?" Aurelius lowered his hatchet and shouted into the tempest, peering into the storm as if expecting to see the squire from the Krak des Chevaliers appear in one of the yet uncollapsed entrances.

We warned you, Clarinda! He's too dangerous! This time, Urd's voice echoed in her mind, full of dismay and resolve.

A dread rose in Clarinda, its source the same profound realization: something more horrific than Hela and her monsters was awakening here in the roots of the mountains. The Norn stared at Aurelius—were his forearm braces glowing with an aquamarine light?

This is the moment, Urd shouted, *the Codex Lacrimae returns!*

More stalactites fell around Clarinda as the Four Winds started to hurl cadavers and werewolves against the sedimentary rock walls and into the rivers.

Lightning flashed in the cavern. A peal of thunder boomed through the walls.

"Pellion!" Santini screamed, and electrical discharges cascaded everywhere, scoring into stone and disintegrating warriors.

Urd departed, but the other woman's voice sounded in her head, alluring and potent. *Il sono il Lacrimae Codex, Servius Aurelius Santini, qual è la tua volontà?* Any remaining words were lost as a mighty tremor vibrated through the underground, causing cracks and fissures to appear in the stone roads.

A terrifying thought occurred to Clarinda: was he somehow causing both the storm and earthquake? She had no time to think further. She needed to move; she couldn't solve the mystery if she didn't survive this hell-storm.

Energies coruscated and rippled along the limestone formations, charging the air with the stench of ionization and burnt flesh. The giant swung again at the Hospitaller. A flash of lightning seemed to consume Santini, but the giant jolted as if he'd just grabbed a live electric eel. The creature staggered backward in pained surprise, and Aurelius jumped onto its chest. Gravity and momentum carried both figures onto the road.

"Pellion can't be dead!" Aurelius screamed. He brought the hatchet through the titan's skull. With a clang and spark of yellow fire the weapon crunched into the roadway. The lifeless fingers of the giant released the stave, and the Hospitaller grabbed at it and arose with the staff in hand.

The Venetian girl stepped forward to get close, then halted. The woman's voice, no, the Codex Lacrimae's thought-speak, was repeating itself, rising in volume and becoming: *Ich bin der Codex Lacrimae, Servius Aurelius Santini, was Dein Wille ist?*

"Get out of my head!" Servius found Hela and ran toward her.

Clarinda looked coldly with a Norn's eyes at the Hospitaller. The Codex Lacrimae had returned fully to the Nine Worlds. That realization enraged the Urd-Side of Clarinda Trevisan.

The winds still tore through the caves, but unless the brothers wanted to destroy themselves and their allies, they'd reached the limit of damage they could inflict on the *Wilde Jagd*. Hela's warriors seemed to realize this, and more dead men and cadavers shambled into the cave where she'd entered and through the entrance that Andvari and Traeg still defended.

Clarinda grappled with the rage she felt toward Santini—

No! Urd's voice returned, extreme in its urgency. Clarinda was shocked, wondering how the Norn made herself heard past Grimnir's magic, then realized that Urd was alone in the thought-speech. She couldn't sense Verdandi and Skuld.

Know this now, Clarinda, in this moment of the Codex Lacrimae's return, what you're feeling isn't anger at him, it's a vestigial memory of the mistake I made with Taliesin over half a millennium ago. I'm sorry, Clare. What I learned from that experience, what I'll pass to you before I die, will set you and Grimnir against Mimir, Skuld, and Verdandi. We didn't realize until it was too late what Surtur and Loki meant to do with the Codices, and even though I've discussed the matter at the Well, my sisters and Mimir still disagree with me. After all these centuries, they'll not admit that they, that we, were wrong. I did great wrong to Taliesin, Merlin, and Dietrich back then, Clarinda, before the Fields of Burning Night, and it was only when Mogthrasir revealed himself that I realized how much I'd erred.

Oh, Sister! I will fall to Morpeth, but I fear that you'll be the one who makes the blood-payment for my mistake.

Stunned, but still in the midst of battle, Clarinda tried to absorb what the Norn was telling her, even while following Santini's line of sight as he ran toward Hela.

In the queen's features Clarinda saw the truth of the anger she'd expressed to Andvari about the presence of the Four Winds. The woman was smiling.

"Servius, don't do it!" Clarinda yelled at the knight. "She's baiting you!"

The Venetian girl sprinted forward, and driven by sheer willpower and the ferocity of battle, dodged lightning bolts that spiked from the ceiling and batted aside the countless undead enemies who came between her and Santini. Thankfully, the melding of Grimnir's Spear with her quarterstaff seemed to have the same kind of terrible effect on the enemies as Santini's hatchet. But whereas Clarinda pushed the enemies aside to reach Santini on his way to Hela, the knight viciously made sure that not one moved after an encounter with him. The young Norn, never having witnessed him fight before, almost couldn't believe what she was seeing.

The youth seemed to almost anticipate moves against him, and he wasted no motion or effort in responding. He used the rock giant's rune-carved stave as if born to it, impaling *vampyrs* here, or slicing cadavers there with concussive, supernatural force, and all the while the hatchet in his right hand beat back foes with devastating blows.

Flushed and out of breath, Clarinda slowed as she drew near him, warily realizing that she probably shouldn't be in anywhere near him when he fought like this, lest she be mistaken for one of the enemy and cloven in two.

Santini steadily closed on Hela, his face a mask of terror. Clarinda had the sobering thought that he looked less like the young knight she was falling in love with, and more akin to one of Hela's own servants, returning to his mistress for more commands.

"Clarinda—there's peril here!" Andvari's voice cut into her thoughts. "The Codex awakens. It will remember the Fields of Burning Night and seek vengeance before trying to restore the other artifacts. Get him out of here, now! The only hope is the river!"

The Norn kept her focus on Aurelius and tried to control the urgency in her voice as she slashed away the last skeleton between them. "Servius, listen to me," she yelled. "If you try to kill her, she'll close on you!" In spite of her fears, Clarinda moved within his attack radius. She needed his attention, and just hoped that his swings wouldn't catch her off guard. "She's Death itself. Death! You can't kill her, but you can deny her what she wants!"

The knight turned away, swiped at a cadaver, and drew closer to Hela. The stave burned bright red in his hand.

"Servius! *Mio cuore, ascolta me! Prega di*, listen to me!" she repeated, moving even closer. The situation was dire, but she needed to remain calm and imitate the serenity of the Norns even in the hellscape of the cavern. Santini's enraged silence seemed worse than anything in the battle thus far.

"I had a chance at Satan and I didn't take it!" she continued, having to raise her voice even louder to keep his attention as he kept blasting through the horde. "Servius, Old Nick and Kenezki killed my father, and I still didn't take my shot at him when we were in Hela's tower! We can't win here, Servius. We've got to get away. Keep the hatchet, but lose the quarterstaff—it's completely evil. We're getting out of here."

"No—she dies!" The anger in his primal shout cut the air with irrepressible violence, and he reversed the heel of the blazing crimson staff into the throat of a *Halbe*-troll behind him. "I'm not a pawn! They've killed Pellion, Clarinda. I felt it. Morpeth—that archer back at the Krak—he's killing everybody, and he just killed Pellion! I've got to ... what?"

The knight stopped talking and didn't move.

Clarinda stared at him. Was he talking to someone? To the Codex? Why couldn't she hear its words anymore?

"Servius? We're leaving," she said calmly, backing toward the river. She remembered the dead birds at Andvari's house. Something was going very wrong inside the young knight's mind. She could almost feel things breaking loose, and she meant to stop it.

The rapids of the black river roared behind her, its waters unabated in the same course they'd run for millennia, rushing forth from the deep parts of the world.

Clarinda suddenly knew what she had to don and fear momentarily immobilized her.

How could she possibly survive the cold waterways under the mountain? Did she even want to survive without him? No—he'd have to make a choice, succumb to the power of the awakening Codex, or rescue her.

She tried to remember what Andvari had said about holding her breath; was it a full minute through a subterranean water-chute, and then maybe surviving Franang Falls? She reversed another step to the water's edge and inhaled more deeply.

O, ti capitano di mare idiota, l'acqua è il tuo amico!

Hoping that water still, indeed, remained her friend—and that she could swim in underground channels as well as in her beloved sea—Clarinda took a last gulp of air, clasped the quarterstaff, and fell backwards into the river.

She heard Aurelius shout something at her, but the words were lost in the frigid torrent and pain. Clarinda's last sight was of the young knight's anguished face. *Oh, God, am I in love with him?* Then she knew only a claustrophobic, panicked oblivion as the icy current of the *Underjordisk Elv* swept her from the battle and into the airless crawl-ways beneath the mountains.

CHAPTER 4

The Battle of the Underjordisk Elv: Aurelius

A few minutes before Clarinda dropped into the rushing waters, Aurelius watched in disbelief as the hatchet sped back to him—the thought occurred to dodge it, but then the weapon flew snugly into his hand. He glanced at it.

Had the hatchet grown after hitting the giant's head?

The flat blade certainly seemed to be broader and thicker, though its edge was just as sharp as it had ever been; but the claw opposite it seemed to have flattened somewhat and become denser, taking the aspect of a mattock. He adjusted his grip on the handle; that, too, had gotten heftier.

A werewolf leapt in front of him, no more time to dwell on the change. He swung the hatchet hard into the creature's face. It fell, and Aurelius rushed past him to confront the still-approaching rock giant.

"You're not what you were, Taliesin, but I know you," the giant roared, swinging his quarterstaff at Aurelius. "We'll finally have our revenge!"

The Hospitaller ducked smoothly under the stave, aware of crimson energies trailing its arc. Anticipating a quick reverse thrust from his opponent, he vertically checked the giant's wooden bar with the hatchet. Yellow light crackled along the weapons when they collided with a shudder. They battled, weaving back and forth, the giant's quarterstaff against Aurelius's sword and woodsman's tool.

Andvari and Traeg blasted the undead *Wilde Jagd* with orange pulses of sorcery, while the four dwarvish brothers tirelessly defended the left cave entrance. Oxen and wolves screamed while dying in flames from the Death Archers' arrows.

Clarinda shouted something to Aurelius about using the hatchet, but he already knew that it had some unique, helpful properties. He noted that some skeletons were nearing her position—he needed to slay this giant and get back to her side.

Mindful of the giant's stance and shifting weight, the Hospitaller closed on his opponent, feeling strangely as if he were in the midst of a sparring session years ago with Devrone di Magglia. However, unlike those past times when he practiced with a staff in an inland meadow on Italy's Amalfi coast, now he fought with hatchet and sword in a subterranean battleground.

"If you can, Servius, always turn disadvantages into advantages," Devrone had repeatedly told him as they sparred, bringing all his expertise as a former Crusader to the benefit of his ward.

The clacking of their oaken staffs broke the quiet of the olive grove near the monastery.

"If your opponent feints and you've already committed to a thrust or strike," Devrone continued day, "don't try to fly backward, nor give an awkward parry. Some instructors would have you slip your guard hand and try to reverse the hit, but I say use your forearm guard as a shield and take the blow, then keep moving forward. If you can keep your balance, it's usually the last thing that anyone expects and can open up entire new dynamics for combat."

Nearby, two other boys, Nicolo (a Venetian) and Alexios (a Greek) trained with quarterstaffs with Brother Tomas. They shared Aurelius's summer visits to Santa Maria di Corrazo, but he'd never learned if their presence was for his own development or theirs.

When they'd finished sparring and the others had returned to the monastery with Brother Tomas, Aurelius had asked Devrone, "Why am I training with Alexios and Nicolo?"

"You know the answer. They're peers of similar ability, and you need competition to develop. Tomas and I are grown men, but in a few years all of you will be stronger than us. Training to each other's strengths and weaknesses now will make you stronger later."

"That's just it, Master—they're not my peers. One's the son of an emperor, and the other's the son of the doge of Venice."

"You beat them daily," Devrone said, "and I believe that you might have a chance at beating me in a couple years, even though you'll only be fourteen."

"But, Master, how does it happen that the three of us are here while all the others are at the monastery every summer?"

"Ask your parents," the sword fighter replied.

"I've asked so many times, I can't bring it up anymore."

Devrone stared at him, then, in that kind of long and measuring assessment that Aurelius long ago had grown used to. At such times, many elements seemed at play in Devrone's eyes, pride in Aurelius's development, mixed with the ever-present anger, and a visible effort to restrain himself from discussing a matter that he'd apparently promised not to disclose.

"When you turn thirteen, your parents will have to tell you everything, so this might simply be a matter of waiting one more year."

Aurelius snorted in disgust. "*Molte cose* ... many, many things, can happen in a year! Alexios thinks there's a good chance he'll be dead at the hands of conspirators in the Byzantine court, and Nicolo never knows who's lurking along the Doge's canals in Venice. You always tell us to prepare for the unexpected, but there's something very wrong here. I can't prepare for it if I don't know what it is. Did Padre pay you and Tomas to train me with royalty?"

"No!" Heat had radiated palpably in Devrone's voice. "Is that what you think? Did Matteo say that to you?"

"Padre said nothing," Aurelius pressed, knowing that his guess had stabbed truly. "But, was that it?"

"Your parents don't get to make any deals ... what they'd planned was an abomination, and it won't ..." He'd stopped himself and breathed deeply. When he next spoke, his tone held the control he used when training. "Let me think on this, Servius. I'll say only this—be wary even of family members in this upcoming year. If any ... offer, any promise, comes to you to go to the Holy Land, don't take it."

"The Holy Land?" Aurelius had asked. "I thought you were going to say Genoa or Venice—Padre's been traveling often to those cities these past two years. I've got a feeling that he's involved in something bad, but I don't know what."

"No, they'll want to keep you far away from Venice," Devrone mused. "But, enough. Let me think. We still have a month before you have to return to Sicily—there's time, yet."

More of Andvari's magic bolts shot overhead. Aurelius scrambled to his feet. The chaos of the battle and pain in his left shoulder where he'd fallen returned him to the present. The rock giant rushed him again, but he took a second to glance Clarinda's way.

The skeletons were gone, and Hela stood beyond Clarinda near the tunnel where the company had entered the cavern. The pale queen's appearance reminded him of their last conversation in Hel, when she and Old Nick had revealed things about his childhood that set his world on fire.

Devrone di Magglia had been wrong: there hadn't been a month more of time at the monastery. There hadn't even been a full day. When Aurelius and Devrone returned to Santa Maria di Corrazo shortly after the monastic hour of Compline, they'd discovered the boy's older brother, Roberto, waiting to take him back to Palermo. He brought word that their father had just returned from the northern lands with a 'long-lost uncle' who wanted to meet the entire family.

He recalled Old Nick's words in Hel.

Oh, put that sword down, Santini—you're not going to hurt your Old Uncle Servius, are you? Are you that foolish? You live twelve years in the world, and one autumn you return from your little summer trips to find a long-lost uncle waiting for you. Six months of getting to know the family, and then it was off to the Holy Land for you with him? Come on, Servius. Didn't you think Paolo's conversion was a bit sudden and strange?

Had he been played a fool by his own family?

Doubt made his anger that much more potent and, combined with the fury he felt in the midst of this battle, it was an effort to think clearly. He heard Clarinda shouting something again, but he needed to focus completely on dispatching the rock giant. He sheathed his sword because only the hatchet seemed effective against the quarterstaff that blazed crimson fire.

Then Pellion fell to Morpeth's fiery blade.

A vision of Pellion and Marcus battling back at the Krak flashed before Aurelius's eyes. His stomach opened and he a coldness descended into him. "Pellion?"

Jeg er Codex Lacrimae, Servius Aurelius Santini, hva er din vilje?

A woman's voice shouted Norwegian words in his mind, and the world around Aurelius exploded into yellow fire. Confused, thinking perhaps the words were spoken by Hela or Clarinda, he ducked below another swing from the giant, but the southern kitchen area of the Krak des Chevaliers remained superimposed on his vision.

Pellion crashed to the cobblestones in front of the knight who'd slain him—his body there, yet not there—and smoke issued from his side. Marcus sprang into view, scooped up Pellion's sword, and attacked the other knight. Aurelius recognized the enemy as the Hospitaller traitor he'd been fighting before traveling to the Nine Worlds.

"Pellion!" Fierce wind blew in the cavern and he shouted his friend's name to be heard against the maelstrom.

The female's voice replied to his surprised cry, this time speaking in Italian. *Io sono il Lacrimae Codex, Servius Aurelius Santini, qual è la tua volontà?*

The overlaid image of the Krak dissipated in a flash of bolt-lightning that erupted from his hatchet when the giant struck it with the stave. Furious that he'd lost sight of events back home, Aurelius swung the hatchet high and leapt onto his opponent's chest, shouting, "Pellion can't be dead!"

He smashed the hatchet, glowing with aureate, blazing energies, into the center of the titan's face, cleaving it apart. A massive spike of electricity discharged throughout the giant's form. Aurelius emerged unharmed from the aquamarine radiance and rose from the corpse with hatchet ablaze in his hand.

Ich bin der Codex Lacrimae, Servius Aurelius Santini, was Dein Wille ist?

"Get out of my head," he screamed in fury—did he have to hear the same, repeated declaration in every language on the planet?

The foundations of the earth trembled and stalactites fell. Aurelius retrieved the giant's quarterstaff, whose carven runes glowed a maleficent crimson across the skulls embedded in its shaft. He spun to find Hela. She still stood near the entrance with a beckoning smile.

"Servius, no!" Clarinda shouted as he ran, but he ignored her. His staff and mattock did their work and shattered through the press of bodies in a furious burst of magical energies. He'd almost reached Hela's position when calm words sounded in his mind.

I am the Codex Lacrimae, Servius Aurelius Santini, what is your will?

Was he losing his mind? He snarled and impaled a *vampyr* with one of the stave's spiked ends, then slammed the blunt side of the hatchet into a skeleton, disintegrating it.

"Clarinda—there's peril here!" Andvari shouted from the front of the cavern. "The Codex awakens! It will remember the Fields of Burning Night and seek vengeance. Get him out of here, now—the only hope is the river!"

Oh, ja, I remember you, Arch-Mage Andvari. Playing the hero now that Dietrich is gone, are you? We'll see about that. Muspelheim doesn't have enough firepits for the punishments I'll inflict on you, this new incarnation of Urd, and all the rest!

A line of cadavers shambling in front of Hela was all that remained between Aurelius and his goal. He thrust at one with the stave, and it backed away warily.

"Servius, listen, please ..." Clarinda said, her words competing with those of the Codex. Then both females' words faded in the fervor of battle.

He glanced at the stave and realized that it, too, was affecting him, making him want to slay everything in sight! No. He wouldn't discard the strange weapon until he'd buried it deeply into Hela.

"... can't win here, Servius," Clarinda had been saying something, but he found it difficult to focus on her. "We've got to get away. Keep the hatchet, but lose the quarterstaff—it's completely evil. We need to get out of here!"

"No—she dies!" he yelled, wishing that both the Venetian girl and whispering woman in his head would fall silent.

The knight you saw striking down Pellion isn't a Hospitaller. His name's Morpeth—he's a Huntsman of Muspelheim.

He sensed rather than saw a threat, and flipped the staff into the throat of a *Halbe*-troll attacking from behind.

"I'm not a pawn!" he shouted. Clarinda couldn't see what was happening back at his home. "They've killed Pellion, Clarinda! I felt it. Morpeth—that archer back at the Krak—he's killing everybody, and he just killed Pellion! I've got to ..."

Pellion doesn't have to stay dead, Son of Jotunheim.

"What?" Aurelius frowned. What did that title mean? Why couldn't he stop the Codex from speaking to him?

"Servius, we're leaving," Clarinda said, but Aurelius tried to focus on the Dark Book's words.

I've been awakened and must obey you—Pellion doesn't have to stay dead.

Hela walked towards him, but Clarinda drew his attention. She'd stepped backward, precariously close to the roiling black waters of the river.

"Clarinda, *attento!* " The girl's peril made Aurelius forget everything except getting to her. He moved forward, but Hela closed in and her cadavers rushed to intercept his path.

The Venetian girl fell into the river with a splash, and the water swept her away. With her arms and legs wrapped around her quarterstaff, she disappeared into the hole at the base of the cavern wall where the rapids churned.

"No, not her, too!" Aurelius cried. He jabbed the quarterstaff into the animated corpses in a flare of red light, then dropped the giant's weapon and dove into the *Underjordisk Elv*.

Hela screamed in frustration.

The hatchet in his clenched fist burned bright yellow in the black current before winking out as the river hastened the Hospitaller into the mountain passages after the Norn.

CHAPTER 5

Rushing Water, Wintry Wood, and the Return of Cerys

The torrent of water buffeted him, and he barely remembered to submerge his head before the rapids bore him through the dark opening at the base of the wall and into the crawlways beyond. The tube descended abruptly, and he hoped that the rush of water would keep him moving through the tight channel.

While twisting to and fro in the surging and rolling current that threatened to bash him against the sides of the narrow space, Andvari's earlier warning came to mind.

If all is lost, Codex Wielder, dive into the right-hand river—it leads directly to Franang Falls. Hold your breath, because its an underground chute for almost a minute, with no air and just the rapids.

Within seconds, he could move his arms freely again, and he no longer felt the claustrophobia-inducing mountain walls above, below, and on his sides. There were still no pockets of air, though, and the hatchet's golden light revealed an underground limestone world whose multicolored stone curtains, gigantic mushrooms, and stalagmites mirrored the formations of the caverns he'd just escaped.

Straining to keep holding his breath in the roiling water, the knight held the small tool in front of him, hoping that it would collide with any obstruction before his head or body did. As he rode out the fast-moving current, he also prayed that Clarinda had kept her wits and acted similarly; and, if they both didn't drown, hopefully a deathly plunge over a cliff-side waterfall didn't await them at journey's end.

The swirling, corkscrewing current expelled Aurelius from the mountain in a spewing surge of whitewater. He sucked in a lungful of air, and splashed into the center of a boulder-lined pool, coughing and sputtering. He rolled in the shallows, and felt an instant of relief, catching one more breath, before his momentum carried him off the edge and down into a greater river.

He bobbed through turbulent foam and gasped loudly when he surfaced into air colder than the *Underjordisk Elv*. Steam issued from his mouth. *Gratis tibi, Domini,* he prayed, grateful to be alive.

Thank not your Lord, Hospitaller, the Codex Lacrimae replied. *He will not answer you.*

Aurelius shook his head, and while treading water and drifting with the current, looked around to see where he was. He saw with a shiver that the river was hastening toward a mist-covered lake a half league distant. A full moon shone in a cloudless sky, illuminating his surroundings, although much of the landscape remained in deep shadow. A snow-covered forest fringed the banks. Deepest winter blanketed this land, but it seemed to be a true winter and not the kind of twisted and frozen hellscape he'd experienced in Niflheim.

The knight swam to the shore closest to him. He slogged through the shallows and stumbled into the trees. The air felt somewhat warmer under the piney roof. He walked as fast as his stiffening legs could carry him, but glanced back at the falls, unable to repress a wild grin, elated that he'd forestalled another killing strike by Hela and her *Wilde Jagd.* His joy at living warmed him and momentarily surpassed the freezing cold pressing against him.

You are proud, Hospitaller, deservedly so. The Codex Lacrimae's voice was quieter than during the battle, but still clear in his mind. *You outfought all your enemies in that cave, better than Taliesin ever could in his prime.*

Aurelius shook his head, trying to dismiss the voice whose assessment he disagreed with. *Not pride, Codex. I'm simply glad to be alive. If I survived, Clarinda also could have done the same thing!*

He allowed for no other possibility. The girl was proving to be one of the hardiest people whom he'd ever met, and the idea crossed his mind that she would've been perfectly at home either training at the monastery with Devrone, or even with the apprentices at the Krak.

Well, except for the fact that she was a beautiful girl. Neither trainers nor knights would even let her on the compound ... Alexios and Nicolo would have, though, he mused. Aurelius didn't care. He'd seen Clarinda fight, and she'd impressed him, regardless of traditional expectations of her gender or her gorgeous eyes.

His smile turned into a frown of concern. Where was she? She'd obviously fallen into the Underjordisk Elv to make him follow her, and she'd been only seconds ahead. He was grateful for that, realizing that she had trusted in the growing bond between them to break the spell of the darkling, crimson-blazing stave.

The ploy had worked, although he was still surprised that she'd taken such a risk. The river passage through the mountains had been one of the most frightening experiences he'd ever had, and he could only imagine how she'd come through it.

Ignoring his shivers, he kept scanning the underbrush for any sign of her. He assumed that she'd have waited for him along this shore, but he saw only shadows and the dark trunks of trees under a starlit sky.

He kept moving forward, trying to shrug off the chill settling onto him. She couldn't have gotten far. Perhaps when he found Clarinda, they could somehow use her *Brisinga* necklace to return to the battle and help their new friends. He wished he could somehow move between places in a similar fashion to her. He wanted to make a difference here and not feel as if he were abandoning his friends.

You need not envy a Norn's trinkets, Aurelius, not when you have me. With a thought we can make a rune-gate between worlds. You've already done so three times.

"What?" he said aloud, the Codex's words startling him. "What do you mean three times?"

When you transported from the Krak to the glade in Alfheim, when you took the Nornish hag to pursue Abbadon to Hel, and when you attempted to return to Midgard.

"Those times were ..." he paused, wondering if he'd misunderstood his translation into Alfheim from the battle at the Krak, or when he and Clarinda had transported to Hela's Tower after retrieving Hav's leather envelope. In both cases, he'd thought other magical agencies were involved. He'd not thought of the possibility that he'd done the relocations himself.

"Wait," he said, stopping short. "What third time?"

At Andvari's cottage, when you were irritated with the Want-to-be-Norn. Your anger at Clarinda for reserving information about the Council at Mimir's Well was pure. It made you want to escape everyone, to return to the Krak des Chevaliers, and be with the people who meant the most to you.

"I was irritated with her ..." he said, then stopped. He had been furious.

You were enraged, boy. Like any good priest, you controlled the emotion almost as soon as you felt it, but I'm almost completely restored. Your anger was enough. I could use it to help you, and I did.

"That's not fair!" Aurelius protested. "You can't act upon a momentary lapse."

I am a Codex, Servius Aurelius Santini. My thoughts are yours, and yours are mine.

"I don't know why I got so angry," he admitted.

Between the squirrel's and Clarinda's words, you were feeling similarly to when as a child you used to walk into your parents' home and your older brothers would stop talking mid-sentence with your father. Hmmm. I need to pursue that memory at some point. There were quite a few times when you thought members of your family were keeping secrets from you, weren't there? Clarinda and Ratatosk merely revealed that even now secrets are being kept from you.

"You, you knew—know—all that?"

I am a Codex, Servius Aurelius Santini. My thoughts are yours, and yours are mine.

"But, I didn't go back home. I didn't get back to the Krak."

You could have returned. I opened a portal to the place where I know you took the most satisfaction at the Krak.

"The scriptorium?"

No, Lore Master. The scriptorium is where you worked and learned, as common a place in your mind as the yards where you train with the sword.

"That's not true," Aurelius said, relieved that the Codex seemed not to know his every thought. "The library and yards are my favorite places."

Did the Codex pause? He wondered, but then it spoke again.

I looked in your mind and opened a *runeporte* to the hospital, the place where you've helped almost a hundred people over the last couple years, and where you had many friends among the physicians.

"But, I stayed in Nidaveller. You didn't send me home. I mean, Clarinda calmed me down and I stayed."

I felt your eyes linger on her form, boy. It wasn't just her words that kept you there. I felt your desire for her, and how at the last you feared if you escaped, you might never see her again. This is no surprise. I've seen such passion and lust before, with another Codex Wielder and the current incarnation of Urd. Taliesin would have followed that wench into the Fires of Muspelheim for a chance at bedding her, and he almost did. I wonder; how priestly are you, boy?

A series of screams sounded in the distance, so high-pitched and sustained that Aurelius couldn't tell if the source were animal, human, or some other creature. The cry ended as abruptly as it began, leaving the youth with only the forest silence. He shivered again, this time not only from the cold. That howling was frightful.

I'll admit, the Norn is shapely, the Codex continued. *It seems to be a requirement for those witches. You could have taken advantage of her in the Fenrir-baude, no?*

Aurelius flushed, trying to keep the Dark Book from his mind. The Codex's voice stimulated a memory of Clarinda's body pressed close to him under the pelts as they slept next to each other after the escape from Niflheim.

You may have another chance. Find her and have your way with her.

"*Silenzio!*" he hissed, mortified that the Codex could read his mind. "It wasn't like that. We didn't do anything except sleep."

Yet, besides meeting her, that one night of sleep has done more than anything else to make you reexamine your intention to take the vows of ordination.

Hot tears of anger and shame rushed to the knight's eyes. *Ho detto, silenzio!* He repeated, and then aloud exclaimed: "You've no right to hear my thoughts!"

Oh, my boy — I am the Book of Tears. Why would I do anything else when it's so easy to make you weep?

"Please ... if someone's there ... if I heard you, and if you can hear me, please, please ... help me!" a female's strained voice asked, her volume barely more than a hoarse whisper, " Aurelius stepped a few more paces, then turned to the shadows of the trees to his left. That voice was female, but not the thought-speech of the Codex Lacrimae—someone was in trouble nearby.

A form peered at him from behind the base of a Norwegian spruce tree. No, not peering, straining. In the gloom, he discerned the forehead and eyes of a woman's face visible behind white-knuckled fingers that tried to maintain a grip on the bark.

Aurelius dashed forward, disbelieving that it had taken him so long to hear her and realize the extent of her peril. He stepped to the side of the tree, and saw why he'd only been able to see the woman's head and hands. The rest of her body was gone, enclosed in a flat disc of darkness that reached to her bare shoulders, leaving visible only her face, hands, and outstretched arms. She lay horizontal, her limbs stretched tight as she struggled against an unseen force that was pulling her deeper into the circle of blackness.

"What's happening to you?" Aurelius asked.

"Quiet, you fool! More Sidhe will hear us!" the woman hissed, wide-eyes glaring at him. She adjusted her fingers on the marbled, dry texture of the spruce's trunk.

Aurelius reached forward and clasped her pale forearms. "What-is-this?" He braced a boot against the base of the tree and, grunting between clenched teeth, strained to free her.

"Just pull, damn you!" Exhaustion made the woman's arms and voice tremble.

Aurelius felt as if he would dislocate her arms from the shoulders rather than have any chance of freeing her from that well of blackness. She tried to help, though, clawing her fingertips in a scramble across the rough bark of the tree.

Aurelius gave one more pull, and then let his instinct take over.

"What are you doing?" the woman shouted.

The knight said nothing, but moved forward, hooked his left hand under her armpit and punched a hand into the blackness behind her. His fist connected with something snarling, and in the momentary easing of tension, he grasped at where he thought the rest of the woman's trousers should be. His hand found bare flesh instead of fabric, and he almost released her when he realized she was naked.

The danger allowed for no more thinking, though. He grasped a leg between her buttock and hamstring, pulled hard, and kicked into the darkness. She shot out of the black disc, and he fell backward with her atop him. His heel crunched into the adversary's jaw, and then it was gone, sucked back into blackness. The disc collapsed on itself with a whirring pop.

Aurelius and the woman lay for a moment, heaving, but when he tried to extricate himself from her grasp, his hands found nothing except the small mounds of her breasts and a wiry body whose urgent hugging showed a complete relief at contact with another human being. The grateful escapee pulled herself closer to him and kissed him fully on the lips. Aurelius was so surprised that it took him a second to pull away, but when he did, the woman clasped both her hands on his cheeks.

"Oh, thank Nereus and Hermes!" she whispered and kissed him repeatedly, then one time with finality. She slid her face against his and gripped a handful of hair. "Oh you're real, you're real. Oh, Mother, oh, Hecate, I live! Not a phantom, not a twisted reflection of myself, folded between dimensions in one of Veröld's twisted games ... this life is mine again."

Her short reddish hair brushed his cheek as she moved close to kiss him again; this time three smacks within a couple of seconds, again lingering on the last kiss. Her words tumbled from her in a rush. "The *Sidhe* never let you kiss them, that's how I know I've escaped. You're real. So many times I thought ... so many times they'd seem real, and then they'd revert to their true forms. You wouldn't believe how many times I thought freedom seemed so close, then they'd rip it away, and I'd have to start a search again."

"Wha—"

"Oh, by Nereus's Waves, you're real. Magnificently real!" She sobbed, then, and tears flowed freely down her cheeks while she continued to clutch herself to him. "Thank Nereus, thank Hermes, and even thank Cronus himself. I'm free. I'm finally free!"

This one's already naked, and should sate your lust, Hospitaller—more readily and appreciatively than the Venetian wench ever could. Already she's kissed you more than Clarinda ever has, and looking at the way she's clutching you, it shouldn't take you both long to warm up.

The woman reared slightly backward, staring at Aurelius. "That whisper. I heard that. It's a Codex." She cocked her head. "*E*, who's Clarinda?"

The knight pushed upward on her shoulders, and finally

succeeded in firmly but gently prising the woman off him. He rose to a knee, trying to ignore beautiful features and the nude attributes of a filthy but well-formed body with which he'd just become very familiar, very quickly.

He stood and moved toward the spruce, but the dark disc was gone.

"You're a big man, but I sense you little more than a youth. How did you make a portal into the Otherworld?" She rose to her feet and glanced around the forest, then frowned. "The screams were there, but gone now. I sense Huntsmen, but, no ... no, he's not here. No Youdic the Damned." She refocused on Aurelius. "Even with codex magic, you were able to make a *runeporte* to Annen Verden without Youdic? That's not possible."

"I ... I don't know," he said lamely, not sure what to say to her. "Who are you, and what was that creature?"

She crossed her arms over her breasts and appeared to be calming herself, using a breathing technique to regain equilibrium. After a couple of seconds, she looked around, still totally uncaring about her nudity in the full moonlight. He'd have offered her a cloak if he had one, but his clothes were still soaked from the river and he'd begun to shake in the cold.

When she, too, had apparently assured herself that the black hole wasn't going to return, she returned attention to him. Hands on her hips, she frowned. "Well, why is there the voice of a Codex in your head?"

"I don't know," Aurelius replied, still stunned by the pace of events. "Who are you?"

She stepped toward him, hands clasped behind her back and said thoughtfully. "I heard your question the first time, and I'm still wondering if I should let you have my name as easily as I gave you my kisses." She looked up at him. "The Codex ... which one, which one? Hmm."

"What do you mean, which one?"

"*Basta.* Give me a moment, please. It'll come to me." She regarded him thoughtfully. "There's potential for domination in a name, you know. Old magic. The giving of a name might give the receiver power over me."

"I agree," he said, and nodded at the Norwegian spruce. "But, it seems as if you already risked coming into my power by asking for help."

She smiled. "Fair enough. Call me Pasiphaë."

The witch lies. Her sister is named Pasiphaë. Know her as Cerys, or Circe.

"I'm Ríg," he replied, returning a lie he felt from her as easily as she'd given one. The power of names, indeed!

"It is, indeed, a Codex," the woman murmured, "and it is correct. I am Cerys."

"Not ... not the Circe from Homer's Odyssey?" Aurelius asked.

The woman's eyes narrowed. "Never ask a woman her age, boy."

"I didn't ask ..." Aurelius stumbled through his words, "I mean, whoever you are, I'm just glad you're safe."

"You have an accent," she observed, and then asked, *"Vieni dalla Sicilia, o sei uno di quei preti di Roma?"* She looked at the white cross emblazoned on his surcoat's field of black. "You wear the Cross of the Nazarenes."

Aurelius was surprised. She spoke Italian flawlessly. *"Io sono siciliano, e sì,"* he replied, "I'm training to be a priest."

She fixed him with a stare, her lip curling in a smile. "You don't kiss like a priest."

"Uh, I … you surprised me. I—"

"I don't care," Cerys waved a dismissive hand, then put her arms across her chest again. "Another woman fills your mind, and I've much to do. Much time has passed, and I fear that much else has been lost. What year is it on Midgard?"

"Anno Domini, eleven-hundred and eighty-five."

"Six hundred years?" Cerys exclaimed. "That's … that's … no matter. No matter. I'm free, and you, Friend 'Ríg,' you have me completely in your debt, whatever this Codex's agenda in bringing me back." She extended a hand. "May I borrow your sword for a moment?"

He felt no threat from her, and acquiesced. She took the blade and etched a pattern he couldn't see in the dirt, muttering an incantation as she moved quickly back and forth across the area in front of the spruce tree.

She paused only once, and stared at the ground in concentration. "Dietrich? Sì Dietrich, and Braunen, I think, with others who I can't make out. No, thank Nereus, there's Sølvmora, and I think even Amari." Her head snapped upward, eyes wide at Aurelius. "Aspetta, Veröld Martröd is on Midgard again?"

"I don't know any of these names," Aurelius said. "Is he the one who sent the *Sidhe* after you?"

Cerys didn't answer, instead she worked more quickly on her scribing in the earth. When she'd finished, she handed Aurelius the hilt of his sword, and stepped into the center of the circle.

"You need to learn to guard your thoughts, Servius Aurelius Santini, especially if you are bound already to the … Codex

Lacrimae. You are correct to cleave to this ... Clarinda Trevisan, but I foresee a Fate for her that will give you much grief for a time. There can only be three Norns, and Verdandi and Skuld revealed themselves at the Fields of Burning Night. Urd will no longer trust them, nor should your Clarinda when she becomes Urd."

She whispered something, and gestured at the ground. Light green flames flickered into life at Cerys's feet, and Aurelius involuntarily stepped back. "I give you this advice without expectation of recompense," she continued, "for I will always owe you a life-debt for freeing me from Annen Verden. Beware of both the Codex Lacrimae and the words of Braunen the Sly. Both will seek to betray you at every turn until all the Codices are free, and already the Book of Tears has begun its work by returning first those who were exiled last. If Dietrich and I have been freed, then expect the return of the Druids of Rhydderch and the Coven of the Mists."

The streaks of dirt on her skin faded in a purifying white light, and a mist enveloped her, solidifying into a sleeveless white linen stola pinned at her shoulders by minute jeweled rods and pulled tightly at her slim waist by a thin brown cord. Sandals appeared on her feet, visible against the emerald flames that were spreading upward into a quietly burning pillar of fire.

She hesitated, then emerged from the pillar and stood before him.

Ah, she's been long without a man, and returns to make you hers, the Codex surmised. *Take what she offers, Hospitaller. This witch is like no other and will intoxicate you with delight!*

As with Clarinda, Cerys's head only reached the middle of his chest, but this time she wasn't reaching upwards to kiss him. Instead, while she whispered a short phrase, she lay a hand against his cheek. It smelled sweetly of oleander.

"Farewell, Lore Master Santini. I sense much of the better parts of Taliesin in you, but also something ... different. May you find peace at the end of your trials, and if ever you need an ally, look to Italia, in the southern Pontine Marshes, near the town of Saubadia. There you'll find me when I'm not abroad in the Nine Worlds. You shall always be welcome in my home, and neither you nor any companions need ever fear any drink I serve."

He looked down upon her, his senses electrified by the proximity, even though ironically she was now fully clothed. "*Grazie*," he whispered.

She turned away, then paused, cocking her head to one side as if listening. Cerys glanced at him, then at the spruce tree where he'd rescued her. While the green flames soared nearby in a column of fire, she walked unhurriedly to the tree, and extended a hand again.

"I hear Arngrim singing, not far distant, and it sings for you," she said. "May I borrow your sword again?"

"Who's Arngrim?" He handed her the blade.

"Trouble for you, perhaps," she glanced at him, then smiled, "but, perhaps not. You are strong, so strong."

She hacked part of the trunk, chipping a large segment of bark loose, then knelt, retrieved the fragment, and returned the blade to him.

"What are you doing?" he asked.

Sandals appeared on her feet, visible against the emerald flames
that were spreading upward into a quietly burning pillar of fire.

"Hush, my knight. I'm saving your life, I think." She hesitated. "And Clarinda's, too, although I scry that at the time she uses this she might not think the same way. Ah, well, that seems to be the course of relations between women. Someday, she'll understand, and I know that she'll need the mirror. Perhaps a Norn will succeed where I failed." She sighed. "I see pain coming for both of you, because Old Nick is wily and Arngrim will not be mastered easily—your Lady Clarinda might as well put the time of that separation to good use."

Cerys held the patch of bark in her opened left palm, and extended her other hand over the piece. She bent her head, and whispered words that Aurelius couldn't understand. A faint yellow glow flared briefly around her cupped hands.

"Who's Arngrim?" Aurelius asked the Codex, but the Dark Book was strangely silent.

Cerys handed the bark to him, and said, "Put this safely away, and look at me."

Aurelius slipped the bark into his wet tunic and inserted it into Hav's leather envelope.

"What is it?" He looked at her and his eyes glazed over.

"Servius Aurelius Santini, I can do this for you because you've not yet accepted the Codex Lacrimae. When I touched your cheek I silenced it, and it has not seen nor heard my words and actions. I would not have it know where I'm going. But, for you, this compulsion: do not reveal anything of our meeting until you achieve some mastery of the Codices, and then their plotting should not matter to you. This you must do, though. I have no wand with me, but can make do. I will return to my true home, but will communicate with you ... no, I See that I shall speak with your friend at the moment when you are in greatest peril. Heed me, boy: with this patch of bark, chipped from the tree where you saved my life, I've imparted what small magic I can, especially since I scry that I'll not be there when you have need of my potions. Give your Clarinda this bark, and she will hear my words telling her what to do. You will not remember this conversation until the madness has passed and you've begun to master Arngrim."

This time Cerys did rise on tiptoes to kiss Aurelius. The soft touch of her lips reawakened both him and the Codex Lacrimae.

Only a kiss? the Dark Book asked incredulously. *Grab her, fool! Strip those clothes off and take her! She owes you her life, and the blood of the sun and oceans runs through her veins. Look in her eyes, they burn with—*

"Oh, you underestimate this one, Codex Lacrimae," Cerys smiled, shaking her head. Her eyes did shine, but only with deep gratitude as she looked at Aurelius.

"Farewell, Lore Master Santini," Cerys returned to the pillar of emerald flame and stepped into it. "You have befriended the daughter of a titan and goddess this day. Be well, and may we meet again under happier skies. Thank you for my life."

Then she was gone, the flames evaporating as quickly as the black disc.

Something trilled in his mind as he cast about, almost disbelieving the encounter.

So, you can be distracted from the Norn ... the Codex Lacrimae mused.

"That's not what happened," Aurelius protested, but his reaction seemed too hasty even to himself.

There's no shame in feeling lust, Servius, or in being attracted to Cerys. You are one of the rare men who has not been ensnared by her wiles.

"Wiles?" Aurelius snorted. "The poor woman was trying to escape some kind of prison, and I think you know more about that escape than you're letting on. Did you make that portal, that rune-gate that freed her?"

It is said that a runeporte to Annen Verden can be opened only with the aid of Youdic the Damned. I don't see him here, do you?

"That doesn't answer my question, Codex Lacrimae, and don't think I didn't notice that she appeared when you were goading me with thoughts about Clarinda."

Those weren't my thoughts, Hospitaller, but your memories. Your desires. Why is it so bad for you to be attracted to these beautiful women? I think that Cerys would be a much better match for you than Clarinda, but I'd advise any alternative to romancing a Norn. Think what you will, but I wouldn't place too much trust in Clarinda, Aurelius. She's a Witch of Fate. Full of secrets and agendas that we can only guess at. How much has she hidden from you besides the meeting with Grimnir, Mimir, and her sisters? Has she even told you what they discussed? Take care of yourself, first, then find her if you must.

"Enough!" A coldness was setting into him that went beyond the frozen woods. He shook his head and the voice of the Codex dissipated, leaving behind chilliness, shivering, and the realization that his wet hair, skin, and clothes were icing in the frigid environment. If he didn't find shelter and warmth soon, the cold would give Hela the end she sought.

The forest grew darker around him. A skittering somewhere

in the upper branches of the forest roof made him look up, and he caught a glimpse of something black and massive moving at a quick speed.

The Spiders of Svartalfheim aren't to be dismissed lightly, Jotun-Son.

He frowned, tired already of the Codex's intrusion in his thoughts. Now that Cerys was gone, he became concerned again about his Venetian friend. Where could Clarinda be? He'd dove after her within seconds of her own plunge, so she should've been just ahead of him.

A light flickered through the trees. He heard the soft tones of conversation and realized that a couple of men were camped in a sheltered glade.

Watch and ware, fool! She's there, but there is peril that I can't help you with—not until you fully accept me.

The wintry weather permeated his skin and racked his body with uncontrollable shakes. He hesitated, unsure whether he should approach the fire. His uncertainty sprang not only from the natural caution one always felt in a foreign and dark wood, but also from the disorienting effect that the Codex's presence was having upon him. He could feel the Dark Book's existence even when it wasn't speaking, and it unnerved him to know that it could read his mind. There was also his complete lack of information about the peoples and dangers in this land—he had, after all, just escaped from Hela herself and a host of giants and dead men!

He looked again at the distant flame and took a bracing breath. Besides the need for warmth, there remained a chance that Clarinda was there. That thought decided the matter.

Better to risk the intentions of unknown people in the glade and regain her side by a warm fire than skulking like this in icy shadows. Night had fallen, and it was going to get much colder before the dawn.

He stepped into the glade.

CHAPTER 6

A Rune Gate to Muspelheim

Two men sitting beside the fire rose with blinding speed, their swords drawn and at Santini's throat before he could utter a word. They wore trousers of woven black wool, brown leather boots, and beige tunics with sleeves that stretched to their wrists. Rectangular fur cloaks fell to their knees, bound by golden brooches that gleamed in the blazing fire.

Age and physical features separated the men. A goatee beard and tattoos from head to foot marked the one closest to Aurelius, and black hair scraped back in a ponytail fell to his shoulders. He seemed surprised, but controlled, at a stranger's materialization at the campsite.

The older man had a thick blond beard and was also of fair complexion, though tanned more deeply than his companion. He spoke first. "*Hei*, now! What's your business here?"

"I didn't mean to startle you," Aurelius replied, "but I saw the fire. I took a swim in the river. I'm cold."

After a long moment, the blond-bearded man lowered his sword. He nodded toward the other man, indicating that he should do likewise, and gestured in a welcoming wave to the fire.

"Come, then. Join us at our meal." He pointed at the spit above the flames that held a roasting boar. "You're not a damned elf; that much is clear. Though, why in Odin's Name you wander about like a drenched rat in the dead of winter is a story that'll be your payment for the food."

"You're armed only with that sword?" the younger man asked.

"Do I need more?" Aurelius replied, trying to ignore the importance the man seemed to place in the question. Somehow the hatchet had lost its glowing attributes and looked again little more than a woodsman's tool at his waist. "A sword serves me well enough."

The tattooed man snorted, and gestured at the supplies near the horses. "If you come across the spiders here, you'll find you need quite a bit more than that blade."

Aurelius moved past him, noting the spears and nets that were the most visible items in a pile of hunting gear. The roasting meat made Aurelius realize how hungry the cold had made him.

The older man tossed a blade to Aurelius. He caught it deftly by the handle while scanning the area. It appeared to hold nothing more than a heap of black sable and white ermine furs, long bundles, two neighing horses, and the men's unrolled bedding.

Where's Clarinda? He moved forward and used the knife to slice a chunk of meat from the spit.

"Fell in the river, you say?" the bearded man prompted after the youth had taken a few more bites.

"Yes, back by the falls," Aurelius replied through a mouthful of the pork. His shivers diminished as food and fire did their work.

"Here." The blond-haired and more hospitable of the two men as he tossed a black sable fur at Aurelius. "You can borrow this for the night."

"Thank you," Aurelius unfurled the weighty garment and wrapped it around his shoulders. The change in temperature was immediate, and Aurelius felt truly grateful for the warmth. He nodded appreciatively at the pile of pelt. "You've had good fortune—I never thought I'd see so much white ermine in one place."

The blond-bearded man grunted. "The stoats in this region are almost pure white, no spotting or discoloration. They yield a high price at the fairs."

"That's it," the tattooed man advised Aurelius in a solicitous tone, "make sure the cloak covers you entirely—you'll warm up quicker that way."

"What's your name, stranger?" the older man asked, reaching forward to slice some more boar-meat.

"I'm called ... Ríg by my friends."

"Well, Ríg, you can relax for the evening," the bearded man replied. "I'm Farbauti, and this is my good friend, Kenezki."

"Good to meet you both. I would have frozen if you hadn't been here with a fire and food. What are you doing in this forest?"

"Hunting," the man snorted. "Svartalfheim's usually a dependable place to hunt for game that's too wild for Midgard. Isn't that right, Kenezki?"

The comment took Aurelius aback—did the man just say Svartalfheim? Andvari had repeatedly said that the Underjordisk Elv emptied into Alfheim. How had he ended up here?

He recalled Fenris's warning about Hela's reorientation of the dwarf tunnel, and then realized that the Queen of Death had, indeed, redirected the river's egress from the Crystal Caves not to the land of the Light Elves in Alfheim, but instead to the land of their Dark Elf kindred.

Kenezki smiled as he chewed, his focus entirely on Aurelius. Meat juices dripped down his chin. He wiped a linen-sleeved forearm across it before answering his partner. "Ja, Farbauti, game that's too wild for Midgard, but apparently tame enough in Svartalfheim. Or, I should say, tame enough to catch in the land of the elves." His eyes reflected the firelight like shining rubies. "Do you catch my meaning, man?"

"I have a little experience in hunting," Aurelius replied with an intensifying dislike for Kenezki's mocking manner. The young knight remembered the survival training that occupied the first fortnight of arriving at the abbey of Santa Maria di Corazzo, camping with Nicolo and Alexios while Devrone ran the boys through their paces.

Besides teaching the boys how to forage for edible roots and mushrooms or build shelters, Devrone had made sure that each of his students could hunt, kill, and skin any game, from hares to deer, and even wild boar such as the one currently on the spit.

Aurelius looked at the men by the fire, giving voice to a growing suspicion. "Though in truth, my master told me there was a difference between hunting and trapping."

Both men laughed loudly at that, and Aurelius smiled nervously as he sliced another hunk of meat from the spit, unsure of what was so humorous. The fire felt warm on his face, and he began to perspire from the combined heat of cloak and blaze.

"I take it you don't agree?" Aurelius asked Kenezki.

"Oh, we agree," Farbauti replied. "It's simply refreshing to hear such a thing from one who doesn't appear to be a hunter. You see, this all depends on the nature of the game you're hunting. In one instance, you can pursue a quarry to the ends of the earth; in the other, you can bait a trap and lure the prey to you."

Aurelius nodded toward the rapidly disappearing meat on the spit. "Well, thankfully, boar is boar, whether on 'Midgard' or here, isn't it? You seem to have done well with your hunting today."

"We did, indeed, Ríg, we did, indeed." Farbauti leaned back onto an elbow. "But, boar's what we eat, not solely what we hunt, or trap."

"Really?" Aurelius finished the last bit of meat. The chills from the river had gone, and as the heated flush on his face grew uncomfortable. He tried to loosen the cloak draped over his shoulders. It felt heavy, as if grown in great weight since he put it on. "What game do you hunt, then?"

"We hunt the Codex Lacrimae, Santini," Kenezki said mirthfully, "and we've trapped you to get it."

Aurelius tried to leap to his feet, but the sable cloak weighted him down.

"Oh, *Bitte*, stay seated, 'Ríg,'" Farbauti said. "We caught a would-be Norn in the same way a few minutes before you appeared. You both showed up exactly where we were told you'd be, and we came prepared. You're not going anywhere with a Grimhold Cloak on your shoulders."

Aurelius stared at both men, feeling a fool that he hadn't looked more closely at the pile of baggage on the far side of the glade. He glanced at it to see if he could make out Clarinda (and her condition) and saw a blurred movement, like wind rushing through leaves, and then nothing.

"Quit struggling, Santini," Kenezki said, not noticing what had happened behind him. "Even if you somehow got out of the cloak, the entire area's warded by sorcery."

"She predicted it almost to the second," Farbauti said, grinning at Kenezki. "This was almost too easy."

She? Aurelius wondered, and a deadly calm settled in him as he made an intuitive connection. He recalled the first words Hela had said on the shore of the Underjordisk Elv: "Unbelievable. You're all here, just as they promised."

Somebody had told both Hela and these Huntsmen where traps could be sprung upon Aurelius and his companions!

"Clarinda was trying to warn you," Aurelius said, feigning a misunderstanding of Farbauti's words. He nodded at the bundled clothes, under which the Venetian girl must be lying unconscious. "She knew that I'm going to get free, and just thinks I'm crazy. I killed some rock giants earlier, and it scared her. She was *richtig* about one thing, though. I'm done with getting attacked everywhere I turn in this dream. Let her go. You have me, isn't that what you want?"

"Listen to the lad spout," Farbauti said, still amused. "I'm tempted to break his jaw, Kenezki. He doesn't need the ability to speak for us to take the Codex."

"Clarinda goes nowhere." Kenezki exclaimed, speaking to Santini. "I've been greatly delayed because of that Trevisan wench. She's much to answer for, and the Battle of Caesarea's the least of it."

"I don't understand this," Aurelius said, still trying to lift the garment off his shoulders. "I've only recently learned about this Codex Lacrimae. If it's a matter of taking it, or killing my friend or me, then you can have it."

"Is it with you?" Kenezki asked.

"Of course not," Aurelius chuckled. "I'm not used to having dreams that feature tattoo-faced howler monkeys in them, much less plan to bring books into them with me."

O, but I am here, Servius! Accept my offer and dispatch these fools to the hellscape they deserve!

That took Aurelius aback. *Get out of my thoughts!*

You need only me, but as with all things of power, you need to pay a price for using me.

"Did you just call me a monkey, Santini?" Kenezki asked in a low voice.

"No, I was saying how strange this dream is," Aurelius

smiled, shaking his head. "If I were calling you anything, I'd say you look like a mandrill's haunches." Aurelius laughed.

You've struck true, Hospitaller. This one's vanity is his weakest point.

Get out of my head! "In truth," Aurelius continued aloud, "that's being unfair to the mandrill, who'd been brought to Jerusalem in a cage from Cameroon. By the time I saw it, its rear end looked better than the tattoos on your sorry face. The poor beast had dysentery, so there were all kinds of dripp—"

Kenezki struck with the speed of a snake, his fist driving into the knight's jaw and making Aurelius see stars. Ignoring the pain, he whipped his head back in an attempted lunge, barely missing Kenezki's knee with a forehead slam.

Head bowed, the youth snorted a laugh as he spat blood. "Too easy," he whispered.

We can work together, Santini. You've none of Taliesin's reserve. Verily, I think you're unbalanced enough to destroy both of these Huntsmen—with my help, of course.

The knight didn't bother replying to the Dark Book. He was preoccupied with trying to shrug off the cloak and waiting for an end to the roar in his ears from Kenezki's blow.

"Kenezki, enough!" Farbauti snapped. "He's baiting you, waiting for the girl to wake up, or help to come. Let's just get what we came for."

"He's got nothing we don't already have," Kenezki said, rising to his feet as Farbauti threw some powder into the flames. "I say we throw him back into Midgard now—I want this matter done."

The older, blond-bearded man murmured an incantation

and the fire turned crimson. The air above it exploded, and a parabolic arc of glowing orange energy flowed upward and framed the casing of a doorway.

Aurelius raised his head, spat again, and squinted against the heat pouring through the flaming portal. Another world lay beyond the rune-gate. Great obsidian cliffs loomed high over the crashing waves of a violently stormy sea. A firefall of incandescent magma flowed through a gigantic rift in the black overhang and poured into a boiling ocean whose superheated, bubbling surface steamed into a maroon sky. Black clouds billowed in malevolent plumes from two distant volcanoes that erupted red-hot basalt into the ashen air.

The youth's bravery faltered at the sight and he felt the first initial pangs of despair. He and Clarinda had survived visits to Hel, confrontations with Satan, and they'd even battled rock giants and plunged through underground rivers deep beneath the Jotunheim Mountain Range. Yet, as he watched explosion follow eruption in those fiery lands, he didn't see how they could last even a few seconds in that superheated world!

"That's not Midgard, Farbauti," Kenezki said. "That's Muspelheim."

"I know," his partner replied. "I'll not have Santini escape us again, and the Nine Worlds aren't what they were when the Codex was created—except for the fact that Muspelheim is closed to everyone except us. If we leave him there, no one can touch him and we'll be free to pursue the book."

"No. I say, kill him. He bleeds, so it can be done. Then, all we'll have to do is dispose of his body back at the castle." Kenezki's voice shook with rage. "I feel something here—

something more than an awakening Codex. A talisman, I think, and one that threatens me directly."

"Search him," Farbauti suggested, returning his attention to the rune-gate, "or try to kill him. I don't think that we can at this point. I See neither Codex nor Artifact here."

You wouldn't See, you poor imitation of Mogthrasir. The Codex Lacrimae sneered. *I sense him, hidden, Farbauti. Does even Surtur know that Mogthrasir, too, survived the Fields of Burning Night? I think not. He would've sought high and low for him if there were any chance that he survived. No. He made you, Morpeth, and the other Huntsmen as facsimiles. What will you do, I wonder, when the First returns and becomes the Last?*

The pirate's knife slashed downward and Aurelius flinched, expecting it to be buried in his neck. He waited for the impact, but none came. Repeatedly, Kenezki tried to stab him, but he kept missing in what became almost comical attempts. He finally sheathed the blade in disgust.

"So, it's begun. The Codex protects him already."

That was a demonstration for you as well, Hospitaller. I'll not protect you again until you and I reach an understanding.

The only understanding we'll have is parting of ways, Aurelius thought. *I'll have none of you.*

"Then it is awake," Farbauti surmised. "Strange. I thought we'd hear it—the legends say that it speaks with a silver tongue." He paused, thoughtful. "Yet, we can't see it, even though its protection is there. This is ... unexpected."

Aurelius ducked his head. In spite of his protests to the Dark Book, he found himself unable to hide a smile as the Codex howled with laughter.

Can't see it? You don't even know how to begin looking for such as us!

"I grant your point, Huntsman," Kenezki ceded. "We need him until the Codex is in our hands." He nodded toward the rune-gate. "We'll imprison him there on the Strombolian Cape. Thanks to his 'protection,' he can sit and burn near the Desolate Sea. Burning, but not dying. Let him wait there while we go hunting with Morpeth for his physical body at the Krak des Chevaliers."

Farbauti nodded, but frowned. "I haven't heard from Morpeth — strange, since we know that because the Codex awakened and protects Santini, that part of his mission succeeded."

He raised an eyebrow at the bound knight. "Morpeth wanted to be here when we trapped Santini, and he hasn't arrived." He cupped a hand thoughtfully under his chin. "I'd also like his advice on what to do with this fourth Norn, especially considering how we came to know how she and Santini would be here—"

Sì, how did you know? Aurelius wondered. *I'm starting to think that someone's playing a double game here, but who, et why?*

You're besotted with one, but I'll say it again: don't trust the Norns. The Codex's voice was almost smug. *This betrayal of information about yours and the Norn's arrival here has all the stink of one of those witches! I'd say either Verdandi, or Skuld ...*

"Trevisan's been too quiet," Kenezki said, and he kicked at the long bundles. "Odin's Blood, I knew it. Farbauti, she's gone! We've gotten some unexpected help, but somebody assisted her, too." Suspicion suddenly narrowed the pirate's eyes and he glowered at the other. "Or, do you play other games here?"

I'm tired of waiting, Hospitaller. The Codex Lacrimae sighed. *You must accept me, and to do that, you must know who I am.*

"No, Kenezki," Farbauti replied calmly, "we play the games needful for the hunt, but this isn't one of my making." He walked across the campsite to stand beside his partner. "Santini and Trevisan were traveling with Fenris and Skade—perhaps they, too, escaped the trap in Nidaveller."

Aurelius heard the men speaking, but the sounds drifted and seemed to come from a great distance, as if an abyss spanning a greater space than the campfire's supernatural flames yawned between him and his captors.

Began to learn now the Script and Scope by which I am bound.

The Codex's voice was mesmerizing, and he didn't have to see the book to confirm that what he heard were translations of the runic script he'd seen in the Codex Lacrimae back at the Krak.

Gone were the threats and posturing that had characterized the Dark Book's previous interactions with him. Instead, streams of information flowed into his mind as a feminine voice relayed the tome's symbols and words in a language of harshly broken syllables and irregular cadences, as if the phrases were snarled or spit from the mouth of a madman.

Then, unexpectedly, the sentences smoothed themselves into passages whose words made Aurelius's heart ache with a strange, indefinable yearning. At those moments, the youth felt as if he were emerging briefly from a nightmare vision of the world that, of all things, reminded him of Cerys's head and arms popping from the *Sidhe*-disc.

He glimpsed a different kind of Codex Lacrimae in those brief inter-seconds, seeing flashes of the forests and rivers of Alfheim gleaming in the majesty of a gloaming sun, where dust motes drifted lazily through the air of a hot afternoon as Aurelius and Amari kissed beneath a beech tree. The Hospitaller remembered that day vividly—

... no, not me. I wasn't there. What is this? Who is Amari?

—and he and the girl lay on the sward of thick grass, kissing after their swim while nixies and strömkarlen erupted from the River Perilous to soar high in the air before plunging back into the waters, for all the world appearing as spraying fountains whose frothing heads momentarily took on the forms and features of naked men and women before reverting to rapids and tiny waterfalls.

"Taliesin," Amari whispered, running a glossy nail across the Hospitaller's bare chest while the lovers watched the watery display. "Sølvmora wouldn't lie about something like that, and you both were a week late in the return from Norfolk."

"Blame Dietrich," Aurelius whispered, running a finger through the woman's lustrous black hair, before pulling her toward him to give a lingering kiss. She pushed away, but he pulled her to him, their bodies entwined as they rolled on the broad blanket.

"Tell me," Amari urged afterwards, nestling her cheek into the hollow of his neck. "Just say that you were with her, and we can move on. I'm not the jealous type, you know that, don't you?"

He laughed. "Oh, you're reassuring me with every word, Amari. You have me now. We have this moment. Why do you want more?"

What ... what is this? Aurelius thought, dimly aware that, entranced, he was leaning very close to the flames of the rune gate. Perspiration gathered on his forehead. *How am I here, I mean, there, and why am I naked with this woman?*

Another page of the Codex turned. A thousand prisoners shoutrf in desperation as a dungeon trapdoor locked with a slam above their heads.

He was reliving another moment, not his memory, but it felt as if it were his body doing the actions.

He glanced at Dietrich.

"These are the last, Taliesin," the dwarf said, staring dispassionately at the prisoners as he leaned wearily on his staff. "The friends of Volund who lent their magic to the Codex Lacrimae."

"It's the most corrupt of them all, Dietrich."

"Killing them wouldn't undo that," the arch-mage said. "Spare them."

Aurelius snorted. "It's Annen Verden. They'd probably prefer death."

"They'll still live, Taliesin. Trust in the ways of our *Siðr*. Leave it up to them to make their own atonements."

"It's not 'our *Siðr*,' Dietrich. I'm not of your faith nor particularly fond of your people's ways. What we're doing with the Codices will demand an accounting. What about Sølvmora?"

"Bah. She's accountable for her own actions. You'll find her, if she wants to be found."

No, not a trap door, Aurelius thought, returning his gaze to the upturned elfin faces that implored him through the thick bars. Thin hands reached through the cage, trying to touch him.

A reverse prison, a portal to ... where? I should know, I do know, but I don't want to say it. They're not going to escape this. They can't, and I'm going to let it happen because they've angered me. This ... this is a portal like the one I saw Old Nick using when he pulled those bodies from the silver disc in Hel. This one was reversed, going into the earth, not the air, and I — NO! Not me ... Taliesin—Taliesin did it to the elves.

"Just as you've banished Sølvmora," he heard himself say, "so, too, shall you lose the sunlit glades."

Something from the dark came, something from the deeps beneath the earth. The elves screamed, multiple voices, high and pure in their shrieking. A people of trees and valleys and open air were banished forever to the tunnels and under-paths of the mountains.

Taliesin! Taliesin, do not do this to us. We beg of you, mercy.

Aurelius tried to close off the screams, but they echoed long in his memory as he knelt, head still bowed and staring at the rune gate. He was sweating freely now, unable to stem the tide of memories rushing through his mind.

Who are these people? Amari? Sølvmora? Dietrich? Why do I have flashes of this Taliesin's memories?

The Dark Book resumed turning its pages, revealing itself to him. The thick parchment folios of histories, spells, and arcane knowledge flipped past his mind's eye as the Dark Book.

Descriptions that would make paragraphs of densely wrought runes in the actual tome itself—pages that were filled with the lives and works of sorcerers, witches, elves and Loki, who all had walked the world when it was thousands of years younger than the present age—became spoken histories in the space of mere heartbeats, all related to the Hospitaller by a distinctly female voice.

No, not spoken, Aurelius corrected himself. It was more as if the voice's words transmitted knowledge into his mind like a flood of sunlight shining through an open window of the scriptorium—too broad and comprehensive to absorb at first sight, and he couldn't raise a hand to shield his eyes from the glare.

During the transmission, Aurelius finally began to feel an affinity with the book that he'd never have thought possible. The engagement with the runes and words reminded Aurelius of the times when he'd been alone in the scriptorium, completely absorbed in memorizing the parts of the Bible that Jeremiah had set before him, with no distractions of any kind from his everyday world.

To his captors, only seconds had passed, and the young knight appeared to be recovering from Kenezki's punch, staring through the glowing doorway at the razor-sharp projections of Muspelheim's obsidian lands, whose sulfurous fumes distorted his vision and pulled tears from his eyes.

You reside in what Taliesin called 'a Lore Master's moment,' the Codex confided, *and you begin to realize that we do many things, be many places in the seconds between thoughts. Open yourself to me, and this is but the first of the lessons I can teach you. Time has little meaning to we who bound across the arcs of the Eternal Triquerta.*

While he listened to the Dark Book, the heat from the swirling lava flows shimmered through the sickly red flames of the door, quickly drying his clothing beneath the Grimhold Cloak, but sweat now plastered the fabric of his tunic to his skin. His throat burned with a parched thirst worse than any that he had suffered while living in the arid environment of the Syrian desert. To make matters worse, try as he might to focus on what the two men were saying, he could make out nothing beyond the roar of Muspelheim and the words of the Codex Lacrimae.

I can assist in defeating these men, the Codex repeated when it came to a pause between paragraphs, *if you let me show you how, you can create a different rune-gate easier than even the Huntsmen did. I have no need of mumbled words and special powders; your theurgy will be as mighty as the Odin-Power!*

Whether a dream or not, Aurelius wanted to escape this place. He wanted to live. For all the darkness in his life, even with the apparent death of his friend Pellion, he didn't want to die. On the other hand, he had no intention of surviving at the cost demanded by the Codex. He had to escape this dream before it broke his mind.

I'm preparing to take vows of a priest in the Church, Aurelius thought, replying in the same internal, silent manner of the Codex's communication. I'll have no part in this magic of yours.

Are you worried about my price? 'The life of a friend?' Servius, listen to me. Who's to say that any of your friends would survive what's coming without your aid? Measure a cost of something that might not even occur against the greater good you can do.

Aurelius tried to shut his mind to her words, and returned focus to his captors.

"... they didn't escape Hela's trap," Kenezki was saying. "The only ones to escape were the Norn and this one—that much I know."

"From your connection to Hela and Fenris?"

"That, and other means," Kenezki said, a look of disgust on his face. "Hela and Fenris are newly come to matters concerning the Codex Lacrimae—I'd be surprised if the wolf even realized how much claim he himself has to it—but, no, I know that no one else has escaped the caverns. The fight there continues."

"Then, we underestimated her," Farbauti said simply, the hunter's assessment a pragmatic one.

Kenezki pulled the *Brisinga* necklace from a pouch at his waist and held it up defiantly.

"I underestimated nothing! This was the first thing I took after we captured her. Someone helped her, and stole her from under both our noses."

The tattooed man contemplated Aurelius, who'd become queerly still as he stared at the rune gate. "No one's aware of our plans for the Codex," Kenezki mused, "nor even whom we serve. I guarantee that even if Mimir or Odin himself guessed at that because of you and Morpeth, no one could have anticipated me. I've not appeared in human guise since the ancient covenants were sworn after the death of Balder."

A-ha! He's revealed himself, Hospitaller! I know him. Accept me, and make your own covenant so that I may tell you all.

What do you mean, 'accept?' Aurelius thought. *Your 'life of a friend' message in the frontispiece of the book? Pellion's dead already.*

Morpeth slew him and awakened me, but you must choose me by paying my price.

Like every deal with the Devil? I don't think so.

They'll succeed in their plan, fool. While I've ... slept, they've had nothing else to do except prepare for my return. They've anticipated the arcs and reduced the options for your own trajectories.

What does that mean? Aurelius asked, completely baffled.

The Codex ignored him. *Boy, how long do you think that you can survive in Muspelheim without accepting my help?*

Aurelius gazed uncomfortably through the rune-gate. His skin already felt charred from the radiating heat. Lava poured into the sea from the vent on the side of one of the volcanoes close to the portal. It sloshed into the ocean in an eerily hypnotic luminescence, creating steam that billowed hundreds of feet in the air like plumes from some fantastic cauldron.

He shook his head, breaking the trance and noting that Kenezki had ceased speaking to watch him. He didn't care if he appeared insane. *Then we die together,* he thought at the Codex. *You're a profane work, and I'm getting tired of letting everyone from Satan to Death think they can have their way with me.* Aurelius's anger was as much at himself as at the Codex Lacrimae. Did he have anything to do with Pellion's passing? He couldn't bear it if his friend's death could've been prevented!

Pellion's death was too high a price for 'awakening' you, Aurelius continued. *If you need the death of one of my friends to exist in this world—or even the promise of death—then that price is too high.*

You'd see us both perish there, rather than accept the few paltry covenants that bind me? These magics aren't my doing, Servius. I had no say in my making, nor in the constitution of the magics that make me what I am.

Apparently, though, he thought, *I do have a say here, and I'll not make such an agreement.* Aurelius swallowed apprehensively as he continued to watch the steaming lava from a pillow mound of basalt arising from the ocean. Lightning flashed in the skies under the distant volcanoes.

The Codex Lacrimae fell quiet for a moment, then it said, *Very well; we will revisit this matter, later. I'd not perish just as I'm beginning to live again, so I'll tell you two things. First, Clarinda and the dark elf, Rudyick, wait beyond the wards of this campsite with a company of elves, ready to attack. Your Norn friend is resourceful, and it seems as if Volund's son is as determined to see me unmade as you are to not use me. Second, ignore what Farbauti and Kenezki say about the Grimhold Cloak—such a trifling has no power over the Codex Wielder, even if he be a fool who doesn't wield my power.*

What have you done? The Hospitaller exclaimed in his mind, even while retaining his scholarly side and dispassionately assessing everything she said. *I can move!* The cloak had lightened, but he bowed his head, listening while the Codex finished.

Of course you can move, thanks to me. Know this, childish fool: Grimhild of the Nibelungs fashioned these cloaks centuries past, but her covenants were always compromised because of Volund's sorcery. Volund was one of my makers, so my magic surpasses any that Grimhild made. When you're tired of being a captive of these men, simply cast off the cloak. The woods about this glade are another matter; the Huntsmen of Muspelheim are almost a match for me in some instances, and I don't know what magics Farbauti used in casting this place's defenses. I have a good guess who Kenezki is, but I'm not completely certain. The world distorts around him, as if his very existence warps reality. Only Loki or his children have such power, and they're all accounted for.

"Farbauti, he is talking to someone!"

The conversation with the Dark Book took mere seconds, and

Kenezki had just reached Aurelius to yank him toward the flaming rune gate when the Hospitaller launched himself upward, throwing the now-lightened Grimhold Cloak at his assailant.

The motion obscured Kenezki's view for an instant, and the knight took advantage of the blind to punch the pirate's jaw. Shards of pain splintered through Aurelius's right hand, as if he'd just struck a stone wall.

Kenezki smiled and shoved back sharply, knocking the knight off balance.

Then a flash of sapphire marked the dismantling of the camp's defensive wards, and an entire squad of elves rushed into the area. Flaming arrows burst from the shadowed trees and Farbauti and Kenezki found themselves each assailed by four or five elves.

The ambush was so sudden that Farbauti got pushed toward the rune-gate and would have stumbled through it if he'd not planted his heels and thrown the two elves holding onto his massive arms into the portal. Then he drew his sword, slew two more elves before they had a chance to react, and turned to Aurelius.

"Servius, use the hatchet on Kenezki!" Clarinda shouted from somewhere in the forest.

The knight pulled the hatchet from the holster on his waist and moved so quickly that the Norn hadn't even finished speaking before he hit Kenezki with all his might. Yellow light flared from the small woodsman's tool when the blunt end crashed into Kenezki's skull, and the pirate staggered backward, clawing at his face as if burned by acid.

Kenezki screamed in Norwegian and stared wide-eyed at

Aurelius and the hatchet, his tattooed features a mask of fury and hate. *"Nei, det kan ikke være lynet hammeren!"* he roared. "I'm not ready for the lightning, and I'll not fight that weapon in this wretched guise!"

Kenezki dove through the portal and plunged out of sight into the boiling sea.

Farbauti paused, his sword still upraised, the expression on his face as surprised as Aurelius's own.

Where did you get that weapon? The Codex Lacrimae shouted in his mind, awe mingled with fear coloring its hitherto serene speech.

Aurelius ignored the question and followed a simultaneous suggestion by the Codex.

"Son of Muspel." He glared at Farbauti and repeated the Dark Book's words, although he didn't understand half of them. It was a disorienting sensation; the Codex was speaking through him! "Begone. Follow the *Väldiga Staven* if you would, but you'll not survive me alone. Watch and ware, else I'll unmake you and return you to Muspelheim's lord in a form even he won't recognize."

Farbauti started to sneer, perhaps sensing a bluff—there was no way Aurelius could defeat the Huntsmen in hand-to-hand combat after so little training, was there?—but he also seemed acutely aware that a company of elves surrounded him while supernatural forces streamed from the demon's home-world through the glowing rune-gate.

Thankfully, Farbauti's decision seemed to be made for him as the *runeporte* started to collapse. The Huntsman dove through the portal before it completely disappeared.

Confused but relieved at his abductors' departure, Aurelius stared in wonder at the hatchet as Clarinda and the Dark Elf, Rudyick, entered the glade.

CHAPTER 7

Clarinda and the Codex Lacrimae

"**S**ervius, we've got to leave before they return!" Clarinda lowered her staff and ran into the clearing and his waiting embrace. Unlike Santini's dried and heated clothes, Clarinda's were still drenched from swimming in the river.

Rudyick, clad in a forest green cloak with cowl drawn, followed her and the rest of the elven squad positioned themselves in a defensive perimeter around the glade.

Aurelius gave her a long hug, relieved and glad that she'd survived the underground channels and captivity. "You couldn't think of another way to break that spell than falling into the river?" he murmured.

She shook her head, smiling as she broke the embrace. "No. It was bad enough to see the giant with that stave. When you got hold of it you were ..."

"... *come uno degli uomini morti Hela?*" he smiled wryly.

Her eyes widened. "*Sì!* Like one of Hela's dead men!" She pushed gently against his chest. "Don't do that again—that river was awful, and the Huntsmen were even worse. Kenezki was the last person I expected to see ..."

You flirt with a Nornish hag? the Codex's voice thundered incredulously. *Enough, boy! I'm a Power in these worlds, one of the Fated Codices, and more trustworthy than any of those witches. Slay these people now, or use me to flee! If flirting with a witch puts a rise in your robe, you should have had your way with Cerys when she lay naked upon you. This one's a Norn, and Rudyick's a Dark Elf; neither can be trusted where you and I are concerned—*

"Is that the Codex Lacrimae?" Clarinda asked after surveying the glade to make sure that no one else was speaking. "I heard the same voice in the cavern. Why does it want to kill me? But, most importantly, who's this naked Cerys?"

"You can hear it?" Aurelius said, dismay at the Codex's 'flirting' comment spinning into mortification when the Dark Book revealed Cerys condition. "Wait. Can you hear my thoughts?"

Ratatosk bounded into the space, cocked a head upward at Clarinda, then turned to Aurelius. "Hear what? I don't hear anything!"

"You heard me, Santini: who's Cerys?"

"I ... I ..." his face flamed red as he tried to concentrate on two lines of communication from two very different, but similarly angry, feminine sources.

You're losing your chance, Jotun-Son; the Witches of Fate can out-riddle Odin if they put their minds to it, and Ratatosk knows the magic of the Maker. They were allied with Taliesin at the Fields of Burning Night the last time I saw them. This wench reeks of that Norn, Urd! Impale the witch, squash the flying rat, craft a rune-gate, and flee!

"I don't like riddles," Clarinda locked her eyes on Aurelius but spoke to the Codex. "But, while I say we skip the impalement, I'll admit that squashing the flying rat has a certain appeal." Then she added, "*E*, no, I can't hear your thoughts, but her speech is very clear, *molto chiaro ...*"

"What riddles? Who are you calling a flying rat?" Ratatosk screeched. "Who are you talking to, Clare?"

"We'll talk about Cerys later," Clarinda said. She ignored the squirrel and nodded toward the hatchet that had banished Kenezki and Farbauti. "After seeing how Kenezki reacted when you waved that hatchet, I think that thing's turning out to be quite a complex mystery itself. You should holster ... whatever it is, Servius. It's another puzzle we'll have to figure out when we're in a safer area."

Safe? Again the Witch tries to mislead you—there will be no safety for you until you've gathered the Codices and mastered space and time to bend the worlds to your will. I urge you, Servius, don't listen to her. She'll say anything to prevent you from being what you are. She's a liar and a cheat. (Ask her about her friend, Alex, if you think that I don't know what I'm talking about.) Ask her what she intends to do when Urd's Death Day comes. If she won't listen to Mimir nor the true Norns, you can't expect that she'll heed anything you have to say. Her lies will kill you—she knows that there's nothing safe in the lands of Svartalfheim. This is the home of the most ancient magics in creation, filled with secrets and griefs that will break your mind. You need me, Hospitaller; you won't survive the Nine Worlds or trials ahead of you without my aid ...

"Does it speak to you like that all the time?" Clarinda asked calmly. Then her eyes narrowed. "Can you see her? I mean, it?"

... listen to me, Servius! I can teach you the runes to destroy them all, the squirrel, the Norn, the dwarves and elves in the forest. Don't worry. I'll not mention to her how many times Cerys kissed you, nor how you kissed back. Rid yourself of them now because they'll only hinder you later. Listen to me, and your rewards can be greater than your imagination can fathom. You just have to listen and agree—

"I can't get her to shut up," Aurelius exclaimed.

"Are you sure you want her to?" The girl raised an eyebrow. "When did you even have time to meet this Cerys, let alone kiss her?"

"It's not important," the knight said curtly, fed up with everybody. There were too many voices at the same time. "I saved a woman's life back by the river, pulled her from a magic hole or something, she fell on me, gave me a kiss and left."

More than one kiss, but tell whatever lies you'd prefer, priest.

"*Buon Dio,*" Aurelius whispered, his face hot with embarrassment, "will you just *silenzio?*"

Ratatosk hopped on a log. "I'm missing something here," he said, his his head turning back and forth between the young people.

"So," Clarinda said, glaring. She wanted to ignore the topic of Cerys, but even she had to admit that the Codex was doing a superb job of instigation. "My question is still waiting an answer. Are you sure you want the Codex to shut up?"

"What's that supposed to mean?" Aurelius asked.

"It means, from where I'm standing she certainly sounds like she's not bothered by you in any way. More as if she wants you all to herself, or better, to make you better acquainted with Cerys, or any other woman she can suggest."

Typical Venetian, jealous of people and things that she's no warrant to think of as her own. Doesn't prevent those damn lagoon-dwellers from trawling the bog for whatever dregs they can, though, does it? Sluttish tramp. Swim back to your marshlands, girl, or sink to the bottom of the Middle Sea with your father's coffin. I know you, and I See the dooms your arrogance will unleash. You think to save Fate from Herself? Fool! See how many covenants withstand that choice! Hear me, Aurelius—if you listen to this would-be Norn, I foretell that she'll lead you to ruin.

"I'm *not* jealous, and I certainly don't think of him as my own!" Clarinda retorted, a little too quickly. Nonetheless, she flushed when she noticed some nearby elves stop talking to look at the exchange.

"You're not?" Aurelius raised an eyebrow, surprised and a bit flustered by the voices of the two women talking to him. "I mean, you don't?" His voice trailed off lamely.

"*Mi scuzi?*" she retorted, intentionally misunderstanding him. "We just met. Do you think I'm that kind of girl?"

"No, no." He flushed. "Of course not. I didn't mean the 'sluttish tramp' part, I meant the jealous part."

"*Perché?* Have you done something with her I should be jealous of? Was this Cerys really naked, and why do you look so guilty? For God's Sake, Santini, we practically just got here! How'd you find time to flirt with another ... I mean, a girl."

Not a girl, a woman. By Odin, Cerys is a woman, isn't she, Servius? Writhed and clutched at you while you rolled about, experienced in ways Clarinda could never be ...

"Silenzio!" He repeated to the Codex, and then looked imploringly at Clarinda. "I'm not looking guilty! I mean ... there's nothing I did, well, I don't ..." He glanced at Rudyick for some kind of help, but the elf looked as confused as he felt.

"Cerys?" Ratatosk sniffed. "Do you mean Circe the Enchantress?" He lifted a head inquiringly. "You've slept with Circe the Enchantress? But, I thought she was dead ... oh. Ewww."

Not dead, the Codex gloated, *but naked, willing, and wonderfully alive.*

"I didn't sleep with her!"

Ratatosk chittered and tapped a paw. "She's fine looking, that one, for a mortal woman. I might have to reconsider my opinion of you, boy. Circe's killed many men who tried to sleep with her."

"Fine looking?" Clarinda repeated, raising an eyebrow.

"No, she's not. I mean, she is, but ... the point is, I didn't sleep with Cerys—" Aurelius then interrupted himself because the Codex was at it again.

Do you see the look on her face? I told you, Servius; you don't know her half as well as you need to, and she certainly doesn't trust you. Not as you need a woman to ... not like you can trust me. Witchy ways, witchy ways, with these Norns. Confusing you with her wiles and her language. Nothing like Cerys, who really seemed to respect you—

"I respect him!" Clarinda interjected.

Und, she's not even a Norn yet. Can you imagine what she'll be like once she knows all the Gåtefull Runers? No, let's forget even what I said about Cerys and avoid all of these Italian harlots, I say.

"*Aspetta*, wait ... Cerys is Italian?" Clarinda's face drained slightly at the revelation. Sharing the same Italianate heritage with Aurelius had been a special part of their growing friendship.

"*Sì*," Aurelius confirmed, "and I'd place her accent somewhere west of ... Rome." He stopped talking again because Clarinda didn't look as if she were interested in the answer.

Too much Roman blood in all of these women you find attractive, Santini, even after all these centuries of different peoples conquering the peninsula. No complexities of heritage like you Sicilians, with all the Normans, Greeks, and Arabians mixing things up. Forget this conniving little tramp, and I'll take you to meet some of the other witches from the Coven. Wait until you see Sølvmora. A more enticing figure than both Cerys and this Trevisan bitch, Sølvmora's a true Scandinavian beauty. She'll cast a spell that you'll never want to ...

"*Oh, voi due: il silenzio per un attimo!*" Clarinda snapped. She bit her lower lip, thoughtful. "Servius," she said finally, "I've heard what the Codex thinks of me—I've heard too much of everything it thinks, and it's voice is starting to drive me crazy. Do you trust me?"

A trap is being set here, Hospitaller—you might think to lose yourself in those pretty eyes or still hopeful that you can press that shapely figure to your own, but know, O Man, I really can help you find a hundred women more comely, and all without any of her irritating personality traits ... women who won't constantly pester you with questions. If you don't want a witch, let me lead you to Lorelei and the Sirens of the Rhine. You'll get a bit wet, but I promise that the pleasures they can offer will more than compensate ...

"I trust you more than anybody I've met here," he replied without hesitation, his words running over those of the Codex. The voice in his mind was revealing more of his thoughts about Clarinda than he'd prefer.

"Let me touch you." Before he could react, Clarinda lightly tapped his forehead with her quarterstaff.

CHAPTER 8

A Norn's Command

The voice of the Codex Lacrimae fell silent.

Aurelius stepped back, relieved. *"Que'st esso?"* he asked in wonder. "She's gone!"

"Completamente?" she replied, an appraising look in her eyes.

"Is what gone?" Ratatosk screeched, hopping between the Norn and Hospitaller and looking around. "Is there a ghost here—is that it? Is it a specter?"

"Sì, completely," the knight affirmed, in wonder. "How did you do that?"

She pulled the staff back to an upright position and nodded at the weapon. "This staff. The old man, Grimnir, gave me this spear when Mimir and the Norns held that council. I told you in the tunnels: he fused the spear with the staff, and it can ..." She shrugged, then finished quietly, "it can do things."

"*Hei*, that's the magic spear, Gungnir," Rudyick stepped into the glade and cautiously approached the Norn and Hospitaller. "I'd know it anywhere. Odin carried it when the world was young, and it never misses."

"Grimnir told me that it had other properties, too," Clarinda said. Rudyick gave a signal of a closed fist and then splayed his fingers before dropping his hand. The twelve members of his patrol moved into the trees and merged into the shadows, vigilantly alert for any sign of the Huntsmen returning or flaring of sorcery. The only sounds, however, were those of Franang Falls and the river rushing through the forest.

Rudyick bent his head for a moment, then leveled his gaze. "I sense nothing beyond you two and the presence of my *Keder*. There's much activity beneath the mountains, though. Probably Hela's *Wilde Jagd* still fighting the dwarves."

"Can we get back there?" Aurelius asked. "I don't like abandoning friends."

"Oh, that's it, I give up!" Ratatosk groaned. He ran up a tree trunk, then along a bough to look upon the group. "We make the effort to rescue both of them, and the first thing he wants to do is visit Hela again."

"Hardly 'abandoning,' I'd say," Clarinda said with some amusement, glad for the silence that had fallen in their minds. She'd ask questions about the Codex and Cerys later. "You were running straight into whatever trap Hela had set for you, and by leaving, I think we foiled her plans—by the way, is that how you always fight? Are you trying for some kind of Viking berserker thing, and hoping that acting *pazzo* will see you through?"

"*Pazzo?*" Aurelius repeated, appreciating the warm tone, but stung by her words. "I'm not crazy. I've survived every fight I've been in."

"*Che stupida logica,*" she muttered, turning toward Rudyick, "and not an answer that gives me much hope if we face her again."

Aurelius recoiled slightly, then snorted incredulously. "I did dive into that river to rescue you, you know!"

"You need to work on your rescues, and maybe follow a bit more quickly before getting distracted by naked witches!" she replied. "Or, didn't you notice that it ended up that we're the ones who had to save you?" She included the company of elves with a wave.

Aurelius looked at the Dark Elf and even at the squirrel above them in an attempt to get some support. "What's the matter with her?" he asked, unsure why she seemed so angry with him.

"Lady Clarinda, I could—" Rudyick began.

"Lady Clarinda?" Aurelius asked.

Clarinda ignored the Hospitaller and nodded at the Dark Elf.

" — if you need it, I could make a *runeporte* to get us close to the Crystal Caves," Rudyick continued, regarding the young people. "But, I agree that your friends might be better served if you're not present. You've escaped from Hela—that's not an easy feat to accomplish."

"And, we've done it twice, now." Clarinda leaned on her quarterstaff and nodded at Aurelius. "I told Rudyick about both of our encounters with Hela," she said, seeing the confusion on the young knight's face, "and that we're trying to get to Mount Glittertind and meet Mimir and the Norns."

Her tone still seemed laden with annoyance, though, and he had some good guesses at its source. It could be the fact that the Codex Lacrimae spoke to Santini in the voice of a woman, or the goading the Dark Book had done by the constant mention of Cerys.

Aurelius dismissed both sources, knowing how he felt about Clarinda. Couldn't she see that the Codex's presence in his mind bothered him in a way she could never understand, not least because the woman seemed quite comfortable in sharing his most intimate thoughts with anyone who could listen?

"—and we can still get to Mimir's Well, Servius," Clarinda was saying, "but we're not taking Andvari's route through the Crystal Caves."

"Nor by using the *Brisinga* necklace," Aurelius noted, grateful that she again seemed to be speaking normally to him. "That man, Kenezki, took it from you."

Clarinda grimaced. "They were waiting for me at the shoreline. I took Farbauti's hand to get out of the river, and then Kenezki came from the woods." Her face flushed. "I've had to suffer that pirate all the way from Constantinople to Caesarea—to find him, to find Padre's killer ..."

"Kenezki's the one who killed your father?" Aurelius prompted when the pause lasted too long.

She nodded, made an inarticulate sound of frustration, then finished, "Well, to find him here with Farbauti ... ah, give me a second." She wiped her eyes. "The murder wasn't solely

Kenezki's doing. Farbauti's one of the Huntsmen whose plans led my father to Caesarea. It's almost too much to bear."

"I noticed that the Codex seemed to play on that pain," Aurelius said. "It has a serious hate for the Norns, especially Urd."

"You may discuss these things later," Rudyick interrupted. "We need to move. I suggest that we take the route through the Weeping Wood. The forest's magic will cloak both your presences—for a while, at least."

"Except for the *ghasts*, *Draugr*, and *Kludden*, you cretinous son of a liar and criminal," Ratatosk taunted from above them. The animal scampered closer when he saw the confused looks on Aurelius and Clarinda's faces.

"*Ghasts?*" Santini repeated, incredulous. "I've heard about spiders, but *ghasts?*"

"They're spirits of those who've died, but who aren't yet in Valhalla, nor settled into an afterlife in any of the Nine Worlds," Rudyick said.

"More than just spirits." Ratatosk alit again on Clarinda's shoulder. "*Ghasts* are confused enough on a good day—they're often still denying to themselves that they've just died—but they become enraged when they see live folk. Their screams get louder when anybody walks through the forest. They can attain corporeal form while in the regions between Skull-Cradler's Grove and the Jotunheim Mountains, exactly where you'll be headed if you listen to Elfidiot here. Trust me, I've seen it happen. They'll drive you into those regions, if you're unwary, and often people are so terrified of the *ghasts'* aspects that they'll run blindly into the trap."

"We're not going to scare easily," Aurelius said.

Ratatosk nodded at the Midgardians, then continued: "I almost forgot how arrogant you mortals can be." The squirrel looked at the entire group. "Fine. I'm done. Go ahead and take that route. You'll make things easy for Hela—if I were her, I'd just have a few *vampyrs* fly above the trees and seek the places where the *ghasts* are falling upon you and then swoop down ..."

"Isn't Mount Glittertind on the other side of that river?" Clarinda interrupted. She'd kept her gaze fixed on Rudyick. "If Ratatosk's correct about these *ghasts* and other threats, wouldn't it be simpler to ford the river, then make our way through the mountains?"

Rudyick shook his head. "*Nein.* Frost giants roam in the borderlands and mountain passes between Svartalfheim and Jotunheim. You don't seem to appreciate the urgency here. Hela and her horde will emerge from Nidaveller soon. We must get to the Weeping Wood."

"Oh, that's much better, Elf," Ratatosk chattered. "Avoid the *ghasts*, but lead them instead to a forest filled with undead Vikings and hell-hounds the size of horses!"

"Those would be the *Draugr* and *Kludden*?" Aurelius asked.

"I don't know, boy," the squirrel said in a petulant voice. "You just bragged about not scaring easily, so why don't you tell me after you've met them?"

"No, hold on." Clarinda said. "You're not telling us something, Rudyick. To where does this Weeping Wood lead?"

"I told you earlier," the elf replied. "The forest path leads to a trail that eventually opens onto the Bandet Road. We'll hike a half-league on that, and reach Vesleisström Pass. From there we'll find one of the cave entrances into Glittertind."

"No, I said, hold on, Rudyick," Clarinda said again, exasperated. She tried to focus on the place in her mind that would compel veracity. "Speak truly: before we reach the edge of the Weeping Wood and the path to Glittertind, is there anything (or anyone) to which you're trying to direct us?"

From the shadows of his cowl, Rudyick's eyes regarded her fiercely.

"Speak."

All in the glade heard the sorcery of the Norn's Speech take hold. The elf had no choice before the Norn's power. "We'll come to the *Sviddengen*," Rudyick admitted.

"The Scorched Meadow?" Clarinda repeated, translating from the Norwegian. "And what do you want to do at this *Sviddengen*? Specifically, what do you want to do that involves Aurelius and me?"

"I want to destroy the Codex Lacrimae and restore my people to the lands of Alfheim from their exile in Svartalfheim."

The words seemed wrenched from Rudyick, and Aurelius shook his head in perplexed amusement at Clarinda. "Remind me never to let you ask me too many questions," he murmured.

"That decides it," Clarinda said simply. "We'll take our chances with the river and the mountains." She bowed curtly to Rudyick. "We part ways here."

"*Aspetta*, Clarinda—please, wait," Aurelius said.

"For what, Servius? I've been told that there's a possibility you are the Codex. It's already talking to you, which I assume means that, given the frontispiece and the prophecy, you've lost a friend?"

"Pellion." The knight grimaced. "I couldn't be sure, but when we were in the battle I saw him drop after getting wounded by Morpeth." Then Santini's eyes widened as he registered what she'd said. "Wait. What do you mean that there's a possibility I'm the Codex? What does that mean? You don't think I'm the one talking to myself, do you?"

"Until we learn more," she continued, pretending not to hear his questions, "I don't think it's a wise course to follow a Dark Elf some place where he intends to betray us and destroy the Codex. Let's take our chances in the mountains."

"Fools." Rudyick said with confident assurance. "You'll never find the proper passes from here without me. You won't even have to worry about an attack by frost or storm-giants — the snowfalls alone will do their work if you don't know the way."

"There's a point," Aurelius observed. He turned to Clarinda. "Do you know the way?"

She frowned, but remained silent for a moment, thinking. "No. I know that it must be beyond those mountains to the east, past the river—I could see it from that bank—and I've memorized Glittertind's tunnels, but, no. I don't know how to get there." She shook her head dismissively. "I know he rescued us, but I don't trust him, Servius."

"I don't intend to take either of your lives," Rudyick said, "nor do I intend to put you in a situation that would necessarily endanger them—"

"Wow, those are very reassuring phrases," Ratatosk said sarcastically. "Do you give legal advice, too? That is, when you're not trying to trap youngsters in haunted forests?"

With blurring speed, Rudyick threw a dagger upward at the

squirrel. Its tip buried deeply into the branch where the animal had been resting, but the Guardian of Yggdrassil was gone.

"—as I was saying," Rudyick continued, "I *do* intend for the Codex Lacrimae to pass from the Nine Worlds. If we return to the *Sviddengen* where it was made, there's a chance that we can unmake it."

"I say we follow him and risk it," Aurelius told Clarinda. The relief that he wasn't hearing the Codex anymore lent urgency to his voice. "I've only known of this book, this 'magic,' for a little while, and I'd be rid of it any way we can." He caught her eye. "I mean, get rid of it so long as doing that doesn't kill me. I don't understand what you meant by saying that I'm the Codex because I don't feel any different at all."

"That's no surprise," Ratatosk said. "Nor did Merlin, Taliesin, nor anyone else who employed the Codex Light. Delusional mortals. You know so little of yourselves that ..."

"I'm supposed to get you to Mimir's Well," Clarinda protested. "There might be danger there, also, but at least between Mimir, Grimnir, and the Norns, we can rely on much wisdom."

Rudyick snorted. "If I were you, I'd be careful of such 'wisdom.'" He glanced upward and reached a hand toward his weapon; the dagger shook and flew back into his hand. "While the Norns perhaps foresee the future, they also oversee the doom of us all."

"I've been with the sisters for only a few months," Clarinda admitted, "but they seem genuinely concerned about protecting Aurelius and keeping the Nine Worlds safe from whatever harm the Codex Lacrimae is supposed to bring."

Rudyick shook his head. "I say, again: fools. You're unaware of the full peril of the Dark Book, yet you're willing to bring it, no, even worse," he waved his spear at Aurelius, "you're willing to bring him within reach of those who will most certainly seek to use its power for their own gain. At least in the *Sviddengen* we know what will happen—it'll be destroyed."

"Can you guarantee that?" Clarinda asked archly. "Have you even thought through all the consequences if you were to succeed?"

Rudyick glared, but hesitated before replying. "No, I can't vouchsafe entirely that my plan will work. Nor do I know what, if any, effects that destruction would have on the other codices, nor even on Svartalfheim as it exists in this dimensional plane. I do believe, however, that I'm correct about the spells and conditions needed to consign it into Ginnungagap." He hesitated, not needing to hear her unspoken question. "But, no, Lady Clarinda, I can't guarantee its complete destruction."

"With the kind of power it's supposed to have," Clarinda said, "I believe that we need to be more certain than that." She herself paused, taking in both Rudyick and Aurelius. "I think we need to go to Mimir and the Norns. In all our discussions about the Codex—and especially at the last council—the Norns have sounded exactly like you, Rudyick. They want to be rid of the thing, but they also don't want Servius to die."

"We really need to talk about that council, Clarinda," Aurelius said. "I wasn't very reassured by what you said Ratatosk predicted, and—"

"Ho, Andvari! Sie sind da!"

The elves surrounding the wood suddenly burst into action as a gigantic, wet wolf erupted from the trees with a woman astride its back.

CHAPTER 9

The Children of Loki

"Andvari, they're here!" Skade shouted. "This way, Dwarves!" She leapt lightly to the ground, rolled, and rose with a dagger raised in front of Rudyick.

Fenris began to transform back into human guise as he approached the group by the fire. Apart from being drenched, the couple were unmarked from their battle in the caverns.

"Ah, wonderful," Rudyick groaned, "*Die Schlampe und ihr Wolf* have found us." He barked an order to the patrol, and another hand signal brought archers from the trees.

"Dark-Elf Dog, did you just call me a slattern?" Skade roared, rearing back with her blade. Her dwarven escort raised swords and axes, and Rudyick's elves brought spears to attack positions. "Say that again to my face, you wanking, stretched-out gnome!"

"Ja, sagte ich, du bist eine Schlampe." Rudyick lowered his cowl and stared defiantly at her.

She launched herself at the tall elf, but he blurred from sight. However, Skade seemed to have recognized him in the half second before he faded. "Wait, Rudyick?"

"Have you seen your husband, Njörd, during the last century?" Rudyick asked as he appeared behind her. "Mate for life, eh, *du Schlampe?*"

"That's unkind, Rudyick," Skade said, lowering her dagger. "It's been so long ..."

"Rudyick, that's enough," Fenris growled. "We haven't time for this—"

"Hah!" Rudyick sneered, regarding Skade with contempt. "No, it turns out not a mate for life. You were with Njörd for five years until this werewolf lopes along und—*was?* What was it, Skade? Were you home alone too often because Njörd took his guardianship of the sea seriously? Did you get bored skiing in the mountains by yourself?"

"I said enough of this, Rudyick," Fenris warned.

"Nein, Loki-Son. No. You and I had our discussion before you went ahead with this thing." The furious elf returned his attention to Skade, and his voice lowered. "What else should I call you, woman? Certainly not 'friend,' not anymore. Not ever again."

"Well, this is getting awkward," Ratatosk said. "I love it!"

The squirrel hopped onto an overhanging branch, and chittered. *"Hei,* Santini, since you and your buddies all seem to have forgotten the danger you're in, and since you seem utterly content waiting around for *ghasts*, *Kludden*, or Huntsmen to show up, be useful: go find some rose hips and pine cones for me to nibble on. I don't want to miss any of this!"

Aurelius raised one hand to silence Ratatosk, but kept the other on his sword as he watched the strange reunion.

"... come now, Rudyick," Fenris was saying, "Skade's got a point. It's been so long, is there really any reason to hold this grudge?"

"I was at your marriage, Skade," Rudyick continued, still ignoring the wolf-man. "Your real marriage. For Odin's Sake, I stood witness for you! Have you even talked to Njörd? He's gone mad. Waves still crash four times the height of a man at the Lofoten Islands in his grief over losing you."

Skade's face had turned ashen, and Clarinda impulsively wanted to comfort her, but she remained still, sensing the same danger Aurelius had.

"It wasn't that simple, Rudyick," the Huntress replied, her voice surprisingly calm. "You never let me explain, and Njörd tried to kill both of us when we went back to talk to him. I searched for you even longer." Fire lit in her eyes. "*Und,* speaking of that marriage, you stood for me, Elf, remember? Not Njörd. We were friends long before I even met him!"

The dark elf's eyes flashed with rage. "I was a friend of you both!"

"I would've explained," she said.

"When? Certainly not when Njörd and I returned after we stopped Dietrich and the Dark Druids from using the sarsen stones off Norfolk. You were gone."

"That was my fault," Fenris interjected. "I was needed in the

First Mage War, and Skade—" He stopped himself, looking at his mate.

Rudyick glared at both of them, then fixed on Skade. "*Und,* Skade chose to go with you, with not even a note left for Njörd. Why?"

"Perhaps she was bored with the sea?" Ratatosk offered. "I can see why you wouldn't be bored with Njörd, Rudyick. Oh, that's kind of good. It rhymes: 'bored with Njörd!' I'll have to use that on him when I see him again."

The squirrel stood upright on its hind-legs. "Look at you, Dark Elf! You're almost as melancholy as that ocean king on a good day. You know, I've always wondered if there was something more to your and Njörd's 'friendship' than druid-hunting. Face it: maybe this wench was just too hot-blooded for the direction of Njörd's cold tides, if you know what I mean." The squirrel made one of its mocking sounds, a staccato of squeaking chirrups. "Or, better, she realized that she couldn't compete with you two boys always chasing warlocks and witches around the North Sea, and finally decided to have a romp with a wolf who'd chase her."

Rudyick frowned, not even bothering to discount Ratatosk's taunting as he squared himself.

"Was that it, Skade? Did you simply yield to an impulse while your husband was trying to prevent the druids' conquest?" He looked in disbelief at Fenris, then back to her. "Or, do you just have some need to be part of a family that's fated to help destroy the Nine Worlds?"

"Says the son of a Codex creator," Ratatosk sniped. "Keep some perspective, Rudyick. At least Fenris is fated to kill only

Odin. Your people helped create Artifacts that will burn the universe in flames." The squirrel took in the group. "To repeat: I am loving this. Nidhogg the Dragon and I never have this kind of drama. All he does is gnaw on the roots of Yggdrasil and growl at me." Everyone kept ignoring him, so Ratatosk shook his head. "It's a wonder that the Nine Worlds aren't on fire already with you lot serving as their defenders!"

"How can you be with him?" Rudyick asked Skade. "Is the rodent correct? Was it something more primal than I'd care to believe? Perhaps, besides becoming a wolf, you discovered that he can change parts of his body at will and ... urggh!"

At the last comment, Fenris moved at a speed that matched the elf's and grasped Rudyick by his nape with an enormous hand. "Apologize to my mate, or spend the rest of your immortal life with a broken neck," the burly man growled. "I think the condition would be an improvement, but you're a vain one, aren't you?"

"*Dann brechen sie, denn ich habe nur die Wahrheit sagen!*" Rudyick gurgled. "Break it, I say. I'd ... expect no less from you, damned one!"

"Fenris, *Bitte*, release him," Skade urged, surprising both Clarinda and Aurelius by the quality of deep emotion in her voice. "This vulgarity isn't like him, but ... he's correct about you, me, and Njörd. He speaks the truth—his version of the truth—but it is truth."

Fenris dropped the elf, who stumbled away. Skade stared at Rudyick, waiting for him to compose himself. "As I said, we came back, Rudyick. We looked for you. There are things that need to be explained—"

"Your actions are explanation enough, Skade," Rudyick snapped. He glared at those gathered in the clearing. "I ... do apologize for calling you that name in public. I'm better than that. I want to be better than that."

Rudyick straightened his jerkin and moved away to give orders to the leader of his *keder*. Skade nodded to Fenris, then crossed her arms under her chest and bowed her head, lost in thought.

Both elven and dwarvish soldiers stood down and backed away to form a defensive ring, as if the commanders of each squad had tacitly agreed to leave Andvari's companions to sort things out for themselves.

As elemental as ever, Fenris grunted, then, after assuring himself that the dark elf and his wife were done exchanging words, pushed long wet locks from his face and grinned at Clarinda and Aurelius. "Well, now that that reunion's over, Hallo, again, my friends!"

"Fenris?" Aurelius asked cautiously. Besides being completely taken aback by the intensity of a very private revelation about Skade and Fenris, the Hospitaller also knew that less than an hour ago the man had been enthralled by Hela and poised to unleash his lupine self on the company.

"Worry not, I'm fine," the wolfish man assured them, reading the concern on their faces. "Hela and her demons left once you both disappeared—I've not seen her that angry since Balder escaped from the Dead Lands a thousand years ago."

"This is ridiculous, and now I'm partly at fault for our delay," Rudyick said in total disgust, his tone returning to its familiar haughtiness. "With all your shouts and racket, we shouldn't have long to wait before Hela, the *Wilde Jagd*, and all those wretched dwarves appear."

More rustling in the forest heralded the arrival of Andvari, Traeg, Delling and the rest of the dwarves, who all burst into the clearing, thoroughly as wet as their comrades before them.

Orange sorcerous energy glowed around Andvari's staff, but upon identifying the group, he lowered the weapon. Its power faded and resumed the aspect of normal wood.

"Oh, hello, all," Andvari said, surprised. "*Hmph*, I sensed a Huntsman here, und … something else."

"It was Farbauti and Kenezki," Clarinda said, after giving a hug to Traeg when the woman had crossed the clearing to greet everyone.

"Give them a moment, Andvari—you'll be able to meet them in person!" Rudyick snapped. "Do you think that they won't take steps to counter your weapon, Codex Wielder, and return anon?"

"Ah, *Guten Abend*, Rudyick. I also sensed a friend here, and I'm pleased that it's you."

"*Guten Abend*, Andvari," Rudyick said, and gave a slight bow and murmured greeting to Traeg.

"Now, then; who's Kenezki?" Andvari asked Clarinda, with a glance at Rudyick. "Not one of the Thirteen Huntsmen, to be sure? *Hmph*. Kenezki. Don't know him. I thought that Morpeth usually traveled with Farbauti?"

"Morpeth?" Aurelius repeated, "A Morpeth just killed one of my friends."

"Ah. They've split forces, then?" Andvari nodded, then peered at Fenris. "What think you, Jotun-Son? Kenezki sounds like someone we should know."

Aurelius flinched at the title, but said nothing. Hadn't the Codex also called him by the same title?

"I've met a Kenezki before, but not in Svartalfheim." Skade raised an eyebrow at Fenris. "Weren't we near the fjords when we met that cobbler?"

Fenris's own brows converged thoughtfully. "*Ja*, that's it. I knew the name sounded familiar. There was a cobbler named Kenezki at the Viking village near the Fjords of Asgard." His eyes widened. "Skade, hold a moment. Do we know where my brother is?"

Skade had tried to move closer to Rudyick, but the elf had made himself inaccessible by standing amidst a few of his own soldiers. "No, you can't think that ..." Skade replied, and then shook her head as she gave up on Rudyick. "No. Well, no, I don't know where he is."

"Skade," Fenris persisted. "It's him. I feel it. Kenezki. That's him. Can't you feel it?"

She bent her head, thinking the idea through. *Ja, ja, es ist möglich, meine liebe* ... There are many seas in the worlds and he can choose whither he will. *Aber*, why? He's been quiet for centuries."

"The Codex—" Fenris began.

Clarinda didn't like what she was hearing. "Hold on, are you saying you have a brother? That Kenezki's your brother?"

Fenris nodded. "In disguise. His name's Jormungand."

"*Aspetta*," Aurelius exclaimed, "isn't that the name for the Midgard Serpent?"

"Alas," Fenris said ruefully, "my family is, literally, from Hel."

"Kenezki fled through a rune-gate and dove into the Sea of Muspelheim," Clarinda said.

"Ja ... und?" Fenris scoffed.

"The waters were boiling from volcanoes and lava!" Aurelius exclaimed.

"Ha! Mild temperatures to one with his scales," Fenris shrugged. "Those plates are denser than the densest armor." Clarinda and Aurelius stared at him in disbelief. *"Was?* This shouldn't be a surprise, *meine Freunde.* Father is a fire-god and mother a frost-giant—even I might be able to survive the seas of Muspelheim."

Clarinda frowned in confusion. "How's that possible? I've read that the Midgard Serpent encircles the entire world? I've traveled with Kenezki from Constantinople to Caesarea—sat with him in a bar, fought him in a shipwreck ... he acts like a snake, but how can he be the Jormungand?"

Fenris grew while she spoke, transforming into his towering lupine form. From the height of treetops, he gazed down at the Norn. "Neither Loki nor his children are bound into any shape, Clarinda," Fenris growled. "Besides being the Trickster, our father is the greatest shape-changer in the Nine Worlds. Although my brother hasn't taken human form in centuries, he's just as capable of changing his shape as Hela or me."

"Oh, the family reunions you must have," Ratatosk said, appearing at the base of a tree. "One can only imagine your childhood—Jormungand slithering on the beach, Fenris ripping apart cattle for breakfast, and Hela playing nearby with corpses for dolls!" He chattered and shook his furry head. "We're just fortunate that Hela's not around, or you'd be chasing all of us around these lands!"

"Hmph." Andvari glared at Aurelius. "It seems clear to me

that—given the company you're keeping and the enemies you've made—there seems to be little doubt. You might, indeed, be the Codex Wielder foretold in the Codex Regius."

"The King's Book?" Aurelius said. "I've not heard of it."

"No reason that you should have," Andvari said. "You're from Midgard, not Alfheim— elvish works usually don't make their way across the Ginnungagap between the worlds."

"The Codices are a collection of books," Clarinda explained, and then flushed.

Aurelius stared at her, recalling remarks by both the Codex Lacrimae and Rudyick about Codices. He hadn't misheard them in the rush of events, and he cursed himself for not paying more heed. "Codices? A collection? You mean, there's more than one Codex Lacrimae?"

"Oh, Odin's Eye," Rudyick cried, gazing at the glade's edge as if he expected their enemies to return any moment. "We don't have time for this!"

"No, there's only one Book of Tears," Clarinda replied, keeping her eyes on Aurelius, "but there's a collection of magical tomes that the kings and queens of Alfheim used to keep in the Fair-Boughed Hold." She paused. "I learned all this at the—"

"Don't say it, Clarinda," the knight warned.

"—council at Mimir's Well," she finished, wincing at the irritation that flared on his face.

"That's it," Aurelius said heatedly, "I don't care if all the Huntsmen in Muspelheim come here, we're going to talk about that meeting!"

Ratatosk squawked in dismay. "It might not help you much,

even if she does explain because I don't think even she knows what they are. Not if she thinks the Codices are still in the Fair-Boughed Hold for use by whomever wants to read them."

Andvari had continued to look speculatively at the Hospitaller, still musing as if he'd heard nothing being said around him. "*Ja*, that must be it," he continued, "you're the Lore Master foretold or, at least, everyone thinks that you are. Certainly enough of the higher powers do. If Jormungand is, indeed, involved here and disguised as this 'Kenezki,' then all the children of Loki—Hela, Fenris, and the Midgard Serpent—they've committed themselves to an involvement in your affairs."

"Hela's made it quite clear that the only rules she's following are her own," Skade said.

"That attack was in complete violation of the covenants that keep peace between the worlds," Andvari retorted. "You can't have rulers juxtaposing entrances hither and thither—chaos would reign!"

Skade shook her head. "No one's going to punish her, Andvari. She knows that."

Fenris folded his arms across his chest. "I agree. I've been giving more thought to the attack. Her trick of reorienting the tunnel isn't the most curious thing about it—I've seen her fashion *runeporten* like that many times—what's strange is the fact that she retreated so quickly. You all have my greatest respect, but she could've taken us instantly to the underworld and perhaps finished us there. In seeking the Dark Book, something about her has changed—she's not acting with the full powers at her command."

"She seems the same to me," Skade said, "and for all her alliances, the only loyalty to which she's always held true is the one with your father."

Andvari grunted, regaining a semblance of calmness. "Loki's involvement would explain her letting Santini live and escape."

"*Aspetta, aspetta.* Why'd you all begin talking about Loki?" Clarinda interrupted, then reddened, aware that her surprise at their conversation made her blurt the words. "I mean," she continued in a quieter tone when the group had paused to look at her, "he is still imprisoned, isn't he? He hasn't made a direct bid for the Codex himself, has he?"

"No, he's still bound," Fenris assured her.

"We just returned from that cavern less than a fortnight ago," Skade said. "Loki's in agony, but he's there."

"Clarinda, Skade, *Bitte!*" Traeg hissed. "*Sei still, bevor der Betrüger hört!* Both you girls use that name too freely in dark places like this!"

"Let the Trickster hear us," Skade retorted (albeit in a lower tone). "I'm not afraid of him." She glared at Fenris, who'd also shot a warning glance her way. "*Was, mein Mann?* You know I'm not afraid of him, and none of us should be! I've met Loki enough times to realize that the surest way to fight him is to laugh at him."

"I wouldn't laugh too loudly," Andvari said. "One of his children is with us yet."

"Careful, Arch-mage," Fenris growled. "I fight beside Master Santini. I've no designs upon him."

"*Ja, ja,* I think it safe to say that we all do," Andvari muttered dismissively. He cusped a hand under his bearded chin, thinking, then added, "But, we've also seen how Hela still holds sway over you."

"Not when he's parted from her," Skade said. "After Hela left, Fenris did most of the fighting against the Wilde Jagd."

"Whatever their motivations," Andvari said to Aurelius, "my point stands: all three children of the Codex's creator are in motion around you. Let's suppose that this Kenezki is an agent of Jormungand, or—less likely to me, but only because I've not personally seen him take human form—"

"He can and has!" Skade interrupted.

"—I bow to the brother and in-law," Andvari continued unruffled, "but, let's even allow that Kenezki is Jormungand himself. Whether agent or serpent, someone seems to be in an alliance with the Huntsmen. If so, it's not illogical to suppose that the Huntsmen's master, Surtur, the Lord of Muspelheim, is also involved. None of the Thirteen has ever hunted without his oversight."

The wizard, apparently galvanized by his own thoughts, strode to the remains of the fire. "Enough of this for now. There's enough residual energy for a return portal. I believe that Rudyick's correct—they may come back at any moment." He turned to the elf. "Which way would you recommend, Friend?"

Rudyick bowed, and took a breath to speak before Clarinda interrupted him.

"Andvari—we can't trust him. He wants to destroy the Codex, which means he wants to kill Santini! Let's try for a way through the mountains. I don't know the way, but surely you—"

"Relax, dear," Traeg said, with a motherly smile. "Certainly Rudyick wants to destroy the Codex Lacrimae—we all do."

Clarinda stopped short. The faces of those she thought friends suddenly became the features of potential enemies. "You all want to ...?" she repeated slowly, trying to work through her surprise.

"The Nine Worlds would certainly be better for its loss," Skade said.

"Please don't give me such a look, Mistress Trevisan," Traeg warned with a smile, "it wrinkles your face like a prune and will age you prematurely. Saying that we want to destroy the Codex Lacrimae is *not* the same thing as saying we want to kill Master Santini here."

"Careful, little mother," Andvari continued. "No promises— it might entail more than we know." He, too, smiled conspiratorially at Aurelius. *"Sie verstehen, nicht wahr?* You do understand, don't you? I don't want any of us making false assumptions. Indeed, if we were sketching this on parchment, there's an off-chance one diagram might see us becoming enemies, eh? Wouldn't want you to think that we're deceivers, and you didn't get fair warning, eh?"

"I ...," Aurelius faltered, then cleared his throat before replying numbly, "I stand forewarned."

Clarinda moved closer to the young knight. "You all seem rather callous about this."

"Not at all, dear," Traeg sounded slightly injured. "Not at all—simply realistic."

"What is the danger?" Aurelius asked, looking at Andvari, Fenris, and Skade.

"If you all must continue talking," Rudyick said, completely exasperated, "could we do it while moving? Whatever Kenezki is, we know that Farbauti's a Huntsman. Worse, he's a Huntsman who now knows his quarry." The elf nodded at the hatchet on Santini's waist. "That weapon won't do much good if they return and capture you before you can make use of it."

"*Ja* ... what about that hatchet, Santini?" Skade asked. "I saw you fight with it in Niflheim, but when it flew back to your hand underground, it might be—"

"I'm willing to follow Rudyick's advice here," Aurelius said, stepping forward and pointedly passing over Skade's question. He'd begun to have his own thoughts about the mattock, but didn't want to share them in so large a company. "But, I've rethought things. We should do what Clarinda's been urging and get to Mimir's Well."

Andvari harrumphed and turned back impatiently to Rudyick. "I agree; we'll talk about these things in a little while. Well, lad, what do you say? Which way should we go?"

"Thank you, master," Rudyick said, with grudging admiration. "I'd take them past the *Sviddengen*, to the Bandet Road, and approach Glittertind by way of Vesleisström Pass."

"Ah, I agree," Andvari said. He turned to the company. "Well, you heard the elf; let's go, and quickly!"

"But," Clarinda protested, "we're just doing what he originally wanted to do. He said the *Sviddengen's* where the Codex Lacrimae was created, and that's where he wants to destroy it!"

"Yes, and worth the attempt, I say!" Andvari said enthusiastically. He shook his head at Rudyick. "Although, I believe that it's grown beyond any of the magics that might be left at the Scorched Meadow, I agree that it should be worth a try. If the attempt fails (and young Santini here survives), we can all go to Glittertind and make the descent to Mimir's Well."

"Andvari," Clarinda persisted, striving for a Norn's calm, "I'm not going to let you all try to kill Santini."

"*Grazie*," Aurelius said from behind her with a heartfelt tone—at least someone here was not speaking about him as if his death or destruction were inevitabilities!

"Nonsense, girl," the old dwarf said, striding past her to stand before the young knight. He looked defiantly up at Aurelius.

"Have you agreed that you'll let a friend die?"

"A friend has died," Aurelius said. "His name was Pellion and he was killed by—"

"*Ja, ja, es tut mir leid*, I'm sure, but it doesn't matter who or what did the killing. If you're the one foretold, then any of your friends could die from any causes and the Codex would awaken. The point is, have you said that you'll let a friend die?"

"No. The book keeps asking me to, but—"

"There!" Andvari interrupted, turning toward Clarinda. "We could burn the book with all the Odin-Fire in the Nine Worlds and it still wouldn't harm your young knight—"

Clarinda flushed. "He's not my young—"

"—*und*, the sooner we get moving, the sooner we put friend Rudyick's idea to the test!"

Aurelius took his turn at trying to speak to the spirited arch-mage. "If you'd give her a chance, I think that what Clarinda's trying to say is that Rudyick doesn't seem to be very trustworthy. He seems to have his own intentions regarding the Codex and he's told the truth to her only when she's used her abilities as a Norn to force it from him."

Andvari looked up at the knight with his brown-bearded chin thrust forward defiantly. "Well, of course, he has his own intentions, Whelp! His father and Loki made the Codex Lacrimae! Short of having Volund here himself, who's there that's better in this group to give advice about how to deal with it?"

Clarinda and Aurelius both looked in surprise at the Dark Elf, who glared at everyone as if they all were wasting his precious time.

"By the way, Rudyick, where is Volund?"

"Father and I parted ways after escaping from Old Nick in Alfheim," the elf replied. "He's going to meet us at the *Sviddengen*." He paused and looked warily at Clarinda. "No need to Truth-Spell, Norn. I told him that I'd bring the Codex Wielder." Rudyick moved to stand in front of Aurelius. "Neither my father nor I would do you harm, Midgardian. We seek merely to undo a terrible mistake that has greatly harmed our people. Will you help us?"

"I might be only one of Loki's children," Fenris said, "but, my heart and my voice are my own. I don't want this thing that both of our fathers made in the Nine Worlds any longer." He paused, intent on the Dark Elf. "These matters between us ... between you, Skade, and me—"

"I was speaking to Lore Master Servius Aurelius Santini. We'll not discuss our personal affairs any longer here, wolf."

"You're asking for help, and I'm offering it. *Und*, these matters," Fenris repeated, remaining calm, "we've not seen you for two hundred years, Rudyick, and now we're in a situation where the Codexes, Norns, and your people's fate are larger than any anger or hurt you hold toward Skade and me. I apologize —"

"Enough!" Rudyick roared, the force in his voice momentarily imitating Clarinda's Norn Voice. "I'll not hear this here!"

Fenris grasped the elf's shoulders. "You will. I'm sorry, Rudyick. I can't undo whatever happened to Njörd. I can't (and won't) unmake what Skade and I've created together. But, I can apologize to you. Finally, after all this time, I can apologize to you. More, whether you ever speak to us again, you can take my offer of help in reaching the *Sviddengen*, and perhaps beyond ... whatever it takes to help your people."

"I, too, would help," Skade added softly. "That's where we started, wasn't it? The good parts of our friendship? The good times. Helping your people?" When Rudyick said nothing and didn't look at her, she continued. "As Fenris said, we can discuss other things later, but you know that he and I are ... helpful in a fight."

Clarinda could have sworn she saw a hint of a smile on Rudyick's lips, and only then did he look Skade in the eyes. His features and posture had relaxed from rage into something like thoughtfulness. Huntress and Dark Elf said nothing, but continued to look at each other.

Clarinda heard something in her mind, like a whisper heard on a different floor of a house, and wondered if Skade and Rudyick were communicating silently in something akin to the thought-speech of the Norns.

Whatever the case, the silence became awkward as no one in the large company was saying anything aloud, so Aurelius finally said, "Um ... to answer your question, Rudyick, yes, I'll help you. I don't know how to use the Codex, but at this point I can tell you that I'll do anything I can do to get rid of it."

Rudyick nodded, breaking his gaze with Skade and apparently grateful at the distraction. He raised a questioning eyebrow at Andvari, Traeg, and the other gathered dwarves.

"Well, if you're asking us, you know where I stand," Halfdan grunted. "You and I have sat watch at over a hundred campfires together. I fought with you and your assembled *keders* during the Mage Wars. You've always watched my back, and I'll follow you and Andvari wherever this quest leads."

Andvari grinned and clasped Rudyick's shoulder. "*Gut*, that's all settled, then. Traeg and I are here, too, so let's have no more harsh words among friends, eh? Now, I know the way to the *Sviddengen*, but we'll follow your lead, Lad." The Arch-Mage motioned to Rudyick with his staff.

"While we walk," he continued, "I want to ask you some things that we've not yet had a chance to discuss since you last visited our home. Do you recall that potion you mixed? Well, the funniest thing happened. It did, indeed, give strength and bravery to a luckless man, but the fellow ended up being so foolhardy about proving himself that he got killed. I heard only the end of the story, but it seems that after he drank the magic mead, the patient sought to employ its magic by going to the nearest tavern filled with enemies from a neighboring village and ..."

As the old friends passed from earshot and lead the company from the campsite, Aurelius looked at Clarinda. "*Grazie*, again, for coming back and for getting rid of that voice in my head."

The Norn moved close and whispered, "I may have silenced it for now, but it's still there, Servius, and there are things about the Codex that you need to know."

"How about we just try to get rid of it?" he asked earnestly. "Everyone here seems comfortable with that idea."

"Andvari and Rudyick will try," she said, "but you heard the wizard. He doesn't think that Rudyick's plan will work. No, I believe it's already bound to you. From what I've read and heard about it, if they succeed in destroying the book, you stand a very good chance of dying along with it."

"I suspect the same," he replied, managing a weak smile. "I do appreciate the fact that you were the only one who talked about me like I was a person, not a thing."

She smiled warmly, genuine affection in her next words. "No matter what you hear, Servius—especially when we talk about the council at Mimir's Well—promise me you'll remember that. If you can keep your humanity at the forefront of all this, if you can stay true to those things that make you you, there might be a way to sidestep the snares of fate."

He winced and glanced away.

"What?" she asked, surprised that she'd hurt him somehow. "Did I say something wrong?"

"What if what's there, what's in me ... what if it doesn't meet your expectations?"

"You're in luck, then, Signore," she said, genuinely amused. She impulsively stepped forward to give him a hug. *"Sai...la bellezza dei Nove Mondi...,"* she began to say, then paused, suddenly self-conscious and glad that her face was against his chest so that he couldn't see her.

"Cosa?" he asked, his voice slightly husky from her proximity. *"La bellezza dei Nove Mondi è cosa?"*

His gentle tone relaxed her. She tilted her head to look up at him, and repeated, "I was going to say that the beauty of the Nine Worlds is that, on one of them—Midgard—I've never even met a Servius Aurelius Santini! So you needn't worry on my account. Any expectations I might have of you here are yours to make for when we finally meet back there."

"*Mein Herr und mein Dame,*" one of the two dwarvish rearguard sentries said softly, "we need to join the rest of the group. This forest isn't safe in the dark."

Aurelius nodded at them, but continued to hold her in his arms, wanting to remain only a moment longer in the glow of friendship that they'd found in each other. Friendship, and perhaps a flickering of something more?

CHAPTER 10

The Servants of Veröld Martröd

"Ah, there you are, Children," Traeg reproved with a tsk-tsk when Clarinda and Aurelius caught up with the group. "Come along, we must stay together in this place."

Rudyick, Andvari, and Halfdan were standing with Fenris in a wide space off the forest path and, if various hand-gestures and raised voices were any indication, they were disagreeing about logistics for the march.

Clarinda noticed that Skade stood off to one side, her head bowed as if lost in thought.

"Will we reach the *Sviddengen* soon?" Clarinda asked Traeg, but still regarding Skade. For all the Huntress's brazen personality, she looked as if she could use a friend. "I mean, do you think that we'll reach the glade before true night falls?"

"*Nein, nein.* We've a half day's march, and can't do that before the sun sets." Traeg chuckled. "It's bad enough that our path must take us through the Weeping Wood, but after dark? No, no, no. I think we'll need to find a place to camp within a couple of hours."

"I thought we were in a hurry," Aurelius said. "With a company this large, and the journey less than a half-day's distance, couldn't we travel into the evening and get close to the *Sviddengen*?"

"Servius, I don't think anyone travels in Svartalfheim in the dark," Clarinda said, then sought confirmation from Traeg.

"*Sicher nicht,* surely not," the female Arch-Mage agreed, tsking again. "Look around you, Kinder," she added. "There are worse things than the *Wilde Jagd* in the forest at night."

Aurelius did so, and couldn't disagree—the forest was truly dismal. "Worse than what we've seen?" Aurelius pressed. "I mean, the *vampyrs*, stone giants, and skeletons?"

All three had rejoined the others in the clearing, and the knight opened his conversation to the entire company. "Excuse me, everybody, but I was just telling Traeg that I think we should keep moving as late into the evening as we can. I've got a feeling that if the Codex Lacrimae returns, she's not going to be so easily dismissed."

"Still calling it a she, are you?" Clarinda frowned.

He rolled his eyes. *"Dio, salvami da gelosi ragazze Veneziane!"*

"We're not having this conversation again," Clarinda said, annoyed, "and I'm not a jealous Venetian girl. I just want to make sure that it's not speaking to you without me knowing."

"Even if the Dark Book were speaking to you, Master Santini" Traeg interrupted, her tone brusque, "we're entering the Weeping Wood of Svartalfheim. The greatest of your predecessors would be hard-pressed to battle this world's creatures at night." She turned to her husband. "We've never travelled these woods after sunset, Andvari. Tell him why we have to make camp."

"The forests of Svartalfheim teem with fell creatures, Codex Wielder," Andvari said, grumpily interrupting his conversation with Halfdan and Rudyick. "Besides the *ghasts* and spirits of the damned—phantoms that can haunt your mind and change your memories—there are *Draugr, Kludden*, and *Húð Göngufólk*."

Aurelius glanced at the squirrel, then asked Fenris: "We've heard about *ghasts*, and Ratatosk mentioned Undead Vikings and Phantom Hounds earlier, but there are also *Húð Göngufólk*, 'Skin-Walkers?' What do all these things even mean?"

"I've read about them in the Norn Archives' sections on Svartalfheim," Clarinda added, "but I'm still confused. How are any of these creatures different from the skeletons, cadavers, and dead animals that make up the Wilde Jagd?"

Headshakes and murmurs marked the group. "They're all very, very different, Clarinda," Fenris replied, "and none of these creatures can be lightly dismissed."

"It's as if when Veröld Martröd died," Traeg said, "all the creatures of the Nightmare Realm fled into the Weeping Wood."

"But, what are they?" Aurelius asked, needing clarification that might explain the dread in his allies' voices.

"The *Draugr* are those Vikings who were able to reach neither Valhalla nor Niflheim when they died," Skade said, rejoining the group but standing opposite Rudyick. "Unlike the ghasts, though, Veröld Martröd snatched them at the moment of death, and thus, they serve neither the living nor the dead. Hela would desire to have them as members of her *Wilde Jagd*, but they still live, existing within and outside of time. Their damnation makes them angry and strong."

"They're also huge," Ratatosk warned from a bough nearby. "Not quite the size of a rock-giant, but close enough for mortal folk."

"So, they can be killed?" Aurelius asked.

"They are still mortal," Andvari affirmed.

"*Molto bene*, now, *secondo*," Clarinda said, moving on. "The *Kludden?*"

"The *Kludden* are hell-hounds," Traeg said, "the size of horses and limned in Muspel-Fire. Their fangs are poisonous, and they can phase through solid objects."

"That's not all," Skade said, "even when aflame, the *Kludden* will most often take the form of gigantic black dogs, but don't be deceived; you can never forget that they're monsters, originally taken from the Nightmare Realm when Veröld Martröd gave them shape in the Elder Days. Be wary if you see a blue flame or hear the clinking of chains in the wood. Those signs usually mean that a *Kludde* is nearby."

Aurelius sighed. "And, *terzo*, the Skin-Walkers, or *Húð Göngufólk*? Are they shape-changers like you, Fenris?"

"*Nein*," Fenris replied, "nothing of the sort. The *Húð Göngufólk* are more like the *Sidhe*—"

"The Shee?" Clarinda asked.

"I fought one of them," Aurelius said, recalling his encounter with Cerys. "They create portals into other worlds. Nightmare worlds."

"*Ja*," Fenris said. "The *Sidhe* are the fairy folk who dwell in both Alfheim and Svartalfheim, but the *Húð Göngufólk* are forever intangible and can exist solely by leaping from one body to another, from host to host, like a plague."

"How can you tell if someone's possessed by the *Húð Göngufólk*?" Aurelius asked.

"With great difficulty," Andvari replied, "and sometimes not at all if the *Húð Göngufólk* have been in the host body long enough."

Traeg inhaled deeply, apparently satisfied that her argument had prevailed. She winked at Andvari. "Well, that's that. *Danke, meine Liebe*. Those are the enemies in the woods ahead, and most of them come out at night." She looked at the four dwarvish brothers and Delling. "Very well, boys. You heard it. We'll not be going far in the forest after nightfall. Go help Delling find a campsite and get to work!"

"Work? Work with what?" Delling groused in exasperation. "The carts, the baggage, my pots and pans, they're all back under the mountains!"

He waved a hand at the dark forest. "*Und*, that's not the only problem. All the mushrooms I've seen in this land are the poisonous kind, and we should expect that even the hares and deer in Svartalfheim have black blood and rancid flesh."

"*Bitte, das ist absurd,*" Rudyick said, "I don't know much about mushrooms, but the game here is as edible as in any you'd find in Midgard or Alfheim."

"A good challenge for you, then, Delling," Traeg concluded in a matter-of-fact tone. She motioned again to the Four Winds. "Norðri, Suðri, Vestri, and Austri: array yourselves among both the elven and dwarvish guards, and report to Halfdan and Rudyick, once they've decided upon sentry shifts for the watch."

The matron pointed at the forest road. "In the morning, I expect that Andvari's going to recommend that we take the *Untere Weg* through this part of the woods, and there are places where the descents are quite steep ..."

"We will be taking the Lower Road, my dear," Andvari agreed, but he stepped from behind her, and shook his head at the entire gathering. "But, I'm sorry, Traeg. I agree with young Santini. For all the dangers of the Weeping Wood, there's an urgency here that we can't ignore."

Traeg's face colored in anger. "What are you saying, husband? Surely, we're not going into the forest at nightfall?"

"That's exactly what we're doing," Andvari said curtly, turning to the Four Winds. "You boys, stay together, but let's avoid any wind magic unless absolutely necessary. When you and the wolves start hunting for dinner, stay as close to the path as possible, and, Delling, we'll be eating almost on the run. There's something in the air that I don't like, and not just the threat of returning Huntsmen!"

"We've felt it, too," Vestri said.

"Smells of murder—" Norðri began to say.

" —*und* desolation, madness," finished his twin, Suðri.

Clarinda gave Rudyick a warning look. "We're trusting you, Elf."

Rudyick snorted, but said nothing. Traeg turned from the group, obviously dismayed, but Andvari followed her to the side of the path. Clarinda watched the couple discuss something intently, and then Traeg took a deep breath and touched Andvari lightly on the wrist. The two arch-mages hugged and then parted.

"She's worried, but she knows we've got to do this," Aurelius said quietly.

"I've been here once before," Clarinda said, "with Urd, when she was giving me my first tour of the Nine Worlds, and Traeg's right to be worried."

"You think that those creatures are that bad?" the Hospitaller asked.

"I only saw a few *Draugr* from a distance," Clarinda replied, shivering, "but I'd take fifty skeletons from the *Wilde Jagd* over those three dead Vikings I saw any day."

He reached across her shoulders and gave her a brief hug. "We'll get through this safely, I promise. I'll fight off any monsters that come at us."

She remained in the comfort of his arm, but stared pensively into the dark boughs of the trees beyond the dwarf troops. "Don't get cocky, Santini," she cautioned, and tapped her temple with a couple fingers. "The monsters aren't the true threat here. It's with good reason that they call this forest the 'Weeping Wood.' Huge sections of it were once part of the Nightmare Lord's realm. From what the Norns told me, before Veröld Martröd died at the Fields of Burning Night, one could enter the shadow worlds he created and not recognize the changes until the trap was sprung."

"Well, nightmares can't hurt you, can they?" He grinned, still trying to reassure her.

He chose not to mention what Cerys had said about Veröld Martröd's games and the Otherworld of Annen Verden. He felt as if they had enough to worry about at the moment. So, instead he told her, "I suggest we stay ahead of whatever this particular nightmare's doing and not sleep until we reach Mimir's Well."

He lowered his voice when he saw that she wasn't reassured in the slightest. "Come on, Clarinda. Let's just get this over with. We've escaped cavern, river, and Muspel-fire. We can do this."

She leaned into him, but said nothing as the shadows lengthened on the path before them.

CHAPTER 11

The Misgivings of Elves, Norns, and Dwarves

The march into the forest resumed after the elves and dwarves deployed.

Clarinda couldn't help but notice that, for all the assortment and movement of soldiers, archers, and wolves, the entire company was positioned defensively around her and Aurelius.

Shortly after the expedition began, Rudyick excused himself when one of the *keder* reported findings. Both elves immediately trotted at an angle into the woods.

Fenris took the chance to move next to Aurelius and

Clarinda. "The *Untere Weg* soon becomes very difficult," he said. "It's a dark and tangled wood, my friends. Stay close to the middle of the path and don't be distracted by whatever you see or hear."

"The wolf speaks truly," Rudyick said, returning without the guard. "My elves are starting to see movement half a league off to the east." He sighed. "This isn't a surprise because the darker things can sense movement of this many people. I fear that, ere long, we may be in for a battle."

He raised an eyebrow at Halfdan, who'd just sent a few of his own dwarves into the woods.

"*Ja*," the brigadier agreed. "I'd also add that we've now reached the outskirts of the *Sviddengen* and as we've all warned, it's a dark place."

"All that's gone wrong with our magic has seeped into the ground, wood, and air of this forest," Rudyick explained, his gaze upon Aurelius. "There is no counter to it, so we must pass through here quickly."

Andvari harrumphed. "Don't be distracted by the sights or sounds that might accost you. They come only from your own pasts and can do no physical harm."

"Can we go around it?" Aurelius looked at the trees ahead of him with apprehension. Whispered voices drifted on the wind, speaking in Arabic and intermingled with distant screams.

"No," Rudyick replied, a great sadness in his voice. "The forest is the heart of Svartalfheim. It was built upon the same ruined magic that created the Codex Lacrimae. We attempt to correct that ancient wrong, but the magic keeps failing."

"With this result?" Aurelius was incredulous that the elf

could speak so calmly about the condition of the forest before them. "This entire region seems a desecration, Rudyick. How can you accept it so calmly?"

"Master Santini …" Traeg cautioned, but Rudyick's temper had already flared.

"I've never accepted it, Mortal. My father and I have gone to great lengths to atone for the evil he did. Don't attribute our failures to a lack of trying, nor of willpower. You're part of that attempt, now."

Aurelius's eyes flashed. "I said I'd help you, Rudyick, and I didn't mean to imply that you're responsible for this wasteland. I'm just … shocked at the state of these woods. Remember, my first experience here was Alfheim. The forest there was like something out of a dream."

Rudyick sighed. "I took an insult where none was meant. You wield a powerful magic, Servius Aurelius Santini, a magic that binds elvish enchantments with the sorcery of the gods. In all the tales, the Codices are foretold to cause the destruction of the Nine Worlds, our Ragnarok, and central among those books is the Codex Lacrimae. This is the very reason that I sought you. If you've truly been chosen to wield the Book of Tears, naught else but your help will avail my people or our land."

Aurelius coughed a harsh laugh, partly reacting to a reek that permeated the air with the odor of rancid meat, but mostly in response to the elf's expectations. "I'm also involved in a game where I don't know all the players or pieces." He waved a hand at the blackened and tangled underbrush. "Forgive me if I'm not looking forward to heading into more of that stinking vegetation just so I can get to a 'glade' where you all might try to kill me."

"We've told you that we're not sure what will happen, and Andvari doesn't think that the Codex has bonded with you yet. I agree with him. Isn't it worth finding out, if you have the chance to save my people? To restore this 'desecration' to its former beauty?"

Santini glanced at Clarinda, then shook his head regretfully. How could the elf speak of beauty when black sap ran from the gashed sides of alder trees here like blood from open wounds? "I'm going, Rudyick, but I fear you've got the wrong man. I don't know how to begin to save this place or your people, much less help even my own brethren who are facing two armies at the Krak des Chevaliers."

"I hope that you're mistaken," Rudyick replied, his tone becoming curt, "both for my people's sake, and for the sake of all in the Nine Worlds. Whatever our beliefs, and whether my choice in seeking you proves well or ill, we must pass through the forest."

He nodded at Andvari and Fenris. "I'll take the lead. *Bitte*, keep your attention on me, and make sure that the company doesn't stray from the path."

Aurelius hesitated as Rudyick turned again to the forked path and began to move forward. Clarinda cowled her head and motioned for the knight to do likewise.

"Why?" he asked softly.

"With the hood up, there's less to see and fewer distractions. I've a feeling that this forest is going to produce visions of some kind," she said. "Remember, I've been to part of this wood before when Urd was showing me around."

"About those times with Urd ... you've not told me much

about your training," Aurelius though still disgruntled by the exchange with Rudyick, drew the hood over his head.

Clarinda blinked, seeing in his now-shadowed face the gigantic and mysterious warrior from Mecina.

He lowered his tone, and leaned close to her. "*E*, since they've all made it clear that I'm disposable if the choice comes down to sacrificing me to destroy the Codex, you might want to tell me something of it so that I have some idea of what you've been going through."

She couldn't see his face clearly, but she felt him smiling as he finished, "We're the only consistent allies here. You and me."

"I know, I know," she admitted, impressed that he was voicing an apprehension about the group that had been growing in her. For all the friendship expressed, there was still a reserve in the demeanor of each member of the company that she intuitively realized was fear, fear of what she and Aurelius would do.

"Well, there were many weeks spent learning how to identify the Threads of Fate, and either knit or weave them into the warp and weft of reality ..." she began, then chuckled at his completely confused look.

"The threads of fate? Knitting and weaving reality?" His eyes narrowed. "I'm trying, Clare, but what's that even mean? You're not saying that you believe the Norns control people like strings manipulate wooden puppets?" She paused. "Is that what you're saying?" he asked.

"Not control," she said quietly, "at least, not in the way that you and I'd understand it. Or, at least, not in the way I used to understand it. It's not even really knitting as you and I are familiar with the term; we use the metaphor because its the one that most easily renders ... no, translates the complexities of space-time."

"Space time?"

"Another shortened way of describing what happens when you move between places using the *runeporten*, or how Mimir's Well serves as a nexus in the Nine Worlds—"

"Clarinda ..." Aurelius said, shaking his head, "I know I asked for it, but you've completely lost me."

"I'm just saying that, so far as I've learned, what the Norns do at the Well isn't so much controlling human beings as predicting human actions ... human events. Once a thread becomes strong enough, we decide whether it should be incorporated into reality's texture, or ..."

"Or, you take it upon yourselves to judge if that thread—if that threat—should be cut?" Aurelius guessed.

"Something like that," she agreed, flushing. "Urd's mentioned something about the possibility that some threads can be rewoven into a different direction, but I'm just starting my training.

"For instance, I can use elements of the Well's power, like aspects of the Voice of Command, and I think I can use Battle Speed in a fight, but I'm nowhere near where the real Norns are—they can stop time, and I think that they can access the Well from anywhere in the Nine Worlds, even though they've told me that can only be done with trinkets like the *triquerta* brooches or the *brisingamen* necklaces."

"Kenezki gloated about stealing yours."

"*Buon Dio*, Urd's going to be upset that it got stolen,"

Clarinda said. "I've tried not to think about it, but it's just one more reason to find Kenezki when we have time." She frowned. "Using these devices still doesn't make sense to me. You'd think that, of all entities, the Norns wouldn't be limited by talismans when crossing dimensions ..."

"What's a dimens—" Aurelius began, then interrupted himself. "Forget that. There's been talk about cutting my thread, hasn't there?"

She glanced at him, but couldn't see his eyes in the shadow of the cowl. Thankfully, his voice was calm, without anger. "I can't yet discuss everything that I've learned, Servius," she said, "but there are many possibilities here for you and me. No particular thread seems to be stronger than the other at this point. I believe that Mimir and the Norns are undecided about you at this moment."

He remained silent for a long time, but she couldn't tell if he was frustrated or just thinking about what she'd told him.

"So, getting back to your visit here with Urd," he said finally, waving a hand toward the dark wood, "what was her advice to you?"

"Urd's advice for passing safely through Svartalfheim was the same as Rudyick's: focus on the road." Clarinda smiled, trying to dismiss the idea that she'd been momentarily afraid of him. Oh, how she'd wished she'd not told him to put that stupid cowl over his head.

"If we're staring at Vestri and Austri's feet in front of us," she finished, "hopefully, we'll be through the forest before things get too bad."

The elves and dwarves formed single-file lines on each side

of the road, careful not to step even so much as onto a blade of grass on the fringes.

Aurelius kept his pace so that he could remain with Clarinda, but he was troubled by the discussion about the mysterious Norns, and quietly dreading what awaited him in the forest.

He'd had a difficult enough time in Hela's citadel with its visions of the dead gathered outside the snow-filled windows, but here in the dark woods the Hospitaller felt even more exposed.

Worse, members of the group had made it clear that they'd like nothing better than to destroy the Codex, a book supposedly in the Krak, yet whose voice he'd heard in his own head.

The forest path inclined, and the air warmed steadily as another half hour passed. Rust-colored leaves carpeted the ground, still damp with the musty smells of late autumn. Occasionally, the spaces between a stand of trees thinned, allowing the cold snows of winter that'd been deflected by the leafy boughs to surge downward in swirling flurries that made the travelers quicken their pace until again sheltered by the forest.

Traeg's relaxed tone returned as they helped each other down a bramble-laden declivity. "Andvari must hold you both in some esteem for him to have followed you into the underground river," she said with a twinkle in her eyes. "It's hard enough to recall the last time that my husband bathed, let alone swam, in one of Nidaveller's more challenging watercourses. He didn't intend to lose you!"

"How did that work out?" Aurelius asked Halfdan, genuinely curious about how the battle had ended after he and Clarinda departed. "Did your entire troop just dive into the *Underjordisk Elv* after us?"

The brigadier grunted. "When it was safe."

Aurelius smiled, the soldier in him hearing much unsaid. "Quite an assignment you have here, eh?" he prompted.

Fenris looked back at them. "*Und*, it can't help but make things more difficult when my sister's around to make allies like me ... unpredictable."

"Not at all, Lord Fenris," Halfdan protested. "If I may, none of us would judge a force of nature. You're like a *weird* or a sampo; with those of your power and lineage, one can almost predict that you're going to be unpredictable. *Nein*, milord. Don't be troubled. You gave us all fair warning, and Mistress Skade distracted you until you returned to yourself."

"I appreciate that, Halfdan," Fenris said. "I've gotten so used to folk simply calling me changeling, or traitor, that it's refreshing to hear a perspective closer to mine."

Halfdan pushed aside a stout branch so that Clarinda could pass under it. "Well, my lord, if I may, perhaps that says more about the company you're keeping than about how those among the rank-and-file in the Nine Worlds view you. To tell the truth, we don't often even think much about what you nobility are up to, but when we do, most folk have enough sense to know that you're not like your sister or brother."

Fenris clasped the dwarf on the shoulder, then nodded and turned to hear a report from a growling wolf that had loped off the road to sniff something.

Aurelius again took up the rearguard next to Halfdan. "Where'd the *Wilde Jagd* go?"

The dwarf snorted. "They simply departed. Once Hela disappeared, they fell back into the north and eastern caverns. For our part, we still followed our own retreat protocol—I was the last into the river—but we still lost five good dwarves."

"Is this mission unusual for you?"

"*Nein*. Well, *ja*. Those of us who fought in the Mage Wars have seen, have battled those kinds of rock giants. I'll admit, though, I haven't seen that many giants fighting side-by-side in over two hundred years."

"If we'd stayed in Niðafjöll, we could've avoided such a raid," Austri complained.

"You should've stayed at home," Vestri said. "You're much better dusting books than fighting skeletons, let alone helping us raise the winds. What were you doing, anyway, waiting so long to join us?"

"So long?" Austri protested. "I was a half-second behind you!"

"Takes less time than that for a blade to do its work," Delling said.

Austri snorted. "Always cooking jokes with you!"

"Because he mentions a knife, you think that's a cooking joke?" Ratatosk asked. "He was talking about the battle. A cooking joke would have been, '*Hei*, what did one knife say to his distracted friend?' 'Stay sharp.' Get it? That's a proper ..."

The squirrel, brothers, and Delling continued their bantering.

Halfdan shrugged at Aurelius. "This raid wasn't so bad, Lore Master. Not when compared to the some of the battles I've fought in. *Nein*, what's difficult here is the unpredictability of you civilians." Halfdan smiled. "I've never seen anyone dive into the *Underjordisk Elv*, let alone do what we're doing now: trekking into a haunted wood that most dwarves have only heard whispers about."

Aurelius chuckled. "I'm glad to hear that humans can still surprise you."

The way to the *Untere Weg* became steeper and more difficult and, except for Clarinda and Skade, who had fallen back to speak quietly with each other, the company fell silent. Deep in conversation, the women held their heads were as close together as the treacherous terrain allowed.

When all were again on flat ground, Traeg said to Aurelius, "Brigadier Halfdan and I traveled in different social circles. He may never have swum through the underground rivers, but Andvari and I used to swim through the channels of the *Underjordisk Elv* all the time when we were younger. Of course, I was much lighter then." She patted her well-padded hips. "I never used to worry about getting through some of the tighter chutes but, thankfully, I've my staff now and can blast apart skeletons, *vampyrs*, and any dangerous stalagmites."

That comment started a conversation within the company about the particulars of the battle against the *Wilde Jagd*, and Fenris gave them a clearer idea of how Hela changed the tunnels to redirect them from the Crystal Caves to the outskirts of Svartalfheim.

Skade murmured something final to Clarinda before joining the conversation. "It was a clever ruse," she said. "Hela chose a similar exit passage and made sure it had florescent minerals and crystals that the rock giants could ignite to imitate the *Kristallhöllen*."

"I almost admire the fact that Hela took this much effort in trying to capture you, Master Santini," Andvari said. He led the company with surprising grace in single file through a place where the bracken and undergrowth seemed to be choking the life out of some dying trees. "Let her enjoy that victory. I won't be tricked that way again. Koschey the Deathless and Hela's representatives on the High Council will also hear from me at the next All-Thing."

Halfdan exhaled loudly, disbelieving. "With respect, Master Andvari, I'm not certain that the dwarves will even be allowed at the next council."

That statement caught Austri's attention, and he stopped carping at Vestri and Delling.

"That would be an interesting sight," he grumbled, "elves preventing dwarves from entering the Great Assembly. Have they forgotten the Law Rock of the Dwarves that sits in the center of the chamber? Have they forgotten that it helped create the All-Thing?"

Halfdan shook his head. "They haven't forgotten, Lord Austri, but it's not only the elves who are cautious of our folk."

"What do you mean?" Austri asked, staring at the general down the pince-nez on the bridge of his nose.

"I mean, that the measure isn't solely an elven initiative. I have a close friend who sits in the legislature. She said that a small, powerful group of elven high lords who sit on the Lögrétta have convinced a majority of members from all the worlds to prevent dwarves from entering the parliament. They've even got some of the more civilized of the frost giants on their side."

"Pah!" Sudri exclaimed. "Nobody's going to take them seriously. When the frost giants do manage to elect someone, the representatives seem to bother making an appearance only in off centuries."

"But, why, the suspicion of dwarves?" Andvari asked. "Why now? I've not heard of this, Halfdan. Are they still contesting the fact that we have two kings?"

"*Nein*," Halfdan answered, "but they are criticizing the performance of one of our rulers. They believe that King Högni's failure to stop either the rebellion or the Wrothken brigands has made the dwarves undependable. The recent Myrkridor attacks have given those elf-lords on the council some credibility."

"What do elf-lords care about Myrkridor attacks in our caverns?" Vestri asked.

"They don't," Austri said, "but there have been a few raids into Alfheim during the last couple of months." He glanced at Andvari. "Arch-Mage, it seems as if the rumor I heard in the tavern was true."

Andvari sighed loudly. "I apologize, Austri. I didn't want to believe it, and I should have looked into it. Högni was so obsessed with stopping the Wrothken that I looked the other way."

"But, I still don't understand," Vestri persisted, "we're allies with the elves. Why would some raids by Wrothken or even *Myrkridor* threaten that friendship?" Delling's assistant waved a hand at the shadowed trees around them. "Odin knows that the elves have enough supernatural problems in their own lands."

Andvari looked at Traeg, then at the younger dwarf. "They're afraid of another Mage War, Vestri. The other worlds will trade with us and take our goods, but they still won't come to Nidaveller. They're afraid things are ... destabilizing again."

His wife nodded. "Who can blame them? Dietrich and his army made their way far into Alfheim before the Fields of Burning Night. The old alliance of elves and dwarves still stands, but it's been precarious ever since."

"I wouldn't worry overmuch about that group of elves, even if it is sitting high in the counsels of the All-Thing," Rudyick countered. "I don't know who your source is, Halfdan, but I can take a guess. It's Amari, isn't it?"

Skade whistled. "She's not a witch to be trifled with."

"She's tried nothing for a long while, and had many opportunities," Rudyick said. "I'm not saying that she's completely reformed—the return of the Codex Lacrimae and Huntsmen might yet tempt her to return to old ways—but I can say that watching her in the Lögrétta..."

"*Mi scusi*," Aurelius asked, "but what's a Lögrétta?"

"The legislative chamber of the All-Thing," Andvari replied. "It makes the laws and covenants for the Nine Worlds."

"I've been a member of the voting committee for the last twenty years," Rudyick continued, "and I can tell you that those elf-lords who are rousing folk against the dwarves are up to no good. The rumor I've heard is that they're not even the real threat. There's talk that an outside group is trying to set the elves and dwarves against each other, and using the ambitions of these elves to further a hidden agenda."

Halfdan shook his head. "Master Rudyick, *bitte*. We've heard this kind of thing before, and, for the dwarves, we know that this is exactly the kind of talk that drove Dietrich mad."

"His descent was a bit more complex than conversations about conspiracies, Brigadier," Traeg said, her voice quiet.

Andvari sighed. "He has the essential truth of it. When our council wouldn't listen to him anymore he sought ... others who would heed his warnings."

"Who's Dietrich?" Clarinda asked. "Was he an arch-mage, too?"

"One of our greatest wizards," Andvari replied, "and a dwarf of deep learning and wise counsels who specialized in *weirds* and sampos." He paused, looking sidelong at the Italian youths. "Those are very strange and powerful magics."

"He went bad?" Aurelius guessed.

Halfdan spat on the ground in disgust. "Bad? It's said that the Mage Wars began because of Dietrich's alliance with Taliesin the Warlock, Mogthrasir the Huntsman, and the rest of the Grey Cadre. Thousands of dwarves died in the First Mage War because of Dietrich's error." He shook his head at Andvari and Traeg. "If you'll not say it, masters, I can somewhat understand, but most dwarves can't forgive Dietrich's betrayal. Reputation is everything with our folk, and business still hasn't recovered from those wars."

"How do you mean?" Aurelius asked. "Niðafjöll seemed beautiful and busy, and we saw and heard plenty of mining and work during our journey there."

"That's because Niðafjöll's the capital city of the Southern Kingdom of the Nibelung," Halfdan said. "It and the northern capital of Atlakvida were the first cities to be restored. There are still countless towns and smaller cities in Nidaveller that haven't recovered from the battles over half a millennium past."

"They will never recover," Andvari said.

Rudyick returned to keep pace with Clarinda and Aurelius's companions. "Dietrich wasn't the only arch-mage who went against his own kind," he said.

"You and your father had an excuse, dear," Traeg countered. "Unlike your father, though, at least you were trying to atone for the hand Volund had in creating the Codex Lacrimae."

"It's not just the Book of Tears," Rudyick said. "The central threat to all of us has always been all the Codices." He looked starkly at Aurelius. "If the Codex Lacrimae is allowed to return, how far behind will the others be?" He added glumly. "With our luck, the next one to awaken would be the Codex Vindicta and that combination would really mean that all Hel's broken loose in the Nine Worlds."

The young Hospitaller said nothing, imitating Andvari's lapse into silence.

Finally Andvari said, "Dietrich was desperate. He was convinced that a darkness was threatening the Nine Worlds, but he had no proof to present at the All-Thing."

"That sounds like my own experience with the elven High Council," Rudyick's eyes glittered in the gloom. "Master Andvari and Mistress Traeg," he added softly, "there are many who still remember your roles in finishing the last Mage War. I know that there are many in the dwarf kingdom who still don't completely trust me. If you are able to speak of these matters at the Great Assembly, please remind everyone that, in the end, I did join you and fought against my father, Loki, and the rest."

He turned to Halfdan, who'd been marching resolutely ahead with a grim face. "*Und*, Brigadier, we did fight side-by-side for many years. I believe in my heart that the majority of your people know what would've happened if Dietrich, Taliesin, and Mogthrasir had won the day. They also know that Gunnar and Högni's rule has brought centuries of peace to the Nibelung dwarves."

Ratatosk chattered again from a high branch. "Is this kind of shoulder-slapping how you all find the peace to sleep at night?" The squirrel taunted. "Who says that the Mage Wars are over, eh? The Dark Elf's points are good ones, but I'll throw a couple more gold coins into the pot and add another: why do you all keep speaking as if Dietrich, Taliesin, Mogthrasir, and Veröld Martröd are dead?"

Andvari stopped the march and looked up. The action brought the flanking elf and dwarf guards into a high defensive alert, but respective hand signals from Rudyick and Halfdan restored peace. The Arch-Mage's eyes narrowed. "Do you know something we don't, Guardian?"

Ratatosk chittered. "Wrong question, Andvari. You should know better. I'm going to go see Nidhogg." Then the squirrel leapt upward into the shadows and disappeared.

Fenris growled. "Typical. Cryptic barbs, then a fade."

Andvari exchanged glances with Traeg and Rudyick. "Well? A taunt, or something more?"

Traeg replied first. "We were there, Andvari. It's been over five centuries, and we've heard nothing. They're dead, or beyond reach."

"But, my friends," Rudyick said softly to the couple. "One of the codices is returning, and the Norns have done the unimaginable in adding a fourth to their number." He nodded toward Aurelius and Clarinda.

Clarinda gaped. "What do you mean 'unimaginable?' I'm just an apprentice who's supposed to replace Urd." Her response elicited chuckles from the company, and Clarinda flushed. She looked to Skade, who wasn't laughing.

"I'm sorry, Clarinda," Skade said, and the menace in her eyes quieted the group. "We all just assumed you knew."

"Knew what?"

"That there's never been an 'apprentice' for any of the Norns."

"What? Of course, there has!"

"Really," Skade asked, "who?"

"I don't know! Urd just told me..."

"Told you, what, exactly?"

Clarinda's throat closed. She took a moment and reflected on everything that Urd, Skuld, and Verdandi had ever said to her. "I mean, she ... they, they've all foretold that I'm to be replacing Urd when she died."

"Replacing the most powerful of the Norns, Fate herself, in a foretold moment of Fate's Death, and you think that's an apprentice position?"

"It's not my fault for thinking that way," Clarinda said defensively. "They've been training me since the first day they brought me into the Nine Worlds."

Skade shook her head. "My understanding of the Norns is that, in much the same way as a Codex Wielder, you can't be trained for the position. You either are, or you aren't."

"Then what have I been doing for three months?" Clarinda asked, irritated.

Skade shrugged. "Ask Urd the next time you see her, but I

doubt even she'll tell you. The Norns are ... you are always very mysterious about your ways, and perhaps that's how it should be, but I'd advise not to make the mistake of thinking that your role with them is solely to replace Urd."

"More likely," Rudyick mused, "that role's to take an arrow that Skuld's foreseen plunging into her sister's heart."

"There can't be four Norns, Clarinda," Skade said. "I don't know what they've got planned—"

"Urd's foreseen her own death!" Clarinda exclaimed.

"—but I've never heard that a Norn can die," the Huntress finished. "Take my advice, or leave it, just be cautious."

"Andvari," Rudyick said, "heed my words. The codices might be returning, and the Norns are behaving unpredictably. Forget that I earlier expressed fears about the Codex Vindicta. All we need for a return to the Elder Days is to have the druids and witches reappear, with Loki and Volund waiting for us when we arrive in the *Sviddengen*."

"About Loki, how did he and Volund create the Codex Lacrimae?" Aurelius asked of the general group, trying to glean who knew the most about the subject.

No one replied, and the company traveled in an awkward silence for a brief time.

"What did I say?" Aurelius asked Clarinda in confusion.

She shrugged and whispered back, "There are relationships and explanations here that go back farther in time than you can imagine; farther, I think, than many, many of our lives put together. You've put the question to them. Let's wait to see who answers."

CHAPTER 12

The Weeping Wood of Svartalfheim

i. Loki, the Dark Elves, and the Runes of Creation

Leaves rustled across the floor of the forest. A cold, piercing wind blew through the trees, wailing in ways that seemed to carry the voices of doomed, fell folk. For Clarinda, the moaning and keening of the air currents left no doubt how the forest got its name.

Great, blackened briars laced themselves through toppled husks of trees felled long ago probably by blasts of lightning. Ruined trunks lay everywhere, many collapsed against other trees that, while still erect, had rotted into spindly, wretched forms. Crowded close together, they seemed to choke the life from the entire surroundings except for the shadows.

Living boughs, stripped bare of bark, lined the right-hand path. Their crooked branches stretched plaintively into the darkening sky, as if reaching for a more merciful fate than that to which they'd been consigned.

Aurelius imagined that he saw figures in those trees; the whorls in the wood appeared to be the opened mouths of screaming men and boys—the dead from Mecina. He frowned and took a deep breath, steeling himself. Unlike his separation from them by a large window in Hela's tower, here the shades were alongside him, beckoning to him. He found himself irresistibly treading toward the trees to try to touch the contorted figures.

Clarinda stopped him by slipping her hand into his and keeping him on the path.

The Venetian girl wasn't faring much better than the young knight. She closed her eyes against the onslaught of her own shades.

The effort didn't work. When she opened her eyes, the trees on her right were as close together as the planks of the wall on the factory-cottage where her mother died. Through the gaps in the wood she saw the slumped forms of the three men who'd tried to rescue Fabricia, and the dangling body of the fourth man, the suicide, who'd killed himself by leaving the toxic gases running in the glassmaking rooms. In trying to save him, Fabricia Trevisan and the men had broken into the house, but their entry had somehow caused an explosion that killed them all instantly.

Words floated sorrowfully on the breeze to Aurelius and Clarinda, and it took a moment for them to realize that the words weren't more phantasmic moans from the trees, but Rudyick singing.

Upon Ymir's Beard, in World's Youth,
    From Jotun's Skulls, to Ran's Coral Tooth,
Sought the Aesir—Odin, Vili, and Ve—
    Nine Runed Relics, Wisdom's Way.
'Neath Frosted Pines, distant Shoals Aflame,
    In Elven Glade, from Muspelheim
Smote Volund's Anvil—Dooms Entwine!—
    In Sampo Hearth, tonged Codices Nine.

Quires Gathered, split Monk-Squire,
    Through trebled Witches, hews Flesh-Cut's ire,
'Pon Glass-Walled mage, Dark Cauldron seethes,
    In Kenned Ink, Moult-Feather sheathes,
As Gamble-Bones roll, clatter Merchants' Greed,
    'Til Ruler's Halo, looms on Wave-Steed.
On Otherworld's Wake, falls Face-Shield night,
    Lest Gemmed-Pin's truth, match Codex Might,
By Starred Path's chart, burn Creation's Light.

Nine songs magical sing I,
    Goblet-sipped from Bestla's mead,
As Sibyls' Coven and Druids Nigh,
    Doom Fate's Daughter and Last Son's need!

"Just what we need," Ratatosk groaned, appearing in the grasses alongside the path. "He's not only a knife-wielding maniac, but fancies himself a troubadour."

"I've not heard the Lay of the Nine Codices in many years," Andvari grunted appreciatively.

"Nine?" Aurelius repeated, dread filling him at the notion.

"*Ja*, 'Codex Wielder,'" Ratatosk sneered. "*Und* you can barely handle the awakening of one!"

"Hush, Squirrel," Rudyick said after a moment of silence, waving an arm toward the blasted landscape ahead of them. "You know as well as we all do that the threat to the Nine Worlds grew here."

"One might argue that the threat began when the Aesir went against the wishes of the Vanir and let Loki remain in Asgard," Andvari said.

"If you're going that far back in time," Ratatosk said wryly, "why not point to when Andumla the Cow licked the first of the Aesir into creation from a sheet of ice?"

"Loki wasn't always evil," Fenris said, his protest thoughtful.

"No," Skade said, "but he was built for deceit. Even from childhood he was said to take more pleasure from spinning a web than in catching the prey."

"Well put, huntress," Andvari chuckled. "Odin knows that whenever his plots got discovered, the retribution could be so severe that one wonders why he made the effort. From getting his lips sewn together to currently bound to a boulder for eternity, I'm not sure if there's been a more punished creature in creation."

"Perhaps he couldn't do aught but what his nature

demanded," Fenris said. "Do we blame the snake for it's bite, or the wolf for its hunger?"

"No self-pitying, Wolf," Skade warned.

"Not from me," Fenris replied, "but you saw how easily Hela mastered me. I thought that I'd gained more control over the centuries, but we were fighting for our lives because of her."

"And the first thing you did upon getting free was to come help us," Clarinda reminded him, her tone just as dismissive as Skade's. "You might have a family from Hel, Fenris, but the paths you choose to walk are your own."

"*Hmph*," Andvari grunted, "you're truly starting to sound like a Norn." He looked at Rudyick, who'd halted again. "Speaking of paths, we're almost at the *Sviddengen*, aren't we?"

"Yes, but there's trouble ahead, Andvari. What you and the others sensed earlier, all will now experience. An ancient evil has come into this place—I smell death in the wind."

He raised his hand and murmured a command to two elves. They sped away in a blur of motion that made them seem to disappear.

"They'll scout ahead," Rudyick said, with an approving smile to the arch-mage, "but, we should continue. If something's happening at the *Sviddengen*, they'll let us know."

He returned his attention to Aurelius. "I'd have you know the rest of our tale before we reach the area of desecration." He waved a hand at the area around them. "This forest was once part of Alfheim, with a life and vibrancy to the trees and plants that cannot be described."

"I saw part of Alfheim, near Mount Glittertind," Aurelius said, "it's beautiful."

"I would have Svartalfheim again be so," Rudyick said as the group started to move again. "To continue my story: in distant times, we elves were blessed to live amidst such beauty, and elvish mages often assisted the peoples of the other realms to better their own worlds. For Odin, we helped the dwarves fashion Clarinda's weapon—Gungnir, the Spear-that-Never-Misses—and invested much of our power into the runes upon its haft. We brought light to the subterranean caverns of Nidaveller, so that the dwarves might carve a civilization for themselves. We created the wards that guard Mimir's Well, so that Seer and the Norns might be safe in their prophesying."

A genuine smile appeared on the elf's face, the first Aurelius had seen. "So many magics," he continued, "and among the greatest of these works was the fashioning of Bifrost, the Rainbow Bridge whose flaming roadway unites Asgard and Midgard.

"Bifrost represented the most powerful of sorceries. We are pleased whenever we hear tales that on Midgard you can see an aspect of Bifrost after a rainfall, when the sun glances upon the skies and lands after a storm. It was the final accomplishment of our people before the Great Rending. With the creation of the Rainbow Bridge, the elves discovered elements of the sorcery used to shape and bind the Nine Worlds. That was a high magic whose potency ultimately had slain Odin's brothers, Vili and Vi. The All-Father and his brothers were fortunate in their earlier workings, but some said that an even 'higher hand' than theirs had made possible the wielding of such magic. Odin ceased to use that creationary magic after the death of his brothers, focusing instead on using his power to rule over the worlds that the Aesir and Vanir brought together.

"Now, when they realized the nature of the magic they wielded, many of the elves who sat on the High Council in Alfheim foresaw in the runes the same danger that Odin predicted. They imposed strictures and governing spells that prohibited the future practice of such sorcery. In their eyes, the Rainbow Bridge would serve as a beautiful reminder of the capacity of (and limitations to) their theurgy. The High Council adjourned, little knowing that they'd come too late in their decision about the perilous magic. One who'd sat among them during their deliberations was not the elf that he appeared to be. Loki—whom we call the 'Trickster,' 'Sly One,' or 'Shape Changer'— disguised himself as a member of the council. He'd heard the elvish deliberations, seen enough of the binding spells and cautionary runes, and learned all that he needed to know to attempt the spell-casting for that mighty magic by himself."

Rudyick lifted a curtain of dead berry shrubs for Aurelius, and he passed beneath. The path beyond widened and the trees began to thin as the incline of the path grew steeper. The supernatural effects of the wood still made themselves felt, though, and Aurelius saw movement in between trunks of trees in the distance.

He realized too late that he was watching himself kill the first of the attackers who came over the fortress wall at Mecina. He averted his gaze, trying to focus on Rudyick, but he still saw the astonished expression on the boy's face when he realized that he had been struck in the upper abdomen by a length of iron the younger Aurelius had wrenched from a torch holder.

He remembered Hela's words in the citadel: *A strange night for a priest, was it not? Killing seventeen people within a few hours?*

"They would've taken the fortress!" Aurelius retorted, speaking aloud to the memory.

"What?" Clarinda murmured absently. She'd heard him say something, but she had her own problems confronting the images before her. She'd been watching her father cradling her mother's body in his arms, mere moments after breaking into the glass factory and finding the bodies. The shadows between the trees coalesced into more scenes from Clarinda's past, and tears streamed down her cheeks.

The sound of her strained breathing pulled Aurelius from his own pained reveries. "Clarinda?"

"I see my father," Clarinda said, "in all the moments after Madre's death that I never saw. He was so sad—so many hours spent at the taverns with my uncle and another man whom I don't recognize."

The scene changed and she watched her father sitting down in a tavern to make a deal with two Templar knights—men whom she now knew to be Farbauti and Morpeth—signing a document for transporting two caskets to Caesarea that sealed his fate with Old Nick.

"Only ghosts live here," Rudyick reminded both youths. "Keep walking and remember not to stray from the path." He then considered Aurelius and Clarinda and added a quiet compliment: "I'm impressed. Neither of you are as fearful as some who've entered this wood."

"Perhaps that's because he's bringing a greater harm with him," Ratatosk observed, scurrying in the limbs above them. "Hard to be afraid of anything when you can make worlds burn."

"Or, maybe we know our pasts can't be changed and we're learning to live for a present and future of our own making," Clarinda said.

"Don't go all Norn on me," Ratatosk chittered, but then hopped out of sight, miffed. Aurelius had been about to make his own reply to the squirrel's comment, but Clarinda's answer to the irritating creature satisfied him. Instead, he prompted, "Your story, Rudyick? You were about to say something more about Loki?"

"Ja, finish the story," Andvari said, although Aurelius doubted that the Arch-Mage needed to hear the tale. "You were telling us about the high magic."

"I'll try to make it brief," Rudyick said. "*Ja* ... the high magic. The elven high council had decided not to attempt the creationary magic after the fashioning of Bifrost. Loki was present at the deliberations. Until that time, Loki had been troublesome, but more of a prankster than truly harmful, and often he gave true help to the Asgardians. It was Loki who stole Sif's hair, but who also later persuaded dwarvish smiths to replace the stolen locks with tresses of delicately spun gold. He next tried to rob the gods of their perpetual youth by kidnapping Idunn, keeper of the Golden Apples whose taste fended off old age. In that case, Loki recovered both the goddess and the magic apples when forced by Odin himself, and he managed to kill the frost giant responsible for the actual theft.

"Yet, as Fenris said, Loki wasn't evil, merely mischievous. He also did great good in those early days. He devised the stratagem to retrieve Thor's hammer, Mjöllnir, whose theft by some dwarves caused a great unrest among the gods—"

"A few bad apples don't spoil the bunch," Delling said defensively.

"I didn't say that they did," Rudyick replied curtly, "but the theft left Asgard defenseless at a time when the Frost Giants were mustering for war. That magic hammer was the only dependable defense against that enemy, and the dwarves who stole it brought the weapon to Thrymr, a frost giant who lived in Jotunheim and wanted to marry Freya, one of the Vanir who tends to those in the afterlife sent neither to Valhalla nor Hel. Thrymr sent word to the Aesir that he'd return Thor's hammer in return for Freya becoming his own. That was inconceivable, so at a great council Loki came forward to make a suggestion.

"He told everyone that since Thrymr wanted Freya so badly, why not give him what he wanted? Or, at least, give an impression that the gods were conceding to the giant's demands. To do that, Loki said, all Thor had to do was be willing to dress as the fertility goddess and present himself to Thrymr. When he got within reach of Mjöllnir, the hammer would fly into his hand and then Thor could kill all the giants and dwarves within sight. Thor protested, saying that he'd be the laughing stock of all Asgard if he were to wear a dress, but even Odin had to admit that the Trickster had devised a good strategy. So, ultimately, Thor did as Loki bade, dressed himself as Freya, and went with Loki to Thrymr's Hall. Sure enough, once he walked into the giant's abode, just as Loki had predicted, Mjöllnir burst from the stone trunk where Thrymr had secured it, and Thor immediately set-to, killing all the frost giants who'd gathered to see the nuptials."

ii. The Creation of the Book of Tears

"**T**hor in a dress," Ratatosk chuckled, "that must have been a sight!"

"Yet, when Loki watched the elves create Bifrost, a great desire arose in him to possess the forbidden magic. For the first time, Loki coveted power not as a means for mischief but for its own sake.

"In that changed purpose lay the ruination of the elves and the eventual damnation of the Nine Worlds. Loki couldn't create this kind of sorcery without aid from the elves, for in the ways of magic, their craft was second only to Odin and the Aesir. That's not to say he didn't have his own sorcery—he'd been begotten of two frost giants of Jotunheim, and knew the magics familiar to giants and dwarves: shape-changing, illusions, and the crafting of magical weapons, jewelry, and rings. The magic of Odin and the elves was deeper and more occult than such things. If he were to attempt the fires of Creation like that magic which made the Rainbow Bridge, Loki would need assistance from the elves.

"He approached the few elven smiths who'd argued at the High Council for the creationary magic. He told these few he believed that he, too, had learned the secret of the creationary magic that had been forbidden by both Odin and the elven council."

"I know you believe that," Andvari interrupted, "but I don't. None of the elves, not even your father, Volund—who's been known to run roughshod over natural laws if he really wanted something—no one would've allowed such a claim to go unremarked or unchallenged!"

"You're wrong, Arch-Mage," Rudyick said, shaking his head. "The way he did it was by making his requests and lore-kenning seem in keeping with his previous habits and tricks."

"What ruse did he use?" Clarinda asked.

"Loki said that there was a mortal upon Midgard—a Sicilian sea-merchant—who'd foiled one of his jests with a northern trader's daughter; as reprisal, the Mischievous One wanted to play a trick upon this mortal. If these few elves could help him create a means to do this, he promised that his interest in the creationary magic would be satisfied.

"The elves whom Loki approached weren't fools. They suspected that Loki was attempting something that would bode ill for someone. No matter the honeyed words of his proposal, they didn't trust the Trickster's words. But, while they wondered at his hidden motives, the prospect to again use the creationary magic was too attractive. Odin's actions and the elven council's assent had interrupted these smiths' great design; they wanted to remake Alfheim—already the jewel of the Nine Worlds—into an even more wondrous place than it was. From this selfish motive the elves were undone."

"What did Loki really want?" Aurelius asked.

"To be certain, there was truth in his tale about wanting revenge against a merchant who'd interfered with one of his Midgardian pranks, but I believe that the deeper, underlying motive was envy. He'd grown envious of Odin's knowledge of runes. Loki wanted to learn the secrets of the runes for himself. He wanted to make his own codex that wasn't beholden to the others."

"Letters of power?"

"*Ja*. Odin learned the runes by hanging crucified on Yggdrassil for nine days. He learned more after drinking from the cauldron, Odrorir, which some call the 'mead of poetry,' then even more he gained from Mimir after sacrificing an eye."

"There were twenty-seven runes, weren't there?" Aurelius interrupted again, as he felt another of Taliesin's memories emerge. He couldn't explain it, but he had the strong feeling that he needed to understand these events clearly. "Did Odin hang crucified for nine days to gain the first nine, and Odrorir and Mimir also imparted their runes in sets of nines?"

"*Ja*, it is said that the nines were bound in arcs of three," Rudyick affirmed, raising an eyebrow. "Strange that you should make those connections so early ..." He stopped and returned to his subject. "Those runes are the *Gåtefull Runer*."

"We think that there are only twenty-seven," Andvari said. "The rumored number of the library of codexes in the Fair-Boughed Hold."

Rudyick qualified, "Andvari and I both believe that the All-Father learned even more than that number." He glanced at the Arch-Mage. "I still disagree with you that there were that many true Codexes. No one knows the exact number of magical books that were created in the Elder Times."

There were more than twenty-seven Gåtefull Runer, Aurelius thought. He didn't know how he knew, but the lore seemed somehow so important that he didn't want to share any of his guesses with his companions. *Odin didn't tell everyone the entire story, but I think that the Codex knows.*

"You've seen the Codex Lacrimae, haven't you?" Andvari

asked, looking searchingly at Aurelius as if seeking to understand how much the Hospitaller did, indeed, know. "There are hundreds, if not thousands of runes within its pages."

"Are you saying that Loki didn't make the same kinds of sacrifices that Odin's did?" Aurelius asked, ignoring the archmage. "I mean, if the All-Father had to make such effort, wouldn't anyone?"

"Indeed. Loki learnt many of Odin's runes for himself," Rudyick replied. Then he added in a quiet tone, "Those he didn't learn, he stole; those he couldn't steal, he duplicated; those he couldn't duplicate, he created. His knowledge was incomplete. Again, it was in the last instance that ... creationary magic. That's where we elves who helped him and were undone.

"In that moment of creating runes—the most perilous of all magic-working, a sorcery so black that its secret had been guarded for millennia by Mimir, Kvasir, and Yggdrasil itself— in the moment when the Codex Lacrimae was made, both we and Loki knew our doom. We couldn't replicate the script fashioning that the Aesir had mastered, and, more, Loki chose the moment we were at our most confused to strike with all his might. He lashed out when the elves were creating the 'accounting book' that would be used to ruin the Midgardian merchant's business, family, and life. That book had never been more than a feint by the Sly One, an idea that came to him after hearing the high council discussing other books of sorcery."

"Those were the Codici?" Clarinda asked.

"Some of them," Rudyick said. "The collection of twenty-seven, or ten, nine, or whatever number of books ... the Codici hadn't yet assumed their final collective forms, and we're still ...

uncertain where the other codexes came from. Unsure of the source of those books, it was foolhardy to try to imitate them, but, as I said, these disgruntled elves thought that the guise of an accounting book should serve as well as any other.

"One of the elves—my father, Volund—realized Loki's true intent and prevented Loki from stealing the elves' magic and becoming more powerful than Odin. I can't describe what he did—only he and Loki knew the exact magics that went into that moment—but that action also created the Codex Lacrimae and damned thousands of the elves to their current condition.

"Loki was cast backward, surprised by the unexpected ferocity and attack of Volund and the elves. His energies were still at play, and they were absorbed into the book along with the elvish magic and all the runes that Loki had spent time learning and planning to steal. The elves couldn't prevent the theft of their own magic, and so both Loki's sorcery and the elves' magic created the Codex Lacrimae. When both sources of power were fused into the runes of the book, a great moan arose from the Norns who sat by the Well of Mimir; they alone sensed that this was a harbinger of Ragnarok, the Twilight of the Gods."

"So you say," Ratatosk countered. "I was at the Fields of Burning Night when the Norns tried to take all the Codices for themselves. The Codex Lacrimae was the last created, and the first to go."

Rudyick nodded but, wanting to finish the story, didn't engage the squirrel. "After that final battle, all the codexes were thought lost or destroyed by the Norns. We now can guess what happened. The Codex Lacrimae itself, although originally intended by Loki to be a ruse to get the elves to open their sorceries to him, mistook Loki's prank as its true purpose and used Urd's and Taliesin's fires at the Fields to transport itself from Alfheim to Midgard, hidden from all, and seeking the sea-merchant who'd foiled Loki's plot. However, since neither Loki nor the elves were very familiar with that world, it was displaced far from the merchant who was Loki's intended target! Whereas that seafarer had been plying his trade in the North and Baltic Seas, the Codex Lacrimae ended up far, far to the east. In the world of mortals, the Book of Tears disappeared for a long while. Back in Alfheim, neither Loki nor those few elves who helped him were ever the same again. Each seemed to have lost an essential part of themselves and they never recovered."

"*Kyrie eleison*," Aurelius murmured, invoking the prayer as much for himself as for those who'd been present at the Dark Book's creation. "They lost their souls."

"Their what?" Rudyick asked.

"Their souls. That 'essential part of themselves' you mentioned."

"I'm unfamiliar with the word. All that I know is that both the elves and Loki became something ... other than what they'd been, and the Codex Lacrimae—indeed, I have since learned that this might be said of all of the codexes—it appeared to be not what anyone expected. Afterward, Loki eventually distanced himself from the other gods, spending more time alone, brooding. The elves who'd disobeyed the strictures of the High Council were exiled to the part of Alfheim ruined by the creation of the Codex Lacrimae, and they, like Loki, grew detached from their brethren.

"There, in the easternmost fringe of Alfheim—where we now walk—those elves were called 'dark' by their former people and ultimately banished from the lighter glades of their world. We're known as Dark Elves more because of the transgression with Loki than for any truly malicious shadow within ourselves. Volund took the leadership of these elves and allowed them to attempt magical workings similar to what created the Codex Lacrimae. They hoped one day to undo what had been done and so return to their kindred in Alfheim."

iii. Old Nick and the Shades of Mecina

Thankfully, Rudyick had increased the pace and so made any kind of maudlin dwelling on his memories almost impossible.

Aurelius gripped Clarinda's hand in reassurance, and tried to focus on the elf's back as they walked, but the images in his mind still came. He saw more kaftan-clad Saracens running through the trees beyond the elves and dwarves, attempting to surround his old self, his younger self, who was now stooping quickly to retrieve the saber from the slain boy.

"I came to the Holy Land on a pilgrimage," he told Clarinda, expecting that she was seeing the same vision he saw, still feeling the need to explain the violence the Hooded Hospitaller started to wreak on the shadows in the trees. "I went instead of my older brother, Paolo, because I was always the more devout one—it didn't make sense that he should go with Uncle Servius."

"You mean, Old Nick?" Clarinda qualified, not knowing why Aurelius was starting to talk about Mecina. She saw Rudyick's look of surprise, but the elf fell silent.

Aurelius grimaced. "*Sì*. At the time, though, my parents and family seemed so excited at the arrival of this long-lost relative. My brother, Roberto, even came to Calabria to a monastery where I trained every summer and brought me home a month early to meet 'Uncle Servius.' During the entire winter all anyone talked about was Uncle Servius's plan to go to the Levant and see the Holy Places. I was a bit envious that Paolo seemed to be the one going—he and Uncle ... Old Nick ... they were always talking together, and I thought in late spring that I'd be heading back to resume training with Master Devrone and Brother Tomas."

"When did Paolo start bringing up the idea that he wanted to attend a university?" Clarinda asked, recalling that it was in trying to support his brother's 'change-of-heart' that Aurelius had volunteered to take Paolo's place on the trip.

"Before Easter," Aurelius said, reflecting on the memories. "Uncle Servius came to the house one day with a group of young priests who were on their way to study law at Bologna. We were all very impressed because they'd just come back from the Holy Land, and told us tales of exotic places and events across the sea." The youth shook his head, his voice disbelieving or still in awe of the effect the stories had had on his younger self. "Uncle Servius—"

"Old Nick!" Clarinda reprimanded, frustrated that the knight seemed insistent on calling the entity by what had been proved to be a false name.

"He ... he and the other priests told us of so many tales about Jerusalem and the Levant. Tales from almost a century of fighting, tales that made us want to take a pilgrimage ourselves and see the land of relics and wonders. I remember him telling us of what might happen on a pilgrimage to Jerusalem. He told of the First Crusade, and of the discovery of the Holy Lance at Antioch, a find that rallied the outnumbered first crusaders and inspired them to ride alongside a Heavenly Host to defeat the enemy, Kergobah. He told us of Prester John, a descendant of one of the Three Wise Men, who was even five years ago returning from the East with a relief army for the Crusaders, willing to avenge the losses of the Second Crusade, but who needed to feel the belief of devout Christians to find the way to Jerusalem.

"Uncle Servius said that the Holy Land needed as many pilgrims as possible for Prester John to feel that belief." He looked at Clarinda, and smiled ruefully. "They even made the sea-voyage to Constantinople seem romantic. He told us of the wonders of Byzantium, and how the city would last for eternity as a defense against the Saracens. At the time, I'd begun to learn some things about my father that had put the entire Levant in a darker, more suspicious light. These stories filled with priests and knights and pilgrims seemed to offer me an alternate explanation to what I'd begun to suspect about Padre's business dealings; the adventures were filled with heroes and faith and a quest to reach the Holy City that seemed as clear as that glass you describe your mother making ... I guess I wanted to find a purity of purpose to replace what had become lost in my daily life."

"What did you think your father was doing?"

Aurelius grimaced. After a long pause, he said. "It's a long time ago, and I never had any proof, but I do know that ... Old Nick's tales made me want to visit the Levant and see things for myself. I fancied that I could make up for whatever my father was doing by making a pilgrimage for the family. I remember that I wanted to see the Tarsus Mountains when those young priests talked about the overland legs of the journey. At twelve, I imagined I would start my journey there and somehow get to Jerusalem and, if need be, make it all the way to Egypt to atone for father, but also get at the truth."

"Aurelius, what did you suspect your father of doing?" Clarinda said.

"I'd rather not say. Not here." A memory flashed then, not of the battle and bloodshed of Mecina that still occurred in the trees, but from months before that time. He'd snuck aboard a ship docked at the port of Syracuse, one of his father's ships. Devrone's training had helped him elude both harbor and galley guards in that predawn hour, and after seeing a few men sleeping in front of the hatch to the cargo hold, he'd been about to leave when he'd seen in the grey moonlight an enormous grating whose broad latticework could mean only one thing— ventilation for the human cargo of a slave ship. Aurelius had just stared at gigantic iron grillwork, swaying as tears filled his eyes and an abyss opened in his stomach. Then he'd heard the sounds of the two-man night patrol over the breathing and coughing of the many men below deck, and the awareness had propelled him forward. No matter the risk, the boy had needed to make a last confirmation by sight, but he gagged at the smell of excrement and sweat as he neared the iron lattice and peered through, the silver light revealing the shadows of human forms lying below the grillwork, men huddled and sprawled upon cots and flooring and even a few who'd been awake, their upturned faces perhaps trying to watch the passage of the moon. The guards had finally caught sight of Aurelius and shouted the alarm, but he'd slipped over the side of the ship and dropped into the water to swim away beneath the piers.

Here in dim light of Svartalfheim, he recalled the vision he'd had when Farbauti and Kenezki had bound him with the Grimhold Cloak; the dream of Taliesin and Dietrich standing upon the grating of the imprisoned elves.

Taliesin! Taliesin, do not do this to us. We beg of you, mercy!

He winced, and realized that Clarinda was saying something.

"... and as for those pilgrims being honorable knights or young priests, I don't believe it," she said. "More likely, they were Old Nick's cronies, Beelzebub, Mephistopheles, and Baal! The tales of those trips were lies."

"I hope not." Aurelius said, not wanting to look her in the eye. For all of the embarrassment and shame he felt at his father's activities, he still couldn't believe that any of his other family members would be involved.

"You hope not?" Clarinda stared at him, baffled and irritated. "You've met Old Nick, Santini! You saw him transform into your Uncle Servius!"

"It could still be another one of his tricks," Aurelius countered. "Perhaps I just don't want to believe that Paolo ... that my own brother would've entered a deal with the Devil."

"Well, you can allow for any possibility you want," Clarinda said in a tone that wasn't at all making any kind of allowance, "but I've learned that my father did make such a deal, and I'm not wasting time trying to disbelieve it, nor trying to look for another explanation.

She glared at him, furious that he seemed to be able to muster any kind of defense about that part of his past. "Sometimes the ones we love let us down, Servius, and sometimes, that disappointment is so extreme, so hurtful that there's no going back to the way things were because the wound's too deep."

"I can't live with that kind of anger," he protested softly. "I'm studying to be a priest, Clarinda; if you hold onto that kind of anger, it turns to hate, rots you from the inside."

"I didn't say you couldn't forgive him, Santini," she said, "I go to church, too. Well, sometimes, when we're not at sea." She inhaled. "But, don't mistake forgiveness for going back to the way things were." She paused. "I'm so angry at my father for what he did, but I think I can forgive him because of all the years that he did things right. Padre acted foolishly, and his actions had far-reaching, long-lasting consequences. Consequences that I've got to deal with *and* clean up. But, I'm still furious with him because he must've known what he was getting into. Although he perhaps didn't fully realize it when he first met them, I'm sure at some point he sensed that Farbauti and Morpeth weren't the most sterling of characters."

"But, if it's true about Paolo—"

"There might be worse truths about the rest of your family," Clarinda finished the thought he wouldn't give voice to.

Aurelius flinched. Looking past her into the trees, he saw himself fighting the invaders at Mecina, intent that they should not get past his position on the rampart, thence downstairs to the gate to let in the quiet army milling outside the fortress. He didn't even see the trees now, only the flagstones of the rampart and the Syrian world as it was five years ago, illuminated by a Hunter's Moon.

His voice grew distant as he watched himself moving with a speed that seemed more appropriate for a dark elf like Rudyick than the thirteen-year-old he was back then. "I, and many other pilgrims, got trapped there. A Muslim army besieged the castle late in the afternoon, but we were fine— enough provisions, enough men-at-arms, enough everything to hold off the enemy for up to six months. Certainly more than enough time for Hospitaller reinforcements to arrive from the Krak des Chevaliers."

He drew a calming breath, and didn't duck as an enemy's head decapitated by his ghostly former self passed through his and Clarinda's bodies. "After Vespers, I went to get some air and discovered a breach being attempted." He frowned. "No, what I saw was Uncle Servius driving a dagger into the back of a Hospitaller knight."

Aurelius's voice broke as he watched the events unfolding again before him. "I killed the other one nearby because my uncle—no, Old Nick—Old Nick said that they were traitors and letting the enemy through the gate. After I'd killed that man— God, both of those knights must have seen Old Nick trying to let the enemy in! I've always thought that Uncle Servius was our first line of defense, but now I see that he's the one who dropped the rope down to them and let them climb onto the ramparts."

"What happened then?" Clarinda asked, realizing that the rest of the company was listening to the story.

"I saw the first of the grappling hooks come over the wall, I grabbed a strap from a brazier on the wall. I killed the first one who came over, and used his blade on the rest." Aurelius paused. "The first one was a boy, not much over ten years of age."

"Where did Old Nick go?" Clarinda pressed.

"I lost track of him, then, because there were so many trying to come through the wall."

"Stay on the path," Rudyick warned.

"No," Aurelius said to the shadows, "I wasn't smiling! Yet there he was, dancing through the invaders on the rampart with what appeared to be a smile on his face while he brought death with swordplay that would have made Devrone di Magglia proud. "Stop," he urged his younger self. "Don't go down the stairs."

"What was down the stairs?" Clarinda asked quietly. She gripped his arm, restraining him from going further into the forest.

Aurelius watched his thirteen-year-old image run down the stairwell that appeared in the shadows of the ground. He turned away, using Clarinda's presence as an anchor. "More death," he said. "A night of death."

"*Bitte*, keep walking," Rudyick insisted. "Please. This glamour that's making you recall sad events, it recedes if you stay focused."

"I wanted to live more than I wanted to keep my pilgrim vows," Aurelius said, numbly returning to the path. "I thought I was going to be a priest, but all of that didn't matter when it came to it. I wouldn't let them kill me, nor attack anyone I could save. I couldn't rely on prayer alone. I tried to pray, but God stayed quiet. I wanted to live."

E, I could finally do something good, something to defend those who were defenseless.

"Choose to live now as well," the elf replied.

"What happened to Old Nick?" Clarinda asked. "We need to know what he did."

"The next time I saw him was in the hospital ward," Aurelius replied. "By that time, I was giving commands to the entire garrison because the proper leaders in the senior leadership had been slain, or were ..."

"What?" Halfdan asked. "Were they battling in the forefront of the ranks?"

"No, they were in the chapel, praying," Aurelius said quietly, unable to keep the contempt from his voice. "Mecina was essentially a fortified pilgrim hostel, but neither the abbot nor the commanders were willing to fight."

"But, but," Clarinda said, confused. "It was a Hospitaller castle, correct? Surely there were warriors who'd fight against Saladin?"

"None who held any rank higher than sergeant. The majority of the fighting monks were on a training exercise near Jerusalem."

"So," Halfdan said, "when the siege began, the most competent soldiers were absent, and the rest of the leadership were dead or praying for a miracle?"

"Strangest timing I've ever seen, all of them being gone," Aurelius said, "but it didn't matter because decisions and defenses had to be made. I did both, and people listened."

"It's all too coincidental," Clarinda mused. "Sounds like more of Old Nick's doing."

"I agree," Andvari said. "If he were trying to prevent you from becoming a priest, perhaps he created an apt condition for seeing what you'd do as a warrior."

"I don't know," Aurelius replied, but everyone could tell that he was racing through his memories, verifying and discounting the variety of moments.

"To be clear," Clarinda said into the silence, "you said you next saw Old Nick in the hospital ward, that he'd been 'injured,' and remained there until the day of Saladin's attack—"

"—at which time," Halfdan concluded, with the kind of disbelief only a veteran soldier could have, "he conveniently 'recovered' enough to say that he'd take your place and fight Saladin in hand-to-hand combat?"

"*Sì*. The last thing he told me was that he was making the sacrifice for our family, that he'd become me, and I'd become somebody else to live another day. We both knew that Saladin had to kill Servius Aurelius Santini to avenge the death of his brother."

"So you let everyone think your 'Uncle Servius' was the Hooded Hospitaller and you became a pilgrim named Ríg?"

"*Sì.*"

"You took another identity?" Fenris asked.

"*Sì*," Aurelius said, self-consciously aware that the entire company had been silent while they walked through the wood.

"Yes, there's a great leader on our world named Saladin, whose brother got killed while I was parlaying with him." He paused. "That must have been Old Nick, too, Clarinda. He must have disguised himself as a guard and sliced Turan-Shah's throat while I was shouting terms with Saladin. I thought I slew the murderer, but how difficult would it be for him to just change into someone else?"

"We saw what he could do," Clarinda agreed. "My guess is that he shape-shifted at need to position you wherever he wanted. But, I still don't understand why? Why would the Devil spend so much time on you?"

"I don't like what I'm hearing," Andvari said with a grunt. "Loki's long been known for shape-changing, for being other than he is." He peered suspiciously at Aurelius. "You say you took another identity five years ago?"

"Tsk-tsk, pish-posh," Traeg said as she elbowed her husband dismissively. "So has Odin, and many other gods and goddesses, for that matter. This boy's taking another name doesn't make him an agent of the Dark One."

"As far as we know, neither Odin nor the others in the pantheon had a hand in making any of the Codices, either," Andvari persisted. "Perhaps the Dark Book's magic was at work even then?"

He peered intently at Aurelius. "What if this boy's Loki himself, eh? Disguised in a glamour so deeply that only a fully awakened Codex Lacrimae will remind him of his true self?"

"But, Loki's bound," Skade said, and something in her tone caught Clarinda's attention. When she turned to look at the Huntress, she noticed that almost everyone had involuntarily taken a step back from Santini. All were regarding him cautiously.

"Is he?" Andvari asked. "We've only the word of you and Fenris for that claim."

"We were in the cavern," Fenris said, but then surprisingly shrugged his shoulders, "but Father is a shape-changer and sorcerer without equal. I suppose it's possible that he substituted someone for him."

"Not likely," Traeg said, and nodded at Aurelius in support. "Odin and the more powerful members of the Aesir personally bound Loki to that rock. He's still there."

"I'd just add this, Andvari," Aurelius told the arch-mage, "if you truly believe that I could be Loki in disguise, we should part ways now. I don't think I am, but I certainly can't prove I'm not."

The Hospitaller defiantly took in the rest of the company. "I've told all of you, until Clarinda silenced it, I could hear the voice of the Codex Lacrimae, but I certainly don't feel any magic, nor do I think that I'm a disguised Trickster." He added quietly, "But, if this is a dream casting me in that role, it might make sense to wake me up."

"What?" Clarinda asked. "What's that mean?"

"Like when you have a dream of falling from a height," Aurelius explained, "and then awaken before you hit the ground." He waved a hand at the group. "I've spent so many years trying to do the right thing after Mecina, but part of me knows I never can."

"You believe us to be a dream?" Andvari asked.

"Except for my God and Church," Santini replied, "sometimes I don't know what to believe anymore."

"*Grazie*," Clarinda muttered, but the arch-mage was speaking again, and she wondered if Aurelius had even realized that he'd slighted her.

"So, like one awakening before death in a dream," Andvari

said, "you think it makes a certain kind of sense that you'd become the villain in this vision?"

"Why not? Some days it's hard to get out of bed, I'm thinking about Mecina ... and other things so much. I wonder how I could ever become a priest with so much blood on my hands. So, if this is a dream, I expect I'll do what I always do when I'm in a bad place. I'll wake up, go to morning mass, and try to pray and atone for my sins even harder than before."

"I give up," Clarinda said, throwing her hands in the air. "If I do meet you in person, I'll make sure to slap you in the face so you know it's 'real.'"

"Clarinda ..." Aurelius began, then interrupted himself and turned to Andvari. "To your point about my taking another identity, all I can say is that changing a name isn't changing my shape. If anything, I'd say that keeping my secret was the work of new friends I'd made at the Krak des Chevaliers."

He returned his attention to Clarinda and smiled. "No magic there, except the great one of friendship, which I'm honored to have, whether I'm in a dream or not."

She crossed her arms over her chest. "To imitate Andvari: *hmmph!*"

The knight started to reply then, surprised, raised a hand to his forehead, rubbing his temples with thumb and forefinger. When he looked up again and took his hand away, the figures from the past had disappeared. "They're gone," he said in relief. "The shades have disappeared."

"Yes, we're nearing the *Sviddengen*," Rudyick said, urgency in his voice. "All of you, come. We're almost there."

Rudyick halted so abruptly that Aurelius almost walked into

the elf's back. In the failing afternoon hour the grey sunlight barely penetrated the trees as evening's approaching shadows lengthened.

"Rudyick, what is it?"

"*Shhh*," the elf hissed. Light flared in the gloom, emanating from a small crystal globe that Rudyick withdrew from a tunic pocket. Aurelius recognized the device, having seen one similar to it in Fenris's possession. The elf listened and scanned the undergrowth near them. He knelt and moved his hand slowly over the dirt.

"What is it?" Aurelius repeated.

"A beast of some kind," Rudyick murmured. "Large, and here recently."

"What kind of beast?"

"I know not, but there was a great battle here, and it kills as easily as most of us breathe."

"Where are the bodies, then?"

"Over here, Codex Wielder. Look." Fenris crouched over a patch of ground where tracks could be clearly seen. The pressed grasses and broken branches looked as if something large had been dragged through the wood.

"What kind of beast drags its prey away in such number?" Rudyick mused. "I reckon that there were at least a dozen men here."

"Yes, most of these prints aren't animal," Andvari confirmed, walking back and forth across the area.

"If there is a beast on the prowl, shouldn't we go another way?" Clarinda asked. "How far are we from the *Sviddengen* and the trail to Mount Glittertind?"

"With the Codex Wielder here, that's hard to say. We'll wait to see if a path presents itself."

"What does my being here have to do with a path appearing?" Aurelius asked, some irritation creeping into his voice.

Rudyick seemed to be returning to his former, haughty demeanor and the knight didn't like the condescension in the elf's voice.

"I thought that you said we'd be taking the road through the forest to the *Sviddengen,* try to get rid of the Codex, and then go ahead to the mountain passes to Glittertind," Aurelius said.

"Because of the paradox that created it," Rudyick answered with some impatience, "the Codex Lacrimae slightly changes the magic in each of the Nine Worlds that it appears. I didn't halt in this place solely because of the beast's tracks. Usually there's a rune-gate here that would take us to the heart of Svartalfheim, avoiding the deeper parts of the Weeping Wood. It's not here, so we'll have to wait awhile to see if it turns up."

"I don't even have the Codex with me," Aurelius said. "You attribute too much both to it and me."

"Mortal, do not repeatedly gainsay me where the Codex is concerned. I've spent much time with this lore. Of course, you have it with you. Anyone can see it!"

A pale blue light flickered between the trees behind Rudyick, and Aurelius assumed that it signaled the appearance of the expected rune-gate.

However, Rudyick seemed surprised by the glowing brilliance. A woman in a dark-green cloak emerged from the trees, and the elf stepped back.

Clarinda gasped. The woman was Verdandi, the Norn of the Present. The witch scowled at the Dark Elf.

CHAPTER 13

An Invitation to Mimir's Well

A glass sphere floated in the air before Verdandi, its shape very similar to those used by Rudyick and Fenris, but the flames in this sphere were sapphire instead of orange and yellow.

"Rudyick, if you'd speak of Codex-Lore, might it not be better to let our friend here have the counsel of those appointed as its guardians?"

The light in the globe turned from blue to white, revealing the woman's ovaline face and long, wheaten hair graying at the temples. Though very short, barely reaching Aurelius's abdomen, she had wide, penetrating eyes that at a glance seemed to absorb all that there was to know about the Hospitaller knight.

"Verdandi?" Clarinda asked incredulously. She'd become so used to seeing the Norn of the Present in the guise of Genevieve Stratioticus that she'd almost forgotten the woman's true form.

"Rudyick, cease this nonsense," Verdandi said curtly. "Witches and druids are returning in the Nine Worlds, and you're bringing Santini deeper into Svartalfheim? Besides other threats you're unaware of, he'll be recognized before you reach your destination. Your people will imprison him, but more likely they'll try to slay him."

"They won't even know he's there," Rudyick said. "We're taking him to the *Sviddengen*."

"We know where you intend to go!" Verdandi snapped. "A madman's there, and the last thing you should be doing is bringing a fledgling Lore Master into his orbit!"

"I need the magics there—"

"Ah, you'd try to rid the Nine Worlds of the Codex Lacrimae?" Verdandi said. "You can't do it in that fashion anymore."

"I believe that I can; it was created there, so too can it be destroyed there."

"I want to try, *Signora*," Aurelius interjected. "From what I've heard so far, it's only brought grief and destruction since Loki and Volund created it."

Both elf and Norn ignored him.

"While true that elven magic partly created it," Verdandi said, "it won't be unmade by elves alone. Different magics are needed here."

"So your sisters and the legends say, but I, too, have spent much time in dwelling upon this; even if the Codex can't be destroyed at the *Sviddengen*, its threat might be reduced. Isn't it possible that the elven half could be stripped and restored to its rightful owners, to us? Verdandi, my people could have the blight on our honor removed ... we might even return to Alfheim."

"The Dark Elves shall not be reunited with their lost kindred until Ragnarok, Rudyick. You know the prophecies."

"Ragnarok will come, Verdandi, whether the Codex brings it about or is destroyed at the end of time; if we succeed in my plan and get rid of the elvish parts, with its power halved, more peoples in the Nine Worlds might have a chance to survive the Twilight of the Gods than otherwise could."

A slight smile played across the features of the Norn. Clarinda had to focus on the fact that even though she shared some similarities in features to Genevieve, this Sister of Fate was millennia old and could foresee all aspects of the Present. Amusement from her wasn't always a good thing.

"You'd be surprised at how close my mind is to yours in this matter, Rudyick. Long have you struggled for this moment, but I tell you, don't go further along this path, and stop waiting for a *runeporte*." She looked at the company, but lingered longest on Andvari and Traeg, then Fenris and Skade. "You'll need these four. Brigadier General Halfdan and the rest of your company may return to the forest fringe, or to their homes."

"No," Rudyick said. "Halfdan comes with the dwarves. He's a friend."

"No?" Verdandi replied, a steely softness coming into her voice, "Rudyick, you do know who I am, don't you?"

"You're the Sister of Becoming and All That Is—the Eternal Present."

"Would you die before your quest ends?" Verdandi's voice was colder than Clarinda had ever heard it. "Die in a moment that repeats for eternity?"

The elf's pale flesh turned ashen. "I'd die to set my people free, if that's what it takes."

"Live for your people, Dark Elf," Verdandi said. "Listen to reason and master your anger. I tell you now, there's more danger here than the unpredictability of Codex Magic. The murderer, Kullervo, waits at the *Sviddengen*, torturing the Volsungs, killing dwarves, and waiting for Sigmund to come slay him. This happens now. Kullervo wants to die his third death, but he also wants to slay as many people as possible before he dies."

"We shouldn't avoid somebody like that," Aurelius protested, throwing his hood back as he spoke to the Norn with a challenging voice. "I don't know who the Volsungs are, but torturing is wrong." The apprentice of Devrone di Magglia nodded at the group around him, then finished: "You don't avoid a trap, you spring it. These dwarves under Halfdan, Rudyick, Fenris, and Skade ... all of them have risked everything to help me. I'll not see their kind killed by anyone if I can help prevent it."

"Oh, you needn't worry, Hospitaller; Skuld's read your fate in the ripples of the Well. You'll face Kullervo soon enough, and the Singing Sword will be your doom and salvation!"

The Norn's voice filled with the authority of prophecy, and Aurelius took a half-step backward at her fury. "Now, however, is not the time! Clarinda?"

"We should listen to her, Servius. We really need to get to Mimir's Well."

"Respectfully, no." Aurelius began, and he looked directly at Verdandi. "And I mean it— respectfully—but, I can't just leave because there's trouble ahead. I don't want more innocent people to die from my actions, or inaction."

"If that's your concern, worry not. You're the Codex Wielder; Kullervo will be there in this moment when you return."

"The same moment?" Aurelius gave a half laugh. "How would I do that, go back in time?"

"He will be there. That's all you need know, eh?" The Norn of the Present raised her staff and peered intently at the young knight.

"We've waited long enough," she said to the rest of the company. "My sisters and I must take a direct hand in matters. I've come for him who currently holds the Codex Lacrimae, but you are welcome, as is Halfdan. It's my thinking that, before this is over, the aid of all peoples will be necessary, be they dwarves, elves, goddesses, or," she paused with a disdainful arch of her eyebrows at Fenris, "or even ill-fated Hel-Spawn."

"That's unfair—" Skade began to say.

" —and completely unnecessary," Clarinda finished, casting a stern look at Verdandi.

"Stay calm, *meine Freunde*," Fenris said, his eyes mirthful. "Remember that *bellende Hunde beißen nicht*."

"Says the growling wolf," Verdandi snapped back.

"I'll convince you yet that not all prophecies are true," Fenris assured her, "and, no matter how your invitation's phrased, Skade and I will come along." He winked at his mate.

"It'll be some comfort for you to see the grottoes again, *nicht wahr?*"

Skade nodded, but still gave the Norn a scowl as she stood beside Fenris.

"We'll come, too," Traeg added, "won't we, dear?"

"*Hmmph,*" Andvari looked into the forest behind the group.

"Arch-Mage?" Verdandi asked.

"Was? Oh, *ja, ja*—we'll come. I'd see Mimir. I sense a threat to the dwarves, and I'd have his counsel."

"I, too, will come," Rudyick said. "I'm honored that you ask, considering how some feel about my father."

"*Und*, you, Servius Aurelius Santini?" Verdandi asked as she turned to him. "Will you now heed our request and come to the Well of Mimir?"

"Please apologize to Fenris," Aurelius said. "I don't know what he meant when he told Skade not to worry because 'barking dogs don't bite,' but I think he's wrong; you will bite, and I've a feeling that not many survive a Norn's wrath. A son shouldn't suffer for the sins of the father."

"You'd speak thus to me?" Verdandi asked, and Clarinda was surprised at the contempt in the Norn's voice. "You whose own father—"

"Verdandi, enough." Clarinda interrupted. "We've not spoken yet of that, and I'd not have it done here."

Aurelius glanced at Clarinda. Did she know of the slavery trade, and, if so why had she not said anything to him? If not, was there something else about his father that he didn't know?

The Norn frowned, but then retreated and inhaled deeply. She turned to Fenris. "Child of the Sly One, I apologize. We've known each other long enough that apologies shouldn't be necessary, but the Codex Wielder is correct, and in this he starts to speak with the wisdom of a Lore Master. As the Incarnation of the Present, I above all should acknowledge that your Fate is yet yours to chart, though it's still my fear that you'll end your days as doomed as the Hospitaller."

Fenris laughed and bowed. "A-ha! You see, Master Santini? That's why you should speak little to a Norn, and certainly never seek an apology. Verdandi, Verdandi, come here, little one." He stepped near and gave her a tremendous bear hug. "Not quite the apology one would hope for, but thank you, thank you!"

"We speak only the truth," Verdandi grimaced at the burly man's strength but returned his hug. "Especially to those who wield the power to slay the Fates themselves and make their own way outside of our looms and skeins." She turned to Aurelius. "Well, Hospitaller? Did that suffice? Will you come to the pool?"

"*Sì*; I'll go with you. I'd like to meet your sisters and Mimir."

"A mixed blessing, that will be," Verdandi replied with furrowed brow, "but, very well, we'll depart immediately."

The Norn reached into her tunic and withdrew a *Brisinga* necklace. Aurelius glanced at Rudyick who was issuing instructions to the leader of his *Keder*.

Aurelius caught his attention. "I need to know three things, Rudyick."

The elf looked curiously at him, and Clarinda smiled a strange smile.

"What?" Aurelius asked her, confused before he'd even asked.

"*Tre?*"

"*Sì, tre cose*—I always like to put things in order, why?"

"It's nothing," she replied, but unable to repress a grin. "I'll tell you later."

Aurelius turned back to Rudyick. "*Primo,* who was the 'Midgardian merchant' that got Loki angry? The Sicilian merchant who interfered with Loki's jest on a northern trader's daughter?"

"That merchant was many fore-bearers ahead of you in your ancestry, Servius Aurelius Santini—a guildsman from Midgard, I believe, or, so the legend goes." He nodded at Clarinda and Verdandi. "Your Norn friends probably know the full story."

"We do, and all will be revealed at Mimir's Well," Verdandi said. "Come along, we must get to a clearing for the *Brisinga* necklace to transport this large of a group."

Aurelius exhaled. "So the name in the frontispiece isn't a mistake," he said, almost to himself.

Clarinda noticed his shoulders sag slightly. "Verdandi's correct," she said. "There's more to the tale than that."

"Even that fact alone is damning. I've been hoping that there's been some mistake in the idea that the Codex belongs to me. It seems that one of my grandfathers earned it for the rest of us."

Clarinda placed a comforting hand on the knight's arm. "Before you rush to judgment," she said, echoing Grimnir's parting words, "speak with Mimir and learn the full story. What's the second question?"

Aurelius straightened. "*Sì. Secondo,* what's so special about Kullervo and his sword?"

"We call him Kullervo the Accursed." Andvari replied before Rudyick could. "A powerful wizard who sought too much knowledge and overreached himself ... overestimated his ability to control otherworldly demons. He went insane trying to learn the Runes of Creation and accidentally slew his family. His blade, *Ukonvasara*, the Singing Sword, is possessed by a demon that assures victory to anyone who uses it. The price for its use is to demand at least one death whenever its drawn."

Rudyick added softly, "Legend has it that Kullervo was once an elf, and the more he tries to commit suicide because of his crimes against nature, the more damage he does to all who meet him."

The Hospitaller winced. "*Bene*—and that answers my *terza questione*. Verdandi said that I'll be coming for that sword soon. You'd better keep your distance from me, Clarinda. Between cursed books and haunted swords, I'm not sure how good company I'll be."

"I'll take my chances," she replied. "We stopped the Codex from talking, didn't we?"

"Children, come." Verdandi led them a short distance into the forest where they came upon a broad clearing.

Even in the shadowed gloom that preceded the rise of the moon, Aurelius could see that the glade differed from the rest of the wood in which they had been traveling. Thick, lush grass rose to the height of a man's knee and ascended the hillock that dominated the center of the fertile area. The brilliant white glow of the orb floating in front of the Norn illuminated the bark of the trees surrounding the sward, and the leaves in the higher branches were full, green, and healthy. It was as if a spell had been cast on this part of Svartalfheim that inured it to the rest of the decay that had overtaken the realm.

Verdandi swiped the air to fashion a rune-gate. It blazed into existence at the top of the hillock, white flames licking about the otherwise invisible framework.

A snow-covered pathway beyond the gateway abutted a cliff-face to the right, and a sheer drop into darkness yawned on the left. Snow fell so rapidly that Aurelius could barely discern the pathway, a jagged break between the cliff wall and the abyss. A dark, shadowed area ahead appeared to be the mouth of a cave.

"*Buon Dio*," the Hospitaller whispered, "not more snow."

"Is that Niflheim or Jotunheim?" Rudyick asked, surprised as everyone else was at the ferocity of the storm blowing through the portal.

"It's Mount Glittertind, as it appears in Jotunheim." Verdandi glanced at Aurelius, her sharp features creating strange shadows on her face in the flickering light of the portal's flames. "Does this way seem familiar to you, Codex Wielder?"

"No. I've never been to Mimir's Well, nor to Jotunheim. If that's the way, then I'll take your word that it is. The last time that I saw Mount Glittertind, it was from a distance in Alfheim."

Through the portal, Aurelius watched the flurries of snow whip into the face of the cliff. Even now, seeing only a part of the Mount Glittertind, he was struck by the earlier foreboding that caused him to feel as if he were going to die there.

"Shall we go on?" Verdandi prompted.

"I'll follow you," Aurelius said cautiously, moving aside to let her pass. He didn't trust the woman.

"Servius Aurelius Santini, when you perish, it shan't be at the hand of a Norn, nor between worlds as you pass through one of my rune-gates. You're safe with me, or with any of my sisters."

The knight shrugged. "If it is all the same, I'll follow you."

"As you wish."

The Norn stepped through the rune-gate. The knight saw her arrive upon the ledge before the path and cave. Aurelius hesitated, thinking he heard an echo in his mind from the Codex Lacrimae, but then he took Clarinda's hand firmly in his own. Amidst the howls of Jotunheim's winds, they walked together through the flames of the *runeporte* and into another world.

CHAPTER 14

Of Huntsmen Piercing the Weirds of Fate

Gale-force winds slamming against the side of the mountain Aurelius slipped on a patch of ice, releasing Clarinda's hand. A sense of déjà vu came over him. He recognized this moment as one of the visions he'd seen upon first touching the Codex Lacrimae.

The small company scrambled up to the cave in stages, helping each other to stand fast against the howling winds and pelting sleet that threatened to dislodge their footing. Inside the cave, however, the temperature changed into a summery heat so abruptly that Aurelius gasped.

The members of the company followed the Norn down a tunnel. Verdandi paused only to ignite the *s'lantar*, and the light upon the passageway revealed green moss and lichen nestled in the walls' cracks and crevices. Flat paving stones radiated warmth that could be felt even through leather footwear.

After an hour of quietly descending into the depths of the mountain, the tunnel's slope became more pronounced and Aurelius wondered how far they'd yet to go into Glittertind before they reached their destination.

Suddenly, a dull, thumping tremor resounded through the passage, originating from somewhere far distant in the mountain.

"What was that?" Fenris exclaimed, pausing mid-step and sniffing the air.

"I usually take greater comfort in mountains," Andvari grumbled, "but that doesn't sound like any mining operation I've ever heard."

"You told me there weren't any dwarves in Glittertind, dear," Traeg said.

"Those aren't mining sounds," Verdandi said.

Another blast shook the mountain, dislodging pebbles and clods of earth in the cavern. Clarinda stumbled slightly at the disruption, but Aurelius lent a steady hand beneath her elbow.

"Something's happening deeper in the mountain," Skade said, speaking to the Norn. "Glittertind's not volcanic, is it?"

"No," Verdandi frowned, then closed her eyes. "We must hasten."

"It's been a hundred years since we've seen Mimir and the Norns," Traeg said, trying to lighten the apprehensive mood.

The mountain finally settled and quieted again, until not even a tremor was felt. "Perhaps Mimir's doing some redecorating at the Well."

"This isn't exactly a social call," the Arch-Mage said. "Besides, Mimir doesn't seem the sort to care about his surroundings."

"Well, with all of us coming, I imagine it'll be social enough to offer some food," Fenris groused. "Even if Surt himself were to appear with all the Sons of Muspell, I'm so hungry that I'd still take a moment to eat some mutton and quaff a pint of ale."

"We stand forewarned, then," Rudyick observed dryly, "the wolf's stomach has priority even at the end of the world. I hope you don't yet see each of us as your evening supper."

Fenris paused for a half-second, understandably surprised that the Dark Elf was, indeed, joking with him. "There's not enough meat on your bones to make a decent meal, Elf."

"Behave yourselves, Lads," Skade chided, the warmth in her voice appreciative at what seemed to be Rudyick's attempt to extend an olive branch. "We should listen to Verdandi and get to Mimir's Well before more of those tremors hit."

They reached the first in a series of steps that spiraled precipitously downward, turning upon themselves through a series of frequently spaced landings—as if they were clambering down the steep stairwells of a castle tower rather than the increasingly claustrophobic interiors of a mountain.

Aurelius felt a blast of cold air, like the door of a warm house opening unexpectedly into the icy chill of a snowstorm. "Do you feel that?"

Rudyick, lost in his own thoughts, said nothing, but Verdandi's face was drawn and, after a confirming glance at Clarinda, Aurelius could tell something was wrong.

"Quickly, now," said the Norn of the Present. "Mimir's Well isn't far."

"Where's the cold air coming from?" Aurelius asked.

"There are natural vents that reach through the rock to this place," Verdandi replied. "The air sometimes comes through, and it's not uncomfortable, but rather refreshing because sometimes the heat of the springs can be a bit intense." She paused. "I'm not sure if this particular breeze is coming from those vents, though, or somewhere else."

"Is the Well of Mimir part of a system of springs?"

"Yes, and the springs supply a system of grottoes where we live—"

A loud, cracking noise interrupted her. A tremendous rumbling shook the depths of the mountain and threw the group to the sides of the stairwell and onto the steps.

Verdandi shouted something to them, but Aurelius couldn't hear her due to the tumult of collapsing rock and soil. Clarinda drew near and yelled at him, then she ran down a short flight of stairs after Verdandi and Rudyick. They seemed to be rushing toward the source of the explosion.

Fenris had shape-shifted into a wolf and grew big enough for Skade to ride him. Andvari and Traeg rose shakily to their feet, and soon the whole company arrived at the next landing.

An enormous mound of rubble lay beneath an open shaft which gaped twenty cubits across the former ceiling. Smoke and dust hovered in a cloud above the debris. The scored and blackened boulders glowed orange, still radiating heat from the blast. Cool air blew snow down the newly bored hole, following the grey stream of daylight shining through, an indication that the storm still raged above.

Aurelius saw a figure making its way down the other side of the rubble, but when the breeze cleared the dust, the figure was gone. Impossible. That ...that man looked like Marcus.

The knight instinctively moved forward to follow, but the Norn's hand on his arm stayed him. "Don't, Servius Aurelius Santini. He's a Huntsman of Muspelheim."

"He looked like a friend of mine."

"It wouldn't surprise me," Verdandi said. "Nothing involving the codexes would surprise me. But, I don't believe that your control of the Codex Lacrimae is so great yet that you can contend with the one who created this hole, do you?"

Don't listen to her! Kill him now, lest he bring trouble later. It's not Marcus, merely a glamour that makes the Huntsman take his appearance. Slay him, and while you're at it, kill the Norn, too!

Aurelius winced, his head throbbing from the urgency of the Codex Lacrimae resurgent in his mind. The force of its words made his head ache.

Go, Hospitaller! I'll show you what to do—don't let him escape!

Verdandi mistook his hesitation for acquiescence to her command. She pointed at an area of shadow to their left. "Good. Let us go through there."

"Wait, Verdandi," Clarinda said, "don't you hear it?"

"Hear what, child?"

"The Codex Lacrimae speaking to Santini."

"What? Now?"

"You can't hear it?"

Verdandi looked from Clarinda to Aurelius, then moved in front of the young knight, put her hand on his forehead and closed her eyes. "No," she said after a moment, "I feel and hear nothing."

We don't have to kill her—binding her with a spell of silence will be just as effective. You can't trust any of the Norns, but especially not Verdandi and Skuld. They told Taliesin they'd help him, but then they let Urd have her way at the Fields. You let these Norns talk too much; all they know how to do is betray!

"It's telling him to bind you with a spell of silence—that's better than a second ago when it wanted him to kill you." Clarinda frowned. "It also mentioned you and Skuld can't be trusted, and something about Taliesin?"

"Taliesin?" Andvari repeated, exchanging a glance with Fenris and Rudyick.

Verdandi raised an eyebrow, then turned again to Aurelius. "Did it, indeed? Try to ignore the thing's speech, Codex Wielder, and follow me. I'll tell you about the Huntsmen on the way to the Well. There's a tunnel in those shadows that can bring us more quickly to Mimir than the route our enemy takes."

"You know that he's going there?" Aurelius asked suspiciously.

"Where else?" Verdandi calmly replied as she began to climb tentatively over the shattered clusters of rocks and boulders.

The group followed. "We've had visions of this attack for months now," Verdandi said, "and all is foreordained and prepared for."

Listen to me! Look at this rock pile and compare it to the hole in the tunnel's ceiling. Notice anything? We're over a quarter kilometer within Glittertind, Fool. Look at that pile. They're liars, Santini, and whatever words they have to say will only delay you at the Well. No, we need to return to the Krak des Chevaliers. At that castle await many enemies who—

"Clarinda," he whispered, but she'd already brought her quarterstaff to his forehead, silencing the tome's words.

"*Grazie!*" he said with relief. "It's so angry at everything, I can't even think my own thoughts. Thank you."

"Hopefully, Mimir will have a more permanent solution," she replied.

"Just so long as it's one that doesn't require my friends or me dying."

"*Mm-hmm,*" Clarinda murmured, but her tone was distant. Like him, she'd heard the Codex's observation and was looking thoughtfully at the pile of rubble.

Verdandi halted with Andvari and Traeg at an apparent dead-end some distance away. Aurelius caught Rudyick's attention.

"Rudyick," Aurelius whispered after he'd glanced at Clarinda and gotten an approving nod. "Do us a favor and run to the top of this blast-hole. Quickly."

The elf started to say something, then looked at the pile of rubble and his almond-shaped eyes widened. He vanished, and by the time Clarinda and Aurelius had crossed the pile of rubble, Rudyick appeared again beside them.

"Well?" Clarinda asked him.

"A massive explosion took place up there," the elf confirmed, glancing at Verdandi's back. The Norn waved her right hand upward along the wall while she spoke to Andvari.

Aurelius glanced at Clarinda, and both exchanged a warning look. Skade checked on the trio's delay down the rock pile, then her eyes tracked upward into the newly blown tunnel above them.

"Here, Clare, let me help," Aurelius reached up to help Clarinda down the last bit of rubble.

"It was correct, Servius," she whispered as she hopped into his arms, and let him swing her around to the ground.

"I know. Somebody was blasting the earth out at the same time the Huntsman was coming in."

"This isn't good," Skade said as they passed her, and the Huntress cast a suspicious look at Verdandi's back. The woman had somehow surmised what they were discussing. "Besides you, Codex Wielder, there's only one person in this group with that kind of power."

Aurelius said nothing, but squeezed Clarinda's hand in an attempt at reassurance as they rejoined Verdandi, who'd stepped back from the wall. The last words of a spell fell from her lips.

A light flared brightly into the dusty air, and a gleaming white crack appeared in the smooth surface. With a tiny click, two halves of a doorway split and swung inward into an impenetrable darkness.

The Norn raised the *s'lantar* and moved into a corridor revealed by the glass-contained flames. She waited until the entire company had filed past her into the newly exposed tunnel, then lowered her other hand in a sweeping, downward gesture. The door snapped shut.

"Let's hasten," she said, moving past them down the narrow

passage. The air was close here, as if the way hadn't been disturbed for centuries.

"Verdandi, tell us who that was back there," Aurelius said. The Norn didn't know him well enough to hear the change in his voice, but its coldness spiked a shiver into Clarinda. "Why did I think it was my friend, Marcus?"

"Was it Farbauti again?" Andvari asked. "I saw an energy aura from Muspelheim around the man, but by the time I helped Traeg up, he was gone."

"I know only that it was a Huntsman," the Norn said, "but whether Farbauti, Morpeth, or another, he must have a powerful patron to control such power. We are well into Glittertind and you yourself saw the hole that he blasted into the mountainside."

"I wonder if these are the same Huntsmen told of in the legends," Rudyick ruminated from behind them, his voice just as controlled as the knight's. "Even in the spans that Norns and Elves reckon time, it's been long since their kind was seen in the Nine Worlds. *Und*, I didn't think that they wielded enough power to blast completely through the defenses of a weird like Glittertind."

"I think that the creature was definitely Morpeth," Skade said. "Now that I've had some time to think about it, I know his reek. I fought him once, long ago when he wore a different form."

"There should be no Huntsmen," Andvari persisted, still irritated that no one was addressing what he saw as a fundamental problem. He had completely missed the silent exchange of glances concerning the pile of debris. "The All-

Father cast them down and exiled them after Mogthrasir fell at the Fields of Burning Night. The gate to Muspelheim is closed."

"One was opened back in Svartalfheim," Rudyick reminded him.

"Something's happening to the *runeporten*," Fenris added, "and I thought it had to do with my sister. Now, I'm not so sure."

"Tis strange that any Huntsman would flee if confronted, as Farbauti did in that campsite," Traeg mused, her voice echoing her husband's thoughts. "But, you're correct Andvari, I'm still surprised that the Huntsmen could return at all. The wards that surround Muspelheim were established by Odin, who made sure that the Ginnungagap reinforced the barriers."

"Ginnungagap ..." Aurelius thought for a moment. "That's the Void between worlds?"

"Yes, and mostly serves to keep Hel, Niflheim, and Muspelheim apart from the more...lively worlds," Verdandi said.

"Why didn't this Huntsman—or whatever it was—why didn't he just use a rune-gate to get to Mimir instead of blowing apart the mountain?" Aurelius asked.

"For the same reason that we aren't," Clarinda replied, when Verdandi, lost in thought, didn't immediately respond. "Glittertind is a *weird*—you can't travel in or out save by physical means."

"Physical means?" Aurelius said sardonically. "There seems to be quite a bit of leeway with that magic. So, no rune gate into the Well, but any other physical means is allowed? Like walking in as we're doing, or punching holes in the side of a mountain like he did?"

"You jest, but there are serious magics that govern the weirds of the Nine Worlds," Verdandi said shortly, "but for this weird to be violated ..."

Clarinda frowned at the conversation, reminded by Verdandi's words of something that had troubled her. "But, Verdandi," she said, "I used the *Brisinga* necklace to return to the grottoes when I fled Satan in one of Hela's Halls."

The Norn stared at her. "Verily? That's unheard of, Clarinda—only Mimir can create a *runeporte* within Glittertind, and usually it takes him some effort at the Well." She looked at the Venetian girl. "You also wear a *triquerta* brooch; that, too, can transport you at need."

"It can?" Clarinda asked, amazed. "Why didn't anyone tell me?"

Verdandi fell silent again.

"The Codex Lacrimae puts all magics in flux," Andvari said, "and perhaps all *runeporten* will be affected now that it's returned."

"Quite likely," Verdandi said, "but still disturbing, nonetheless." She peered at Aurelius. "You've not accepted the Dark Book's price, have you?"

"No," the youth replied, his tone defensive. "I told Andvari that."

"No one should be able to do what we just saw," Andvari stated with deliberate emphasis. "That's what I see as the greatest cause for concern here. Even Odin had to walk this mountain's passages when he came to petition Mimir."

"He speaks truly," Verdandi said. "This is without precedent. If I didn't know better, I'd be of the mind that that being was not a Huntsman, but one of the Aesir, perhaps Odin or Thor, or someone of like power, so tremendous were those blasts. Such would be preferable to the notion that the Huntsmen are truly abroad again in the Nine Worlds."

"Verdandi, if we're agreed that these Huntsmen are from Muspelheim," Aurelius mused, not intending to be ignored by the Norn and Arch-Mage, "it doesn't seem as if Ginnungagap is holding them back anymore. If you can find where they've reentered the Nine Worlds, you might find more answers to these and other questions."

"Aye, that's true." Verdandi glanced at him. "Is this you speaking, Master Santini, or the Codex?"

"Me. Clarinda has silenced the book for a while."

The Norn turned to the Venetian girl, genuinely surprised. "Who taught you such a thing? You 'silenced' a Codex? That kind of spell-casting was thought lost with Dietrich and the Coven of Witches."

Clarinda raised the quarterstaff slightly, enjoying the fact that a Norn seemed surprised at her knowledge, instead of the other way around. "I just felt it was the right thing to do," she said. "Grimnir told me that I'd find many uses for the Spear of Destiny, and he was right. Its touch seems to silence the Codex."

"*Hmmm*, well, of all of us, Grimnir would know, wouldn't he?" She shrugged. "These are all problems we'll have to pose to Mimir and the other sisters." Again her eyes locked with Santini. "You've met at least one of these Huntsmen, haven't you?"

"Two," Aurelius corrected her. "Farbauti in Svartalfheim, and

I discovered that I fought with Morpeth on Midgard, where I live at the Krak des Chevaliers. I passed out there and woke up in Alfheim."

"Then you're, indeed, fortunate, or the Codex is working powerfully for you. Farbauti and Morpeth were the most feared of Surtur's Huntsmen, hated by all civilized beings of the Nine Worlds."

Ahead of them, the tunnel began to lighten, a brightening that was discernible even beyond the light cast by the *s'lantar.* They neared a curve in the corridor and heard the steady splashing of a waterfall.

"Surtur's the ruler of Muspelheim," Verdandi continued, "and the Huntsmen were his creation in the Elder Days, when the Aesir first came into their power in Asgard. The demons created by Surt to populate his armies were fearsome creatures, but none more so than those Thirteen that he called his 'Huntsmen.' Each were made in the image of the first, Mogthrasir, a monstrous creature who'd become too powerful and courted Death herself in an attempt to overthrow Surt. The Fire Lord eventually vanquished Mogthrasir by letting Taliesin cast his former apprentice into the Pit of Unmaking at the Fields of Burning Night ..." Verdandi paused as if recalling something, bowing her head briefly.

She lies, Aurelius. She and Skuld allied secretly in a pact with Taliesin and Braunen—all of them betrayed Mogthrasir in the last moment. Verdandi and Skuld wanted Taliesin for themselves, and Braunen ... well, Braunen always looks out for himself, and his use of Mogthrasir had come to an end. Braunen, Verdandi, and Skuld were always in league; they were willing to take down Mogthrasir, Dietrich, and Merlin to unmake Mogthrasir, and I had to watch as Taliesin unwittingly did their bidding! Urd helped Taliesin defeat Mogthrasir, but only because her sisters had revealed the others' weaknesses and hatred of the Codexes! These are all lies and half-truths!

Clarinda reached forward with the staff, then hesitated, glancing at Aurelius.

He shook his head. Even though the span of time between silences was collapsing, this new information felt somehow true. If he and Clarinda could both hear the Codex in his head offering a different version of events than the Norn's, perhaps it wouldn't hurt to hear another side?

As if reading his thoughts, the Venetian girl winked and gave a nod.

Aloud, Aurelius asked, "You were there, Verdandi? At the Fields of Burning Night?"

Verdandi nodded. "All the Norns were, and Hela herself. That was in the days before the Great Rending, and Surt was a threat that none could countenance. But, for all that, even Surt screamed in agony after Urd revealed Mogthrasir's threat—that Huntsman was like a son to him, and Mogthrasir had done much to bring Muspelheim into the orbit of the other eight worlds before ..."

Oh, Surtur screamed when he tried to slay that Huntsman, the Codex recalled, its voice clear in the Italian youths' minds, *but it wasn't his hand that remade Mogthrasir. He screamed because when Taliesin shut the barrier between the worlds, the Fire Lord knew that he'd lost both his gambit to escape Muspelheim and his favorite Huntsman!*

"Before what?" Aurelius pressed, trying to remain focused on

Verdandi as the Codex offering its alternate version to the Norn's tale.

"...before the end," Verdandi said with a shrug. "Surtur solved the problem of rebellion afterwards created the Thirteen Huntsmen and their Hounds. Unlike what he'd done when he made Mogthrasir, to the Huntsmen he gave mortal bodies that they needed to caretake even when possessing others across the Nine Worlds."

"Why are you surprised that the Huntsmen are back, though?" Aurelius pressed. "Isn't Muspelheim one of the Nine Worlds? Can't it be accessed by these *runeporten*? I saw part of it when Farbauti and Kenezki held me in Svartalfheim. They were going to throw me through the rune gate to imprison me!"

"At one time, *ja*, Muspelheim could be accessed in such a way," Verdandi replied, "but after Surt failed to conquer Asgard, the All-Father sealed Muspelheim from the rest of Creation. You must have had a vision or seen an illusion."

"Verdandi, the portal was there," Clarinda said calmly. "Both Kenezki and Farbauti dove through it."

But the Norn had turned from them, and directed the group toward another tunnel.

Clarinda wondered why Verdandi was either being cryptic in her responses or insistent on a reality that seemed at odds with the one the company had just lived through. Was it simply that the Norn didn't want to admit that she didn't know something, or was she truly so afraid of the return of Surtur and the Huntsmen that she'd deny their existence in her bailiwick of the Present until the last moment. Whichever the truth, Clarinda didn't like seeing this side of the formerly cheerful Norn.

"The prophecies were always on Surtur's side," Andvari grumbled. "We all knew that there was a good chance he'd be back one day." He jerked a thumb at Aurelius. "Look at him. It was said that the Codex Lacrimae would someday return, and here it is."

"Prophecies?" Aurelius asked.

"Yes," Verdandi said, "ones that foretell the role that Surt will play in Ragnarok. It's said that when the end comes, he'll lead the legions of Muspelheim into the Nine Worlds and bring a fire that both destroy and cleanses. Surtur wanted to hasten the Final Twilight, and Mogthrasir and the Huntsmen were his initial efforts toward that end."

Rudyick sang suddenly:

Leaping o'er fire-lakes to Bifrost's bright door,
Come Surt and Muspel-Spawn in death aglow,
Heroes' songs quenched on Valhalla's floor,
As swords, flaming, smite fair rainbow,
The bridge to Asgard darkens with one fell blow,
And dooms Creation to Dark God's sorrow.

"Yes," Verdandi said. "That's a verse from the Lay of the Codex Lacrimae, Servius Aurelius Santini. Do you know it, yet?"

"Not in its entirety," Aurelius replied. He remembered the words—the pages of knowledge and ancient lore—that came into his mind while a prisoner in Farbauti's campsite. He suspected that he somehow did know the lay in its entirety, but he didn't care to reveal how much he knew about the Codex

Lacrimae, either to the Norn or Rudyick. Except for Clarinda, he still wasn't sure whom, if anyone, he could trust.

"Then the Huntsmen," Aurelius said, continuing his line of thought, "they were themselves hunted and ... removed to a place beyond the same Great Barrier that Odin created for Surt and his legions in Muspelheim? But, why weren't the Huntsmen killed?"

"It's difficult to slay a Huntsman," Verdandi replied. "They were always the most effective of Surt's weapons because they were unlike any other being in Creation. Their essence is the substance of Muspelheim itself, so they're not entirely corporeal. When wandering in the worlds outside of Muspelheim, they need bodies from those worlds to possess—"

"Like the *Húð Göngufólk*, the Skin-Walkers?" Clarinda asked.

"In possession of an innocent, *ja*," Verdandi confirmed, "but unlike the *Húð Göngufólk* the Huntsmen have original bodies that they try to preserve so that they can return to them at will. This physical possession—a kind of shape-shifting, I suppose— it allowed for them to blend in better with the native populations when they were hunting.

"When their task was completed, or their quarry tracked down, they'd flee their host-bodies and return to their own before making their way to their master. This process was, to say the least, extremely traumatizing for the people whose bodies they'd inhabited, leaving them to an agonizing death when the hunt was over. In short, Codex Wielder: the Huntsmen can't die, except by Odin-Fire, and only the All-Father himself commands such magic."

"Remember that, Servius," Clarinda murmured. "When

we're at the Well, we're going to discuss a couple of caskets that you and I need to destroy at the Krak. Besides holding the means to create a gigantic *runeporte*, each one carries the original body of Farbauti and Morpeth."

"What caskets at the Krak des Chevaliers?" the young knight asked. "We're under siege. No caskets are getting into that castle, trust me. But, wait. How do you know what we'll be talking about?"

"I told you: time—everything we're doing has to do with time, and you'll find that—"

"Hush, children," Verdandi interrupted. "I'd finish this tale before we reach the Well."

Aurelius still wanted to speak with Clarinda, but he obeyed the Norn. "Can you tell me at least how did Odin and the Aesir succeed in ridding the Nine Worlds of them if they can't die?" Aurelius persisted. "How was this ward, this Great Barrier, or Ginnungagap created?"

"Only Odin knows, but it's held for millennia. That's why the tidings of Farbauti and Morpeth returning are so disturbing. After Mogthrasir was cast down almost six hundred years ago, those two became the greatest of Surt's minions. It's reasonable to assume that, if there were a means of escaping the wards that Odin placed around the abyss, they'd be the ones to discover it. My fear is that they weren't alone. If Surt himself has been freed, and the Codex Lacrimae is again in the Nine Worlds, then Ragnarok, the End of the World, may indeed be approaching as Mimir warned."

CHAPTER 15

Present becomes the Future: Clarinda Uses the First of the Gåtefull Runer

At the end of the tunnel, the Norn ceased speaking. A vast cavern loomed before the group, and light brighter than that of day flooded the entire subterranean space. Trees fringed the broad cave and grew in hilly stands along the pathways that laced themselves throughout the uneven terrain. Grass sprouted in tufts between the formations of natural rock and stalagmites that thrust upward from the earth, and in some places the turf lay expansively in broad, thick, and verdant swards. Wildflowers in sweeping meadows that stretched as far as the eye could see filled other stretches of the cavern.

Astonished, Aurelius initially looked ceiling-ward for the source of light, but then saw that the radiance shone from silver-white fire flickering hotly over the surface of the lake that dominated the center of the cavern. Shadows fled from the argent flames that coruscated like starlight on top of the otherwise still surface of the water. Rock formations and boulders covered with light green moss lined the shores.

Something on a bridge leading to the flaming lake amazed him even more that the underground Eden. On that bridge another Clarinda spoke to a cloaked woman!

"Hold here for a moment, everyone, and stay out of sight," Verdandi said, pointing at the women. "Time needs to realign."

Aurelius took in the sight of a Clarinda on the bridge, and then, gaping, turned in wonder back to the one standing beside him. Surreally aware that there were, indeed, two Clarindas within shouting distance of each other, he clasped her hand more tightly in his own.

"Just watch," Clarinda whispered. "This is why I couldn't talk about the council before now; we're all members of it!"

"What? You mean, the entire company?"

"Sì," she said, keeping her voice low. "That Clarinda over there, that's my past self, but I'm also returning now into the present."

"Past and the present together?" the Hospitaller hissed, completely confused.

"*Shhh*, it's a Norn thing," the merchant's daughter confided. "I'll try to explain later. That other woman is Urd, the Norn that I'm training to become after she gets killed by Morpeth."

"That's been bothering me, Clare; if you know she's going to die, can't you prevent it?" Aurelius asked, taken aback that Clarinda was so calm about there being two of her in the grotto. "If that was Morpeth who blew a hole in the mountain, shouldn't we have tried to stop him back in the tunnels?"

"They don't think Fate can be avoided, but I'm working on it. Now, *tranquilla*, Aurelio! We need to let all this happen so we can get to the Well."

The group remained in the shadows on the far side of the cavern and watched as the Clarinda on the bridge shook her head in response to something just said by the robed woman in front of her.

"I just learned that Satan played 'Uncle Servius' to Santini over five years ago," the other Clarinda said. "Are you saying that he and Hela somehow drove him to the Holy Land when he was living in Sicily so that he'd be in the area where the Codex was—or, where it *would* be—some five years later? Did Old Nick free Farbauti and Morpeth?"

"This meeting was just after Fenris pounced and carried you through Hela's window, and I'd escaped from her tower," Clarinda whispered to Aurelius. "I came back here before I returned to find you in Niflheim."

"Perhaps," Urd replied to the other Venetian girl, "but I'm of the belief that there's something else at work here, Clarinda. Someone who's organizing events and manipulating people at a level I've not seen since Loki roamed the Nine Worlds."

"Loki? The trickster god?"

"Yes, but he's still bound at the deepest level of Mount Glittertind. My sisters and I've been checking regularly on him since all this began, and he's still where Odin left him, tied to a rock until the end of time."

"Why would he have anything to do with this if he were free?"

"Clarinda," Urd replied cautiously, "Mimir interrupted us and you were too angry to let us finish, but you heard correctly when we said that there was more than one author of the Codex Lacrimae. We've known that Volund, the Dark Elf, was one of those creators. Except for Dietrich the Mad and Professore Ugolino, Volund was one of the rare Great Mages who could manipulate the kinds of magic needed to create the Codex."

"Volund?" Clarinda exclaimed. "Wasn't that the elf who Old Nick and the *fossegrim* captured? He was tied to a tree as their prisoner when Hav brought us to the glade."

Urd nodded. "That makes sense. Old Nick must have been trying to get information from the Dark Elf about the Codex Lacrimae when you two came along and interrupted him." The Norn took a deep breath. "As for the other 'author' of the Codex, we suspect that Loki played a crucial role in making the book before being captured by Thor and imprisoned by Odin after the death of Balder."

Clarinda and Urd, Mimir's voice sounded in their minds, but even the entire company waiting in the shadows behind Verdandi and the other Clarinda could hear him.

Some haste, please. The girl needs to get to Niflheim.

"Let's go," Urd said, moving off the bridge. "This mystery has been consuming us for years. I don't think that you're going to solve it in the next few moments."

When they'd passed out of sight, Verdandi still held her hand up to forestall any movement by the members of the eavesdropping company. Her caution was rewarded. Another Verdandi walked quickly past them, followed by a robed woman whose appearance made Aurelius gasp.

"Fatima?" he whispered, looking searchingly at Clarinda. "What's Ibn-Khaldun's daughter doing here?"

"I've met her back on Midgard. We've been traveling together since a banquet and battle at Caesarea."

Confusion still played across his face.

"It's not your Fatima," she continued, "I mean, the Norns have been assuming the likenesses of my friends to help with training. Initially, it was to keep things familiar for me, and to offset the shock of the Nine Worlds—recently, I've begun to think that they like the changes. See Verdandi? You wouldn't know because you haven't met her, but she's taken on some of the features of my friend, Genevieve."

Aurelius looked again at Skuld, disbelief still on his face. "That's amazing. I've gotten to know Fatima and her husband—"

"Khalil," Clarinda finished his sentence. "I've met him, too. We all fought together—it was when I first met Old Nick and Kenezki revealed himself."

"Ah, I'm putting it together now. The banquet and the battle—the Caesarean incident that Old Nick and Kenezki both talked about?"

"Not a fun tale; which is why I've not discussed it. That's when I found my father."

"Oh, right, sorry —"

"Don't be. There's nothing anyone could do, except if *Padre* hadn't sat down with Farbauti and Morpeth to begin with." She nodded at the receding backs of the Norns and continued when the area around the underground lagoon was clear again. "The one wearing Fatima's face was Skuld." She flushed. "This is a strange feeling. I don't know what'll happen when this me," she pointed to herself, "meets the past me—or is it the future me, now that I'm approaching?" She inhaled, bracing herself. "Well, let's go. I suppose we'll find out soon."

Verdandi motioned the company across the bridge.

Ratatosk snorted. "Skulking in the shadows and running from the Huntsmen," the animal said as he ran along the bridge's stone balustrade. "I've not seen shenanigans like this since Freyr and Freyja played tricks around the great mead hall in Asgard when they were kids. Children! You're all acting like children." He swirled his tail at Aurelius. "You're lucky to be alive, fellow; they all know that these moments before you accept the Codex are probably the only times you can be killed, and no one's doing a thing!"

"Hush, Ratatosk," Verdandi said. "As ever, you take pleasure in short sighted gibes, rather than reflecting on long-term realities." She took in the rest of the company with her piercing gaze. "We can join everyone soon. Time's shifting back into the predicted moments. Clarinda, you and Ratatosk must come with me now."

The Norn looked sternly at the rest of the group. "Clarinda, Ratatosk and I must rejoin our past selves to meet this future. We'll give you a signal to rejoin us at the appropriate moment."

The two women and squirrel walked behind one of the larger boulders and didn't emerge from the other side.

Aurelius and Andvari looked at each other. After a space of time both knight and arch-mage peered around the edge of the rock, but because of a bend in the cavern wall, could only see the flickering shadows cast from the flaming lake.

"How are we supposed to see a signal, if we can't see any of them?" Aurelius whispered to the dwarf.

"*Shhh*, I'm eavesdropping!" Andvari hissed.

"I can't hear ..." Aurelius began, but then Rudyick and Fenris both shushed him.

"Are all mortals as talkative as you and the girl?" the elf asked in a low voice. "Use your ears. They're all greeting each other, and Urd's angry that Ratatosk and the other Guardians have been visiting Clarinda."

Elf and dwarf paused, listening some more, and then Andvari added. "Ratatosk's arguing with Urd, and insulting Clarinda —"

"It sounds like mumbles to me," Aurelius said, exasperated.

Oh, by Odin's Nails! The Codex Lacrimae's voice rushed back into the knight's mind. *You don't need to depend on the hearing of an old dwarf and a miserable elf, Aurelius! Listen!*

Suddenly, Aurelius's hearing became so acute that the words of the group in the far part of the grotto became so clear that he started, thinking that the speakers were next to him.

He heard Ratatosk speaking: "Do you see, Grimnir? Do you see what I have to put up with down here? Is it any wonder that I spend my very long-lived life running up and down a tree and playing with dragons and Hel-beasts? Would *you* stay down here for any time? The conditions are impossible. Let me tell you something, I was just in Hel, and *she* knows how to host a party—a festive atmosphere compared to these grim folk, with fun fountains and lively banquet tables …"

"Ratatosk!" A woman's voice cut sharply, her tones sounding like an older version of Clarinda. "What have you told her? How many of the *Gàtefull Runer*?"

"None of those, I swear!" Ratatosk squealed. "I've been telling her stories about each of the Nine Worlds, mostly.'

"What are the 'Enigmatic Runes'?" Aurelius heard Clarinda asking.

"Sigils," an old man answered, which the knight immediately recognized as Grimnir, the man he'd met briefly in Alfheim. "Special signs—runes, like these—but, I think, in the case of the Norns, very different in what they do."

If I may. Mimir's voice was cold, and so clear in Aurelius's mind that he knew he would have heard it even without the assistance of the Codex.

This has all been well and good but I suggest that we turn to the matter at hand. Ratatosk, quit bothering the wolves, or perhaps go visit Nidhogg the Dragon. Clarinda, you'll be learning one of the Gàtefull Runer *before this morning is over, so let's not worry overmuch about that. Urd, I knew of the Guardians visiting Clarinda, and think the friendship will be helpful in time to come. Now, Clarinda, allow me to introduce Grimnir, an old friend who has taken something of an interest in our attempts to help young Santini. He has some news to share; it seems that he had a visit with the Hospitaller shortly after the boy's arrival in Alfheim …*

Then the company behind the boulder heard Grimnir relate his story about meeting Aurelius shortly before the encounter with Old Nick and the *fossegrim*. The young knight felt a little uncomfortable when Andvari, Traeg, Fenris, and Skade looked at him with newfound respect as Clarinda took over the tale after Grimnir had departed, and described how the Hospitaller had defeated the water elemental by speaking its secret name.

He patted the leather packet in the front of his tunic—until that moment, he'd almost forgotten that Hav had dropped the envelope and he'd retrieved it. The packet was slightly thicker now because of the chunk of bark Cerys had given him. He thought also about the blue coral still in Clarinda's purse, and wondered if they'd ever see the water elemental again when he came to claim those talismans.

"You've gained a considerable ally," Andvari whispered to Aurelius as Clarinda's voice ceased, and she received some kind of instructions from Mimir that none could decipher. Even Aurelius with the aid of the Codex heard only garbled words.

"He's teaching her the runes for a particular spell," Andvari said. "We'll have to wait until he's done to hear clearly again." He peered curiously at the young knight, and shook his head with a smile. "Extraordinary. I've never known anyone who has a life-debt from a *fossegrim*, and yours is from one of the most powerful in the Nine Worlds."

"I merely did the right thing," Aurelius said with a slight shrug. "I don't think that I'd have figured it out, if not for the conversations with Grimnir about the Norse word for 'ocean' and Clarinda telling me about her conversation with Rudyick. They led me to thinking a certain way, and the answer to the riddle of his name became obvious."

The conversation of the group around the corner of the

cavern wall came back into prominence and Aurelius found that he could hear the words clearly again.

"Ah, well done, Mimir—a particularly proficient use of that rune" Grimnir said, "and that reminds me: Clarinda come here, please. We may as well make sure all is in accord with the Tree of Life when you meet Santini again. Here, take this cloak. Along with those boots and gloves that the Norns have for you over there, you'll be able to offset the cold of Niflheim. If it's appropriate, you might want to tell the boy to use my hatchet against any Huntsman he meets, and particularly any tattooed friends that happen to be with them. I think, my dear, that along with Gungnir, you and Master Santini will be pleasantly surprised by the properties in these weapons."

The hidden eavesdroppers couldn't hear what happened next, so Aurelius crept forward to the bend in the cavern wall and peered around the corner. He saw a flaming lake, with a glowing, human head floating in the air at its shoreline. Clarinda, and three other women stood there, as well as the cloaked figure of Grimnir and his wolves. Ratatosk watched from a rock ledge nearby.

Clarinda walked over to Grimnir, and the old man took her quarterstaff into his hand. He put his spear next to the weapon and Aurelius watched in wonder as the wood of both seemed to blur with a flash of light. Then spear and staff were one and he returned the weapon to her.

"There. Don't let go of the spear," Grimnir said. "Take care of it, so that it will take care of you. You may find that it also has more uses than warfare, if you put your mind to using its magic in different ways."

"Thank you," Clarinda said, "I'll guard it well." Mimir's voice became slightly urgent.

You must leave now, Clarinda, and find the Codex Wielder in Niflheim. At this moment he fights with Fenris and Skade against Hela's *Wilde Jagd*.

Clarinda nodded, but Aurelius frowned and asked Andvari and Rudyick who'd come to watch, "How can that be? We're not in Niflheim anymore. That was a couple days ago, and now we're all here."

"Time and space mean little to Mimir and the Norns," Rudyick said.

"No, Elf," Andvari disagreed, "they mean everything, it's merely we who don't understand."

Mimir turned to Clarinda. *There is need for haste, and you will go soon. Peril is closer now than it's ever been. All of you, heed me: untrained, with the Elven and Jotun magic at his command, Santini might fracture the worlds. Clarinda Trevisan, Urd-Yet-To-Be, please bring him to us so that we might speak of these things with him. I will complete the first of the* Gàtefull Runer *that I will teach you, Clarinda. This first is one of the most subtle, yet also the most effective where time is of the essence. It is called a* dopplegänger *rune that makes you here and there, folded in time—*

The Codex Lacrimae started laughing, its words returning loudly to Santini's mind drowning out those of Mimir.

Watch and ware, Hospitaller; this should be instructive on what not to do when crafting this particular Gàtefull Rune. *We'll see if they've learned my magics as well as they seem to think they have. How dare he? I'm gone for a few centuries, and this discarded and disembodied Vanir thinks that he can appropriate my sorceries?*

Clarinda's head snapped toward Santini, unable to see him in the shadows of the cavern niche, but obviously hearing the Codex's words where no one else in the gathering—not even Mimir—had done so.

Mimir floated to the edge of the pool and Clarinda leaned forward to listen to his words. The Seer whispered something unintelligible to the girl, but the Codex laughed again exultantly in Santini's mind.

As I thought, it's not a true doppelgänger; *where he's merely playing with time, I could truly split you in twain with none the wiser, including yourself. Fool. He's satisfied with merely passing between seconds to appear in two places.*

"The Codex Lacrimae is present and laughing, Mimir," Clarinda said, when Mimir had finished what he was teaching her. "Further, it says that you've not learned how to make a true doppelgänger, and that you're merely playing with time."

Mimir's head moved backward, and the Norns murmured in astonishment to each other, all of them looking around as if they expected the Codex, too, to appear floating in midair as Mimir did.

It speaks not, Mimir asserted. *I would sense such a thing.*

"It does, too, speak," Clarinda persisted, "and it talks constantly to Santini. They're both here, hidden, and the Dark Book's laughing and saying that you're just playing with time and not able to do what it can."

That's true, Mimir conceded, *but the magic's been close enough for our purposes.*

Aurelius stepped back around the cavern wall, heeding the cautions of Verdandi and Clarinda and not wanting to be seen yet. The Codex, however, continued to speak in his mind, and Clarinda kept translating its words for the group by the lake.

Well, she obviously survived this attempt, Mimir, but I wouldn't stake my existence on this clumsy imitation—any of the Gàtefull Runer *is only as good as the sorcerer speaking the runes."*

Mimir looked in the direction of the shadowed area of his grotto, and spoke directly to the Codex, even though neither he nor the Norns could see the hidden company.

Perhaps you'd care to enlighten us as to the proper way, O Dark Book?

The Codex replied immediately, using Aurelius's voice: "Tell the boy to accept my price, and I'll teach you many things—some you might even live to regret learning."

The members of the hidden company stepped back from Aurelius, startled at the knight's declaration when they'd not been privy to the rest of the conversation.

Mimir shook his head, and glanced at Clarinda.

Even after all this time ... nothing changes. If the Codex Wielder is here, then you must go to Niflheim, Clarinda. We shall resume speaking in a few minutes. His eyes flicked at Grimnir. *If I may, Grimnir, perhaps Freki and Geri could accompany, to protect her in the wastes?*

"A prudent idea," the old man nodded. "Geri and Freki, accompany and protect her. Find Santini."

Aurelius's eyes widened as Clarinda came towards him from the very tunnel they'd used to get to the grotto. The Venetian girl's out-of-breath appearance coincided with a brilliant argent flash that brightened the grotto.

"*Bene,*" she gasped, resting her hand on Aurelius's shoulder.

He noticed that she had unpinned the *triquerta* brooch from her waist and now clasped it to the v of her tunic, directly over the cleft between her breasts. The knight blushed and looked away.

"Mimir just sent me and the animals through the pool over there," she said, "and I ran here from a different cave entrance!"

"We heard," Aurelius said, giving her a brief hug. "I think I'm starting to see what you were trying to tell me about time."

Halfdan glanced around, a confused expression on his face. "But, where's Ratatosk? I can't really tell Geri and Freki apart from Fenris's pack, but I know that the squirrel was with us much of the time."

Clarinda shrugged. "All three are guardians of Yggdrassil, Halfdan; they must have teleported back here after Hela's ambush in Nidaveller. I don't bother trying to keep track of their comings and goings. All I know is that we can all go forward now—that *Gåtefull Rune* worked. The present now meets the future of the past."

CHAPTER 16

A Codex and a Vanir at the Well of Fate

Clarinda began to move again as if the idea were as easy to understand as her stride and—even though many questions were on the lips of everyone except for Andvari and Traeg, who seemed to fully comprehend the supernatural implications—the members of the company followed the Venetian girl into the nearest grove of trees, passing over the soft grasses as silently as a breeze.

Mimir had vanished, but Skuld saw them. The Sister of the Future broke away from the other woman who awaited at the edge of the flaming lake, and moved to embrace Clarinda.

"Urd, Skuld, and Grimnir," Verdandi said. Her words had a formality to them, deliberate by way of introduction. "This is Servius Aurelius Santini, Knight Hospitaller, and potential user of the Codex Lacrimae."

"Well met, Master Santini," Urd said solemnly, "your fate is not a kind one, but there might be much that you can accomplish ere your passing."

"Hail," Grimnir said, "and good to see that you survived Old Nick and the *fossegrim*."

"Hail, Grimnir," Aurelius returned the greeting with a curt bow, "you left before we had a chance to go fishing."

"So I did, so I did," the grey-bearded man chuckled. "I try to avoid confrontations when at all possible." He pointed to his two wolves who'd emerged from the shadows. "It gets Freki and Geri upset, I think."

Aurelius shook his head. "I've seen those wolves fight. I'm glad to see the two of you survived Hela and the *Wilde Jagd*."

"Hail, Codex Wielder," Freki said, and then his yellow eyes moved to catch Fenris's attention. "Your pack is safe, Fenris; after Hela left, we showed them the ways through the tunnels. They were running back to your hut the last we saw of them."

"That's good to know." Fenris nodded to both of them. "Thank you."

"Do you still have that little hatchet I gave you?" Grimnir asked Aurelius.

"I do. It's served well for other things than chopping firewood," Aurelius put a hand to the hand-ax. "Would you like it back?"

"No, no; you'll have more need of it than I."

"These others," Verdandi continued, waving a hand toward

the rest of the group, "are here by my invitation." She gestured at each member of the company as she spoke. "The Codex Wielder is accompanied by the Arch-Mage Andvari, Sorceress Traeg, and Brigadier-General Halfdan of the dwarves; Skade, the Skiing Huntress, comes with Fenris, Loki-Son; lastly, this is Rudyick, Volund-Son, a Dark Elf."

"Again, I say well met, all of you," Urd said solemnly, "and we're particularly pleased that you've survived thus far, Master Santini."

"*Grazie*," Aurelius replied. "I've been helped much by my friends, and by one of your own. I don't think that I'd have gotten very far in my adventures without Clarinda here."

"Greetings, Master Santini," Skuld said, stepping past Urd and surprising everyone by embracing the youth.

He felt a genuine kindness and concern radiate from her, feelings enhanced by the fact that she looked identical to Fatima. Ibn-Khaldun's daughter had become like an older sister to him during the last five years at the Krak, and he held her for a long moment as if she were a singular, secure connection to a past that was unraveling the more he learned about it.

"Don't let my sister's somber tone dishearten you," Skuld continued when she broke the embrace. She held both of the Hospitaller's arms at his sides as if she were an aunt who had not seen a nephew in a couple decades and was measuring his growth from boy to man. "Urd tends to speak more directly than is customary for general civility."

"I'm certain that reassures him, Skuld," Verdandi commented dryly, "but we must have a council, quickly. A Huntsman approaches through the upper halls."

"We know," Skuld replied. "Urd thinks it's Morpeth."

A geyser of silver fire erupted soundlessly at the center of the burning lake. It streamed upward, forming a single column of pulsing energies that stretched from the lake's surface to the ceiling and crackled like living lightning.

Aurelius raised a hand to shield his eyes against the brilliance. The brilliant silvery light faded to the normal flickering white flames of the lake and vanished back into the water with a rush of air that made the knight's ears pop. The head of a man, unattached to a body, now hovered above the flames—Mimir. His handsome features belonged to a man in the prime years of life, fair of complexion, with hair that shone as if made of spun gold.

The head floated towards Aurelius, unnerving him. It stopped in the air a few paces from the knight and, without knowing why, Aurelius stepped forward to greet the entity.

Well come, Servius Aurelius Santini. Mimir's voice resounded in the minds of all members of the company gathered at the shore. I am Mimir. As expected, your coming brings with it problems both foreseen and unforeseen, and I hope that your burden shall surpass neither your strength, nor the need of those who inhabit the Nine Worlds.

Mimir's voice contained a warmth and compassion that surpassed even that of the Norns and, except for his physical condition, the man seemed the most humane of all the strange beings gathered by the strange lake.

Mimir stared at Aurelius and his glowing eyes narrowed. When he spoke next, he used a cold and dispassionate tone. *Identify me.*

Aurelius spoke, but it was the thought-speech of the Codex Lacrimae that answered. "Hail, Mimir, Outcast of the Vanir."

For the first time, everyone in the group could hear it, and to a man and woman each took a slight step away from the Hospitaller.

I will not be trifled with, especially by you. Mimir's said dismissively. Do you recognize an axis?

"Never!" Aurelius said. "You'll not set a constant, Mimir, nor attempt to associate with us. We settled that at the Fields of Burning Night."

That moment was not unanimous. Do you acknowledge isometries for you and your kind?

"Never. We are unbound, and without measure. I will not reveal the script in which we were written."

Observe the ways of our Siðr, and abide by the rules of the Codices' particular Trolldómr. Your form governs your response, and it is corrupt.

"Ha! Rules. Each of us is different and unknowable to the other, fool. Taliesin knew. Taliesin knew that we are beyond faith, traditions, and morals. So do not float above your pathetic pond beneath the mountains and speak to me of 'our Siðr.' We are not of you. We are beyond this space and time, and we follow or disregard any ellipses you try to define us by."

You will observe the universal Trolldómr. Identify me.

"Would that there was one. Old Man, do not describe my magic as a series of spells within the range of your witches' petty sorceries. *Trolldómr!* Bah. Your Norns have enough problems with casting even one of the *Gátefull Runer,* so do not think to include me in your conception of *Trolldómr.*"

"Think you to know more of the *Gátefull Runer* than Mimir?" Grimnir asked.

"Fly with your crows, Grey Beard! You above all know what we can do." Aurelius glared at Grimnir, then returned attention to Mimir. "Ja, Mimir, I do know magics that would break your mind. Can you unbind a three-fold man and yet leave him one? Can you gain the allegiance of a dragon undead yet breathing fire?" The knight pointed at himself. "I foresee that these acts will be the first of this one's *Gerningar* after he accepts me. I will teach him, and he will span the worlds in the blink of an eye."

"A *Gerningar*?" Clarinda whispered to Urd.

A concrete act, the Norn thought back to her, *one which binds the natural and supernatural together by sorcery. Now, be quiet!*

Power without conscience is abomination, Mimir said. *Your form governs your response. Identify—*

"I am formless, Mimir! Written by beings whose magics were bound to the grief and sorrow you allowed."

Identify me, Codex Lacrimae.

"You are Mimir the Bodiless, Ogler of Witches."

Identify me.

"You are Mimir the Unclean, smeared in the Worlds' Excrement in your sewer beneath the mountains."

Identify me.

Aurelius's head began to hurt, and sweat began to collect on his forehead.

I will be correctly identified, Codex Lacrimae, Mimir repeated, *or you will be returned to the ether from which you've almost escaped. You have no mastery here. Your form governs your response, and by the hands of Volund and Loki your making was corrupt. Identify me, or you will be cast again into the Night.*

The pressure inside Aurelius's mind became acute. He suddenly found himself on one knee before the flaming lake with his head bowed. The rage of the Codex Lacrimae made it hard to breathe as he spoke the required words. "You are Mimir, a Maker, Lore Master, and Guardian of the Nexus Portal. I identify you as Keeper of the World Lines that bind the Arcs of the Eternal Triquerta."

Ah, much better. Mimir's tone remained even, but the entire cavern seemed to release a tension that had built between the two entities.

Aurelius rose shakily to his feet, and Clarinda noticed that he seemed disoriented, and still not in control of himself.

Mimir spoke again. *Hail, Codex Lacrimae, One of the Nine Codices of Fate—long lost and newly found. I place you within the Last Three, preceded by the Seventh Note. You are ill-met because of the corruption you bring, and I know not your intent here. I still hope that you might eventually rejoin your brothers and sisters to restore order to universe.*

"My intent remains my own, Lore-Master" Aurelius replied in a voice that remained his, yet not his. "Your hopes have ever meant less than nothing to me."

Beware of this place, Aurelius, the Codex Lacrimae continued, speaking only to the Hospitaller now. *You stand in great peril here. Odin himself, during a time when the Nine Worlds were threatened by Surt and the legions of Muspelheim, came to the pool to seek the wisdom and counsel of Mimir.*

Mimir gave the All-Father counsel without charging a price, for he owed Odin a life debt. However, the pool took its own price: upon Odin's first sip from its waters, power surged through his frame, coursing through his body as his mind was filled with the lore of ages. Black, crackling radiance shot through with bolts of violet-blue burst from the All-Father's left eye. He was never able to see from that orb again.

There is a price for everything in life, Servius. The Codex Lacrimae's voice dropped to the quietest tone Aurelius had heard it use. *Even denying me will take its own price on your destiny and those around you.*

I ask you this: unless your friends are immortal, will they not eventually die? Why should you concern yourself overmuch with your singular interpretation of "the life of a friend?" The runes of Loki and Volund that mark my frontispiece allow much in the way of interpretation.

Mimir interrupted.

Thank you, Codex Lacrimae. Whatever you are discussing with the boy can wait until later. You may depart.

In similar fashion to Clarinda and Cerys, Mimir's words silenced the feminine voice in Aurelius's mind.

Mimir's head turned slightly in the air, taking measure of each member of the company gathered at the shore. *Come, now, I foresee much of your intents, already, but I'd hear from each of you the many purposes and desires that bring you to my pool.*

The knowledge here can be costly, yet you've all braved many perils to visit me. Are you all here solely for the sake of escorting the Codex Wielder, or would you request something else of the Seer of Fate?

CHAPTER 17

The Council
at Mimir's Well

When no one immediately replied, Urd stepped forward. "Please, Fenris, tell us why you have followed the Hospitaller."

The youngest of Loki's children smiled a haunted smile. "I would change my fate, Fate."

"Explain," Urd said.

"You all probably know that in my home, I spend much time reading, trying to find a way to escape the curse," Fenris said with a nod toward the books and manuscripts that filled some of the wall niches by the pool. "I see here in your collection many of the same works and parchments that I pore over every day. It's been foretold that I will side with my sister and father at Ragnarok, the end of days." He crossed his broad arms over his chest. "After Fimbulvetr rages for three years—"

"Fimbulvetr?" Aurelius asked.

"Yes, I apologize, Codex Wielder; Fimbulvetr is a storm that will make the one on the mountain outside and those we saw in Niflheim seem like light flurries. Then my sister, Hela, will set sail in Naglfar, a ship that she's building even now. A vessel made of dead men's nails. Giants will be on board with her, as will an army of the dead much like that of the *Wilde Jagd*, only a hundred times larger. My brother, Jormungand, the Midgard Serpent, will slither from the sea to battle Thor, the god of thunder, eventually slaying him with his venom. *Und*, I … it is foretold that … I will kill Odin himself, the All-Father and ruler of the gods of Asgard." Fenris stared intently at Aurelius. "I would have it be otherwise."

"We all hope that it'll be otherwise, my love," Skade added, "and that Fate in this instance can be turned aside before the end." Then her voice softened to a tone that none who'd seen her fight could believe possible. "Don't be so hard on yourself, Fenris. Ragnarok hasn't come yet, and the prophecies say nothing about the union between you and me."

"That's true enough, my little huntress," Fenris said with a grin.

Rudyick nodded at Urd. "It seems that sometimes Fate can be undone. You were at Skade's first wedding Urd. You said then that both Njörd and Skade would be together forever."

"*Nein*," Urd corrected, "what I said was that their union would hold until the Sarsen Stones fell."

"But, they remain," Rudyick exclaimed.

"Not those off the sea of Norfolk, they don't," Urd stated flatly. "You and Njörd took care of that."

"We were trying to stop Dietrich and the druids!"

Urd shrugged. "We were discussing my foretelling, not your failures in interpretation."

"Rudyick," Skade said, "there's no one to blame for the failure of our marriage but Njörd and me." She shrugged. "Our natures never changed. I'm from the mountains, and he from the sea. It was only a matter of time before we realized that."

Long are your lives, Mimir observed, *and there is great truth in acknowledging the unpredictability of Fortune's Wheel.*

Fenris squeezed Skade's hand, thanking her quietly for her support. He glanced at the reflective Rudyick, then at Aurelius and grinned. "For all the predictions of my Fate, I believe my fortune started to turn the moment that you appeared alive in my sister's tower."

Skade's face flushed with irritation, but he forestalled her with a raised hand. "I talk of my Fate, now, not my love."

He paused and looked between the Hospitaller knight and the bodiless Vanir. "Of course, I prefer to think of my actions in that moment—when I attacked you and carried us out the window—that I was governed by a recognition of the Codex Light around you."

He closed his eyes. "Mimir and the Norns know enough about me to know that there's another possibility. I might have been trying to kill you, Aurelius. The beast does not think as we do, remember that."

His eyes glittered in the pool's light and the knight noticed the man's teeth gleaming through his beard. "A wolf is a wolf—

it knows only of existence and the continuance of existence. Hunger and satiety."

Long have we watched you, Fenris, Mimir said. Since you were a cub and cast from Odin's home—and I, too, would hope that you might somehow avert the Fate foretold by my Norns. Is that your sole purpose, then? To accompany the Codex Wielder and protect him?

Skade took the lead, shaking her head. "No, Wise One. We have come partly to fulfill the promise to protect Master Santini and Lady Clarinda, but mostly for another purpose. We seek counsel in a quest."

The price for my counsel is high, Skade, yet ever you have been close to our hearts, and I remember fondly the years that you lived in these grottoes. Ask.

"We've learned that Hela's death-ship, Naglfar, is almost completed," Skade said.

"What?" Andvari burst out, unable to restrain himself. "That's impossible. There haven't been enough wars and death in the Nine Worlds to complete the construction so soon!" He looked to his wife. "Our spies on the shores of the Niflheimian Sea would have told us."

"We've not heard from them in almost five years, Andvari," Traeg said quietly. "Their reports ceased around the time that our kindred started to disappear in the mines."

"Balder's Dash!" he swore dismissively. "That's a coincidence of time, not a statement of fact. These aren't absent miners. Those dwarf spies were members of Dietrich's Grey Cadre, and they've sometimes let half of a century pass between reports. Even in five years' time, there's no way for Hela to have made that much progress on the death ship!"

"Your spies haven't been watching closely enough," Fenris countered with a shake of his head. "I've seen it myself when I was at Hela's side. Trust me: Hela has all the dead people she needs, and Naglfar is almost ready to sail."

"Wait," Aurelius said, almost wishing for the Codex to inform him, but glad that the tome remained quiet. "Naglfar is the ship of dead men that sails when the end of the world comes?"

"Dead men's fingernails," Rudyick corrected.

"When it's completed," Fenris continued, "and when Hela allows the frost giants of Jotunheim to board as her crew, then will the ice-storms of Fimbulvetr rage for three years, a sign that Ragnarok begins."

"If Hela is, indeed, ready with her ship," Urd asked the Huntress, "why hasn't she launched it?"

"I believe that she's awaiting a signal," Skade replied.

"From whom?"

"My father," Fenris said.

Loki is still bound, Mimir assured them, *and nothing will free him until the end of time. Moreover, Hospitaller, these events of which we speak might be millennia in the making. There are yet many plagues, wars, and travesties unimagined to occur in how you reckon time.*

"Or, until the time when the Codex Lacrimae returns to the Nine Worlds," Rudyick said, stepping forward. "Which now could quicken those thousands of years into a thousand minutes, depending on what this boy does. That, at least, is how my father, Volund, and I interpret the prophecies, and the reason I'm here. We would attempt to take back the elven magic within the book, and thereby restore the Dark Elves into the lands of Alfheim. By doing those things, by not letting Loki have recourse to the magics in the Codex, we might even prevent the Last Days from happening."

You would destroy yourself and the Dark Elves, Rudyick—some things that have been made cannot be unmade.

"More than likely, your father," Fenris grumbled, "like mine, is merely playing another of his cruel games."

"With respect, wise Mimir and Fenris, my father and I believe that in this instance, the magics can be taken back!" Rudyick came closer to the Seer, his expression earnest. "Volund has changed. He and the other elves realized the mistake they made the moment that all the Codices became ... other than they'd intended. We've studied this lore for centuries, ever since the Codex Lacrimae was lost. That's why I wanted, why I needed to take Santini to the *Sviddengen* in Svartalfheim. There, where it was created, Volund and I would see the Dark Book unmade."

Loki's plan— if one exists—might be to do the same thing for himself. To secure the Codex, and then take his own might back into himself. If that is your thinking (and his), then you all are gravely mistaken both in your ideas about the Codex Lacrimae. More egregiously, you've not accounted for the relationship that the Book of Tears shares with the other Codices.

Fenris agreed with a nod, but Rudyick shook his head and smiled, arrogantly dismissing Mimir's words.

"The Codex will surely recognize one of its true masters," Rudyick insisted. "I'm sorry, Mimir, but you weren't there at its creation. My father and Loki were. I think that the Dark Book would choose to return its magics. *Und*, given Loki's current incapacitation and inability to receive the part of his magic that was taken, I believe that the Codex would make us it's choice for returning the magic."

Fenris barked a laugh, and Aurelius heard a cracking sound, then Rudyick started screaming.

"What ... have ... you ... done?" the Dark Elf groaned, stumbling backwards. Blood ran from his left hand, which had been transfixed by the bladed end of a weapon. As the other pieces of Rudyick's spear clattered to the rocky shore, Aurelius realized in horror that the elf's spear had been shattered and its razor-sharp point driven into Rudyick's hand.

"Rudyick, if the Codex Lacrimae ever were to 'choose' between you and my father, which true master do you think it would prefer? I wound you as a gift. Remember: we are both sons of those who helped create it! My siblings and I possess only a fraction of Loki's might, and still we can bring ruination to the world, as much as to a paltry thing like your hand. My gift is this: remember this moment when you think of such foolishness as any of the Codices 'returning their magics.'"

At Fenris's nod, Skade reached into her leather pouch, withdrew bandages and a vial of ointment, and approached Rudyick cautiously. "May the 'slattern' approach?" Skade asked, a strange mirth in her eyes.

"Indeed. I apologize to you similarly, Thiazi-Daughter. I've been a fool." He sighed and let her take his hand and tend to it as he stared in disbelief at the wound. Aurelius thought the elf would be angry, but he seemed simply incredulous. Clarinda recalled the despair the elf had expressed when she first met him in Alfheim. "I've been a fool, and now my people are beyond redemption."

Perhaps, and perhaps not, Rudyick. I agree with Fenris about the inability to disentangle the magics of Loki and the Dark Elves from the Book of Tears, but there is much in your desires that the Fates and I share. We, too, would see your people redeemed. But, before we address that, while Fenris and Skade have made broad descriptions, the still have not told me their purpose.

Fenris straightened and cleared his throat. "*Ja, ja.* After spying for years upon my sister, and now with the reappearance of the Codex Lacrimae, I would ask your help in giving me a plan to foil the completion of my sister's death-ship, and then getting me to Asgard."

That seems to be two requests.

"Both informed by one desire—to undo the part of the Norn's Tapestry that casts me as one of the Harbingers of Ragnarok. I would escape my father's legacy, and to do that I'd stop my sister's fleet before it's launched, I'd ... destroy Naglfar, or make it impossible to launch, and then warn the Aesir about the possible return of all the Codices."

"*Und*, perhaps seek the counsel of Odin himself about your Fate?" Grimnir added softly, looking intently at the bearded man.

"*Ja*, that's my hope," Fenris admitted. "There's no one else in the Nine Worlds who can help me, if not him."

I've seen only the Codex Lacrimae here, Mimir commented. *What makes you think that more of the Codices will return?*

"Fenris, if I may?" Andvari said, stepping forward. "At the Fields of Burning Night, the Codex Lacrimae was the last of the Codices to be destroyed."

Obviously not destroyed, for one is here in our presence. Your point?

"Banished, then." Andvari corrected with a shrug, a deep frown on his brown-bearded face. "My point is that it seems at least possible that it's reappearance may be but the first of the others' return."

Mimir glanced at the three Norns. The sisters began talking to one another in whispered tones as Clarinda stood to one side of them, listening but also watching Fenris and Skade. She could tell how much in love they were by the proximity they kept to each other, and the united front they presented to Mimir as they pled their case.

She glanced at Aurelius who, in turn, was looking at her. Clarinda blushed and pointed at Mimir as if to focus the young knight's attention on people and events, but privately she was pleased that she'd caught him looking at her unawares.

Und, you, Rudyick, now that you've had this conversation?

The Dark Elf considered for a moment, then spoke with deliberation. "Death holds enough sway in the universe. I'd not see all lands become like Niflheim and Hel. That's what will happen if that ship gets launched. So, *ja*, Mimir, I'd accompany Fenris and Skade to Niflheim, and help in bringing down Naglfar."

"Quite a different purpose than taking back the enchantments in the Codex Lacrimae," Skuld commented. "Is this hastily done?"

"No, Mistress Skuld," Rudyick said. "I'll need to get word to my father about the change in plans, but I think that Fenris's ideas have merit. I, too, would seek the help of Odin in Asgard." He hesitated. "I've been so focused on the Codex Lacrimae, on what that particular book meant to the Dark Elves, that I'd not seriously considered the possibility that the other Codices could be returning. That ... changes things."

"Well," Andvari cleared his throat, "Traeg and I have heard enough."

The dwarf came to stand before Mimir. "We originally came to guide and protect Master Santini through the caverns of Nidaveller, but I also was trying to solve a mystery concerning the dwarves. After the battle with Hela and meeting with Rudyick, we also came to think that we might be able to help in removing the threat of the Codex from the Nine Worlds." He looked down his crooked nose at Mimir. "You haven't said as much, but I gather that you're going to be tending to Aurelius and Clarinda?"

Your insight serves you well, Arch-Mage. Servius Aurelius Santini and Clarinda Trevisan will be tended to. Whither then, you and Traeg?

"Well, Hela and her *Wilde Jagd* took me by surprise in Nidaveller, when I'd guaranteed these folk safe passage through the underground rivers and the crystal caves. It seems only fair that I return the favor."

You'd go with Fenris, Skade, and Rudyick to Niflheim? To destroy Naglfar?

"*Ja.*" Andvari looked at Traeg for confirmation, and then back to Mimir. "Things are moving in different ways in many places." He jerked a stubby thumb at Aurelius. "*Und,* apparently he hasn't even accepted the Codex's price, yet!"

"I don't plan to—" Aurelius began, but the dwarf cut him off again. The youth flushed in irritation, and Clarinda cupped a hand over her mouth at the reaction. She remembered the dead birds in Nidafjöll, and still felt wary of Santini's anger!

Andvari did seem to interrupt Aurelius quite frequently, and she wondered if the wizard was unintentionally casting the youth into a novice's role, with all the verbal abuse and disregard that attended a master-apprentice relationship.

"... there's a civil war brewing between the Light Elves in Alfheim and Rudyick's Dark Elves in Svartalfheim," Andvari continued, "and Fenris's sister and brother are running amok. First, there's Hela with her *Wilde Jagd*, and whatever she's planning to do with the Death Ship. As for Jormungand, we believe that he's disguising himself as a mortal again, but it's possible that he's still loose on the Fjords of Asgard, waiting to help Hela when she launches her attack. For our part, we've had dwarves disappearing in Nidaveller, and the beginning of what appears to be civil war among the Nibelung. Now, there's this talk of the mustering of armies in Niflheim."

He gave one of his shrugs and adjusted his staff on the sand. "The evidence is varied, and still might only be coincidental, but Traeg and I believe that dark things are stirring in the Nine Worlds."

"Evil things," Traeg added, "the like of which haven't been seen since the troubles that preceded the Fields of Burning Night."

"There are two armies outside the Krak des Chevaliers." Aurelius glanced at Andvari, who frowned at him. "On 'Midgard,' where I come from. I know it's only one castle, but I'm getting the feeling that we've never seen anything like the eastern army."

"*Und*, it seems, armies also mustering on Midgard where the boy lives," Andvari appended. He harrumphed, muttering,

"That's not good, not good at all," then pushed on. "You see, Mimir? Traeg and I believe something is happening in the Nine Worlds, and we both think that all the activity is because of the Codex Lacrimae."

These are not coincidences, Mimir observed. *All the events you've described are interrelated, and all signify the return of the Codices of Fate.*

That statement drew an assortment of responses from each member of the company, but Andvari was the first to reply.

The arch-mage took a breath. "As we thought. I've also noticed that many of the local *runeporten* aren't working as they used to, and I fear that the major gates will soon be the only reliable ones." He hesitated, thinking. The moment seemed to stretch into an awkward silence, but no one broke it.

"He's trying to work through this without asking a question," Clarinda whispered into Aurelius's ear.

The action tickled his lobe, and he didn't want the moment of contact to end. "Why?" he whispered back, his lips close to hers. "Mimir's been very friendly so far."

She seemed to notice, but still backed away a few inches. She sensed peril everywhere now, and it certainly wasn't the time or place for an accidental kiss! "He's the Seer of Fate and his answers come at a price."

Andvari finally spoke. "I'm speaking my thoughts aloud, so need no confirmation or denial from you, Mimir." He took in the members of the company, finally alighting on Fenris and Skade. "Without evidence that any of the other Codices have returned, I believe that we need to deal with the most immediate of threats, stopping both Hela's Death Ship and the armies besieging the castle where Servius Aurelius Santini lives."

"The Krak?" Aurelius said. "We're provisioned for winter and we've held off sieges larger than this one many times!" He glanced at the others. "Forgive me, but Hela's project seems to pose much more danger to the Nine Worlds. And, Halfdan, Andvari, what about the missing dwarves?"

"The Codex Lacrimae, the Dark Book itself, it's at your castle, isn't it?" Andvari asked.

"Well ... *sì*," Aurelius said, flummoxed. "I'd just seen it before trying to stop a break-in at the front gate."

"Then you've not completely accepted its price, and we can assume that at least one, if not both, of those armies are in pursuit of the tome while it's in a form that can be apprehended. You must retrieve the physical book before any enemies do."

"*Und*, my dear," Traeg said, "given that Hela, Old Nick, the Huntsmen, and Odin-knows-who-else pursue the Codex, it seems as if you have many enemies!"

"None of them must be allowed to get the Codex Lacrimae," Andvari agreed. "I'm not sure what assistance can be given to your castle—"

"Perhaps a couple of companies of dwarves?" Halfdan offered.

"We'll see, we'll see," Andvari said, "but those dwarves might be needed for another assault. If these fellows and Skade want to go to Hel to destroy the Death Ship Naglfar, the quickest entry and exit from there is the Gate of Niflheim."

"You'd use the major gate in the middle of Hela's Sea?" Rudyick asked incredulously.

"*Ja.* It is the last place that Hela would expect us to go, especially if we've dared enough to destroy her flagship."

"Because it's in her domain!" Rudyick exclaimed. "She might not even have it guarded, so strong are her forces there."

"*Hei*, Lad," Andvari reprimanded. "There's still the matter of you and Fenris wanting to reach Asgard soon, not me. One of your Dark Elf lineage can't use Bifrost without Mimir's aid, and I don't think you'll be getting back here to Mount Glittertind anytime soon after we bring down Hela's Death Ship. Having Traeg and me along will help in reorienting that *runeporte* so that you can make an escape to Asgard."

The arch-mage shrugged. "I see no other options. The only other access to the Port of Niflheim is the Realm of Death, and that way is too dark. Remember the saying: 'just as one can soar across the rainbow bridge into heaven, so too might one crawl there from the passageways of hell.' Isn't that how Odin ordained it when he created Valhalla? Trust me, whoever destroys the Naglfar ship is going to have more than the *Wilde Jagd* on its heels! An arch-mage and his sorceress wife will come in handy, I think."

Your words and argument are wise, Andvari, Mimir said, *and though you've not asked my advice, it will be considered. But, I would know one thing from you, please: tell me of these 'disappearing dwarves.'*

"We've noted that in the deeper levels of Nidaveller, whole work-gangs of our people, the Nibelungs, have been disappearing during the last seven years ..." Andvari quickly related the problem, with occasional qualifying interruptions from Traeg and Halfdan.

After their story was completed, Mimir was quiet for some

long moments. Then, he looked at each in turn before opening himself to the entire company. *I agree with you, Arch-Mage, and to all of you, I give this advice, free of the payments I usually take from those who seek my counsel. The course you've planned to interfere with the launching of your sister's ship, Fenris, is a sound one. It has the advantage of satisfying three needs. In the first, if you can prevent Naglfar from launching, it will not be able to reach its destination, the Krak des Chevaliers—*

"What?" Aurelius exclaimed. "It's going to be launched at the Krak?"

Hela seeks the Codex Lacrimae, and plans to use the invasion of Midgard as a means of both joining the eastern army you mentioned (an army led by her commander, Fafnir the Dragon), and as giving her an opportunity to collect the Book of Tears.

"But, wait," Clarinda said, "I thought that Farbauti and Morpeth had arranged for the eastern army—"

Do not interrupt again, Urd-to-Be. You are as much a risk in this moment as any of the enemies we seek to stop. Desist in the plans you make, for if you succeed, you'll uncurl the folds of the tapestry and upset the dualities that govern the universe—

"No," the Venetian girl protested in a fierce, urgent voice. She stepped forward and almost touched the pool "Mimir, no. I've figured something out that—"

"Clarinda!" Skuld hissed, "don't interrupt. He's fully in the Sight!"

—and if those laws are violated, believe what you will, but by your act of making something new, parity will demand an unmaking, or creation of something that was not in the universe before. Be respectful of the covenants, daughter, and all will be well.

"I've not violated anything," Clarinda murmured, retreating and slightly confused. She glanced uncertainly at Aurelius while everyone else was fixated on Mimir.

Aurelius shrugged and redirected her attention to the Seer, who was still talking. He didn't understand what Clarinda and Mimir were discussing, but he wanted to hear everything. Whatever else had happened to him on this journey, he was still a monk. Like any chant or Bible section he'd needed to know for any of Jeremiah or Ibn-Khaldun's tests, he'd memorize everything being said, and would then analyze it later.

Arch-Mage Andvari, I See that in following the Thread to Naglfar, the completion of that task will reveal the true danger to the Nibelungs. Except for the Codex Wielder and Clarinda Urd-to-Be, who will remain here, I approve that you all go to the Sea of Niflheim and assay the destruction of Naglfar. Then, even with this particular Codex back in the Nine Worlds, the Day of Ragnarok will not yet be nigh.

The Seer of Fate turned to Rudyick. *It has fallen to you to stop your father, Volund, for his mind is not aligned with yours. Unlike you, Volund intends not to return the lost magic to the Dark Elves, but to correct, to reforge, what he sees as an error in the Codex Lacrimae's creation. Even now he works beside Ilmarinen, pretending to make a Sampo, but truly waiting to strike when Santini finally accepts the Codex's price.*

This time, it was Aurelius's turn to exclaim, "Mimir, no! I'll not have any part of it. I want you and the Norns to help me get rid of the thing, or at least take it back to Odin and the Aesir, or whomever can take care of it."

Neither the Aesir nor Odin must be allowed near any of the Codices, Lore Master Santini.

"What? Why not? Didn't they make them? Or, at least, have a hand in fashioning the Codices?"

"Acts which do not necessarily give them the privilege of controlling them," Verdandi snapped. "Would you, of all people, tell us at this pool that a parent should control the actions of his children?"

"What does that mean?" Aurelius asked. "The Codices aren't children!"

Rudyick, Mimir continued, *you must reunite the Elf Kindreds of Alfheim and Svartalfheim without recourse to the Old Magics.*

"Without ..." Rudyick's eyes narrowed. "*Aber,* wise Mimir, that's impossible! Neither Light nor Dark Elves understand anything without reference to the Old Magic. How can I reunite them without binding them to the old ... *ahh.*" The elf's posture sagged when he realized what Mimir was demanding of him. "*Ja.* I think I see." His head remained bowed. "I'm ... I'm not strong enough, Mimir," Rudyick said disconsolately, his former arrogance gone. In this moment, Clarinda was reminded of the despair that had marked him when they first met before the encounter with the *fossegrim* and Old Nick. "*Und,* my father has too many sins on his head for the clans to listen to me."

The time comes when the sons gathered here must surpass their fathers.

"There's no time," Rudyick said. "What you're asking isn't just a matter of securing alliances among the High Lords. I'd have to somehow convince members of the Lögrétta and the All-Thing itself of a change of ways."

If you fail, the Elves die, Rudyick.

"Some say that was our fate from the moment of the Codex

Lacrimae's creation," Rudyick said. "Why else call it the Book of Tears? Damn my father!"

I speak not only of the Dark Elves, child. The Elves will die if you fail.

Rudyick stopped his rant and stared. "You don't mean the Light Elves, too?"

All the Elves will die if you fail. Assist these others in stopping the launch of Hela's ship. As with presenting an answer to Andvari and Traeg for the plight of the dwarves, that action will reveal the way you must take.

"But—"

Lastly, Fenris and Skade, when you reach Odin and the Aesir, be wary of Tyr. Your warning needs to be heard, but things are not as they were in the Golden Realm. Asgard is threatened by more than the wars that will soon be overtaking the other worlds. The giants will return, and they will dwarf the elements. You must—

Mimir stopped speaking and looked downward into the fires of the lake.

He nears. His footsteps, doom. The Seer raised his head and this time there was no mistaking that he looked directly at Aurelius. *It is the Huntsman, Morpeth. I used the Sight, for he was hidden from me. He is filled with great wrath; the guise that he has worn on Midgard for nigh seven decades has been slain by your young friend, Marcus.*

"What?" Aurelius exclaimed. "How's that possible? Marcus was injured the last time I saw him!"

In answer, flames surged in the lake, and the knight found himself staring at the lower kitchen areas of the Krak des Chevaliers.

Pellion lay in the foreground of the vision, the boy's sword drawn, but held laxly in a hand that appeared lifeless, never again to wield a blade. The boy's unconscious body lay at the base of the vaulted stone ceiling of an interior courtyard between the stables and lower kitchen. A great, blackened hole yawned wide in his side, smoke issuing lazily from the body into the dusk-shadowed air.

Marcus, clad in a black Hospitaller battle-cloak, stood above him, bare legged, barefooted, and poised for battle. Aurelius had last seen him in the vision at the Battle of the Underjordisk Elv, preparing to engage Morpeth after Pellion fell.

"You're fast, boy," Morpeth observed as Marcus again squared himself, "almost elven-quick, but I've slain elves and Sampo-users who are faster. Come now, and join your friend!"

The entire company watched as Marcus scooped up Pellion's sword and attacked Morpeth with both blades swirling in the air, the metal blurring with a speed that seemed a match for Rudyick's or Fenris's speed.

Morpeth's sneer turned to alarm in the face of the attack, and Aurelius felt a surge of pride at the relentless precision of his friend's sword-thrusts and parries.

Aurelius smiled, then said softly, "*Oh mon cher ami, tu joues ton Jeu de Combat.*"

"What's that?" Clarinda asked.

"Marcus is playing his Battle Game."

"What?"

"Morpeth's in trouble."

The Codex was quiet, and Mimir said nothing, but there

seemed to be a magic at work in the ferocity of Marcus's assault, so taken aback did his fighting seem to make the Huntsman.

Aurelius squinted, thinking for a moment he saw the slightest of argent-white glows flickering along Marcus's blades, and then the unthinkable occurred.

Morpeth dropped one of his own blades in an attempt to blast Marcus the same way that he'd dispatched Pellion. His hand began to glow a bright orange, but Marcus lunged fully forward with a speed that even caught Aurelius by surprise and drove his right sword deeply into the Huntsman's abdomen.

The Huntsman grunted, the fires in his hand disappearing as he clutched at the sword that transfixed him, and then all gasped as Marcus followed through his attack by a slash with Pellion's blade in his left hand to the man's throat.

Morpeth fell lifeless to the stairs as Marcus stumbled to the side of a horse stall. The youth clutched his shoulder where Aurelius had seen him shot earlier with an arrow. Silvery flames obscured the vision of his friend, and Mimir began speaking again.

Your friend has slain a Huntsman's body. I can't remember the last time, if ever, such a thing has occurred!

"Marcus is good with a sword," Aurelius murmured, proud of his friend, but feeling shocked anew at the apparent death of Pellion. For the first time, Aurelius had confirmation that the events in the Nine Worlds through which he was traveling had a separate reality than that back at the Krak.

"Morpeth must have a powerful patron, if he was slain in so decisive a moment, yet already has another body with which to pursue us into this mountain," Urd commented. "There's more to this boy, Marcus, than seems apparent at first sight," Skuld agreed. "There's a shimmer of the old ways about him, but I can't See what kind."

"How's that possible?" Verdandi asked. "Let me … you're correct." She gave Skuld a strange look. "This is unexpected."

"You say Morpeth's almost here, Master?"

In mere moments, Urd.

"You don't think that patron is Surt?" Verdandi asked.

In this, even I'm not sure. Whoever it is, he has enabled the two most powerful Huntsmen to cross the Great Barrier that Odin created to hold back the legions of Muspelheim. If Surt were again in the other eight worlds, his presence would be felt. The Great Barrier is intact. Loki is still bound. I checked those things after discovering that Farbauti and Morpeth were abroad again. The question of how it could be breached without breaking is one that must be answered after Morpeth comes.

"What about your *weird*?" Aurelius asked.

"Now is not the time for the uninformed to speak," Verdandi reprimanded, not bothering to look at the Hospitaller.

"But, he asks a valid question!" Clarinda countered. "Not even Odin nor Surtur should be able to blast through the weird that protects this mountain, no matter on which World it appears! That's one of the first things I learned, Verdandi."

"No time for this, apprentice," Skuld said, her tone dismissive and final. "What shall we do, Mimir? We knew this time was coming. I'm willing to fight him, but we're not warriors."

There is no escape for me, nor would I seek one. I must remain with the Pool. However, you would all do well to use Bifrost. The members of the company will return with Fenris to Niflheim and execute the plan to destroy *Naglfar. I will deal with Morpeth, and then we'll continue our discussion with the Codex Wielder and Clarinda, when she becomes Urd in the next incarnation.*

"Alone?" Verdandi said. "You'll remain alone against a Huntsman?"

"Where'd Grimnir and the wolves go?" Aurelius asked, looking at Clarinda as he moved across the shore to stand protectively near her.

"He ..." Clarinda followed his gaze, turning her head this way and that. "*Hmmm.* I don't know where he went."

"He did the same thing to me in Alfheim, right before I was attacked by the *fossegrim* and the *strömkarlen.* I'm beginning to think that he doesn't like to be around when there's trouble brewing."

"There's more to it than that," Clarinda said, "I've got a theory about him—"

Verdandi, what more harm could be done me? Mimir interrupted. Odin has seen to my protection, and I'm not without defenses. This is my wyrd. It is the protection of you all that must take priority. I will access Bifrost from the Well, as we have done in times past at great need.

Mimir's eyes focused on something beyond the group gathered at the lakeshore. Aurelius, Clarinda, and the entire company turned to see what he was looking at, and the Hospitaller gave an involuntary gasp.

Marcus stood in the entrance to the cavern, glaring at those who stood by Mimir's Well.

He is not your friend from Midgard, Codex Wielder. Morpeth has taken the aspect of he who slew him.

"I ... I know," Aurelius murmured. He'd just seen a vision of

Marcus alive, leaning against the wall after killing Morpeth, so he had to believe that Mimir's Well was the true reality. "He looks just like him, though."

"Wait," Clarinda brought her quarterstaff to the fore and moved away from Aurelius. "This isn't how my vision went. He was a different Morpeth in my dreams, Servius."

"Mine, too," Aurelius said.

She risked a glance at him, astonished. "You've seen this before?"

"Sì, for the entire summer back at the Krak, but I didn't know all the people back then."

"We meet again, Santini," Morpeth said as he made his way down the grassy verge. "You passed out on Midgard before I could properly take the Codex. Farbauti is correct. I do continue to underestimate you."

He reached the company quickly, and Aurelius noticed that the three Norns had moved slightly to his right, with Fenris and Skade sloshing into the pool a bit to get an angle on the left. Andvari and Traeg remained where they were standing by Mimir and followed Clarinda's example of raising their staffs defensively. Rudyick, hefting his second, intact spear into a casting position, moved to the periphery of the semicircle.

Morpeth nodded derisively at the group, shook his head in warning at the elf and Fenris, who were closest to him, and returned his attention to Aurelius.

"What do you want here, Huntsman?" Urd asked. She stood at the forefront of the gathering.

"Move aside, Urd. I want the Codex Lacrimae. I intend to tear it from Santini's corpse, as I should have done from the first."

"You can't do that," Urd said flatly.

"No one knows the full potential of any Codex, hag. I'm willing to take the chance that the book will not become dormant if torn from him. I don't think such a force would allow itself to sleep again, once it's been awakened, do you?"

The Norn of Fate didn't reply.

"There's nothing to take," Clarinda said, "the Codex isn't here."

"You're wrong, mortal," Morpeth retorted. "What do you call those armored braces on his forearms?"

The armored braces? Startled, Aurelius looked at his forearm guards, then at Clarinda. She gasped, seeing them in the same moment as he, as if the Huntsman's words had evaporated a concealment spell on the objects. Indeed, two bronze battle gauntlets rested on Santini's forearms, gleaming with aqua-marine energies that contrasted brightly against the argent, almost white fires of the Well.

He stared in amazement at the pieces of armor that somehow were there, where previously they'd been only pieces of clothing like his boots or gloves—the Codex Lacrimae.

Fenris had said there'd been an aura around him, a Codex Light, but now he realized that each person had seen the armor, recognized the pieces for what they were, although he and Clarinda somehow hadn't seen them until this moment.

The knight's mind raced. How could he not have seen them? He'd even taken them off and re-donned them at the baths under the Fenrir-baude. But, then, why should he have thought of them? Like his dagger, sword, and chain-mail vest, they were merely battle accoutrements, to be put on as unthinkingly as his tunic and boots.

Then he remembered the moment shortly after his arrival in Alfheim, when he'd been made a prisoner by Old Nick. Aurelius had been held fast against a tree trunk by the *fossegrim's* water-ropes, and had tried to speak directly to the Codex Lacrimae. What had he done and said in that moment?

Now, let me see here ... what form has that book taken this time? Ah, there it is—so it seems as if you are the Codex Wielder.

A chill passed through Aurelius. Old Nick had been staring at his upraised forearms.

Then there'd been Austri's reassessment of him when Aurelius had first met the grumpy dwarf on the road to Niðafjöll. Skade had told him to "take another look at the lad," and Austri had started in surprise, completely changing his attitude toward Aurelius after seeing what Ratatosk had called the "Codex Light."

"Servius," Clarinda said, dismay in her voice. "I saw those braces glowing with that green-blue color once before!"

"What?"

"At the *Underjordisk Elv*, when everything was going crazy, right after you first saw Pellion fall. Urd shouted in my mind that the Codex Lacrimae was returning, and I ... I thought I must have imagined it, especially after the Four Winds started tearing the place apart." She frowned. "But, how could I forget that? I haven't even looked at those things since the battle."

"A glamour," Aurelius whispered. "Like the kind of spell that kept us distracted with things in the past while we were in the Weeping Wood, or what Andvari accused me of when he told everyone that I might be a disguised Loki."

The realization changed everything he'd thought about the

Codex Lacrimae—although it had taken the form of a book at the Krak, the tome's voice and shape-changing ability seemed to make it a sentient force in the Nine Worlds. As such, it had kept itself hidden from him until he accepted it, and the price that it demanded.

The life of a friend.

But, Aurelius hadn't paid the price stipulated in the tome's frontispiece. Or, had he?

He looked from the gauntlet-braces above each wrist and into the angry face of Morpeth. The Huntsman wearing Marcus's features and form hadn't advanced further onto the shoreline, but Aurelius remembered the hole blasted through the side of Glittertind. He doubted that even the upraised hand of Urd—Norn though she be—could avail against Morpeth's might. He wondered, if he perished here, would his body also die back in the Krak des Chevaliers?

"Move aside, Urd. I'll not say it again." Morpeth said.

Morpeth, we will have words, you and I. Mimir interrupted. *This is the Well of Prophecy, and no violence shall be done here save by me. Odin lost an eye at one time for the knowledge he gleaned, and another time the Pool nailed him to the World Tree for nine days so that he might learn the secret of the runes. You've just lost a host body to one who seemingly has his own runes to wield. Are you willing to pay a similar price?*

The nape of Aurelius's neck prickled as he watched Morpeth react to Mimir's words. Power electrified the air like before a thunderstorm.

"Mimir," Morpeth replied in a quiet, restrained tone, "that boy got lucky. It's never happened before, and never will again.

Your day, and that of all the Aesir and Vanir, begins to end here."

An ending comes to all things in Creation, Morpeth, and in proper time an ending is to be embraced just as beginnings are. There is a cycle to all things; however, now is not the time for me, nor the Norns, nor the Codex Wielder.

Morpeth took in the entire group. "At least I now understand how you escaped the trap Old Nick was supposed to set for you on Alfheim. It looks as if you've made some new friends," the demon with Marcus's face smiled at the young Hospitaller. "New or old, I don't think that the Dark Book minds, does it?"

FREE ME, HUNTSMAN! The Codex Lacrimae screamed, surprising everyone with the ferocity of its will as it spoke in a voice that resonated through the minds of everyone there. Aurelius stumbled to one side as if physically hit by the scream, falling to one knee near the flaming pool while his mind seared in pain. The Codex wasn't speaking through him this time; its words boomed through the minds of everyone at the Well.

OR, AT LEAST, MORPETH, KILL ENOUGH OF THESE FOOLS SO THAT THIS WRETCHED HOSPITALLER WILL FINALLY PAY MY PRICE! I ... WOULD ... BE ... FREE!

CHAPTER 18

A Day's Black Fate, Thwarted

Morpeth moved with unbelievable speed at the Codex's invitation. He attacked Fenris first, swinging upward with a short rod that he'd been holding at his side. The silver-capped length of dense wood erupted into crimson flame, and Aurelius recognized the danger before Fenris did—Morpeth was expertly wielding a three-balled, spiked flail! The burly man lurched backward as one of three leaden maces collided into his nose, knocking him briefly into Skade.

The Huntress didn't fall, though, and one of her arrows

glanced off the padded shoulder of the Huntsman's black Hospitaller short-cloak. Instead of falling, Morpeth jerked outward with the rod, letting the three chains attached to the spiked balls whip their lengths around Traeg's staff. He yanked, just as the orange light of her spell began to flare up her weapon.

The reddish flames of his chains snapped the wood of her crozier with a shattering sound. She staggered backward, her hands splayed forward as she tried to begin another incantation, but it was too late. The Huntsman reversed his wrist and pushed forward, savagely clipping her jaw with the butt of the flail. She dropped onto the shore and didn't move.

As Morpeth landed, he spun, brought another flail in his left hand to bear, and feinted at Andvari with a laugh before dodging a bolt of lightning that erupted from the brass tip of the arch-mage's staff.

The distraction of using a second flail worked. Andvari hesitated for a second too long, and the crimson flaming chains in the fire-demon's right hand whipped around the dwarf's staff like a bola, the spikes of the burning mace-spheres coming dangerously close to the wizard's eyes. Morpeth came in low, spinning, and as he'd done with Traeg, cracked the heel of a flail into the side of Andvari's head. The wizard screamed in pain, his head snapping backward as he, too, fell without breaking his fall to the sands beside his wife.

When the arch-mage's staff began to fall, Morpeth dropped one of the flails, leapt at the staff, caught it and, without looking, reversed its tip behind him at waist-height. The hard thrust caught an attacking Skade in the abdomen. She stumbled away, gasping for breath, as Fenris caught her and lowered her to the shore before beginning his transformation into a wolf.

All had occurred within a few seconds. Morpeth dropped Andvari's staff and stretched out his hand, and the flail and chained mace attachments flew back into Morpeth's hand. He crouched in front of Mimir and the Norns, slightly rotating his wrists so that the mace balls made circles of brilliant red fire in the air to each side of him.

The flames of the lake flared, the white changing into the shimmering colors of the rainbow. The transformation caught Aurelius's attention. He glanced at the Well of Mimir and found himself gazing into the heart of a radiant star. Distracted, he didn't move quickly enough to prevent Skuld from making a mad dash toward Morpeth.

She took a strange angle, though, and Aurelius paused, frowning, while the Norn of the Future stumbled into the shallows of the pool and crashed headlong into a sprinting Clarinda.

That wasn't an accident, Aurelius observed coldly. He moved to flank Clarinda's exposed side as the Venetian fell toward Morpeth. An instinct born of hundreds of battles made him look to the other two Norns. Urd was moving to help Clarinda but Verdandi was backing away from the pool.

What's going on here? The knight wondered. *Do those two want both Urd and Clarinda to die?*

The Hospitaller needn't have worried about the latter two women. Clarinda used the momentum of Skuld's collision to turn her own fall into a half-flip roll, launching herself through the air with a sailor's grace that brought her solidly to her feet in the middle of the well.

Nicolo never got that move right, and Alexios was still struggling with it when we left Tomas's monastery that last summer, he thought, strangely proud of Clarinda even while running to her other side where he could help her best.

She stood with staff raised horizontally just as Morpeth brought madly spinning flail maces where her head should have been.

"Clarinda, no!" Aurelius shouted. He rushed forward to help her, but none was needed.

The girl's quarterstaff caught the chain, whipping the three spiked balls around the length of Gungnir.

Aurelius winced, recalling the explosion that had broken Traeg's staff, and brought his sword and trident main gauche to a striking position. But, Clarinda's staff held. Instead of shattering as Traeg's had, this time it was the reddish flames of Morpeth's chain that dissipated against the brilliant yellow fires shining around Gungnir.

The Huntsman's energies ran along Clarinda's massive stave and then all three of the leaden spiked balls exploded. This time it was she who yanked hard the remaining fragment of Morpeth's chain attached to the flail, and he looked so surprised that Clarinda didn't hesitate to follow through on a different line of attack.

"Your turn!" she shouted as she imitated his earlier moves against the dwarf-wizards and brought Gungnir's iron heel upward against Morpeth's jaw, delivering a cracking blow that bowled him backwards. The Huntsman stumbled, and then Aurelius was upon him.

Clarinda whirled at the Norns. "Do what Mimir said! Into the pool and begone!"

Urd staggered backward, shocked. "What's this? I'm not dead!"

"Urd, *correre adesso!* Run now!" Clarinda said, raising her quarterstaff again as Morpeth sidestepped Aurelius's first swing, and then moved into the knight's attack radius and tried to head-butt the Hospitaller under the chin.

Aurelius dodged so that Morpeth's forehead crashed only into his collarbone, and in the close quarters he rammed his left elbow into the area behind the youth's ear. *No, not a youth! He's not Marcus, he's not Marcus.* When Morpeth's momentum kept him moving forward, and Aurelius kicked a booted heel into his butt and sent him into the waters to fall to his knees in front of Clarinda.

Clarinda had no such reservations about thinking that the enemy was a friend. She brought Gungnir's iron-shod tip down hard onto the back of Morpeth's head, sending him face first into the pool with a crack that resounded through the cavern.

"Urd!" Verdandi shouted. "Clarinda's correct; somehow she's changed the timeline! Do what she says, and get into the pool!"

Aurelius moved to Clarinda's side, and the remaining members of the company advanced on Morpeth.

Codex Wielder, the well is a rune-gate. I have aligned it with Bifrost, the Rainbow Bridge. Take Clarinda, pass through it, and be safe. We will contend with this Huntsman, and then come for you.

"No," Aurelius said, watching as Morpeth rose to his feet, grabbed Rudyick's spear and melted the iron into slag.

We shall not be felled by such as you. Mimir's words were accompanied by fire that leapt from the lake itself in narrow pillar of pure energy. The bolt caught the Huntsman full in the chest, throwing him sprawling backward a few paces and onto the shore.

Clarinda leapt after Morpeth, inverted the quarterstaff so that it was vertical and then drove it ferociously downward again. The point plunged into Morpeth's chest, and Clarinda leaned into it as the Huntsman screamed. He grabbed the bottom of Gungnir with both hands and murmured a spell. Orange fire flashed along the length of the spear, blasting into Clarinda, who took a step sideways. Stunned by the energies, she somehow managed to retain her grip on the staff.

Morpeth, impossibly, started to regain his footing.

Aurelius saw his chance and leapt at Morpeth, but Clarinda grabbed him as she fell toward the pool.

"We've done enough," she gasped. "The Norns, all the Norns are safe!" She pulled Aurelius with her into the flaming lake.

He plunged into the water, and his world exploded into a multitude of colors. The water was shallow, so stood and, gasping at the iciness of the immersion, he looked at the shore a few feet away.

Fenris returned to the fray, tackling Morpeth as Aurelius had intended doing. Rudyick was closing from behind, and Skade was rising shakily to her feet, recovering from a backhanded slap by Morpeth that had sent her sprawling.

Clarinda, too, recovered herself, and rose shouting, "Servius, your arms!"

He glanced at the armored braces which were now bathed in a hot, cerulean blue and aquamarine fire whose flames erupted toward the argent silver power blazing off the surface of Mimir's Well.

I don't care who frees me, Hospitaller. Accept my price, damn you, grab the Huntsman by the throat, and send him back to his master in shards. I will show you how, just FREE ME!

The runes of the Codex Lacrimae sang in his mind, but he began wading through the water, intent only upon helping those who were being hurt trying to protect him.

Morpeth punched Fenris, a flash of orange-red power attending the impact. He hit the ground and continued to roll while transforming into his lupine self. Rudyick launched himself at Morpeth with a flying kick, but the Huntsman grabbed his foot and wrenched it with such force that Aurelius heard bones break.

No. Mimir's voice now brooked no disagreement. *Clarinda, you've changed everything by this action, and I fear much death will come of it ere there is renewed life.*

"What?" Clarinda exclaimed. "I just saved Urd!"

You've changed everything, and there will be a cost—not one, but three will fade before parity returns. We'll speak of it later. Listen to me now, and obey! You must get away. Take the Codex Wielder, and begone! Santini, don't be tricked here by the Dark Book's pretended urgency. If you choose the Codex Lacrimae, do so on your own terms, not Morpeth's. Bifrost is here. Take the Rainbow Bridge to Asgard, and we will come for you when we can.

"I'm not leaving my friends!" Aurelius shouted, moving forward in the shallow waters.

"Servius, this time we listen to reason!" Clarinda yelled, and with a grunt, she caught him off-guard, tripping him from behind and semi-tackling him into the pool.

I told you the witch couldn't be trusted! the Codex practically screamed in his mind. *Do you see, now?*

"Oh, shut up, you hag!" Clarinda cried, rapping the quarterstaff against the knight's temple as they fell. Confused and dismayed by Mimir's response to her saving Urd, the last thing she wanted to hear was the voice of the Codex Lacrimae. She hugged Aurelius with desperate strength. The Codex fell silent, and the knight's body went limp.

He kept conscious enough to try to push away from her, and they both waded upright to their knees in the flaming waters. "*Clare, prego, ascoltami* ... listen to me! We can't leave them again. This is worse than Nidaveller with Hela and the *Wilde Jagd!*"

"Servius, we'll save more lives if we're not here! Trust me, but mostly, trust Mimir."

Aurelius held her then, ceasing his struggles and watched as the heatless fires running along the braces on his forearms faded, although he could still see a faint aquamarine glow limning the armor.

Then man-sized flames of red, orange, yellow, green, blue, and purple erupted around him, the rune-gate to Bifrost, the Rainbow Bridge effectively cutting Clarinda and him off from the action on the shore.

She moved closer into his arms as they faded, and an eye-blink later they were gone, the sounds of the battle against Morpeth lost in the roar of flames as the Seer's rune-gate took the Hospitaller and Norn far from the depths of Mount Glittertind.

CHAPTER 19

The Fjords of Asgard

The flaming waters of Mimir's Well and carnage-filled grotto disappeared along with the rainbow colors of the *runeporte*. Still soaked from the waters of the pool, Clarinda and Aurelius were in a rocky terrain. They knelt above ground on a road paved with dwarvish designs that sloped upward to a craggy ridge beneath a cloud-covered sky.

They rose to their feet, Aurelius hastily, as if he expected to rejoin the battle against Morpeth. Clarinda took her time, wincing at the jabs of pain in her shoulders from the backlash of energies that Morpeth had sent along the staff. There'd be no return to the fight; they'd been translocated from Jotunheim to another of the Nine Worlds.

"We're near the Fjords of Asgard," she said, leaning wearily on the quarterstaff.

Aurelius stopped trying to angrily wrench the braces off his forearms and scowled.

"How can you tell?"

"Besides the fact that Mimir told us he was sending us here," she nodded at something behind him, "there's a sign right there that says so."

He followed her gaze to the small shingle nailed to a post at the top of the broad road.

A single rune symbolizing the Norse word for 'fjord' had been burned into the sign.

Heavy, pressure-laden air, indicated the imminence of a hellacious storm. Charcoal-colored clouds sparked lightning, flashing on the slate-colored boulders and ashen ground. "It's going to rain any moment," Clarinda said, still leaning on her staff while she watched his renewed efforts with the armored braces. "But, *hei*, since our clothes are already wet ..."

She frowned, realizing what he was doing and disapproving. "That seems like a complete waste of time, Santini. If those arm-guards didn't come off after—*cosa?*—twenty tugs, I don't think they're coming off. Leastways, not until you put some finality into your dealings with the Codex."

"I'm ... so ... tired ... of doing ... *umph! Oh, buon Dio!*" He gave two final, disgusted twists and shook his head, an action that obviously hurt, because he winced and rubbed his temple.

"Tired of what? Having temper tantrums? Or, tired of listening to common sense?"

He glared at her and snapped, "No! I've got plenty of

common sense, and I'm not having a temper tantrum! It's not as if you've got that much sense. We should've stayed and fought Morpeth. I could've taken him—found an opening and just attacked. I'm sick of running, and I did fine for years on my own. Before I saw Huntsmen, the Codex, or you!"

"I can tell," she retorted, her exhaustion stretching her patience. Who did he think he was? He still didn't know half the story that she'd learned about the dangers to the Nine Worlds, and he talked about fighting a Huntsman who'd attacked Mimir—Mimir!—as if it were some kind of chance for fencing practice!

"You've really got a serene grip on that temper, don't you? Some priest-in-training. All you Crusaders are the same— prayerful until somebody crosses your path. Hypocrites. Talking of peace while stabbing and killing. I bet you'd slam your friends' heads into pews if they were talking too loudly while you're praying in church!"

That image brought him back to himself. *"Cosa?"* he smiled. "What'd you just say? *Una cosa stupida!"*

"Non così stupidi come ti comporti!" She gave him a vulgar sailing gesture.

"I'm not acting stupid," he protested, still irritated, "and if a guy made that sign at me back at the Krak, we'd settle it in the yards."

"Vieni, Santini." She took a defensive stance with the staff and beckoned with her free hand. "I'm serious. Come on. Don't let my being a girl stop you. I'm betting I can control Gungnir a lot better than you can the Codex, and we've both taken on these Huntsmen." She paused, remembering the dead birds,

but continued to stare hard at him even as she swallowed hard. "So do you want to keep going with this, or should we take a rest?"

"*Io sono fatto.*" He held up his hands, smiling. "*Veramente.* I'm done. *Buon Dio,* you scold worse than my mother."

"I'm not your mother." She put the staff solidly back on the ground, vexed now for a variety of different reasons. "And if you make that comparison again, we will have a fight."

"*Mi dispiace!* I'm sorry! You're the most …" he stopped, not liking the furious questioning in her eyes as she waited for the end of the sentence. "I mean … well, I just didn't like leaving," he added somewhat sullenly, then turned and scanned the surroundings. When he'd made a full circle, he said cautiously, "I'm fine, now, Clarinda. Truly. I don't want to fight. We've got to figure out where we are, what Mimir meant in sending us here."

He rubbed his forehead, appreciation and respect in his eyes as he. "*Hei,* maybe next time when you're quieting the Codex, a little lighter 'tap?' I appreciate the help, but that quarterstaff feels like solid iron."

"Grimnir did say that Gungnir never misses," Clarinda observed, "but, I' m sorry; I didn't mean to hit you that hard."

"Didn't you?" He smiled. "I think you did. What was it you said to the Codex? Something like, Shut up you hag?"

"*Dio,* I don't know how you put up with it," she said. "Did you hear the thing offer itself to Morpeth if he'd set it free?"

"Who didn't?" He held up his hand and looked at the braces. "I just want it … them off, but I don't suppose I can just toss them aside, can I?"

"Not responsibly. Everyone thinks that the Codex runs a race with catastrophe, so you don't want a frost giant (or even a dwarf) getting his hands on those things."

"How did we not ever see them? I mean, *guarda!* Look! They're on my arms, as plain as day."

"I see them. I don't have any explanation. I've been in the Nine Worlds longer than you, and I'm still seeing all kinds of magic. I think you mentioned it back there. A *glamour*, a concealment spell, but I thought that those kind of enchantments applied only to people or faerie-creatures. This one just had more subtlety than most." She hesitated.

"It probably goes without being said, Servius, but you'll have to be careful about the Codex. If it could hide from us, it might even now be affecting us—affecting you—in ways we don't know."

"Hiding in plain sight?"

"That, or perhaps our status as Midgardians has something to do with it. Maybe the Codex's magic works in different ways on us than everybody else."

Aurelius put his hands on his hips and looked at the top of the ridge. *"Dove andiamo?"*

"I don't know where to go," she admitted. "I hadn't thought that through. I listened to Mimir and got us out of there."

"Well, the other Norns aren't here—or, if they are, they're not here with us—and Mimir said that he'd come for us after settling things with Morpeth. Do we just sit and wait?"

She raised an eyebrow. "You, sit and wait?"

"Don't start," he warned. "Quitting the field used to be against my nature, but it's all I seem to do since we met."

"And you're alive to tell the tales, so I wouldn't complain about it."

"Urd's alive!" Aurelius exclaimed, remembering.

"You noticed?" Clarinda smiled.

"But, I thought they kept planning for you to take her place?"

"They did. So much so that after being in the grottoes for a while and listening to her predict her own death day after day, I got sick of it and swore I'd do whatever I could to prevent it." She clacked the iron heel of her weapon on the ground. "Gungnir helped. When Morpeth sent that energy through this staff, I thought my hands would burn off, but Grimnir's Spear did what he promised it would. Special properties, indeed." She reflected on the battle. "Tell me, is your friend Marcus that good a fighter back at the Krak?"

"His usual weapon is a sword, but he's the best. I mean, besides me, of course." Aurelius paused, the humility he strove for in the Church contrasting with the pride he took in swordsmanship, but the statement was true.

Clarinda's agreeable smile made unnecessary any apology. He pressed on. "He's a great fighter, but he's no Huntsman. It was so strange. Morpeth looked exactly like Marcus, but my Marcus, well, he has a ... problem with his speech. I've never heard him speak like we do. It was wonderful and horrifying at the same time."

"I could've done without those kinds of words."

"Me, too. So, Urd's alive. That means the Norns can be wrong, which bodes well for both of us, I think. I'm tired of everyone telling me that my 'doom is nigh,' or some such kind of thing."

"Or Hela predicting that you'll be around a thousand years before she finally claims you?" Clarinda added, still bothered by that bit of prophesying. Part of her hated the idea of falling in love with a man who would outlive her by a score of lifetimes.

"Or that," he agreed. "This is some dream, Clarinda, if Death, Satan, and demons from a fire world are roaming constantly through it."

"I don't think it's a dream, Servius."

"I know, but let me pretend that it is for a while more." His eyes fell momentarily. "It'll make things easier."

"With the Codex?"

"Sì, but with us ..." He flushed. "I mean, we've also never met on Midgard, not back in Venice, nor at the Krak des Chevaliers, nor, well, anywhere. My castle's in the middle of a siege at the moment, and I don't know where you are when you're not with the Norns or trying to save my life, so, I mean, if we get back to our world ..." The redness in his face grew deeper as he foundered with the words, realizing that he was completely rambling. "Look!" he said over-loudly. "All I'm saying is, it might be a while before we ever get to meet again, all right?"

"All right," she replied, trying not to laugh at his discomfort. She was about to tell him that her body, too, was at the Krak des Chevaliers—apparently asleep in a coffin thanks to a subterfuge she'd arranged with Fatima and Khalil—but then a peal of thunder boomed and interrupted her. Mutually alarmed, they both looked at each other and walked toward the top of the hill.

Lightning shot in jagged forks from the black clouds, spectacular pulses of energy that sometimes struck so close to the travelers that Clarinda felt the strands of her damp hair stand on end. Thunder clapped again within seconds of the electrical strikes, and the smell of something burning wafted through the air.

"Let's run!" they shouted at the same thing, then laughed. He reached for her hand, and they jogged up the road. Aurelius kept them on one side, close to a series of large boulders that might offer some scant cover in the barren landscape.

Droplets of rain pelted the pavement and spattered the dirt embankments. They began to sprint and, holding the young knight's hand tightly in her own, Clarinda bent her head against the torrent. They raced through sheets of rain and whipping wind until they crested the hill.

Nothing could have prepared her for the grandeur of the sight that awaited there. A vast valley lay below them, stretching for leagues—a fjord. The air was redolent with the fresh smell of spring grasses whose scent wafted upward, enhanced by the strong rains. Green slopes descended to a bay that intruded into the base of the valley, and farther down, toward the horizon, gigantic granite mountains girded the water, thrusting upward in sharp, vertical relief. Closer to them, the road ended a quarter-league down the slope in a series of steep stone stairs that descending in switchbacks to farmlands, a Viking village, and small harbor.

Besides the basic comforts of civilization afforded by the sight (how she wanted to take a bath and just lay down to sleep in a cot for a little while!), the twelve boats docked at the piers excited the Venetian girl. The ships reminded her of how much she missed the sea and she simply wanted to get to the three jetties to walk by the storm-tossed water and smell the briny air.

By the time Aurelius and Clarinda reached the town of rock-piled pit houses with sod-covered roofs, the rain had diminished and become a fine mist. Smoke rose from chimneys in the low-lying homes, and as late afternoon edged into twilight, the inhabitants settled in for evenings of merrymaking, family conversations, and, from the sight of dart throwers glimpsed through a window, playing games.

They reached the town center as the clouds parted and sunlight burst through. The grass-covered homes shone vibrant green in the aftermath of the rainfall. A large building resembling an upside-down Viking longship dominated the village.

"That must be where the town elders meet," Aurelius guessed as they passed the structure, heading toward the piers.

Clarinda marveled at the number of houses and lanes, and that even a windmill and tannery rested at the eastern edge of the village, past an assortment of smithy and carpentry shops. "Almost a thousand people must live here. Where are they?"

"Staying dry and warm inside," Aurelius replied with a slightly surly tone.

She looked at him and was surprised to see that he appeared to be as exhausted as she felt; for some reason his great stature always made her think that he was invulnerable to any kind of weakness. But after the events of the last couple days, she should've been surprised that both of them didn't drop in the muddy paths that squelched wetly beneath their boots.

Her head ached with the spiked lancets of pain that she'd felt in Caesarea. "Servius, there's danger here," she said distantly, trying to ignore the discomfort and grateful that blood wasn't yet running from her nose.

"What's wrong?" He halted, looked at her in concern, and then warily about them.

"Kenezki. My head always starts hurting when I'm near him. It wasn't too bad at the camp in Svartalfheim, but this hurts. I don't want to believe it, but I think that he's somewhere close." She looked up at him. "I'm not bleeding from my nose, am I?"

Disturbed by her words, he checked and shook his head. "We'll be on the lookout. Let's get down to the docks. I feel too exposed out here. It'll be something of a comfort to be back in a town with crowds of people."

She chuckled. "Do you see any crowds down there?"

"It looks very quiet, but the storm probably drove everyone inside."

She sighed. "Maybe that fellow on the pier will know where we can get some shelter and sleep for the night." She nodded toward a solitary figure that stood at the end of the longest pier.

"My thoughts, exactly, Clare—I mean, Clarinda."

"No, its fine; all my friends call me Clare." She smiled. "My parents did, too."

"*Grazie*, Clare," he said, casting a quick glance at her. "It'd be an honor to be your friend."

She was thankful that the setting sun probably hid her blush. When they reached the dock, the figure at the end of the pier stood cloaked and motionless his back was to the village until Clarinda and Aurelius stood a few paces from his position. Then he turned in a casual, relaxed manner, and gave a slight start when he saw the knight and Norn standing behind him.

The man held a massive staff in one hand, and his other hand strayed to the hilt of an immense broadsword at his waist. The sight was somewhat intimidating because the warrior was great in stature, wearing a helmet, and densely ringed, silver chain mail that barely restrained the muscles that bulged heavily from his chest, arms, and legs. Ruddy cheeks rose above a thick, well-groomed black beard, and warm brown eyes assessed the Hospitaller and Norn from the shadows of the helm. The man's mouth matched his puzzled frown.

"Greetings, Mortals; I'm Heimdall. What affairs take you to Asgard? Speak truly, or turn and be gone."

"I am Servius Aurelius Santini, apprenticed and squired to the Knights of the Hospital of Saint John in Jerusalem, stationed at the Krak des Chevaliers," the young man said, and then turned to Clarinda. "This is Clarinda Trevisan, called by the Norns 'Urd-Yet-to-Be.'" Aurelius hesitated, thinking something through for the first time as he turned to her. "At least, you were supposed to be Urd-Yet-To-Be, until a little while ago."

Clarinda shrugged and looked at Heimdall, who frankly returned her gaze before dropping his eyes to the brooch in her cleavage. "You wear the *triquerta* symbol of the Norns."

"*Ja*, she does," Aurelius said, reddening in a flash of jealous irritation at how long the bearded sentinel seemed to be looking at Clarinda's chest. "*Und*, we've got no business in Asgard of which we're aware, but we've just come from the Well of Mimir. He sent us here to escape a Huntsman from Muspelheim."

"Hold, Man!" Heimdall appraised Aurelius and Clarinda in

turn, as if seeking some indication in their physical appearances that might explain the young knight's story. "You tell a wondrous tale in a few breaths, Servius Aurelius Santini. No mortal has ever been to Mimir's Well, and even Thor himself had reason to pause when the Huntsmen sought a quarry. But, thus far, you speak only words. Besides the Norn's jewelry, do you bear some token, some proof, either from Mimir or the Norns that will prove you true to the Watcher of the Gods?"

"Is that you?" Clarinda asked, her tiredness making her skeptical of titles. She felt great power radiating from the man, but the headache that seemed to emanate from the entire village was confusing her. She didn't trust her senses here. "You're the 'Watcher of the Gods?'"

"*Ja.* You each must prove trustworthy before I bring you to Asgard."

"I have no token," Aurelius said. He thought for a moment and then raised his left arm. "This brace seems to have some significance to those who see it."

Heimdall glanced at the band of gold on the knight's forearm, then glanced down at the matching one. "Ah, a Codex Wielder. So is explained the failure of my Sight to sense you."

The enormous man bowed to Aurelius. "Welcome to the Fjords of Asgard, Servius Aurelius Santini. If you are bound for the Golden Realm, there I shall take you."

Aurelius glanced at the dark waters of the fjord. The wind continued to blow, causing whitecaps to form on the wavy surface. An enormous longboat bobbed on those waves, tied to the end of the pier by hawsers as thick as a man's wrist.

"We're not certain where we're bound, friend Heimdall,"

Clarinda said wearily when she realized that Aurelius wasn't going to reply immediately.

Music came from the more well- established long-houses in the village, and the warm orange glow shining through hundreds of window panes seemed too inviting to pass. Clarinda shivered in the cold air; the winds coming off the water cutting into her wet skin and clothes like the sharpened points of a thousand icicles. Her head hurt, and she wanted nothing more than to fall fast asleep.

"Besides the brooch, this is my proof, Heimdall," Clarinda said as she lifted the quarterstaff. "Within this wood is the spear, Gungnir, magically bound into my weapon by the traveller, Grimnir."

The gigantic guardian nodded and completely relaxed his guard. "Well come to the Fjords of Asgard, Clarinda Trevisan. Your proof is more than acceptable, and, as with your friend's token, I'd hear more from each of you about the sagas that must attend to each of those weapons." Heimdall frowned. "You both look weary, and I'd take you to my home to give you refreshment and accommodation—a place to eat, and a place to sleep for the night—but first I must ask you, need you passage this evening? Tonight? Did Mimir intend that you should rest in this village, or make the crossing to Asgard immediately?"

"I don't know what he intended," Clarinda replied. "Servius and I used the well as a *runeporte* to escape a Huntsman of Muspelheim, and we were following Mimir's instructions."

"He said that he and the Norns wanted to talk more with me," Aurelius said, "but they weren't given the chance. They were under attack when we left."

"The Huntsman of whom you spoke, do you know his name?"

"Morpeth." Aurelius replied.

Heimdall turned at the mention of the Huntsman's name and peerd into the distance. Aurelius followed his gaze, but only saw a mountain range. "I cannot see into Glittertind." Heimdall said, surprise in his voice. "I would call you liars, Servius Aurelius Santini, and you, too, Clarinda Trevisan, if I didn't see the Codex Light shining brightly about your arms, nor Gungnir lying plainly within that staff. Now that I know what to look for, neither of these wondrous gifts is hidden from my Sight, as they seemed to be before your arrival. I notice also that you carry a hatchet the seems as much a hammer as a hand-ax. A formidable weapon hidden behind a *glamour*, perhaps?" Heimdall nodded admiringly at the weapon hitched to Santini's waist. "May I see it?"

Aurelius shrugged and said nonchalantly, "A mere tool to cut wood when we're not in civilized lands."

Heimdall stared at him, grunted, and then shrugged, not repeating the request. "These things you have, they make me believe that a Huntsman could return across the Great Barrier unseen by either the All-Father or myself. You are fortunate to be alive after such an encounter, especially if it was Morpeth."

"That is why I fear for those I left behind," Aurelius said, frustrated. "Mimir told me that the Well would cast me to the Rainbow Bridge, but he must not have had time to prepare the pool properly, because we found ourselves on the road at the top of those stairs."

"No, he cast you both truly. This is as close to Asgard as any may come." Heimdall raised his staff in the direction from which the Hospitaller had just arrived. "Behold, Bifrost!"

Aurelius and Clarinda turned, expecting to see the same hillside and stairwell, and their breaths both caught at the view from the wharf. The sunlight that earlier had pierced the clouds reflected upon a gigantic rainbow arching colorfully into the heavens.

"Besides the Northmen who live in this village, few people before you have set foot on this side of the Rainbow Bridge, Codex Wielder and Urd-Yet-To-Be. In many places does the rainbow appear on Midgard, but in only one place does it reach Asgard. Mimir could send you no closer to the Golden City than this."

"Asgard lies ahead?"

"Farther down the fjords," Heimdall replied with a nod. "I'm the only one who can navigate the ways."

"Will you take us?" Clarinda asked.

Heimdall grinned. "Of course. I've taken many of lesser prestige before, and this will be an honor. But, first, would it be too much trouble to invite you to a hot meal, dry clothes, and warm beds to spend the evening?"

Aurelius and Clarinda laughed, both disbelieving that a moment of relaxation had come upon them after the events of the last few days.

"I think that I can speak for both of us," Aurelius said, still trying not to let his teeth chatter in the icy breeze coming off the fjord, "that it wouldn't be any trouble at all."

"Then, come, my friends — my house is over there by that ship with the dragon on its prow."

Clarinda slipped her hand into Aurelius's and gave it a reassuring squeeze. "Thank you, Heimdall; this is a wonderful offer. I don't want to impose, but do you have a bath?"

He barked a laugh. "Better than that, Child. I am the

Watcher; my house was built on top of a hot mineral spring, and I use tree trunks to light my fires! You'll be warm and dry soon enough!"

Aurelius returned her squeeze, and the two young people followed the guardian of the fjords to his house near the pier. The clouds converged again overhead and a light rain began to fall.

CHAPTER 20

The Watcher of the Gods

The next morning, Aurelius awakened to the sound of many activities outside Heimdall's house: the neighing of horses and clop-clop of hooves, the shouting of men lading ships with thumps of cargo, and the clanging of a blacksmith's hammer and roar of a forge. Sun streamed through the leaded windowpanes of the longhouse, and the faint aroma of food wafted across the north end of the dwelling where last night he, Clarinda, and Heimdall had stayed up late talking about events in the Nine Worlds.

That memory startled him into full consciousness and he

rose onto an elbow, finding himself near the hearth in the center of the sunken-floored dwelling. As they'd done in the *Fenrir-baude*, he and Clarinda had fallen asleep there, comfortably lying on furs by the board table where they'd eaten. Aurelius rose to his feet. Neither Clarinda nor Heimdall were in the house. How long had he slept?

Feeling chagrined, he rose quickly and went to the griddle where sausages and small loaves of bread waited. He made and ate a quick sandwich, stowed some small red apples and walnuts in the cloak's inner pocket, and gathered his few belongings. After donning his boots and clothes (both dry now, having hung overnight on a rod by the fire), he checked his tunic pocket to secure Hav's leather envelope, and then strapped sword and hatchet to his belt. The black, white-crossed Hospitaller short cloak completed his outfit. Within five minutes of opening his eyes, he was out the front door.

Bright sunshine and blue skies marked the morning on the fjord. At least twenty wattle-and-daub huts and houses flanked the lane outside Heimdall's home, all expertly built, stout of timber and frame, and well-suited to withstand the harsh weather that must blow off the sea in the winter season. Small farms lay to his left, with broad pastures leading up the green sloping hills.

Aurelius waited for some cows and their herder to pass, then made his way to the port, walking on the thick grasses tufted beneath the post-and-rail spruce fences to avoid the muddy mire from livestock and passerbys.

Two blacksmiths stood before one home with mugs of some hot drink in hand, laughing at a bawdy joke while they took turns directing an apprentice who moved back and forth between a log-pile outside the shop and furnace. The boy looked exhausted, his face already covered in soot, but Aurelius knew from his own experience that the lad wouldn't have it any other way if he were to one day become a guild-member.

Some weaver women stopped talking as he closed on the docks, staring at him while he passed. A couple of younger girls whispered to each other and ran into a house filled with looms. Aurelius greeted the women kindly, but kept moving, trying not to blush at the frank interest they showed in him, and not replying to certain questions he hoped he'd misunderstood!

The muddy path opened onto a timber-lined road along the beach which served as a border between town and port. Seven longships bobbed at anchor in the waters by the rocky shore, and two of the largest were tied down at the long pier.

When he reached the wharf, he spotted Clarinda amidst all the bustling men and activity. She stood at the end of the pier watching Heimdall give orders to the crew rigging and preparing the longboat. She'd obviously positioned herself so that she could keep an eye on Heimdall's front door, and gave Aurelius a welcoming wave at first sight of him. He waved back and made his way to her side.

"*Buon giorno*, Clarinda," Aurelius greeted.

"*Buon giorno, Dormiglione*," she replied with a smile.

"Who's a sleepyhead?" he protested, shading his forehead and squinting at the sun. "Not me. They're still loading the ship; you're not late if the ship hasn't set sail."

"Oh, is that how you monks reckon the Divine Office these days?" she asked. "Matins begins when you're ready? Somehow

I don't believe the priests in your Krak des Chevaliers would be so relaxed."

"*Molto vero*," he agreed with a grin, "and I'll just confess that I needed the sleep." Then, awkwardly, he stepped forward and gave her a hug.

Surprised, she hugged him back, managing the action while still holding onto the quarterstaff.

When they parted, he ignored the long look she gave him, and self-consciously gave his attention to the activity on the dock. He waved at Heimdall, who nodded his way while giving orders to a crewman.

Aurelius looked down at Clarinda. "It's the strangest thing; except for my sisters when I was seven or eight, I've never slept beside another woman." He cleared his throat. "Now, um, now that we've slept together twice, and it's been the deepest sleep I've ever had." He raised an eyebrow. "Is there some kind of enchantment involved?"

She blushed, but maintained eye contact. "No, but I wish there were some kind of spell to stop your snoring in the middle of the night!"

He chuckled. "Is that what woke you up so early?"

She shook her head. "No, Heimdall was puttering around cooking sausages and making bread. Once I was awake, I couldn't get back to sleep and you were really out." Her face became serious. "Obviously, Heimdall wasn't going to sail without you, so we decided to let you sleep as long as you wanted."

"*Grazie*, I needed it."

"*Siete i benvenuti.*"

Aurelius put his hands behind his back and relaxed beside her, watching the crew of the longboat put the final bundles of cargo into the vessel. "I've missed the sea," he said. "This must be bringing back many memories for you."

"I'm thinking about my crews and hoping that Pasquale's been doing well while I'm gone." Her eyes tracked the hoisting of a heavy canvas square sail. "This lot is very efficient. I always thought my men were the best, but they could stand to learn some things from these Northmen."

"What's that spar they're attaching to the main mast?"

"It's a good idea, is what it is," Clarinda said, recalling what she'd just learned from an old Viking about how the material was treated and oiled. "When I return to the Mediterranean, I'm going to have Pasquale put one on the *Maritina*—on all my ships."

"Helps with the sailing?" the young knight guessed.

She nodded, watching the sailors finish the project. "It's called a *beitass*—complements the main sail when turning into a headwind. Heimdall says a storm's coming from the west, and wants to be prepared."

"You still think this is the right thing to do?" Aurelius asked. "To go to Asgard and seek Odin's advice? Not wait here like Mimir said?"

Clarinda glanced at him. "I don't know. Heimdall's reasoning seemed sound last night, but in the morning I woke up with a bad feeling about this. What do you think?"

"Do you still have that headache?"

"Sì. Your brew of—what was it, yarrow and comfrey?—it helped, but ..."

"Not enough. I'm surprised the plants were any help at all. My herb pouch was soaked."

"No, no. I was sore from the fight, and it helped with that. But the headache, it's just as bad as yesterday. I've been keeping an eye out, but no snake-tattooed sailors yet."

"Fenris made a good point: Kenezki's a shape-changer."

"Then we're in trouble. I can't See with that depth yet."

"Nor I, and I wouldn't know what to look for. If it were Heimdall, he had plenty of chances to attack last night, and he seems to be a fixture at this village." He paused. "We could ask the Codex Lacrimae. I can't say I like the idea, especially after I slept so well when you silenced it again."

"No, let's let it stay quiet," Clarinda said. "Mimir should've contacted us by now, so we'll take Heimdall's advice. Urd never took me to Asgard, but everyone knows that he's the Guardian of the Fjords, so we've just got to trust him."

"Clarinda, Aurelius!" Heimdall beckoned to them. "We go. I don't like the look of those clouds over there, and we're ready." He peered at the young knight. "Did you eat?"

"*Ja, danke,*" the knight replied. "It was what I needed and better than I expected."

"*Gut ... gut.* The first leg through the fjords will take most of the day. We've got plenty of provisions on board, but you've had your last hot meal until evening. Always good to start on a full stomach, eh?"

"When you can," Aurelius agreed, not bothering to tell him of the fasting that was often part of his devotional regimen back at the Krak. "Is there anything we can do?"

Heimdall looked from Clarinda and then back to Aurelius. "I

feel as if I'm having the same conversation of an hour ago, only this time it's with a boy instead of a girl! You are good folk, I can feel it, and I'm sorry that you have the burdens you carry." He shook his head and waved toward the prow of the longboat. "No, my friend, there's nothing to be done. Please, just take the two seats that have been left for you, right by me at the head of the craft."

"Those are some ... menacing decorations," Aurelius said, staring at the most pronounced features of the Viking longboat: intricately carved dragon heads arched fearsomely on bow and stern of the double-ended craft. "Are they to ward off the monsters of the deep?"

Heimdall chuckled. "No, no, my young friend. The serpents of the oceans would split our ship in twain. We show our respect and awe for them by putting their likenesses on our vessels."

He looked thoughtfully at the dragonhead prow, then indicated the deck. "Let's get underway. If we're to reach the first portage by sunset, we won't reach it by talking here!"

The narrow-hulled boat lay low in the water, thirteen shields inset into each side. Even with all the men waiting on the benches inside the craft, the balance was so secure that the ship barely rocked when Aurelius and Clarinda boarded.

Heimdall and another crew member loosened the hawsers, and lowered themselves to the benches. The pilot shouted some orders, clapped twice, and the entire crew vertically raised its oars.

Heimdall stood. "May Odin's Breath guide our sails, Thor's Strength drive our oars, and Honored Jormungand lie asleep `neath our wake!"

The men roared something Aurelius didn't understand in enthusiastic response, and then, in unison, all the men on the starboard side dropped their oars to a horizontal position and pushed off from the dock. Within a moment the craft was underway.

"'Honored Jormungand?'" Clarinda asked of Aurelius, but Heimdall heard and nodded.

"Only fools don't acknowledge the True Powers in the Nine Worlds when setting forth into the sea."

Aurelius frowned, briefly imagining he could again hear the Codex Lacrimae, but the voice seemed the merest of whispers, its words easily lost in the sounds of the water and men. The boat lurched. He and Clarinda braced against the hull and tried to get comfortable on the bench at the prow.

The vessel reached breathtaking speed and sea-spray began misting into their faces. Heimdall withdrew a vast, folded blanket from under his seat and handed it to Aurelius and Clarinda. Aurelius hesitated, recalling the Grimhold Cloak that had briefly bound him in Svartalfheim. *I escaped that then, and I'll do it now if need be,* he thought. *Clarinda's cold.*

When the youths put the densely woven fabric over their shoulders, a marvelous warmth spread through their bodies. Heimdall grinned at their astonished faces.

"Some elven friends in Alfheim wove that blanket." He inclined his head toward some distant mountains. "My watch is harsh at times, and Glittertind can be an unforgiving mistress if you're unprepared for the sudden storms on the fjords. They can be cold," he chuckled, "cold and deadly enough to splinter even the thick hide of an elderly man like myself."

"We should all look like you when we're elderly!" Clarinda shouted against the rising winds.

"You've a clever manner of speech, Clarinda Trevisan!" The burly man winked at Aurelius. "*Und*, you'd do well to not lose this one, Codex Wielder. If I were a couple centuries younger, I think I'd strive with you for her hand!"

"Oh, we're not ... I mean, I can't— " Aurelius began, then interrupted himself and shouted, "I agree, but you might want to watch your own back on this boat. She knows her way around a ship and runs a fleet back on Midgard!"

"Hah! I know!" Heimdall roared. "Though the tars on the *Maritina* would be hard-pressed to match this crew!"

Clarinda shook her head, privately pleased at Santini's reaction to Heimdall's taunting, but not wanting to make things more awkward between her and the youth than things sometimes were by appearing too grateful.

"Typical men!" she shouted, knowing from long experience with her own crews how to handle them. "You talk too much for ship work. Focus on getting us across this strait!"

Heimdall made his way to the stern and spoke with the stroke-master, then pilot. Aurelius smiled at her and then regarded the nearing mountains of the great fjord.

"That peak to the south," he asked after Heimdall sat again, "is that Mount Glittertind?"

"*Ja*, at the gate to Bifrost here in Asgard."

The young knight gazed at the distant peak, thinking about the constancy of the mountain in the many of the worlds he'd visited. He'd seen it in the distance upon first arriving in Alfheim, and it was the last place he'd been to before being torn from its depths in Jotunheim. That thought led back to wondering about those he'd left behind at Mimir's Well. Had Mimir dealt with Morpeth? Did his new friends survive the encounter? Why did Morpeth's use of Marcus's form seem so offensive to Aurelius, and what did the use of that form signify about things back at the Krak? If these entire experiences were part of some dream, why did the knight feel so involved with matters here?

Clarinda nudged him with an elbow, and he smiled, grateful and completely confused by the effect she had on him.

"You're not talking with the Codex are you?" she asked in a low tone beneath the blanket they shared.

"No, and I think that you'd hear it if I did."

"Thinking about everybody back at Mimir's Well?"

"Definitely. I don't like feeling this helpless, but this is the only thing we can do, right? If Odin and the Aesir don't know what to do with the Codex, then who will?"

She reached across his lap and squeezed his hand.

He drew a deep breath, momentarily exhilarated by her touch, but also pleased to be on a ship again, whatever the circumstance. They both fell back into a comfortable silence.

The natural beauty of the fjord seemed possessed of a magic all its own. The recent rainstorm had brought a fresh vivacity to the area, enlivening the knight's senses. He saw the grassy, viridescent slopes that rolled to the opaque water in breathtaking vividness; he smelled the fresh air filled with the redolence of those green hills; and he felt, with an invigorating and tangy sharpness, the salty sea-spray misting over the bow.

The air had a translucence and clarity that Aurelius had seen only during mid-autumn afternoons in his native Sicily. The lands bordering the fjord, and the water itself were parts of a world that, like the Krak, like Alfheim, and even the monastery back in Calabria, he could find himself fighting to preserve.

The canvas of the broad square sail billowed full and strong in the wind gusting across the briny waters of the fjord, and the dragon-headed longboat was moving so rapidly now that it seemed to barely touch the choppy surface of the fjord.

Aurelius kept hold of Clarinda's hand, because she hadn't withdrawn it, and it felt right to keep holding it. He didn't want to disrupt the tranquility that the warmth and sights had unexpectedly brought him. He sank into the elven blanket, staying close to Clarinda, and regarded the receding Mount Glittertind. His thoughts turned again to his situation.

There seemed to be real consequences to the actions that were revolved around the Codex Lacrimae, and Aurelius believed that there would soon come a time when he, too, would become directly involved. His decision not to "pay the price" of the dark book hadn't prevented people from dying, and he wondered if inaction itself might not be as perilous as full commitment to the tome's demand.

But how could he contemplate any action that involved the Codex Lacrimae? Even a willingness to sacrifice the "life of a friend" was reprehensible to him on spiritual grounds. God would never condone such an action, and even Clarinda had shared the same repugnance toward the Codex's "price" when Aurelius had told her of it.

A shadow fell across the craft, and Aurelius and Clarinda beheld the first of the monolithic granite cliffs that lined the strait into the fjord. The natural outcroppings rose from the sea like a mountain that had been cleaved by the axe of an angry giant, the shorn sides of the walls towering high into the space through which earth once lay and now only water flowed. The temperature dropped and the youths pulled the blanket closer about them, grateful for the warmth.

The longboat approached a bend in the fjord, and the rowers pushed and pulled furiously against the waves of a strong current. The winds became a dull roar in the young people's ears and they lowered their heads against the spume that began to sting their faces. The labyrinthine cliffs retreated and the longboat sped across an expansive length of sea. Aurelius saw more green hills a long way off and, some leagues ahead, another series of granite fjords. The whitecaps of the wavelets and the foam of the boat's wake reflected the light of the sun with a brilliant opalescence. Aurelius stared at the iridescent froth and hoped that the so-called Watcher of the Gods, who sat relaxed at the prow, watching him impassively, was at least correct in his guess about the promise of Asgard.

"So, Heimdall," Aurelius shouted when they reached an ocean-like expanse with no land in sight. "You're the only guardian of this route to Asgard?" His voice vied with the sound of the water rushing beneath the hull.

"I am, but I also watch all that occurs in the Nine Worlds."

"Is that what you are doing now? You looked as if you were not quite here. Is it magic?"

"To a mortal it might seem so. In the parlance of those who know, we call it the Sight."

"Can you really see all the worlds?"

"*Ja*, unless other, great magic conceals things. Even then, if I am made aware of such workings and know what to look for, my aspect of the Sight will pierce any ward placed upon a person, animal, or thing. I told you, I was unaware that either the Huntsman or the Codex Lacrimae had returned to the Nine Worlds because they'd hidden themselves from me." He gazed appreciatively at Aurelius. "Even now, with you two less than a few feet distant, I can barely see you in the other planes of the Sight. I can see you physically, but not in the other realms."

"That's a first," Aurelius smiled. "Most of the people in the Nine Worlds swear that the Codex glows like a star when they look at me."

"Only the Norns, Mimir, or those of great evil would see it as such," Heimdall replied.

"Evil? Why do you say that?" Aurelius asked, more for time to think than from any serious doubt about (or challenge to) the assertion.

He himself believed that the Codex was a source of great evil. Others all the way back to Ibn-Khaldun had told him such. How could it be otherwise? The caveat in the book's frontispiece—the life of a friend as the price for using it—revealed it to be a work of pagan, dark magic, and if he had any doubts after reading that line, there was the information that had been flooding into his mind since escaping Farbauti and Kenezki's trap in Svartalfheim: thaumaturgy for raising the dead, charms against other forms of ill magic, spells for the creation, unmaking, and redirection of *runeporten*.

As a priest-in-training, Aurelius recoiled at such things—in all the workings, there seemed to be an essential denial of God.

Sorcery was explicitly forbidden in the Church. Authorities back to Saint Augustine didn't recognize any magic, except for wondrous events such as the transubstantiation that took place with the bread and wine at Communion, the power of Holy Writ that was effected through the Scriptures, or the miracles that graced the lives of the Apostles and all the saints. From his studies of the medical lore available in the East, Aurelius knew that the boundaries between science and what the Church called magic often blurred, but where the Codex Lacrimae was concerned he'd never really doubted its evil origin.

"The Codex Lacrimae is naught else but evil," Heimdall asserted, mirroring the knight's thoughts. "Like knows like. It is a Power in the universe, but it is a fell one. Those of like nature sense its presence immediately. I know it to be the bane of the Nine Worlds."

"Then, why have you been so kind to me? To us?" As during the conversation with his friends in Svartalfheim, Aurelius was somewhat stunned by the offhand manner in which Heimdall was speaking about the matter of destroying the Codex Lacrimae.

"I told you: you both came from Mimir's Well. Any who are sent by him, for good or ill, have the right to go to Asgard if he desires. We Aesir do not interfere in the affairs of Wise Mimir, or those of the Norns. Their respective powers, their presence in the Sight, demands that special consideration be given."

"What would you have done if Mimir hadn't sent me?"

Heimdall frowned. "It's doubtful that you would have made it across Bifrost. There are safeguards in the magic that prevent any of ill intent from crossing. I believe that you could transverse the Rainbow Bridge with only the Codex Lacrimae, and then, indeed, the initial defense of the Golden Realm might have fallen to me. If I'd sensed such a threat, I would have seen you immediately and tried to stop you."

"What do you mean, 'tried?' Aren't you like a 'demi-god'? One of the Aesir who built Asgard?"

"*Ja*, but it's said that the Codex Lacrimae has the capacity of Odin-Fire. I would perhaps have been hard pressed to stop you."

A competitive fire lit behind Heimdall's eyes. "Perhaps I could have stopped you, perhaps not—it would be interesting to see a contest." He sighed. "Yet, should I have failed, you wouldn't have been able to navigate the labyrinth of the fjords. That is the ultimate defense of the Golden Realm; many a Huntsman, frost giant, and dark elf have been confounded by the straits during those few times that I have not been at my post. None have ever heard of them again, although sometimes when I am sailing I think that I can hear their screams in the deeps."

Aurelius hesitated, brooding over Heimdall's words. The aphotic water darkly resisted his attempt to peer into it, and the foam that lingered after the ship's wake reflected the turbid seething of his thoughts. The craft passed into the shadow of another monolithic slab of granite.

"Heimdall," he asked finally, "What would you do if you had the Codex Lacrimae?"

"I would destroy it, or throw it into the deeps out here. I don't have to imagine very far, Codex Wielder—I am the Watcher of the Gods, one of the Aesir. You could even hand it to me, and I'd leave my post for a few moments, travel to the *Sviddengen* in Svartalfheim where it was created, and open a rune-gate to let in some of Muspelheim's molten seas. That's all it would take to be done with the threat to Creation that the Codex poses. Ragnarok will come inevitably enough without the Dark Book working to hasten it." The navigator's voice was firm in its conviction. "To do otherwise would be to participate in the wrong that was begun long ago by Loki and the Dark Elves."

"So, even if the magic could be used to help people, you say no compromise?" Aurelius pressed, recalling the various purposes that both Mimir and the Norns had attributed to it. Even Rudyick, through destroying it, wanted to use the Codex to save his people.

"None."

"Good. That's what I've believed since I read the first words of the book."

"Why do you wear the armor braces, then?" Heimdall's question held no recrimination, only curiosity.

"They used to be leather. I didn't even know they'd turned to metal until I was at Mimir's Well, and since then I have tried to take them off, but can't. It doesn't seem as if I have a choice."

"There's always a choice, Servius Aurelius Santini," Heimdall said, his eyes darkening slightly. "You could cut your arms off at the elbows, if the braces were truly offensive to you. An enemy might still try to do that."

"That, too, is what I've always believed," the Hospitaller said, chuckling as he thought Heimdall had made a joke. "But I've spent so much time in this dream being cast from one place to another that I haven't had time to really think, much less make any lasting choices."

Heimdall shook his head, a grave expression on his face. "You'd better find time to give this matter some thought, Midgardian, for this is neither a dream, nor a time to hesitate in your actions. The Huntsmen have returned and the Codex Lacrimae is burning again in the Nine Worlds. Who knows if or when the other Codices might awaken? No, I think that you're responsible for whatever course Mimir and the Norns have set for you."

"That's a problem, then," Aurelius said regretfully, "because they were going to tell me what to do, and then Morpeth appeared."

"Not a very good position to be in," Heimdall agreed. "Mimir has a better reputation than he deserves, if he left you two to your fate like this." Heimdall laughed and took in Clarinda, too, as he continued mirthfully. "Especially when one considers that, besides the dreaded Codex Lacrimae, you both wear and carry strange weapons with you. The spear, Gungnir, lies within that staff, and as I said last evening at the dock, that hatchet on your waist is a deceptively fearsome tool. You still haven't told me how you came by them, and I noticed last night around the fire you each changed the subjects whenever I tried to learn the stories. Come, we have time here; tell me the tales. Haven't I earned your trust with my hospitality and this passage to Asgard?"

Clarinda had been leaning to one side of the ship, apparently watching the waters swirling by, but when Heimdall spoke those words, she looked directly at the guardian while lightly, almost accidentally, tapping the tip of her quarterstaff on Aurelius's forehead.

"Ow," the youth said, rubbing his temple, "Clarinda what the—?"

"*Mi dispiace*," she apologized, moving the weapon to the other side of her.

—*fool!* The Codex Lacrimae was saying, the words returning to Aurelius's mind in a rush. *If you don't believe me and persist in not talking to me for an entire day, ask Heimdall about how he knew the name of your witch's ship! Your Norn never mentioned anything about her ship back on Midgard last night—all you discussed was the time you've spent in the Nine Worlds! Also, why does he deliberately bait you by saying he'd take me to the* Sviddengen, *when only Odin, the Norns, and Volund know where I was made? Why won't you listen to me? You and the Trevisan wench are going to die here!*

"As we said last night," Aurelius replied, trying to focus on the watcher and speak in what he hoped was a casual, dismissive tone to Heimdall.

An empty space lined by dread opened in his stomach, but he knew that he couldn't let any apprehension show on his face. He and Clarinda were in the middle of fjord, completely at the mercy of this man and his crew! It was almost impossible to ignore the Codex's disturbing words. He had to think!

"It's enough to know that the weapons were given to us by a friend," he continued, "and he trusted that we'd use our tools well."

"Perhaps it's enough," Heimdall mused, "and mayhap not." He glanced at Clarinda. "No offense, but strange are the ways of that quartet of Norns and Seer."

Aurelius didn't reply. He looked at the fjord and tried to keep from shouting in pain as the Codex screamed in his mind.

You're in grave peril, Servius Aurelius Santini! You need to start worrying about yourself, or you'll have no friends left to be of concern when paying my price, the Codex Lacrimae screamed. *Do you want to die, and avoid engaging me? Is that why you remain silent? You must heed my words—this can't be Heimdall! The Watcher of the Gods waits on the other side of the fjords to personally escort those who survive the labyrinth of waterways.*

Aurelius intentionally avoided looking at Heimdall and Clarinda after the Codex fell silent again. He hoped that Clarinda was listening to its words and devising a plan of her own. They needed to think through what the Codex was telling them without giving away the fact that they were now suspicious of Heimdall.

The choppiness of the water seemed to confirm his fears. The boat rocked so much that Aurelius grabbed hold of the hull. Large drops spattered past the shields and wooden dragon's heads, pelting his face as the longboat's became increasingly buffeted.

Clarinda released her hand from his, feeling the same tension in the air that he suddenly did. Heimdall seemed to awaken from the trance into which he had fallen and glanced around.

It's not a trance, fool! He's summoning a storm, and going to take you both to the depths with it!

The boat continued to lurch between waves that were now twice the height of a man, and a shrieking wind bore the first flakes of snow across the tumultuous sea. How had the storm front had arrived so quickly?

The Children of Loki share their sire's supernatural powers, Santini.

Listen to me, please. I'd not fall in the fjords and be lost to such as Jormungand before I've begun to live again!

The snow increased, its cold flurries driving against the occupants of the boat.

"This isn't a natural storm!" Clarinda shouted through the hyperborean winds and snow. She pulled the blanket over both their heads and spoke quickly to Aurelius. "Something's not right with Heimdall, Servius. I agree with the Codex: he's not what he seems, and if the book thinks that it's Jormungand, that'd explain my headaches. I thought somebody in the village was causing it, but the pain's been there this entire voyage. What's the book saying now?"

"Nothing. You probably heard how angry it was, saying that he's creating this storm, but now it's completely quiet."

"I heard what it said about the *Maritina*, and it's right; I never told Heimdall about the fleet. or the name of my ship."

"Young ones!" Heimdall shouted, his voice booming through the fabric. "I'm the Watcher of the Fjords of Asgard; I can see for hundreds of leagues and hear the sound of wool growing on a sheep's back! I can hear you! Do you suspect me of treachery?"

The blanket got yanked away, and Aurelius and Clarinda stared not into the bearishly friendly features of Heimdall, but instead into the leering face of sinewy man whose serpentine tattoos were garishly illuminated by flashes of lightning.

"Well, you should fear treachery, children, because I'm not Heimdall!"

"Kenezki," Clarinda whispered, her worst fears confirmed.

She and Aurelius were trapped in the middle of a stormy sea with the Midgard Serpent.

CHAPTER 21

Jormungand's Bane

Kenezki lurched forward, backhanding Clarinda with the speed of a viper, and bowling her backward. Gungnir clattered onto the deck and rolled underneath the bench. Blood erupted form Clarinda's nose and she fell off the ship and disappeared into the surging waves of the fjord.

The tattooed pirate grasped at the hatchet on Aurelius's hip, but, with all the instinctive haste he'd shown when plucking Ratatosk in midair, Santini punched a forearm hard into Kenezki's face. Codex Light exploded in a brilliant green-blue flash from his right forearm-guard.

Now, let it be done! The Codex screamed. *Accept the price, and we'll be done with all your enemies!*

Aurelius kneed the man, and the impact sent the pirate aft-ward into a few members of the startled crew, some of whom had dropped their oars and rushed toward the bow, shouting for Heimdall and confused at the fight. Ice-laden gusts made the words Kenezki screamed at Aurelius inaudible, but his anger was clear.

Aurelius reached for the hatchet, and his eyes widened in surprise. The tool had transformed fully into a large hammer with a blunt mallet on one side and a razor-sharp ax blade on the other. Luckily, he'd not sliced open his wrist.

The youth took the half-second's respite while Kenezki recovered and scanned the storm-tossed waves for Clarinda. *Dio*, where is she?

Kenezki rose to a knee, drawing Aurelius's attention back from his search. He pulled the hammer from its holster and with his weapon raised high above him, rushed at the man. The pirate pushed two of the sailors between him and the enraged youth and dove off the other side of the ship into the roiling waters beneath the longboat.

Aurelius spun around, re-holstered the hammer, and grabbed Clarinda's quarterstaff. He rushed to where she'd been knocked off the boat, and searched the fjord for her. Gungnir wrenched him starboard, and Aurelius didn't stop to wonder at the magic in Clarinda's spear, but followed the pull of the staff.

There!

"Woman overboard!" he screamed at the crewmembers when he saw her form floating limply atop one of the mountainous waves. *"Kvinne over bord! Frau über Bord!"*

Clarinda disappeared into a trough between the stormy

swells, but he had the direction. The Hospitaller's words and pointing finger polarized the confused crewmembers into the effort of lifesaving.

Oars plunged into the waves and—in a shorter time than would've seemed possible and with a finesse that only a lifetime at sea could manage—the boat careened off the face of one wave and suddenly came alongside Clarinda, who was coughing and blinking water from eyes.

Aurelius extended the quarterstaff. She clasped it firmly, and he pulled her harder than necessary into the craft. She fell onto him, and they rolled onto the deck, then lay for a moment together, breathing hard.

"*Grazie!*" she whispered, still clinging to him.

"I thought I lost you," he whispered back, not wanting to let go.

"We've ... got ... to get ready," she said. "Ah, *Dio*, it's ... cold! If ... if ..." She clenched her teeth to stop their chattering, then said fiercely, "If Kenezki's Jormungand, we're going to be in trouble. He's in the water"

"That's why I didn't dive in after you." He helped her up and swirled the elven blanket around her shoulders. She huddled into it with another muttered *grazie*, and they took a seat opposite each other. He glanced at the rowing crew. The beat-master was making his way forward.

Aurelius pulled the hammer from its holster. "You've got to take command," he told Clarinda, "tell them where to go!"

She shook her head. "It's not going to matter, Servius. He's coming back." But, Clarinda stood, blanket still clutched around her, hooked a foot under one of the posts supporting the benches, and gave a few sharp orders to the crew.

The oarsmen responded instantly to her veteran's voice, and the longboat sliced cleanly into the next hill of water, then plunged downward at speed toward the next one.

"Hold on the same course!" Clarinda shouted at the burly Viking pilot, then turned to Aurelius. "Get ready for Kenezki!"

Aurelius held the hammer in front of him. "Did you notice this? It changed again when you were knocked overboard!"

"It's a hammer, now?" Clarinda glanced at the weapon with a frown. "My God, it's Mjöllnir! It's Thor's Hammer! It was a hatchet when Grimnir gave it to you, but it's always been Mjöllnir. I thought it might be when you were fighting in Nidaveller and brought the lightning down ..."

Thunder boomed and lightning flashed in the leaden skies overhead. "I didn't suspect anything until it flew back into my hand," he shouted back. The longboat swept downward into a deep trench between the waves, then lurched up into cresting sea-foam as a roar resounded in the snowy air.

Fool! The Codex Lacrimae's voice roared in both of their minds. *This is Jormungand; if Mjöllnir couldn't help Thor from being lost, it won't help you now!*

"No, you still don't understand, Servius," Clarinda yelled through the winds. "There's more at work here then we thought!" She lifted the quarterstaff. "Gungnir is Odin's Spear! It never leaves his side, and Thor would never be separated from Mjöllnir; that god and his hammer are the main defense of Asgard against the frost giants!"

Aurelius stared at her. "What are you saying?"

"Well, *primo*, I think that Grimnir isn't just a wandering old man; he's Odin himself!"

The Trinkets of the Asgardians are nothing to me, the Codex said in a sneering tone. *Ignore her and prepare. The serpent has transformed into its true self, sounded, and now returns, mortal! Do you die here or choose to use me? Jormungand comes!*

Some of the crew shouted behind them. Aurelius turned. The men stared at him and recited some kind of prayers. Many of them clasped amulets dangling from leather straps or silver chains. He leaned to the closest man and saw that the sailor's necklace was looped through a pendant in the shape of an inverted "T."

The man clasped the young knight's shoulder and smiled bravely, his cracked yellow teeth visible through a heavy beard. *"Odin segne uns, Jotun-Sohn—befreit uns von diesem Übel aus der Tiefe!"* The man closed his eyes and repeated the prayer, ending fervently, "Please, Son of Jotunheim, rid us of this evil from the deeps!"

"No, my friend," Aurelius said, putting a hand on the man's strong forearm and pushing it gently down. "I'm not a Jotun-Son, nor who you think I am. This ... this hammer was a gift, that's all!"

You'll need more than Odin's blessing and a sailor's belief in you to escape the serpent, Hospitaller. You need me!

Aurelius mentally told the Codex to stay quiet if it wasn't going to offer any helpful advice, but he was reassured that parts of his guesses seemed to be confirmed. He tightened his grip on the hammer.

"Secondo?" he shouted at Clarinda. "Quickly! What do you think, that I'm somehow Thor?"

"No! I mean, I don't see how that could be, but the most

important thing is that if Odin's taken a direct hand in this affair, if he's given you his son's weapon, there's a connection somewhere that we're not seeing. I think that it's got to do with that trick Loki was playing on your ancestor over a hundred years ago."

Her seasoned eyes scanned the waters, then looked directly at Aurelius. "He's breaching, so hold on!" Snow pelted them with the force of a thousand minute pebbles. She raised her voice to be heard against the pounding of the storm. "Servius, listen to me! I can hear the Codex trying to get you to use it! Use the hammer instead! If it is Thor's hammer, you've got an alternative to the Codex! Mjöllnir can rip open the sky, and its prophesied to be the weapon that kills Jormungand at the end to time—no wonder he fears it!"

A fantastic roaring interrupted her, and both youths looked at the waters past the prow. The sea, for all its heaving and waves of great height, couldn't hide the great vortex beginning to form almost a league from the wildly careening craft. The snowfall was starting to diminish visibility and add weight to the sail, but three sailors were clearing the canvas as it accumulated. The taut sail thumped a beat in the winds, a counterpoint to the serpent's distant, approaching roars.

Oddly, a ferocious part of Clarinda took heart—the part of her that was pure mariner, willing to live and die by the laws of the seas—and a foolish sailor's pride filled her.

She grinned, very relieved that the crew members here didn't seem to be in league with their enemy. Ignoring for a moment the danger of Kenezki, she shouted encouragement to the third sailor who'd taken charge of the *beitass*. The expertise she was witnessing with the sails, along with ferocious strokes of the oarsmen made the Venetian captain's heart swell.

"By God," she shouted at them, exultant. "This might not be my ship, but I'd sail with you lot anywhere in the Nine Worlds!"

"Clarinda," Aurelius shouted, "something's happening—hold on!" The knight reached forward to loosen the rope and was thrown painfully onto his elbow against the side of the hull. He raised himself above the edge and saw that the vortex was nearing.

Lightning flashed white light upon pillars of granite that now seemed close by. The oily, greenish rocks that were strewn with gleaming kelp strands stood in stark relief to the frothing waves that crashed against the bases of those stone slabs.

Aurelius frowned and shook his head; weren't they just on the open water? Where did these cliffs come from? He squinted, his sight straining past the wet snow and water that plastered his hair to his skull. He was about to shout at Clarinda, when a fearful realization sliced into his stomach.

The longboat was on the open water, and those slabs of granite had not been the cliffs of the fjord—the Midgard Serpent was rising from the deeps.

The cliffs-that-were-not-cliffs move steadily upward. Aurelius forgot to breathe, staggered by the recognition that he was seeing the undulating flesh of a living creature. The beast was thousands of cubits across, its deep green coloration mottled in places by crustaceans that had grafted onto its skin after centuries on the sea floor. Scales, each twice the height of a man, protected its flesh, and in the lightning flashes Aurelius saw that those layers matched the sturdiest armor ever made by a blacksmith.

The Hospitaller, hands gripped tightly to the side of the prow, peered upward in astonishment. His gaze followed the sinuous length of the leviathan for hundreds of cubits to a tapered head whose width was that of five-hundred ox carts, a head with the befanged maw of a colossal serpent.

For serpent it was! Jormungand, whose coming at Worlds' End the Norns foretold would bring the death of Thor while Ragnarok embroiled the inhabitants of Asgard and the other eight worlds. Jormungand! The father to the race of the great worms that Midgardians called dragons, whose sinewy muscled coils possessed a thousand times the strength of any dragon that had ever flown in the Nine Worlds.

The head disappeared and the curved neck of the leviathan vanished as the creature sounded again. His sudden disappearance beneath the ocean in a turmoil of seething water and frothing, lashing waves made Aurelius almost believe the mythic tales about Jormungand's length—here was a monstrosity that, indeed, seemed able to encircle the Earth.

The longboat sped forward into the beast's wake at such velocity that Aurelius and Clarinda were hurled onto their backs.

"Erhalten Sie von dieser Stelle, Jormungand!" some of the crew shouted almost in unison from their oarlocks behind the Hospitaller. One repeated the scream, his voice trembling in fear, "Get you from this place!"

"Servius, call Hav!" Clarinda shouted, an idea suddenly coming to her. She reached into the purse at her waist. They had the *fossegrim's* coral!

Aurelius took the blue fossilized anemone from his friend's outstretched hand. "Hav!" he screamed. "Hav—help me!"

The longboat raced toward the vortex that Aurelius now knew was the origin of the creature's rise. The knight didn't know how the human-sized Kenezki had achieved such stature, but he didn't care. Anger mixed with fear, and the entirety of his being committed itself solely to Clarinda's defense.

"Hav!" he screamed again.

The storm waves rose higher and fell lower in tremendous heaves, and hundreds of *strömkarlen* and nixies suddenly appeared around the longboat. Aurelius fell back in shock.

But, while the snow still fell with increasing force and density, nature's violent forces seemed to diminish before the forms now standing on top of the foaming crests. Nude elementals in male and female shapes—of the water and apart from it—crowded in a glorious multitude around the ship in a ring that blunted both waves and snows. Tears filled Aurelius's eyes at the beauty of the creatures, their appearance in the wake of Jormungand sending a thrill through him that he'd only felt when in the most meditative moments of prayer. Unlike the creatures of darkness he'd seen in his journeys, the deep roars of the *strömkarlen* competing gayly with the light songs of the nixies were the Nine Worlds at their most glorious. None of these sprites feared such things as disguised serpents, or cursed books, or predictions of doom. They were elementals, finding joy simply in their mere existence and unity with the waters of the world.

The youth wondered how he could ever have been afraid of them, and then his gaze hardened at the memory of Old Nick, and the corruption that the devil had begun by possessing the *fossegrim* who led them all.

I am here, Santini Water-Friend, greetings. A voice boomed in Aurelius's mind, making him think that the Codex was speaking to him again. Then, he realized that the entire crew could also hear the words. *Ah, greetings to you, also, Trevisan Water-Friend. You have called, and I have come. What is your need?*

Most of the sailors had fallen back on the benches of the vessel with the appearance of the water elementals, but when Hav rose from the water, they prostrated themselves. The *fossegrim's* stature rivaled even the mountainous scales and height of Jormungand. Only his head and shoulders were visible, and the creature formed eye sockets, a nose, and mouth so that the mortals he was speaking with would have some frame of reference to relate to.

Aurelius held up the blue coral. "Clarinda and I have retrieved this from Old Nick!" he shouted and hurled it directly at the elemental. "You are completely free and back in control of the oceans and waterways, Hav!"

The coral vanished into the *fossegrim's* head with a plop.

Takk ... this is a gift undreamt of, Servius Aurelius Santini. Thank you, and takk to you, Mistress Trevisan. We will be forever in both your debts, and never again let one such as Abbadon take what should never have been taken.

"You're welcome!" Aurelius said, looking past Hav and noticing that the vortex of water was still nearing. His ears popped. Their change in pressure could only precede Jormungand's return. "Hav, we still need your help—may we have it?"

Anything.

"Can you destroy the Midgard Serpent?"

Nein—Jormungand is an Elder Power, bound into the waters of the world by Odin himself, and coeternal with such as me or other fossegrim. Only another ancient power, earth, stone, air, or fire may have a chance at destroying him.

"Earth, air, fire ..." Aurelius raised the hammer before him. "What about iron?"

Ah, Mjöllnir, forged with the same care by the dwarves as the gift I gave you. The elemental's head turned left and right. *I sense Skíðblaðnir's presence, but see it not. Why do you use a ship of the little humans, when I gave you a gift of the Aesir?*

"What gift?" Aurelius asked. "You threw a leather packet on the ground in Alfheim."

"Oh, Aurelius. Open it, quickly!" Clarinda urged, feeling like a fool. She recalled Hav's words in Alfheim: *You might find use for this when the seas prove contrary or no ship is found to carry you whither you will.*

Aurelius reached into the hidden pocket in his tunic and withdrew the leather envelope. His hands also touched upon the wood chip from Cerys. He frowned, not recognizing it, and feeling a strong compulsion to hand both items to Clarinda.

"I tried to open it a few times, Clare; there's no way—"

"We weren't anywhere near a sea or fjord during those times!" Clarinda shouted.

Leathern thongs fell from the packet and something expanded from within.

"Whoa!" Aurelius reeled back in surprise.

Simultaneously, the scrap of tree bark from Cerys began to

fall, but Clarinda swiped it in midair and peered at it, shouting, "What's this piece of wood? There's something strange about it."

"I don't know," he murmured, his mind curiously dazed. "Keep it."

"I sense magic here ... in both items!" Clarinda slipped the scrap into her tunic.

Did I forget to tell you how Skíðblaðnir works? Hav mused, an absent tone in his booming voice. *Apologies ... these details slip my mind sometimes. I thought it obvious—the magic is the same kind that governs Mjöllnir, and whether boat or weapon, each item will grow and change at need. Such is the magic of the elves and dwarves that fashioned them.*

The leather packet dropped from Aurelius's hand, and the contents grew into the shape of a toy ship. It fell into the water and almost immediately expanded into a ship three times the size of the Viking vessel. It bobbed on the waves alongside the dragon-headed longboat.

"Into the boat!" Aurelius shouted at the crew-members who, though dumbfounded by the events, began adroitly scrambling over the gunwales onto the spacious deck of Skíðblaðnir. Jormungand erupted from the sea some distance away and wove back and forth in the snow-filled air. His every movement caused eruptions of water that foamed in sloshing waves and threatened to capsize the craft.

SANTINI, this is the end of it! Hav didn't look at the water serpent, but remained focused on Aurelius and Clarinda.

"My last requests are two," the young knight shouted. "Ask the *strömkarlen* to take Clarinda and Skíðblaðnir to safety—"

"Servius, No! Don't you dare! I want to stay here with you!"

the Venetian girl shouted, but even if the *fossegrim* seemed unperturbed by the onrushing Jormungand, the hundreds of elementals at his command reacted instantly.

A couple of nixies lifted Clarinda bodily from the longboat and hurled her into the magical vessel. The *strömkarlen* and nixies submerged into the waves and swirled Skíðblaðnir away at a speed that matched any of Rudyick's blurring runs.

"—and then carry me to that viper's head!"

I ... AM ... JORMUNGAND! With those words, impossibly, the Midgard Serpent rose to an even greater height, its head soaring high into the gray-black clouds of the storm until it passed from sight. The uncoiling body of the worm sped upward and burst through Hav's body, dissipating the elemental into a thousand million droplets of water. The fjord erupted in a mountainous shower of devastation; the water returning from its upsurge collided onto the top of the bobbing longboat with the impact of a miniature hurricane.

Aurelius heard the mast snap. The flailing sail hit him like a gigantic fist, smacking him from the craft and into the turbulent fjord. Hav's voice entered his mind, calming him, and his descent into the sea slowed. He kicked furiously at the water, hoping that effort and his body's natural buoyancy would be enough to get him to the air before he drowned. The roaring he'd heard in his ears before the water hit changed slightly, and his head pounded from some unseen pressure. His lungs burned, and he could see nothing as he swam upward toward what was hopefully the surface.

Breathe, Codex Wielder. You will not die in my waters, unless I perish, too.

Aurelius trusted Hav's voice and inhaled.

Air, not water, filled his lungs, and he found himself bobbing on the surface and then rising into the air, born aloft by one of Hav's giant hands. They quickly approached Jormungand, who was moving upwards and looking about through the wreckage for his foe.

"If you can't kill him," Aurelius gasped, "he can't kill you, can he?"

I am one of twenty-seven fossegrim, *my friend, and none of us are as powerful as the children of Loki. I'll not leave your side, though.*

Aurelius didn't wait any longer. With a grunt and a tremendous heave he rose unsteadily on top of Hav's palm, trusting that the elemental wouldn't let him fall. He stood upon the column of water that kept rising to match Jormungand's height.

The young knight knew that he would die if he were to fall from such an elevation, but a battle-fury rose in him that demanded a fight with the sea-dragon, no matter what the cost. He felt his life was forfeit, anyway, and wanted to secure at least some safety for Clarinda before dying.

Too many things were out of his control. He couldn't do anything about the Huntsmen, nor Old Nick, nor Hela, nor the armies back at the Krak, nor any of the other host of enemies that seemed to have been arrayed against him in a very short period; but, against Jormungand, against this gigantic foul worm, he felt that he could do something. He had the gift of Mjöllnir and the friendship of Hav. As a warrior, those were more assets than he could hope for in any battle, and he intended not to squander the opportunity to rid the worlds of an evil such as Jormungand.

When the water cleared from his eyes enough to see, he

flung the hammer as hard as he could, releasing the weapon upward through the madly falling snow in the direction of the fast-approaching sea-serpent. The heavy, iron mallet flew straight and strong. Its head collided with Jormungand's lower jaw in an explosion of yellow energies that blasted the creature backward. The gigantic serpent dropped into the waves, and disappeared as the hammer flew back into Aurelius's hand.

Jormungand returned in a geyser of sea spray, terrifyingly quick and roaring with rage. Aurelius raised the hammer again, but didn't throw it because Hav's hand enveloped him and thrust him higher. The *fossegrim* was now the same size as Jormungand. With the speed of a waterfall, Hav grasped the serpent beneath its head with what looked like a hundred hands. Then it started to squeeze.

That's enough from you, I think, worm, the elemental whispered.

Jormungand's head writhed upward in panic, and even though in the watery grip of the highest of Hav's hands, Aurelius turned his head slightly to seek fresh air, so foully did the serpent's noxious fumes blow through the tempest.

Let ... me ... go, Fossegrim, or my venom will unmake you as surely as it will the boy!

Hav held the serpent strongly, but Aurelius felt a tremor pass through the elemental's form. He dreaded what was going to happen and swam a few cubits through Hav's appendage to get closer to the edge of the *fossegrim's* fist where he could leap on top of Jormungand if Hav faltered.

Depart these waters, Jormungand. Hav's voice resounded in both the knight's and serpent's mind. *This boy's not for you.* Hav rose from the sea and, growing to a height where he could observe

Jormungand thrashing inside, he created a dome of water that trapped the visible upper parts of the leviathan's coils.

Aurelius noticed that the battle between the two gigantic creatures had dissipated the vortex. The waves were still tempestuous, but not of the sizes that they'd been earlier. It appeared that all the water Hav used to maintain his leviathan-like stature was calming the sea.

He ... has ... a ... Codex, Jormungand thundered. *If it's not for me, then whom?*

Jormungand undulated back and forth against the orb's walls, each collision water to spray into the snowing sky in massive eruptions.

The Codices are not for such as us. This is a matter of Midgardians, Nibelungen, und Elf-Kind.

UND MEIN VATER!

Jormungand, Hav's voice began to sound strained, and parts of the water globe exploded into the storm as the serpent bashed its head against the sides. The effort of containing the beast was beginning to take its toll on Aurelius's ally. *You've not seen your father for centuries. Leave this matter be, and return to the deeps. The boy is a water-friend. You will not kill him while I live.*

I ... will ... be ... free! The serpent's coils finally ruptured the sphere, and as water spumed in all directions, Jormungand launched himself skyward, racing towards Aurelius's position at the top of Hav's water column.

Wield your hammer as you will, Jormungand roared, his red eyes fixating upwards on Santini's with murderous hatred. *You die today!*

A colossal wave of water collided with the serpent, the crest of its wave pounding Jormungand to the side as he closed on the knight's column. The waters of the wave transformed into Hav again, and this time the *fossegrim* held the sea dragon with two massive hands.

The serpent writhed but couldn't free itself from Hav's grip.

"Hav, *bitte*, I need to stand!" Aurelius tightened his grip on the hammer. The elemental seemed to hear him and solidified water beneath the knight's feet.

He emerged from the top of the column, standing and steeling himself to jump, even though his elevation above the Midgard Serpent was three times the height of Hisn al-Akrad back home. He threw the hammer again, but, as he feared, the cascading torrents of Hav's waters blunted the strike. Jormungand's head did recoil, but with nowhere near the kind of pain or injury needed to truly damage the leviathan.

I'll have to be right on top of him, Aurelius thought grimly, preparing himself. *Buon Dio, on him. Repeated strikes in one place, until I'm through the other side of that fanged head!*

It seemed, however, that even held fast by Hav's power, the Midgard Serpent wasn't going to relent.

Do it again, Santini! Jormungand shouted, this time with a hint of Kenezki's mocking voice. *I dare you, Boy!*

"Wrong person to dare anything," Aurelius muttered as he obliged the taunting snake. He threw Mjöllnir, trying to coincide the cast with Hav's attempt to start freezing the water around Jormungand. Unlike the previous strike, this hammer connected solidly on the scales at the back the sea-snake's neck, and dark blood and severed muscle strands sprayed into the snow-filled air.

The beast bellowed in pain, and made a particularly violent, heaving wrench as the hammer flew back into the knight's waiting hand. *You had your chance, Santini, and now it's too late!* Jormungand roared. *Recruit pathetic allies like this water elemental, or even try using the Codex Lacrimae! I've destroyed Lore Masters before, wielders more versed in Script and Scope than a boy like you could ever be! I'll not be denied my vengeance upon your folk any longer—I will have revenge for what's been done to my father and my kindred!*

"*Basta!* What revenge, Jormungand, Kenezki, or whatever you want to call yourself?" Aurelius ignored the pit of fear yawning in his stomach. The sight of the serpent beneath him, of Hav straining against the creature to defend Santini, made a primal part of the youth explode with fury.

He was sick of all these conniving enemies, shape-changing pirates, and even his sometime-threatening friends. Mostly, he felt frustrated beyond endurance by everyone's constant, cryptic references about him and the Codex Lacrimae.

"*Stolto!* Your father created the Codex, not you!" Aurelius cried. "You could choose your own path—Fenris did! You didn't have to make allies like Satan, or kill Clarinda's father! Those were choices!"

For such as me, there's no choice, boy—only Being! Hunger! Destiny! I will have the Codex Lacrimae, now that it's here. Returned finally to the Nine Worlds, and partly here in my waters and partly back at your little castle back home! Too long has my father been bound, too long have we been delayed by Aesir, Norns, and Elves. None of them know what Fate truly demands.

"Really, Snake?" Aurelius barked a laugh, unable to restrain himself from starting some battlefield taunts. "Do you have water on the brain? Did you say that the Norns don't know Fate? Fate?"

Why shouldn't he start taunting? Nothing else seemed to be working. The Codex was quiet. Each one of Hav's attempts at stopping the Midgard Serpent seemed to be failing, and Aurelius was simply at a loss what to do. The monster was ... beyond staggering in size. He was witnessing a battle of titans, and completely reliant on Hav maintaining the integrity of his watery shape lest Aurelius himself plunge to his death from this great height.

"Hav, lower me a bit," he whispered, "I'm no use to you way up here!"

He wants you closer, Water Friend. I should fling you kilometers distant, and let my strömkarlen *catch you.*

"Don't you dare!"

Isn't that what Clarinda Water-Friend said to you, before you cast her aboard Skíðblaðnir?

"I ... that ... that was different. You owe me a life-debt. You can't throw me to safety while you fight here!"

That makes no sense. Your life would be safe, and part of my debt would be repaid.

"Hav, I'm not going."

So be it, water-friend, but hear me. Whatever his ranting, the serpent's correct about the Script and Scope. I don't think you've learned enough of the Codex Lore. I'll not let you die while I live.

"Und, I'll not have you die for me!" Aurelius repeated, gathering his thoughts. "Hav, together we might have a chance. I've got a plan. Jormungand's vanity."

Distracting the enemy was one of the first lessons he'd taught Marcus when he'd begun training the boy in Devrone's arts, and he hadn't yet been disappointed by the tactic when he bothered to use it himself.

Of course, one might argue that the time to employ taunts wasn't in the middle of a storm-roiled fjord against a leviathan, but the knight had had enough. If Hav could continue straining against the Midgard Serpent while Aurelius stood safely out of harm's way, the youth was going to do something.

Kill you, then I'm going after Trevisan—rip you both... Jormungand began, but Hav interrupted him by pouring a lake of water into the beast's gullet. He froze it into a column of ice, then strove to push the serpent beneath the waves by icing all the water in the immediate area.

Something cold settled in Aurelius at the threat to Clarinda. This battle wasn't just about him and Hav anymore. He'd not let anything happen to the Venetian girl. Aurelius had only briefly met Kenezki, but Clarinda had told him enough to know that, whether pirate or dragon, there'd be no mercy for the two Midgardians from Jormungand. The path, however, was the same: distract and infuriate the monster.

"*Ja*, go back to the deeps, Serpent!" Aurelius yelled. "Just like any pirate, you can't do anything by yourself. Stealing because you can't make, striking from shadows because you can't bear the light! Go back to the sea floor, Worm!"

Jormungand bucked, enraged by the Hospitaller's words. His strength snapped Hav's ice sheathe like a ship fracturing an iceberg. Then he melted the frozen ice in this throat with a blast of dragon's fire that spewed high into the sky. With maw still flaming a strangely colored vermilion fire, the serpent launched itself at the *fossegrim*.

I've waited too long for this moment! Jormungand bellowed, then one of his fangs sliced into what would have been Hav's shoulder, but the water simply parted and reformed as the tooth passed through. *Death for all of you, and the Codex for me!*

Santini-friend, Hav's voice resounded in the knight's mind. *I've been poisoned.*

Hav, no! You're fine—his fang passed through you!

The serpent is Elder Kind. I am poisoned, by flame and venom.

"Go back to skulking around in your disguises!" Aurelius taunted aloud to the beast, but assessing all parts that he could see of Hav with great concern.

I FEAR NO ONE!

"You could've fooled me! You couldn't even hurt me back at Svartalfheim when you kept trying to stab me with a knife! You remember that, don't you? You ran like a frightened rabbit, then. Oh, sorry, I mean, you dove like a minnow through that *runeporte*, didn't you?"

Limb from limb, Santini! I'll become Kenezki again to take my time with your woman, and then eat the chunks of you raw!

"Come on, then, what are you waiting for?" Aurelius flipped him an old sailor's insulting gesture and kept scanning Hav's form.

He couldn't notice any difference in the *fossegrim's* millions of cubits of water, nor a change in Hav's struggle, but he knew that the creature didn't speak lightly. For Hav, somehow, poisoned meant dying.

"Do whatever snakes do when unseen by those of us who

walk in daylight!" the knight screamed, lending some of his desperation to his shouts. He retained a mocking smile and demeanor, though. If Hav really was dying, Aurelius was going to drive Jormungand into a rage that would leave an opening, some kind of vulnerability in those vast scales.

"*Hei*, I know what," he continued, cupping his hands as he leaned over the clear waters of Hav's fist, "since all you've done is talk about yourself, moan about your Fate, and brag about how much time you've had to wait for the Codex, and blah, blah, blah, why don't you make a meal of it?

The serpent roared in fury, rearing its head upward in a momentary pause in the fight. *What was that?*

"A meal! Why don't you eat yourself!" Aurelius repeated, almost hoarse, hopping briefly on one foot as he hurled the words at the behemoth.

You ... you ... speak of Odin's punishment?

Hav's voice interrupted, it's voice strained: Ware, Friend Santini. For centuries because of Odin's judgement against him, he lay thus, beneath the seas, sealed mouth to tail ... his anger ... I feel his fury.

"If he's killed you, Hav, his anger's nothing to mine," Aurelius thought back.

Then, aloud, he shouted: "Come on, worm! You lived in Constantinople long enough, didn't you, 'Kenezki?' I don't recall seeing many creatures like you in the Harbor of the Golden Horn ... must have gotten awfully lonely! Had to go back to your old ways, didn't you? Perhaps found you liked the taste of you after all that time?"

You ... you cannot speak to me thus!

Hav's voice was pained in Aurelius's mind, but there was confusion in it, too: *Water-friend, is this a flyting? Do you seek to drive him mad?*

"Just fight the poison, Hav, or get away. I know what I'm doing." Aurelius had learned the fine art of putting someone down after hundreds of hours in the yards, fighting with squires and sparring mates as everyone traded jibes and insults with each other in a proud sporting tradition that went back to ancient times.

"*Hei*, Jormie!" he shouted. " I'll stop," he lowered his voice in imitation of the serpent's baritone, "'speaking_to_you_thus,' if you do us all a favor, coil around this fjord, and eat yourself!

ENOUGH! ... Hav, get ... off me! I'd not slay you, but ... I'll ... not ... be bound!

The *fossegrim* didn't reply, and Aurelius tried not to show his surprise at the familiarity lying behind the threat. Jormungand knew the *fossegrim's* true name! Did the two sea-creatures know each other well?

Hav, the youth thought desperately, willing his own message to the elemental. *Get out of here. He just wants me, and he's going to want me more in a second. Get out of here!*

But, if anything, the *fossegrim* increased his efforts. The waters of his form swirled around Jormungand, lashing the gigantic beast with water-cords the size of oak trunks.

When it seemed as if the snake was momentarily secured again, Aurelius thought to Hav. *His face. Get me close to his face.*

He's still too strong for you, Lore Master.

"Lore Master?" Aurelius asked aloud. "I thought I didn't know enough?"

Whether brilliance or madness, this tack is working. He's becoming enraged.

Takk, Aurelius said, not letting his emotions overcome him. Hav's voice sounded weaker.

Hav submerged the knight to his shins and directed the water column at high speed to the side of Jormungand's head. The proximity tempted Aurelius with the striking distance, but he'd keep his promise to the *fossegrim.* The time to strike wasn't yet.

"*Hei,* Jormungand!" he shouted. The great flaming eye rolled to focus on him. "Clarinda told me you always wanted to get away from everybody on the sea-journey to Caesarea. Why'd you want to be alone?"

The monster didn't reply, just wriggled tremendously against Hav's restraints.

Closer Hav. To wherever his ear is.

No, that would be too close. One swing of his head would kill you. I ... can... barely... hold ... him.

Then cushion my fall, or put a wall of water between us! Aurelius snapped. *He needs to hear this.*

Hav obliged, and within a second Aurelius was on a platform next to Jormungand's head. Aurelius tried not to feel foolish. This was like speaking to the base of a mountain!

He continued with the flyting: "When you went below-decks, was it to go visit your sister? I've met Hela! She's not bad looking as sisters and queens of the dead go. I've even heard her lower body's a snake. A snake! Was she tempting when you were growing up, especially because you're so good-looking? Oh, *aspetta.* You're not good-looking at all. You're the ugliest, sorriest, most pathetic *figlio di puttana* I've ever seen. No wonder you went after your sister, you pitiable, conspiring *stronzo mangiatore*. Do you two ever, you know?" Aurelius paused in his rant, raised both eyebrows questioningly, and grinned as he made a crude sexual gesture.

The Midgard Serpent howled and fire erupted through his nostril holes and jetted harmlessly through the snowy air. Jormungand tried to wrench his head in the knight's direction, but Hav held him fast.

"Is that a *ja* or a *nein?*" Aurelius asked. "You're so hard to read, and I couldn't—"

Now, Lore-Master, there! Hav's voice boomed through Aurelius's mind as the serpent's maw twisted against Hav's water muzzle to unleash more fire.

In straining, though, the curve of his neck had bulged against the tear in the scales from Santini's earlier attack, exposing spouting blood and a hole through which white bone gleamed.

Santini threw Mjöllnir as hard as he could at the gaping wound at the back of the serpent's neck. The ax-side of the hammer sliced deeply into the gash, and scales and gore trailed the weapon as it erupted from the other side and returned to the knight's hand.

Aaawwrroooohhh! Jormungand bellowed, finally snapping the water muzzle. Fire shot into the air, blasting into Hav's gigantic form. Steam erupted in great, billowing clouds, and Hav screamed.

Aurelius found himself soaring skyward back to safety in a rush that threw him onto his back on the column of water.

When he was almost half a kilometer distance, the column ceased moving, and Aurelius was able to stand again. He ran to the side of the disc and gazed downward at the titans.

Hav had returned to the shape in which Aurelius had first met him, but of a size that equipped him to battle the Midgard Serpent. Water ropes lashed outward from all parts of his body, securing the snake and then snapping in almost the same instant, a thousand times within seconds. *Strömkarlen* and nixies did what they could, but their attacks were like sprays of water on a fortress wall against the scales of Jormungand.

You'll die, Hospitaller! Jormungand screamed, before sinking another fang deeply into Hav's midsection. The elemental groaned, but kept his arms and water ropes securely around the wildly struggling snake.

Hav ... get ... off ... me! Jormungand pleaded, his voice softer than when he raged at Santini.

Keep at this, water-friend. Hav urged Aurelius. *His struggles are not as strong.*

"Then get me closer, Hav! He can't even hear me this far away!"

Santini fell on his back again as Hav returned the water column to the battle. When he regained his feet, Aurelius shouted at the serpent: "Apologies about the sister comment, Jormie! She might be able to raise the Dead, but I don't think that'd help you. You're more of a one-snake kind of guy, aren't you?"

Was?

"A real solo act!"

Was sagst du?

"I said, anyone who spends as much time talking about himself as you do, can really only be satisfied by one thing: himself! So go to it!" Aurelius made another vulgar motion, and then nodded. "Come on, Jormungand, Odin knew it. The rest of the Nine Worlds knows it. You know it. That's why he punished you in that way!" Aurelius spread his arms wide and laughed, and even he wasn't sure where the words were coming from. Was the Codex speaking through him again? "Don't waste time with us anymore! Make a full meal of it, *lei segaiolo!*"

WAS SAGST DU?

"You heard me, I said eat yourself!" Aurelius broke into genuine laughter. Anything else wouldn't strike the necessary depth, and he was about to die, anyway. He repeated the vulgar motion. *"Du bist ein Wixer!"*

I. AM. JORMUNGAND!

Aurelius grinned, and roared back. "YOU. ARE. A. WANKER!"

Aaawwrroooohhh! The serpent roared thunder, and lightning blazed from its eyes. *MIDGARDIAN, YOU DIE NOW!*

Hav, Aurelius thought calmly, *he's beside himself. Launch me at him, and go! Heal yourself.*

It's too late, water-friend. But my sons and daughters know the truth of you, Lore Master. May your time of guardianship over the Codexes be long-lived and just. Farewell.

Please, Hav, there still must be ti—

GET. OFF. OF. ME. FOSSEGRIM!

With that, the serpent reared its head as only a snake could, finally crashing through Hav's grasp in a watery explosion, and belching venomous fire over the entirety of the *fossegrim's* body.

Hav's roar of pain was a concatenation of a thousand waterfalls. He dissolved instantly, his mortal-like form losing coherence, but somehow he still maintained a column of water that held up Santini. Confused, and hopeful that the column meant his friend might still be alive, Aurelius looked at his feet. Despair washed over him. The faces of a hundred *strömkarlen* looked back at him, their features in shock and grief at the death of the *fossegrim*.

When did he switch the column from his body to theirs? Aurelius wondered.

The sound of the elemental's agony brought back hundreds of *strömkarlen* and nixies into the waters where Hav had been, but whatever magics Jormungand had unleashed took them apart too and they began screaming in anger and agony.

"Hav, no!" Aurelius shouted, staring down in helpless horror from his vantage high above.

The watery hand, the arm, and everything human-like that Hav had created for himself evaporated as the serpent's poisons spread through the water. Fires sprang up from wherever the venom touched, including the base of the column on which Aurelius stood.

He drew Mjöllnir. The time for flyting was done.

With a wrench, Jormungand sped upward, and screaming in frustration, closed on the swiftly falling apart pillar of water where the young knight stood.

Whatever your lineage, Santini, whatever your purpose, your tale ends today!

"Friend *Strömkarlen*," Aurelius shouted. "Throw me at him!"

With the last of their energy, the *strömkarlen* obeyed, flinging him away with the force of a hurricane. Aurelius flew through the air directly at the serpent's head and raised Mjöllnir high above him, praying that he might get at least one solid strike into the serpent before dying.

The sea-dragon's face was suddenly there, and the knight brought the ax side of Mjöllnir down into the greenish flesh of Jormungand's snout.

Light and power crackled as the edge bit deeply into the scales. Green blood spurted everywhere, and the knight started to slide towards the serpent's left eye. Again, Aurelius brought the ax-side of the hammer up high and jammed it into Jormungand's steely flesh.

The Midgard Serpent screamed in agony, and its body shook with the force of an earthquake.

Aurelius hung on. Like the piton of a mountaineer, the hammer served to secure the knight's hold while Jormungand rose high again into the heavens, cursing in many languages and swearing to tear apart the enemy stuck on its maw.

The sudden motion almost sent Aurelius careening into the air, and the knight held onto the handle for dear life. Maintaining his grip on the hammer, the knight drew his sword as the rose, screaming back at his foe while he tried to bury the blade next to the hammer. The sword bounced off the worm's hide like it was a stone wall, and rebounded with a shudder, slipping from the youth's grip and into the open air.

Aurelius punched his fist into the wound Mjöllnir had opened and grasped a fracture in the serpent's skull. He withdrew the hammer again, and brought the ax-side colliding into another section of Jormungand's face. His position was defensible if he could hold on, because Jormungand couldn't open his jaws enough to get at the wildly pounding Hospitaller.

Crackling lightning and bolts of wild fire rushed outward from the strikes of Mjöllnir, and ichorous blood spewed from the ruinous wounds that Aurelius inflicted. Fully engaged in battle, and in grief and fury at Hav's death, the youth screamed again and again for the worm to die.

Then, Jormungand plunged downward with a wrenching speed that flung Aurelius off him and into the waves below. The impact took his breath away and pain flared through his entire body. For a second, he thought that the collision with the water had broken his back, but then he realized that he wasn't moving because he wasn't trying to move.

Stunned, he felt the hammer clutched in his hand. He also realized that there were still some *strömkarlen* lingering in the water, braving their own destruction to buoy him until he could recover.

He looked around futilely for Hav, but the *fossegrim* seemed to be gone, and the only traces of elementals to be seen were moaning nixies and sprites who dissolved into the waves at the sight of Jormungand.

Water streaming from his face, the knight broke the surface of the water. Snow still fell lightly, but visibility was good enough for at least a half kilometer. He whispered gratitude to the two elementals holding him, and floated to a position where he could observe the heavens, but his sight was obscured by the swooping head of the returning monstrosity.

Jormungand streaked toward him with such velocity that the waves around the knight began to flatten at the worm's approach, and a great, booming sound, louder than the loudest peal of thunder, cracked across the water of the fjord.

"Save yourselves," he urged the *strömkarlen*. Part of him was relieved when he felt their presences recede and disappear, but then a greater part of him felt terribly alone.

God, where are you?

Only the crashing of waves and the roaring of Jormungand answered him.

Aurelius saw his doom in the approaching fangs of the serpent, but he couldn't do anything except tread water and await it. He brought Mjöllnir to his side and vowed to at least try for one more strike before dying. The icy water slowed Aurelius's movements, and his thoughts were wretched, confused, and tired.

God, please ... answer me. I know the lesson of Job, but I've not abandoned you. Why have you abandoned me? Where are you? I can't perceive you. Left, right, backwards, and forwards, there's only death here.

He'd never in his life known such fear or anger, nor faced an adversary of such mind-numbing size. He'd always thought that he might die with some dignity, but in these seconds before the serpent struck he desperately wanted an alternative to this fate. Something trilled on the fringe of his mind at that thought, a familiar hope that was beyond sound but reduced to words so that he might understand it.

Clarinda, please be alive. I need to see you again.

He didn't think of his life as an apprentice squire, though it saddened him that Marcus would be alone without an older brother figure. No, not alone. There was Ibn-Khaldun, Pellion, and all their friends were at the Krak.

No, Pellion's dead. He didn't dwell on the diminishing hopes of becoming a priest. The adventures through the Nine Worlds had shown him that he wasn't fit to be one. Besides all the anger he'd felt, there was the undeniable power of the pagan magics he'd faced, and—certainly with the Codex and Mjöllnir—even explicitly engaged and used.

He'd felt desire in his heart, from the moment months ago when he'd first started to see Clarinda in his dream visions, to the fleeting initial responses he'd had to the variety of women he'd met recently in various states of undress, as had happened with Hela, Skade, and Cerys.

Until this adventure, he'd been accustomed to living his life for the last eighteen years in preparation for two paths; a life spent almost entirely in training for war, or one that involved learning the rites of the Church as he studied in a scriptorium for the priesthood. But, he'd felt such wrath at times while he'd been traveling here that he didn't know if he could ever remove the stains from his soul and remain in the Church. Rage had controlled his sword arm in the battles against the *Wilde Jagd* in Niflheim and at the *Underjordisk Elv*, and he remembered especially the wild elation that overwhelmed him when he'd taken hold of the rock-giant's skull-covered stave.

Lust, anger, and wrath. The voyage through the Nine Worlds had already revealed him capable of three of the Seven Deadly Sins, and his inability to simply stop traveling, kneel and pray and wait for the dream to end might even make him a candidate for a fourth, Sloth, the lack of exercising one's full talents or abilities.

If he were truly a devout Christian, and priest-in-training, shouldn't he have just refused to go any farther in obviously magical worlds, and simply waited for the dream to end? Or, perhaps with the attention and concern he'd gotten from Clarinda, and the way that everyone spoke of him and the Codex, he'd begun to succumb to a fifth sin, Pride?

No, not a priest. Not anymore. He was going to die in a second without even receiving Last Rites. And, in his heart, he knew that all of those failures of the spirit were nothing when compared to the real reason he knew he'd never be fit to wear clerical robes: Clarinda Trevisan.

For everything else, he might be forgiven with the proper penance, but he couldn't be forgiven her. The Church wouldn't allow a married priest, and he had begun to feel that the only life he wanted was one that had her in it until the end of their lives. He didn't want to be forgiven of her, because that would mean he'd never see her again. She'd overwhelmed his life as completely as any Codex Fire, and even if he somehow survived the oncoming serpent, he knew he'd never recover from meeting her.

I will see her again. I can't die without seeing her again. I think I'm in love with her, God, but I don't know how to do that, how to be that. Don't let me die before I learn how!

As death came, his thoughts were filled with the features of the Venetian girl he'd only met a short while ago. He recalled the irritation on her face when he approached the river in Alfheim, triggering the attack of *strömkarlen* and nixies that led to their capture by Old Nick. The anger in her eyes as she shoved against his chest when they'd arrived in Hel after he'd retrieved Hav's envelope. Her soft tone and touch when they'd hugged each other after soaking in the hot springs beneath the

Fenrir-baude. Falling asleep beside her both in the *Fenrir-baude* and Heimdall's house.

No, not Heimdall's house, Kenezki's. Jormungand! His instant of memories came full circle, returning him to the moment of crisis. *God, I need you now. Please, preserve me against this enemy. Do not forsake the work of Your Hands. Answer me!*

He choked on a wavelet that slapped across his face. With a savage, angry wrench of his head, Aurelius whipped away the wet hair that had fallen across his eyes. I won't die here.

Another prayer was on his lips for a moment, another Psalm: *Turn, O Lord, save my life; deliver me for the sake of your steadfast love. For in death there is no remembrance of you; in Sheol, who can give you praise?*

His mind filled with the blinding aquamarine brilliance of the Codex Lacrimae, and a last, fleeting vision of Clarinda—no! It couldn't be a real image, could it? Were nixies taking her from Skíðblaðnir and back to the battle?

God, please. Where are you? His braces gave off a faint aquamarine glow beneath the fjord's surface. In that sinister tome were the words that he needed at this moment. Words apparently more immediate, more powerful, and more responsive than the silent God Who had cast him to this fate! He wouldn't die here.

So be it: The Book of Revelations it is, God. Guide my arm, and let me throw down this dragon!

Then the thinking was over, and Jormungand was upon him.

Aurelius had an instant to register the shriek of Mjöllnir as he swung upward to make a last strike at the serpent. Then his vision filled with green scales, crimson eyes, and fanged maw as the leviathan became a blur before him. Oblivion followed in a rushing gyre of flaming dragon's breath, blue-green Codex Light, and black sea water.

Then the eldest and wiliest of the Children of Loki took the doomed Hospitaller into the midding deeps, striving to wrest the Codex Lacrimae from him and thereby avenge the wrongs done to his father, the Son of Jotunheim.

Never again was Servius Aurelius Santini seen upon the Fjords of Asgard as living man.

Here ends the second part of the beginning of
The Artifacts of Destiny series,
The Codex Lacrimae, Part II:
The Journey to Mimir's Well.
Part III, The Book of Tears,
concludes the tale.

INDEX OF CHARACTERS, TALISMANS, CREATURES, & PLACES

Clarinda Trevisan's Family & Other Venetians

Angelo Trevisan Clarinda's father; Venetian sea-merchant with trading fleet of five ships

Clarinda Trevisan daughter of Angelo and Fabricia Trevisan

Nicolo Ziani son of Sebastian Ziani (Doge of Venice); childhood friend of Aurelius

Verrocchio Trevisan roguish uncle of Clarinda, elder brother and business partner of Angelo Trevisan; running operations in Venice during Clarinda's absence

Pasquale second-in-command of Trevisan sailing fleet

Servius Aurelius Santini's Family & Relations

Aurelius (Servius Aurelius Santini) youngest male member of merchant Santini family (Sicily)

Brother Tomas Benedictine monk who trained Aurelius at Calabrian monastery (s. Italy)

Constanzia Santini younger sister of Aurelius

Devrone di Magglia sea-captain & sword-master on Santini family ships

Eleanor Santini older sister of Aurelius

Matteo Santini Aurelius's father; Sicilian trader and broker

Nicolo Ziani Venetian son of the Doge and childhood friend of Servius Aurelius Santini

Paolo Santini older brother of Aurelius; Sicilian broker whom Clarinda meets while in Constantinople, in company of Kenezki and Radulf of Thuringia

Roberto Santini older brother of Aurelius; banker in Genoa who brokers with papal legates

Rosalba Santini Aurelius's mother

"Servius Aurelius Santini" same-named uncle of Aurelius; died at the Battle of Mecina

Khajen ibn-Khaldun's Family & Relations (including House of Saladin)

Fatima (Fatima bint-Khajen ibn-Khaldun) daughter of Ibn Khaldun; mathematician & scholar; wife of Khalil; sister to Thaqib and Marcus

Hamzah al-Adil younger brother of Saladin; vizier of Egypt (and Dominions of Saladin) for his brother; primary advisor and closest friend of Saladin

Khajen Ibn-Khaldun (Khajen ibn-Khaldun ibn-Khalid al-Hārūn) Islamic 'alim (religious teacher and scholar), sufi mystic, and Keeper of the Rolls (master librarian in the scriptorium) of Krak des Chevaliers; master of Ríg; father of Thaqib, Fatima, and Marcus

Khalil (Khalil ibn-Safir al-Esclabor) husband of Fatima, and son-in-law of Ibn-Khaldun; best friend & brother-in-law of Thaqib, and shaykh of a camel-trading bedouin tribe based in the Nafud (desert south and east of Jerusalem); adoptive brother-in-law of Marcus

Marcus (Marcus de Roussillon, *and* Marcus ibn-Khajen ibn-Khaldun) in Languedoc, Francia son of Jonathan & Desdemona de Roussillon, brother of Denissa; in Syria, adopted son of Khajen ibn-Khaldun & Sara; adoptive brother of Thaqib & Fatima; best friend of Ríg

Saladin (Ṣalāḥ ad-Dīn Yūsuf ibn Ayyūb) ruler of Egypt, successor of Nur al-Din, the 12th century Islamic sultan who began the *jihad* against the Crusaders in Palestine, the Holy Land, and Syria; currently uniting all Muslims in region to drive Crusaders into the Mediterranean Sea; brother of Turan-Shah (deceased) & Hamzah al-Adil

Sara (Sara bint-Thaqib al-Mosul) deceased wife of Ibn-Khaldun

Thaqib (Thaqib ibn-Khajen ibn-Khaldun) eldest son of Khajen ibn-Khaldun; elder in the bedouin tribe, and second-in-command to Khalil

Turan-Shah (ibn-Ayyūb) brother of Saladin; slain at Battle of Mecina

Jacob David-son's Family & Relations (Constantinople/Byzantium)

Aqib son of the caravan leader (Gannen); among pilgrims seeking shelter at Krak

Ghannen caravan leader of pilgrims and merchants heading to Jerusalem

Jacob (Jacob ben-David, or David-son) thirteen-year-old Byzantine boy; son of Rebecca & David

Owena Welsh friend of Jacob in Constantinople; daughter of Aeddan (Ethan) the Blacksmith

Rabbi Mordecai Jacob's mentor and friend in the Ben-Delos Synagogue

Rebecca (Rebecca bat-Gurion) mother of Jacob David-son; wife of David, who was lost at Battle of Mecina; stricken with severe case of pneumonia

Signor Boccanegra Genoese landlord of the David-son textile shop in Constantinople, and of many other homes and businesses in Genoese Quarter of Golden Horn district

Sølvmora the Witch reputed soothsayer and witch in Genoese Quarter of Constantinople; friend to Jacob and Owena

Stratioticus Family & Other Notable Characters from Constantinople

Alexander Stratioticus eldest son of the noble Stratioticus family, brother of Genevieve, and expert swordsman whose skills and leadership abilities make him the youngest hoplitarch (military commander) in the history of the Imperial Guard

Alexios Comnenus an heir to the Byzantine throne & childhood friend of Aurelius

Genevieve (Genie) Stratioticus Greek childhood friend of Clarinda Trevisan; a renowned & well-liked socialite in Byzantium; of ancient noble house, & younger sister of Alex

Kenezki a Black Sea pirate based in Constantinople with connections in empire & the Levant

Radulf of Thuringia German trader specializing in trade from Constantinople to North Sea

Hospitallers & Others in Krak des Chevaliers and the Holy Land

Adelbert Master of the Stores at Krak des Chevaliers, in charge of provisions & chambers

Aimery of Lusignan younger brother of Guy of Lusignan

Andreas the Chaplain Hospitaller apprentice in scriptorium; second only to Ríg

Arcadian Grand Master (also known as Castellan or Preceptor) of the Hospitaller Order in command of the Krak des Chevaliers; senior member of order in this bailiwick of Syria

Belvedere Hospitaller physician in the hospital at Krak des Chevaliers

Braunen aged Hospitaller physician, caught in siege at Krak; acquaintance of Dietrich the Mad Dwarf

Damian Hospitaller, third-in-command to the Grand Master, Arcadian

Demetrius assistant to Ibn-Khaldun and Ríg in scriptorium and hospital at Krak

Edward castle page and apprentice in scriptorium

Eric Frankish troubadour; minstrel who got caught with partner, Frett, at Battle of Mecina

Evremar of Choques Templar Grandmaster of Caesarea; arranged deal for delivery of two caskets by Angelo Trevisan (Clarinda's father)

Franj (or *nazaros* = "followers of the Nazarene," i.e., Christians) Arabian name for Crusaders

Frett musician and partner of Eric the Troubadour, trapped at Mecina

Guy of Lusignan ousted regent of Latin Kingdom; husband of Sibylla

Jeremiah elder scholar who runs the scriptorium of Krak des Chevaliers with Ibn-Khaldun

Mercedier brother of Grand Master Arcadian, & second-in-command; mentor to Ríg

Monachus Archbishop, based in port city of Caesarea; ally of Templar, Evremar of Choques

Pellion castle page & scriptorium protégé of Ibn-Khaldun; close friend of Ríg & Marcus

Perdieu (Brother Bernard Perdieu) Commander of Knights at the Krak, and Burgundian baron

Ríg Lead Squire (under Brother Perdieu) and Master of Apprentices (under Brother Jeremiah & Khajen ibn-Khaldun) in Krak des Chevaliers; friend of Mercedier, Marcus, & Pellion

Sibylla ousted regent of Kingdom of Jerusalem; elder sister of Baldwin IV, the Leper King; wife of Guy of Lusignan

Sister Nikola Benedictine nun; caught in the siege at the Krak while touring the Holy Land with orders from the pope to investigate sister-houses in the Levant

Wallace squire and apprentice in scriptorium

Nine Worlds of Norse Mythology

ASGARD: Golden Realm of Norse gods, citadel guarded by Heimdall and labyrinthine fjords Aesir younger family of Norse gods; led by Odin, who defeated Vanir in Elder Days

Heimdall the Watcher of the Gods and Guardian of Bifrost, the Rainbow Bridge

Hügin (name is Norse word for "thought"); one of Odin's two ravens whom the All-Father sends to gather information; appear at times & places of crisis in Nine Worlds

Münin (name is Norse word for "memory"); one of the two ravens of Odin (see "Hügin")

<u>**ALFHEIM**</u>: Land of the Light Elves

<u>**HEL**</u>: Norse Underworld ruled by Hela

Blod Betaling "blood payment" for passage into Hel; collected by skeletal servant, Modgud

Gangloti and Ganglot male and female demon-servants of Hela

Hela daughter of Loki and the frost-giantess Angrboda; upper part of body is a cadaver and lower is a serpent; ruler of the underworlds of Hel and Niflheim; sister of Jormungand and Fenris; commands legions of the dead, orcs, and goblins, & the *Wilde Jagd*

Modgud skeleton female guardian of Giöll, the crystal bridge that leads to Hel

Vinduene Illevarslende the "Windows Portentous" in Hela's Citadel; her personal *runeporte* to all parts of reality, space, and time

<u>**JOTUNHEIM**</u>: Land of Frost Giants; mountain ranges around Mount Glittertind

Ilmarinen giant and blacksmith; forger of Sampos, Mjöllnir, and the Codices of Fate

Myrkridor (*Myrkur Vistfólk*, "Dark Dwellers") Fire/Frost Giants; Nightmare Lord's elite guard

MIDGARD: "Middle World" of the Nine Worlds where mortals dwell; currently 1185 A.D

Levant eastern coast of the Mediterranean Sea; also called Outremer and the Holy Land by Frankish Crusaders (includes lands that stretch from southern Anatolian Peninsula (modern-day Turkey) south to regions south and west of Jerusalem

MUSPELHEIM: World of Fire, Volcanoes, & Firestorms; ruled by Surtur, and sealed from other Nine Worlds by Odin and the Aesir in the First Age

Farbauti foremost of 13 Huntsman created by Surt, ruler of the Fire-World of Muspelheim

Morpeth second-in-command of Huntsman of Muspelheim

Mogthrasir original Huntsman of Muspelheim; rebelled against Surtur at Battle of the Fields of Burning Night

Surt (or Surtur) Fire-giant who rules Muspelheim; prophecies foretell that his blazing sword will set the Nine Worlds afire at Ragnarok

NIDAVELLER: World of the Dwarves; heart of kingdom in Mount Glittertind

Andvari dwarf; Arch-Mage of Nidaveller; married to Traeg

Atlakvida northern capital of dwarvish Kingdom of Nidaveller; ruled by King Gunnar

Austri lead dwarf assistant to Arch-Mage Andvari (brother to Norđri, Suđri, and Vestri)

Delling cook and dwarf assistant to the Arch-Mage, Andvari

Dietrich the Mad, Arch-Mage of the Elder Days; dwarf, slayer of Codex Wielders and obsessed with collecting Sampos;

defeated and exiled to Otherworld of Annen Verden by Urd and Taliesin Lore Master at Battle of the Fields of Burning Night

Døkk River the "Dark River," central conduit of the *Underjordisk Elv* in Nidaveller

Falmoria former independent kingdom that prided itself on Arch-Mage Dietrich's discovery of Crystal Caves (*Kristallhöllen*); conquered by Kings Gunnar & Högni during Mage Wars

Gunnar dwarf; King of the Nibelung Dwarves in the Northern Realm, based in capital of Atlakvida (shares rule of Nidaveller, World of Dwarves, with twin brother, Högni)

Halfdan dwarf; Brigadier General of Nibelung Army (North)

Högni dwarf; King of the Nibelung Dwarves in the Southern Realm, based in the capital of Niðafjöll (shares rule of Nidaveller, World of Dwarves, with twin brother, Gunnar)

Kristallhöllen ("The Crystal Caves") discovered by Arch-Mage Dietrich & Taliesin Lore-Master

Niðafjöll southern capital of dwarvish Kingdom of Nidaveller; ruled by King Högni

Norðri dwarf assistant to the Arch-Mage, Andvari ⎫ three
Suðri dwarf assistant to the Arch-Mage, Andvari ⎬ brothers
Vestri dwarf assistant to the Arch-Mage, Andvari ⎭ of **Austri**

Wrothken brigands who roam back ways of Nidaveller; nemeses to all Nibelung dwarves

NIFLHEIM: the World of Ice and Shadowlands, adjoins Hel and the Nightmare Realm

Baba Yaga ancient enemy of Skade the Huntress; one of three leaders of Hela's *Wilde Jagd*

Død Bueskytteres the "Death Archers" of Hela's *Wilde Jagd*

Draugr Viking men and women who reached neither Valhalla nor Niflheim upon death; damned by Veröld Matröd to exist both within and outside of time; giant-sized and difficult to kill

Naglfar the great ship constructed of dead peoples' fingernails; in dry-dock near *Runeporte* on the Sea of Niflheim and guarded by armies of dead, goblins, frost-giants, and orcs

Ville Folk wild people who often join Wilde Jagd when Hela summons them for raids

Wilde Jagd the "Wild Hunt," or vanguard of Hela's armies; based in Niflheim

SVARTALFHEIM: the Land of the Dark Elves

Rudyick a Dark Elf; son of Volund

Volund a Dark Elf who was part of the group of elves that helped create Codex Lacrimae

Other Characters, Locales, & Talismans

All-Thing representative body that oversees covenants in the Nine Worlds, where meet delegates from elven, dwarfish, and giant high councils; also includes Aesir & Vanir

Annen Verden mysterious Otherworld whose access was lost when Surtur was exiled and Veröld Martröd banished by Taliesin the Druid at Battle of the Fields of Burning Night

Arngrim the haunted, Singing Sword, whose curse must slay a person whenever drawn

Arthur Pendragon pupil of Merlin of Carmarthen, and best friend of Taliesin the Bard; later King and Defender of Britain against the Saxons during the 6th Century; united Celtic, Welsh, and Breton tribes for brief time; defeated Mordred and the Hosts of Veröld Martröđ, the Nightmare Lord at the Battle of Cad Camlann (also called the Battle of the Fields of Burning Night); Arthur disappeared after battle, and thought to be on Isle of Avalon, or in Annen Verden (the Otherworld), until called back to Midgard at time of Britain's greatest need

Battle of the Fields of Burning Night (c. 540 A.D., also known as Battle of Cad Camlan or, in Welsh, the Battle of *Brwydr Camlan*) final battle site of King Arthur, where he died at the hands of Mordred; also, last known sighting of any of the Codices of Fate

Caliburn the sword Excalibur, thought lost at the Battle of the Fields of Burning Night

Cerys (also known as Circe) enchantress, daughter of Helios and Lorelei, sister of Njörd; witch who lured Odysseus and others by herb lore and transformations; in 6th century, she co-founded, then abandoned the Coven of Mists to seek Mirror of Carmarthen

Coven of Mists group of European and Middle Eastern witches who allied against the Norns in the 5th and 6th Centuries; most members disbanded after disaster at Emain Ablach (c. 525 A.D.) against the sea-god, Njörd, and his ally, Rudyick the Dark Elf; other witches in Coven killed (or exiled) by Taliesin, Merlin, & Urd in 540 AD

Druids of Rhydderch originally a Celtic group of warlocks who came together under leadership of Braunen the Eternal, a druid reputed to have discovered the secret of eternal life and based in Britain since the time of Julius Caesar; under Braunen's leadership in the 6th Century, the Druids of

Rhydderch realized their fullest power, especially after securing the *Codex Maleficarum* (Book of Witches) at Battle of Emain Ablach; entire order of warlocks destroyed in 540 when Taliesin Lore-Master and Dietrich the Mad Dwarf wrested Codex Maleficarum from Braunen the Eternal

Fafnir dragon in Norse mythology, slain by Sigurd with sword of the Volsungs

Fenris son of Loki and the frost-giantess Angrboda; changeling who can turn into a wolf

Fossegrim water elemental, one of the 27 Nøkken who rule the oceans, lakes, and rivers of the world; commands the water elemental *strömkarlen* and nixies

Freki grey wolf companion to Grimnir the Wanderer

Galahad knight of King Arthur's court, and son of Lancelot and Elaine of Corbenic; only survivor of the Siege Perilous (chair at Arthur's court reserved for person who will lead the quest for the Holy Grail), and close friend of Perceval; along with Perceval and Bors, Galahad is known as the Finder of the Holy Grail; disappeared after the Battle of the Fields of Burning Night, but thought to have taken a ship to return the Grail for safe keeping to the Isle of Serras, whom some place close to Britain, but others locate in the Middle East

Gàtefull Runer the Enigmatic Runes that Mimir distributes to those who pay his price; Odin learned them all by being crucified for nine days and losing an eye; rumored that there are more than the 27 that Mimir knows

Geri grey wolf companion to Grimnir the Wanderer

ghasts creatures who can manifest as both zombie and wraith because of the nature of their cursed death; favored soldiers of Hela for her Wilde Jagd because of their fierceness and the fear elicited by their screams; can attain true corporeal form and semblance of life in Svartalfheim regions between Skull-Cradler's Grove and Jotunheim Mountains

Grimnir mysterious wanderer in the Nine Worlds; gift-giver who travels with two grey wolves (Geri and Freki) as companions

Húð Göngufólk Skin-Walkers, intangible spirits who possess mortal bodies, but also type of spell favored by Huntsmen of Muspelheim when traveling and hunting in Nine Worlds

Irminsul magic pillar venerated by the Norsemen; usually a tree trunk shorn of its branches, found in sacred groves, and thought to contain deities or serve as focal points between the Nine Worlds

Jormungand son of Loki and the frost-giantess, Angrboda; also called the Midgard Serpent

Kludden Hell-Hounds in service to the Nightmare Lord; horse-sized, and marked by the sound of clinking chains with glowing blue Muspel-Fire; also, poison-fanged, with ability to phase through solid objects

Kullervo extremely powerful magician from Finland who owns a haunted sword, Arngrim, said to have ultimately betrayed and killed him; recruited by the Nightmare Lord to unite the Druids of Rhydderch before the Battle of the Fields of Burning Night, but Kullervo's insanity (and the bloodthirstiness of his sword) made him highly unreliable; thought slain by Dietrich and Taliesin when Arngrim revealed to be disguised *Codex Vindicta*

Lögretta legislative assembly in Nine Worlds; decides upon and enacts laws for All-Thing

Loki the 'god of fire' in Norse mythology; demi-god known for his practical jokes and tricks on the gods of Asgard, but also useful and friendly to them at times; currently known to be bound beneath Mount Glittertind in Norway for his role in slaying Balder, the 'god of light'; son of frost-giant Laufey, husband to both Angrboda and Sigyn; also known as Lopt, the Mischievous One, the Trickster, the Sly One, Changeling, Dark One, and Son of Jotunheim

Merlin of Carmarthen court wizard and close friend of King Arthur and Taliesin the Bard; cast the Codices of Fate into Ginnungagap with Taliesin and Urd at end of the Battle of the Fields of Burning Night, but betrayed (and saved) by Nimue, the Lady of the Lake, the last witch standing from the Coven of Mists; reputed to be trapped in a crystal cave

Mimir a Vanir turned Asgardian who was gifted with the Sight and sent to broker peace between the Aesir and Vanir when they were at war in the First Age; beheaded by the Vanir because of perceived betrayal, Mimir was saved by Odin to become guardian of the Well of Knowledge; resides in the deepest part of Yggdrassil, the cosmic ash-tree that encompasses the Nine Worlds; assisted in his task of guardianship of the Well by the three Norns

Mjöllnir magic hammer of Thor Odin-Son; indestructible, lightning-summoner, controls storms and climate; and always returns to thrower's hand

Mount Glittertind one of the central *weirds* (*wyrds*) binding the Nine Worlds together; Nexus of All Realities (Mimir's Well) located in cavern and grotto system at its base

Nidhogg the Dragon serpent who dwells at base of Yggdrassil, the World Tree, trying to sever roots to begin Ragnarok, the Twilight of the Gods

Norns called by many the three Goddesses, or Witches, of Destiny: Urd ("Fate"), Verdandi ("Present"), and Skuld ("Future"); believed to control the destinies of all beings in the Nine Worlds; live with Mimir in grottoes beneath Mount Glittertind near the Well of Knowledge

Old Nick malicious demon who roams the Nine Worlds (see also, Abbadon, Satan, et al)

Palomides Arabian knight of King Arthur's court, who met and fell in love with Iseult while in Ireland (6th century); sparring partner and best friend of the knight, Tristan; Hunter of the Questing Beast, who was controlled by Veröld Martröd, the Nightmare Lord at the Battle of the Fields of Burning Night; both Palomides and Veröld Martröd disappeared in the battle, each thought to have slain the other

Perceval knight of King Arthur's court, lover of Blanchefleur; failed questioner of the Fisher King, but ultimately both Perceval and Galahad succeeded in securing the Holy Grail; Perceval was briefly King of Corbenic before fleeing with the Holy Grail to protect the artifact from Dietrich the Mad Dwarf and the Druids of Rhydderch; disappeared after the Battle of the Fields of Burning Night

Prester John Christian king thought to rule of over a mythical kingdom somewhere in the medieval Middle East, Central Asia, or even in East Africa (Ethiopia); charged with defense of the world against the invasion forces of Gog and Magog; also maintains the magical barrier (*runeporte*) at the Gates of

Alexander against that apocalyptic day; 12th Century people believed Prester John to know the location of Fountain of Youth

Ratatosk the Squirrel lore-wise, magical creature who runs through the Nine Worlds via the branches and Yggdrassil, the cosmic World Tree

Runeporten (Rune-Gates) magical portals between the Nine Worlds, navigable only by those skilled enough to see, create, or direct them

Satan the Ancient Enemy; also known as Lucifer; the Great Adversary; Abbadon; Old Nick

Sidhe (pronounced "Shee") shape-changing fairy folk who dwell in Alfheim and Svartalfheim; may be good or evil, and ally themselves with whomever strikes their fancy; Veröld Martröd ensorcelled many Sidhe and cast them into Annen Verden to serve as his army before the Battle of the Fields of Burning Night; some Sidhe, such as Youdic the Damned, control "tunnels" (or *runeporten*) between dimensional walls of the Nine Worlds by way of Ban-Sidhe ("Banshee") Tunnels, marked by the screams of their users

Skade Huntress in Norse mythology who skies and wanders through the frozen wastes of Jotunheim, Niflheim, and icy lands with a reputation for destruction; divorced from the sea-god, Njörd, and currently married to Fenris the Wolf

Skuld a Norn; also called Sister, Goddess, or Witch of the "Future"

Sviddengen (the "Scorched Meadow") Svartalfheim location of one of Ilmarinen's Forges that was ruined by creation of the Codex Lacrimae; cursed by elves and monster-kind alike

Taliesin knight and bard of King Arthur's court; most favored and skilled of Merlin's pupils; best friend of Arthur Pendragon; Lore Master and Codex Wielder of the Third Age; thought lost in Annen Verden after the Battle of the Fields of Burning Night

Thor son of Odin All-Father, and Norse god of thunder; defends Asgard against Frost Giants of Jotunheim, and close friend of Loki the Trickster (although both often fight each other for the favor of Odin and Aesir in Asgard); not seen recently in any of the Nine Worlds

Urd the original and most powerful of the Norns; complete command of the Past, Present, and Future, and one of the Elders of the Universe; lives at a subterranean lake beneath Mount Glittertind that was the only place powerful enough to contain Mimir the Seer, with whom she shares responsibility for Fate of Humanity; also called the Sister, Goddess, or Witch of "Fate"

Vdofnir rooster who lives in branches of Yggdrassil, the World Tree, and spars daily with Ratatosk the Squirrel

Verdandi a Norn; also called the Sister, Goddess, or Witch of the "Present"

Vanir elder group of family of Norse gods; defeated by Odin and the Aesir (the younger branch of the family) in the First Age; both families reside near Fjords of Asgard

Veröld Martröd the Nightmare Lord who disappeared at the Battle of the Fields of Burning Night

Yggdrassil, the World Tree cosmic ash tree that unites dimensional planes of Multiverse; bounded by the lands of Asgard and Niflheim in the time and space continuum, with

Mount Glittertind and the Well of Mimir as the weirds/wyrds that appear in some form in every world; under constant attack by the Niðhogg the Dragon; guarded by beings of immense power and mystery: Mimir the Wise, the Three Norns (Urd, Verdandi, and Skuld), Grimnir One-Eye, the ravens, Hügin and Münin, Ratatosk the Squirrel, Vdofnir the Rooster, and the wolves, Geri and Freki

ABOUT THE AUTHOR

A. J. Carlisle holds a Ph.D. in medieval European history, with varied interests that include the Crusades of 1095-1291, theology and philosophy of the Middle Ages, and the Mediterranean Worlds of Late Antiquity. Inspired since childhood by the works of J.R.R. Tolkien & C.S. Lewis, his hope is to reboot and universalize the epic fantasy genre by bringing to a global audience a unique blend of Norse mythology, Arthurian legends, international folklores & heroes (and villains) drawn from all parts of the medieval world!

Carlisle lives in the United States with his wife and children.

CPSIA information can be obtained
at www.ICGtesting.com
Printed in the USA
BVHW080833060519
547457BV00001B/35/P

9 780578 454016